# All the Perfect Days

# MICHAEL
# THOMPSON

sourcebooks
landmark

Copyright © 2025 by Michael Thompson
Cover and internal design © 2025 by Sourcebooks
Cover design by Matt Roeser
Cover image © Esgoty/Shutterstock

Published by Sourcebooks Landmark, an imprint of Sourcebooks
P.O. Box 4410, Naperville, Illinois 60567-4410
(630) 961-3900
sourcebooks.com

Cataloging-in-Publication Data is on file with the Library of Congress.

Printed and bound in the United States of America.
VP 10 9 8 7 6 5 4 3 2 1

*Henry & Maeve, this is for you.*
*Just don't read it 'til you're older.*

# 1

Charlie Knight hadn't expected an old lady's arthritic ankles to consume his final moments. But he also hadn't expected the extraordinary pressure that was building and swelling inside his head, so obviously his expectations counted for little.

He stumbled back, colliding hard with his own desk. A jar toppled over, and a rainbow of jelly beans cascaded to the floor. Charlie barely noticed.

Edna Bradley looked up at him, startled.

"Doctor?"

Charlie didn't answer. He couldn't. His skull felt entirely too small for his brain, for the pressure that was growing there, that had barreled out of nowhere and was now—certainly—going to end his life while an eighty-four-year-old woman patiently held out a papery-skinned foot for him to examine.

"Charlie? Are you all right?"

He leaned against the edge of his desk and tried to focus.

*If this was happening to somebody else—what would you do?*

If it was Edna. Or his dad. Or a stranger on a plane, with that urgent call for any doctors on board to please make themselves known to the cabin crew. That had happened once, and when Charlie had stood up, the other passengers had actually *cheered*.

Nobody was cheering today.

And worst of all, he couldn't see an answer, couldn't find space in his mind to *think*, and the only space left was occupied by a white-hot rage that this, *this*, was going to be the end of him. That he'd be taken out by some almighty brain explosion, just when he was about to do something big. Something *spectacular*. That his life was playing out like a cop movie, the ones he watched with his dad, the ones where the detective would turn to his partner and declare he was buying a yacht once they solved one last case. From that second on, the hero was guaranteed to take a bullet in the chest. Denied that peaceful retirement, and getting a blaze of glory instead.

*But that's not it at all*, Charlie thought desperately, angrily, as the pressure expanded and squeezed; his head felt set to burst open. *I'm not winding down. I'm just getting started.*

And for it to happen in front of one of his favorite patients too. One who'd known him since he was six; one who brought shortbread biscuits to every appointment and still dressed up for the occasion.

He stared at Edna, but then he stared *past* her, because something else was happening to the cozy little office. And this was something he could *see*.

A poster on the wall—a colorful diagram of the respiratory system—was changing, dimming slightly. So was the one next to it, the digestive tract. And the next, a full cross section of the body's muscles. The next one too. All of them. The pictures were fading.

No, not fading.

They were *draining*.

The colors oozed out like someone had pulled a plug from a bath. The spongy pink lungs and the yellow stomach acid turned a dull, lifeless gray.

Charlie didn't want to look. The colors slipping out and dripping away to nowhere at all turned his stomach up and over. He wanted to close his eyes but just couldn't bring himself to do it, because now he was looking at the floor, and that was different too. The bright colored jelly beans resembled tiny gray kidneys, the blues and greens and reds having bled to monochrome. A light gray here, a darker charcoal there.

Edna's voice cut through.

"Charlie? What's wrong, dear?"

It was like looking at a black-and-white photo of his patient, wearing a flowery blouse that Charlie *knew* had once been colorful and cheery. Cheeks that were rosy with spots of blusher a shade too bright, now with just a faint shadow to mark where the color used to be.

Everything was gray.

And still that squeezing against the inside of his skull, with one more element to it now: something shifting and swirling behind his eyes. It was an aneurysm, or a clot, or a tumor, something built for bursting and hurting and killing.

*There was something inside that swirling, shifting pressure. Something hiding, trying to push through.*

He reached for Edna, only to find her hand already resting on his arm. And that angry, indignant corner of his mind that insisted it wasn't his time yet made way for a burst of sheer gratitude that of all people to be with him at the end it would be her. A brief flash of Edna—Mrs. Bradley—standing in front of a classroom, in front of a tiny Charlie Knight, amidst a sea of innocent, curious faces. He put his hand on hers and held tight as the memory vanished, crushed by the awful, consuming pressure.

A moan filled the room, a low, guttural groan, and he knew it was coming from him, and he just didn't care because the thing in his head was building, squeezing against his eyes and his brain, straining against the walls of his skull, and he knew this was it.

Then it stopped.

The noise continued until Charlie closed his gaping mouth—with an effort, it seemed, for his mind felt detached from the rest of him. Then the room was silent.

Edna was staring at him, glasses askew, her own mouth hanging open.

Charlie blinked slowly. Deliberately. Still trying to connect the brain to the body it normally controlled.

"Lord above, he's having a stroke," Edna blurted, and put that gnarled hand on the arm of her chair, pushing herself unsteadily, painfully to her feet.

Charlie blinked again and the color was back, solid and clear and *there*, as though it had always been. The spilled jelly beans were bright and sharp against the clean floor. The embroidered flowers around the buttonholes of Edna's blouse were purple again, and the handle on her walking stick once more a faded navy blue. The arteries on the posters high on the wall, dull gray a moment ago, now a deep crimson. As they were supposed to be.

Charlie assessed himself, his brain now functioning at something near full capacity, and made two quick conclusions.

The first was that he felt completely normal.

The second was that *something* had definitely happened.

"Edna. Are you okay?" Charlie asked his patient. She was standing, grabbing for her stick without taking her eyes off Charlie.

"Am *I* okay?" she replied. "Of course *I'm* fine, Charlie. I'm getting you some help."

He shook his head and strode to the window, sliding it up with ease. Fresh air would help. Maybe it was a gas leak, making them see funny things.

"Edna, slow down." He took her arm and guided her back into the chair. "You need to take it easy. What did you see?"

"Lord, you hit the desk hard. Lucky you didn't break a hip."

"Not that. The room." He gestured around his office, at the examination bed, the blood pressure cuff, at the posters, all in full color. "How it went kind of dark. Like a cloud in front of the sun, right? All gray."

Edna pushed her glasses back up on her nose and peered at Charlie.

"It didn't turn gray?" Charlie asked again.

Not for her, apparently. And as relieved as Charlie was that Marwick Family Clinic hadn't sprung a carbon monoxide leak, the alternative was troubling. Because it must be something bad. Something that affected only him. And *something*—even a little *something*—could be enough to disrupt his plans.

A deep breath.

"Let me take another look at your foot, Edna," he said, and she tried to wave him away, as though her creaky old ankles were the least of anyone's concerns now.

"Doc, I would've said you're too young for a stroke, but my great-nephew had one last winter and he's younger than you. He's only forty-one."

"Edna, I'm thirty-eight. It wasn't a stroke. I'm fine."

*I'm fine. I'm fine. I'm fine.*

Maybe if he said it enough times, he'd believe it.

"Really, Doc. Just thirty-eight," Edna repeated, with a flicker of a wicked smile. "And going silver already."

Charlie grinned. She was letting him off the hook. Trusting his judgment, perhaps, or just letting him believe what he needed to.

*I'm fine.*

"Let's see that ankle." He swept aside a cluster of jelly beans with his shoe and squatted down again.

Where he'd been when it started.

But this time, nothing happened.

The arthritis in both ankles was worse: a steady, painful progression that he could do little to stop. Then he shone a light in Edna's eyes, checked a suspicious spot on her arm, updated her blood pressure medication, and had a chat about the sudden onset of summer.

"Cicadas have started again," Edna remarked, looking toward the open window. "They're a bit early."

Charlie knew it too, and almost hated himself for it. For knowing it was at least a couple of weeks too soon for that buzzing drone to descend on Marwick. For knowing what *normal* was. He'd loved that noise once; it was the soundtrack of every summer he could remember.

Now it made him restless.

*Almost, Charlie,* he told himself. *Count the days.*

"You're all set, Edna." Except for the delicate part. "You don't need to mention me spilling the jelly beans to anybody, do you? Or anything else. It was just an accident. I'm fine."

"You keep my secrets, Doc," she said. "I'll keep yours."

He smiled gratefully, though he suspected Edna Bradley had a few secrets she didn't share with her doctor.

*Suppose it goes both ways then.*

"If I see Mum, I'll tell her you said hello." He picked up the Tupperware container that had somehow survived the carnage on his desk. "And thanks for the shortbread."

Charlie helped Edna to the door, only stopping there because she shooed him off. He closed it behind her and pressed his ear to the wood, listening for her cane tapping toward reception. She wouldn't say anything, he knew that. But if she did, the receptionists would have to tell the boss, and then MaryAnn would ask him what was going on and he'd have to explain what had happened.

Which was what, exactly?

Charlie had witnessed the colors run out and the room go gray. And he'd felt that awful pressure inside his head, a balloon inflating in a shoebox.

And once the color vanished, and his head was about to

burst, he'd seen something else: something moving and shifting and turning in his mind like smoke.

But that wasn't quite right. He didn't see it, he *felt* it. A sensation right behind his eyes, so close that he could *almost* see it.

Something that made no sense at all, because why would a *number* be appearing in his head?

It made no sense, but it happened. He was sure of it: as sure as he was of the jelly beans on his floor or the dusting of silver hair that Edna had gleefully pointed out among the brown. What he'd felt emerge from the pressure in his skull was a number. Just a small one—a single digit—and suddenly Charlie scrabbled on his desk for a pen, desperate to get it out of his brain.

He wrote the number 4 and circled it, expecting to feel better now that he'd cleared it from his mind.

But the relief didn't come. In its place was a growing sense that something was very, very wrong.

Something that might just stand in the way of his grand escape, from the place where everybody knew him, where they brought him biscuits and asked after his parents and where he knew exactly when the cicadas were supposed to start their drone.

He only needed six weeks.

But six weeks could be a lifetime.

# 2

Charlie could still hear the neurologist's braying laugh as he turned off the highway. The grating haw-haw-haw was stuck in his head, and stayed there right up until he approached the single-lane bridge into Marwick. Then, thankfully, the rhythmic bump of the rivets across the old wooden span took its place. Another car coming toward him stopped and waited for Charlie to finish crossing, and he waved in acknowledgment, not registering that it was too dark for the other driver to see him.

If only he'd been able to convince himself he was fine.

*If only Edna had been a one-off.*

Then he could've avoided asking Matt Rowan for a favor and avoided hearing that awful laugh until they next met for dinner. Their twice-yearly meal wasn't due for another three months, by which time Charlie planned to be long gone, and may never have to hear it again. Never have to haul himself from Marwick to Abercrombie, because dinner was always in Abercrombie and never in Marwick, because Dr. Matthew Rowan was now used to people coming to see *him*, and not the other way around. Because he was already doing something spectacular.

Charlie was past the other car now and watched its taillights behind him as the driver slowly made their own way across the bridge. A visitor, judging by the speed: not used to such a narrow deck and a little nervous about knocking off the side mirrors in the dark. They were lucky. If it had been a few hours earlier they would've had to contend with a bunch of kids too, balancing on the dusty, splintery railings. Charlie had seen them on his way out, and the sound of them counting each other down before hurling themselves over the edge and into the water below had made him smile. It was more than two decades since he'd done a somersault, but he could still feel the slap of sunburnt skin against the surface of the river. The water had always been so cold, even on the stinking hot days. On those days, the water was heaven.

Matt Rowan had actually done him two favors: squeezing him in for an appointment and reminding him why he had to leave.

"This is between us, right?" Charlie had asked, and the neurologist rolled his eyes. "Sorry. Of course. Thanks. Matt, something a bit weird's going on."

"Weird," repeated his friend. "There I was, thinking you'd gone to medical school. Must've been another Charlie Knight." *Haw-haw-haw.* "Give me symptoms, yeah?"

"Uh, okay. Hallucinations. Maybe optic neuropathy—colors mostly. But quickly, you know? Like they fade for a moment, or run out, then come back. And something else too." Charlie had thought about how to describe it on the drive to Abercrombie and still hadn't landed on the right words. "This one's a bit hard to explain."

Matt stopped scribbling on the pad in front of him, pen poised above the page, and looked up as Charlie continued.

"It's like a strange sensation. There's pressure—heaps of it—and then it's like I'm seeing something behind my eyes, but kind of *feeling* it, rather than seeing it." Charlie paused; he knew how it sounded. "Sounds crazy."

"No, not crazy. But yes, weird." The neurologist squinted through thick glasses at Charlie, as though his magnified eyes could see straight through the hair and the skin and the skull and diagnose exactly what was going wrong inside Charlie's head. "When did it start?"

*With Edna's ankles. And then every patient since then.*

"A few days ago. On Monday."

Matt frowned.

"Is it happening right now?"

"No."

The frown deepened.

"When, then? Random times? Watching TV? Light sensitivity?"

"I don't think so." Charlie chose his words carefully. "It happens when I'm with patients. When they're telling me their problems. As soon as they start talking—I don't know, it's like a trigger. And it's not just at work. It happened yesterday afternoon, at the supermarket. The cashier jammed her finger in the till." Matt smirked, and Charlie felt a rising hatred for his friend. "She thought it might be broken, so I had a look. And it happened then too." He shrugged. "One moment everything's fine, then the next moment it's not."

Then he told him about the numbers, and Matt put down the pen entirely.

And now, as he watched a stranger's car reach the other side of the Marwick Bridge and accelerate away, Charlie's phone was ringing, and he just *knew* it was going to be Matt Rowan with his test results.

With bad news.

"Hi, Charlie. Where are you, mate?" Malcolm Knight's voice always had a smile in it. A cynic might have said he did it to help sell houses, but Charlie had heard the same smiling voice now for thirty-eight years. It came from a good place.

"Oh. Hi, Dad. Just crossed the bridge."

"Ah, gotcha. I just stopped at your place on my way home. Thought you might like a beer, but everything was locked up tight. If that grass gets any longer, people will think you've skipped town."

"Yeah. I was actually..." *Actually what, Charlie? Actually seeing a neurologist because you reckon a tumor is making you see things?* "I had to duck out."

"I would've mowed your grass for you, but it was getting a bit dark. Though you do need to cut it back, mate—in this weather, you'll end up with snakes."

"All right, Dad."

"And have you still got a key for next door?"

"I do. Why?"

"Cos someone's left a light on in Ruth's place. Duck in and

switch it off for her, would you? Don't want the cleaners racking up her power bill. Poor old thing."

"All right, Dad," Charlie said again.

A few seconds passed. The only noise came from the car, gliding through the silent streets of Marwick. Past the school where Edna Bradley had taught him. Past the park where he broke his arm when he was eleven, trying to hang under the slide like a sloth. Past the house where he'd had his first kiss with a girl named Kylie, who'd left Marwick not long after, leading him to believe he was a woeful kisser. Past the vacant lot he'd been running by when he'd received the worst call of his life. Past the tennis court where he played every Friday night, unbeaten for the best part of a decade. Past the clinic where he worked, when he wasn't begging off for the afternoon because his old college roommate could squeeze him in for a neurological consult.

It was, Charlie knew, all quite depressing. His entire life, summarized in four blocks. The very definition of a small existence. Derailed once, by that phone call seven years ago outside a vacant lot. And now derailed again, perhaps permanently, by whatever had taken hold in his head.

"Everything okay, Charlie?" Malcolm asked, and Charlie smiled ruefully. Even over the phone his dad knew how to read him. "Everything all right at work?"

*Just tell him. Tell him everything. Tell him about the neuro. Tell him you're scared, but you're in good hands. And tell him about the move. You can't keep either secret forever. Cos one way or another, soon that place will be abandoned, and someone's gonna need to mow the grass.*

"All good, Dad. Work's fine."

"You just seem a bit quiet. Now, you haven't forgotten about your mum's party, have you? Next week. Saturday."

Charlie groaned; he *had* forgotten. Although at this rate, he didn't know if he'd still be alive come Saturday of next week. And that kind of made RSVPing a little difficult.

He did know one thing though: he couldn't say anything now. Not about his brain—until he'd heard back from Matt Rowan and knew his treatment options—and certainly not about leaving town. Because if he mentioned leaving Marwick, Malcolm would surely suggest a joint celebration, which was objectively a terrible idea. Lorraine Knight barely returned Charlie's calls now. The odds of her letting him blow out her candles? He had a better chance of curing whatever cancer was growing in his head.

"It's just a barbecue, but it'll be a big one—you only turn seventy once. I left you a couple of voicemails, but you might not have heard them."

Good old Malcolm, graciously giving his son an out.

"Sorry, Dad. It's on the calendar. Who's going?"

"Everybody! All her friends from the golf club. Aunty Cate, Les, the kids." He rattled off more names, a potent mix of friends and family and colleagues. "So yeah, it'd be great if you can make it. It'll mean a lot to her."

"You reckon?" Charlie asked.

"Come on, mate," Malcolm replied, the smile still in his voice, but a little weary. "She wouldn't have invited you if she didn't want you there."

"Unless she just—"

A beep interrupted him. Incoming call. Charlie's stomach flipped as Matt Rowan's name flashed up. This was it.

"Sorry, Dad," he said again. "I've gotta take this."

"All good, Charlie. Saturday next week, mate. And don't forget to turn off that light."

Charlie sighed. The cleaners forgetting to turn off his elderly neighbor's light barely registered on his list of concerns. Not when he was 99 percent sure Matt had dire, fatal news. He'd pulled every string imaginable to get Charlie an emergency MRI, and now he was calling at night with an update.

After-hours probably meant terminal.

"There's nothing there." The neurologist's voice seemed distant; much farther away than the twenty or so miles that separated Marwick and Abercrombie.

"What do you mean, nothing?" He wouldn't put it past Matt to be setting up a joke at Charlie's expense. *No brain at all*, he'd say. *Haw-haw-haw!*

God he hated that laugh.

"No tumor. No mass, no unusual shadows—nothing. A healthy brain, from what I can see. You're all clear."

Charlie felt numb. *No tumor.*

"So what's causing it then?" he asked.

"Charlie! You should be thanking me! You're not going to die. You haven't had a stroke, there's no aneurysm, no lesions, no damage of any kind, in fact." Matt sounded almost annoyed that he hadn't found anything exciting. "So it's not physical. It probably only leaves stress. Which, if I'm honest, Charlie, would surprise me. Because…let's be real here. You're a pretty laid-back guy. And general practice isn't really high-stakes stuff.

You misdiagnose strep throat, you're hardly going down five million bucks in a malpractice suit, are you?"

He brayed hysterically. The relief Charlie had felt at Matt Rowan's news was fading, draining away like the colors did when he saw a patient. And in its place was that prickly, gnawing urge to get out and do something.

Something spectacular.

"Hey, but seriously Charlie, no disrespect," Matt continued. "I've got nothing but admiration for you, buddy. You're the front line. Nothing gets to us if it hasn't gone through you guys first."

Charlie could picture his friend leaning back in his chair, maybe polishing his glasses, a satisfied look in his mole-like eyes.

And it might've been that imagined expression, or the comment, or a combination of both, but Charlie bristled, and he said something he hadn't said to another person within hundreds of miles.

"It could be stress. I'm moving."

If his life had been a fantasy movie, Charlie thought, that's the moment that the town would've heard him. The trees lining the road would have swayed and reached toward the car, maybe the streetlights would've flickered, and the Marwick Bridge behind him might have crumbled into the dark river below. A town, refusing to let him go, doing what it needed to trap him there. More than it had already done.

But the trees didn't sway, and the bridge didn't crumble, and as Charlie's headlights played across the front of the Marwick Hotel, the only activity came from a small group enjoying post-work drinks on the grand old pub's veranda. A few familiar faces glanced up, and Charlie told himself the look in their eyes was curiosity, not betrayal: *Whose car? Oh, it's only the doc.* One or two waved into the darkness at him, and he waved back, knowing they couldn't really see him behind the glare of his lights.

"Rubbish," the neurologist scoffed. "You're leaving? Come on, where are you gonna go?"

"London. I'm getting back into emergency medicine." Charlie paused, and while it was the truth, it still didn't sound grand enough. Not for Matthew Rowan and his serious-looking office, where serious art hung on the walls. No human body posters in sight; these were oils and watercolors. "I've been headhunted."

Headhunted was a bit of a stretch. Charlie had actually been one of hundreds of applicants, the online job ad triggering an alert he'd set up. He'd done three interviews: two online and one in person, which had meant flights and a week of annual leave. (He'd told MaryAnn he was off to the beach, a fib that almost came undone when he returned home without a tan.) At last the hospital had made him an offer, and he'd accepted it without hesitation.

"Well, congrats." Matt sounded unsure, irritated, as though Charlie had just upset the power balance between them. Which, Charlie supposed, he had. "Didn't see that coming; thought you loved being a GP. What'd your folks say? And your boss, what's-her-name, she would've hit the roof. I reckon you're her retirement plan."

"I haven't told MaryAnn yet."

"Can I be there when you do?"

"I haven't told *anyone*. So you can't either. But I've got six weeks. Less now. Just over five."

Matt was still talking, proposing one last farewell dinner that neither of them probably expected to attend, when Charlie pulled up outside his house. It was exactly as his dad had described: dark and abandoned, the lawn long and unkempt, and according to Malcolm Knight, probably harboring snakes. Malcolm said he needed to mow it. Hadn't he also asked him to do something else?

"Hey, Matt? Sorry, but I've got to run. Somebody's left a light on in my neighbor's house."

"Oooh, an emergency in Marwick. You're gonna miss those," Matt mocked, and Charlie hung up mid-*haw*.

He pulled his house keys from his pocket and flipped through to one that didn't match: the spare key his neighbor had given him in case of emergencies. He hadn't needed it much since Mrs. Longstaff had gone into care, but when she'd been living next door he'd checked on her daily. It'd been his recommendation that she move; the constant juggle of oxygen cylinders and eight different pills morning and night was just getting too much for her. She still expected to come home at some point (she needed some hope, and Charlie would never want to take that away), so paid someone to come in once a week and dust the blinds, vacuum the floors. It wasn't the first time they'd left a light on.

Charlie turned the key and pushed open his neighbor's door.

The entry hall was dark, but at the end of the hall there was a line of light under the kitchen door. Charlie could still smell Ruth Longstaff's menthol cigarettes; the scent had infused itself into the walls and the furniture.

But there was something else, something new. Another

smell: fragrant and fresh, like citrus. A new cleaning product. Perhaps mint too, but definitely citrus. Like the orange blossom that dotted his parents' property.

His shoes left scuff marks on the polished wooden floor, and he wondered if he'd said too much to Matt about leaving Marwick, whether his news could leap the miles between Abercrombie and his hometown and spread before he'd figured out how to share it the right way. The careful way. He yanked open the door to the kitchen. Matt was right though about telling MaryAnn; she'd be—

A shriek almost deafened him.

Something small and very hard hit him square in the face, an inch below his eye, before falling and shattering at his feet. Then another slammed into the wall beside him, and a third bounced off the fridge. Both hit the floor and exploded into a million tiny shards.

Charlie threw himself backward into the hallway, half rolling, half scrambling back until he could kick the door closed. Another impact, another smash, and now something was seeping under the door, into the dark hall.

Something that smelled like lemons.

Charlie put his hand to his stinging face and felt warm blood. What on earth just happened?

The door flew open, and a figure was standing above him, arms raised as though trying to make herself seem bigger, more threatening.

A silhouette, gorgeous in the kitchen light.

"Charlie?"

That voice.

He squinted up at her and took in the black hair piled in a messy bun and those big dark eyes.

*Oh no.*

*Not now.*

"Oh my God, Charlie. It's *you*. And you're bleeding."

"Of course I'm bleeding, Gen. You just threw a—what *did* you throw?"

"Uh…I think that was patchouli oil. The last one was lemon though. Can't you smell it?"

"Why, Gen?"

"Why patchouli? First thing I grabbed."

"No!" He swiped roughly at the blood now trickling down his cheek. "Why are you throwing bottles at me in the first place?"

"Well, why are you breaking into my grandma's house? It was just self-defense, Charlie—I didn't know it was you. I reckon I could defend myself against *you* without having to smash anything."

She extended a hand and he took it without thinking.

Her skin was soft and warm, and he tried to ignore the rush he felt race along his arm as he got to his feet.

*No.*

He let go.

Charlie had too much on his mind for this.

The colors, the pressure, the *numbers*. The numbers that meant nothing, but were filling pages in a notebook, hidden deep within his desk.

And his deadline. His departure date: five and a half weeks, to take up the job he was *supposed* to do seven years ago.

To get his life back on track.

But no.

Genevieve Longstaff was back.

Just in time to ruin everything.

# 3

Edna Bradley died on Friday morning.

Charlie didn't find out straight away; not until after his first appointment of the day, during which a curious thing happened.

It takes a special kind of hypochondriac to have a usual seat in a waiting room, but Simon Lopez was that kind of hypochondriac. He leaped up the moment Charlie arrived to collect him and led the way into the doctor's office. Charlie felt almost redundant.

"Does this look infected to you, Doc?"

No greeting, no small talk, not even a mention of the fresh nick on Charlie's cheek, too high for a shaving cut. Simon held out one hand, thumb extended like he was hitching a ride, and Charlie squinted at the nail.

The pressure came on quickly behind his eyes: the intense, squeezing sensation. But now, after dozens of patients, Charlie was ready for it. He was ready too for the color to leach from the room, and when it did, he paid little attention, noting only that Simon Lopez's pallid complexion didn't really change that much. Then the swirling, churning feeling inside his skull spat out a number—the sense of a number, really—and as the colors washed back into the world and the pressure melted away, that big number was the only thing left behind.

Simon rotated his hand, trying to give Charlie a better look at his thumb. He winced, as if to encourage a more dire diagnosis.

"I squashed it the other night. The latch on the gate at the park is busted. Reckon the nail's gonna go black, maybe come off. But—touch this bit here—it feels kinda hot too, so I thought it might be infected. Tried to book in yesterday afternoon, get on top of it early, but you weren't here."

Charlie had no doubt that Simon had tried to make a preemptive appointment about his sore thumb. On a normal day, when he wasn't ducking to Abercrombie for a quick brain scan, Charlie could allocate fifteen minutes to each patient. Allowing for emergencies and overruns, and a sandwich at his desk, he'd usually see up to thirty patients before heading home. One hundred and fifty individual appointments per week. And on any given week, Simon could be reasonably expected to occupy up to three of those slots.

Charlie gazed at his patient, who was still grimacing at his own thumb. If he had to guess Simon's age (which he didn't, because he had thrice-weekly access to his medical record and knew exactly how old he was), he would have said close to midfifties. His face had that gray tinge, a smattering of old pockmarks, and an almost greasy sheen that Charlie suspected came from too many potato chips, not enough sunshine, and too much time spent convincing himself that he was actually sick. Simon was in fact forty-three; just five years older than Charlie. But while Charlie went for a run most mornings and still played a-grade tennis, Simon freely admitted he avoided exercise because of the likelihood of injury. It meant the five-year age gap looked closer to twenty, although genetics probably played a part too. Charlie had his dad's broad shoulders, whereas Simon had inherited the physique of a bowling pin.

"Your thumb looks okay, Simon," he said, and his patient's face fell. "It's a bit swollen, and you're right, that nail might go black. But it's not infected."

Simon shuffled out, looking dejected. Charlie waited a few moments, making sure he wasn't about to burst back through the door with something he'd forgotten. Then, satisfied he was alone, he opened his desk drawer and rummaged deep within it. Buried beneath medication pamphlets, Edna Bradley's Tupperware container, and three copies of *The Lancet* that he still hadn't read, was a small black notebook.

He pulled it out and opened it to the first page. The first line: Edna Bradley. Below her, the name of every patient he'd seen since then, and next to each one, the number he'd felt form in his brain. Downloaded to the page, cleared out of his head, then hidden away where nobody would see. Until Matt Rowan had called, he'd been so sure it was a tumor, pressing on strange parts of his brain and causing odd things to happen, like John Travolta in *Phenomenon*. But he didn't have a tumor, he hadn't developed telekinetic powers, and he wasn't going to die, so it seemed more like an anomaly than a phenomenon. *Anomaly*, starring Charlie Knight. Not quite a Hollywood blockbuster—it was something weird, for sure, but something minor, something private. Something he didn't need to declare to his new employer at St. John's Private Hospital, especially since he'd already signed the contract. Because a side effect of stress—if that's what it was—would pass. Probably once he was on the plane.

Charlie considered whether he really needed to add Simon's name to the book; he was already there from Tuesday, when he'd fronted with a stomach complaint. Under questioning, Simon revealed he'd eaten two large bags of Doritos while updating his website. Charlie diagnosed indigestion and patiently took Simon through—for perhaps the twentieth time—the foods he *should* be eating. There was his entry: Simon Lopez, 14190.

Charlie's brow furrowed.

14190.

It wasn't the same number he'd felt when Simon held out his thumb.

He turned to the next page, to the blank space beneath the last name there, and scrawled *Simon Lopez* again. Then, letting the pen lead the way, the number he'd felt appeared in ink: 14187.

Close, but not quite the same. Possibly human error, but Charlie doubted it; when he wrote a number down, it was like it flowed from his cerebral cortex, straight down his arm, into the pen, and onto the paper. But it was curious, wasn't it, that the numbers seemed to—

A soft chime from his computer interrupted his thoughts.

Next patient is here. But can you return a call first? It's
urgent.

Charlie could see Lisa was typing another message, and
he waited, because if Lisa said it was urgent, then it probably
was. She had impeccable judgment for someone so young. She
needed it, to make up for the chronic hopelessness of her desk-
mate, Toby.

The message appeared, and Charlie's eyes went straight to
the phone number he was supposed to call.

Charlie knew that number: Marwick Aged Care and
Hospice.

His heart sank.

Edna.

"It was the shampoo," the day supervisor said, raising his
voice over the noise threatening to drown him out. Charlie had
called right on Morning Music Hour, and somebody was hammering out "When the Saints Go Marching In" on the piano. It
seemed an oddly appropriate choice when one of their residents
was just being wheeled off on a gurney, although the rendition
was perhaps a little too jaunty. "At least, I reckon it was the
shampoo. It just makes the tiles so slippery," he continued.

*Oh, Edna*, thought Charlie. *What a terrible way to go.* His
imagination filled in the gaps of the supervisor's story. Edna
Bradley squeezing shampoo into her hand, a little of it drib-
bling through her fingers and onto the tiles. Her weight shifting slightly, a foot finding the slippery patch and shooting out
from under her. The panic she must've felt at that moment, and
the pain, and the *sound*, that horrible crunch when she hit the

tiles. All those children's faces, all the shortbread, all the kindness, all the memories, gone in an instant. One sudden, lonely, awful instant.

Charlie closed his eyes as a deep sadness washed over him, a longing to have been with her at the end.

To have put a hand on her arm.

*Oh, Edna.*

"They think she was only there for half an hour or so," the supervisor said. "The cleaner goes in every Friday morning. Not the first time she's found a resident who's passed away, but still, not exactly in the job description." The man paused, and when he spoke again, his voice broke slightly. "Not a good morning, all round."

Charlie murmured his agreement.

"Anyway, you were listed as Edna's regular GP, so I wanted you to know. We'll miss her, that's for sure. And her shortbread. She took over the kitchen once a week to make another batch, left a god-awful mess, but it kinda became like currency here."

Charlie chuckled softly. "What, bribery?"

"Can't say for sure. But I don't remember ever seeing Edna taking her turn as the bingo caller. Always someone willing to fill in for her. Bit of shortbread probably changing hands. I don't know…" He lowered his voice again as the mystery piano player stopped. "But it kinda feels like she's been snubbing her nose at this—at death, I mean—for a while now. I thought she'd outrun it forever, the way she was going. But it probably just caught up with her. Caught her out. Not like she didn't make the most of it though."

*Snubbing her nose at death.* It was unusually profound for

the supervisor, who'd always struck Charlie as someone who was probably biding his own time at Marwick Aged Care and Hospice until something a little more *lively* came up. The pianist started again ("Ode to Joy" now, but still played at the speed that'd made "When the Saints" sound like a polka), and Charlie thanked the man and hung up.

He pulled the Tupperware container from his drawer and opened it: there was one shortbread biscuit remaining, the last he'd ever have from Edna Bradley. He picked it up, raised it slightly to the sky as though saluting the baker, then bit into the sweet, crumbly cookie, smiling sadly as the pieces dissolved on his tongue.

Edna was dead. And to think the last time he saw her, he was bumping into his desk, knocking jelly beans over, and pretending everything was okay, when in fact everything was not okay, and the number 4 had just appeared in the smoky haze of his misfiring brain.

She'd been so gentle, so kind, so vital. She'd held his arm, made fun of his salt-and-pepper hair, and promised to keep his secrets—and now she was gone, a tragic end to a wonderful life, and to a strange, strange week. A lot had happened in just four days.

*Four days.*

Charlie's stomach dropped away, taking the shortbread with it and leaving a gaping hole into which all reason, all logic, all sense of what was possible and *normal* threatened to collapse.

*No way.*

*It's just a coincidence.*

Four days ago.

His computer chimed again with another message from Lisa:

Just a reminder. Jamie Clayton and his dad are here. Not to rush you, but he's getting a bit angry.

He assumed Max Clayton was the one getting angry. Jamie was only six.

Charlie jumped up from his chair, suddenly dazed and a little unsure. He didn't want to leave his office, didn't want to see a patient; he wanted to stay right there and process this thing that had just occurred to him. This thing that was completely impossible yet seemed to make sense, like two pieces from two different jigsaws coming together and just *fitting*.

But Jamie Clayton's dad was *getting a bit angry*. And he'd be taking it out on Lisa, who didn't deserve it, and he'd be taking it out on Toby, who may be trying to defend Lisa's honor, because poor, hopeless Toby had a crush on his colleague, the kind that made him say and do stupid things.

"There he is," Charlie said at the waiting room door, offering Jamie a high five. "One of my favorite customers." He wasn't supposed to have favorites, but Jamie was one of them. Abigail Wilson, a sweet young woman with a developmental disorder, was another; there was so much intelligence behind those eyes, and Charlie knew exactly what to say to make them sparkle with delight. Edna Bradley was on the list too. Well, she used to be.

*Four days.*

Jamie knew the way to Charlie's office. It was, after all, his fifth visit that year—not quite his record, but close. The boy's dad followed behind, eyes fixed on the phone in his hand.

"Good to know appointment times are flexible," he muttered without looking up. "Some of us have got places to be." Max Clayton seemed more snarky than angry, but Charlie could see red rage-blotches fading on his close-cropped scalp. Perhaps he'd used up all his temper on the young duo on reception. Charlie felt an entirely unprofessional urge to punch Max in the face.

"All right, then," said Charlie, ignoring Max entirely and talking just to Jamie, a slight boy with two very large front teeth. "Why aren't you at school?" he asked, eyes narrowing playfully.

"Cos I'm sick," the boy replied.

"Sick!" Charlie cried. "What are you doing in here then? I don't want sick people in my office! Gross!"

"No!" Jamie laughed. Even his little chuckle sounded painful, catching in his throat. "You're the doctor! You have to see sick people!"

"Oh yeah," Charlie replied. "I suppose I do. So what's the problem this time? Broken leg?"

*The trigger.*

His overloaded brain refused for a moment to allow space for the churning, wriggling mass behind his eyes, but then it gave way and he felt the number form. A huge one. Then the room sharpened, the colors returned, and he was back.

A very big number. Much bigger than Edna Bradley's 4.

*And four days later, she was dead.*

Jamie was still laughing.

"Not my leg. It's fine! See?" He held out his skinny right leg and swung it about.

"Oh, of course," Charlie replied, recalling where he'd left the conversation just a few seconds earlier. "Okay then, give me a look at that throat." He pulled a tongue depressor from the jar, and Jamie was already saying "ahhhhh."

"Have you done this before, Jamie? Are you sure *you're* not the doctor here?" he asked.

The boy shook his head, tongue swaying from side to side. It was like dealing with a miniature Simon Lopez, but before the paranoia kicked in.

Simon Lopez. The thought jarred in his mind.

"Come *on*." Jamie's dad urged, still staring at his phone. His scalp was almost back to a normal color. "I've gotta go. Just give us a letter saying he can go to school, or they'll try to send him home again."

*Simon Lopez. Two visits, two different numbers, just a few digits apart. Three numbers between them.*

*When was Simon in last?* Charlie swiveled to his computer. *Tuesday morning. And then again today. Friday.*

He counted the days on his fingers.

*Three.*

Simon's number—that massive number—was counting down. Edna's must've done the same.

And when it hit zero…

"All done," Charlie announced, choosing to focus only on what was in front of him—an act of self-preservation, because if he thought at all about the numbers, about the *days*, about Edna, about Simon, about the tick, tick, tick down to zero, then it might just make his head explode. "Tonsillitis again. No school today. But should be right by Monday."

"Christ almighty." Max Clayton rolled his eyes, looking up at last. "You lot would keep him home for a paper cut. The kid isn't staying home. He's going to school."

"He can't."

Charlie prepared a prescription for medication: a sticky pink mixture that he hoped would actually make it into the poor boy. Jamie's dad took it, and Charlie caught a glimpse of the man's phone and the screen he'd been so absorbed by. He felt a little flash of anger.

"Max, he needs to take it easy," Charlie said. "Watch TV, keep the fluids up, early to bed."

Max shoved the prescription into his pocket and sneered at Charlie.

"Easy for you to say. I've gotta be somewhere at ten. I can't just drop everything so he can watch *Paw Patrol* all day."

"*Paw Patrol*?" Jamie interjected weakly. "I *hate Paw Patrol*! I *like Rusty Rivets. Paw Patrol*'s for babies."

"Yeah, well you won't be watching either. Come on."

Jamie's face fell, and that urge to break Max Clayton's nose returned. But it would be unprofessional, Charlie knew that, despite how good it might feel and how richly it was deserved. He'd be struck off, then he'd be fired, and London wouldn't happen, and so to distract himself from the temptation, he let his mind return to the numbers. He thought of Jamie's number. He thought of writing it into his black notebook, and of what it meant.

It was a huge number.

And if each one was a day, like it had been for Edna, then Jamie had decades and decades ahead of him.

He just had to get through this decade first, with a pig of a human who could barely tear himself away from his phone.

Charlie felt his anger take a more pointed form. Maybe it was time for a little chat with Max.

"Hey, Jamie?" he said. The boy turned. "If you run out to reception and see Toby—he's the guy with the brown hair, floppy, looks a bit like a puppy—he's got some photos on his phone of his lizards. Ask him to show you." Toby wouldn't be happy. He was trying very hard to be cool in front of Lisa, and his secret collection didn't help his image.

Jamie took off at a run, and Charlie closed the door behind him.

Rough math: young Jamie Clayton had another eighty-five years of life. Eighty-five years that could be sabotaged by the man whose scalp was getting blotchy again and whose face was twisting into an impatient scowl.

"What now?" hissed Max. Foamy spittle caught on his lip.

"Jamie's a great boy," Charlie started, keeping his voice quiet. Calm. Max narrowed his eyes, and a vein emerged in his forehead. Charlie hadn't seen that since they were in high school. "And I think we both want him to get the best start."

The scalp blotches turned a furious red.

"Well you can mind your own business, Knight." Max had never called him *doctor*. Max Clayton was stuck twenty-odd years in the past. "He's *my* kid. I'll decide what he—"

"I saw your phone. I saw where you need to be at ten o'clock. If you take him to the races today, I'll find out, and I'll report you to child services."

Max made a noise, a protest forming in the back of his throat.

"And if he doesn't get that medicine, I'll find that out too, and I'll report you."

"I can't just—"

"And if I see you in here again, glued to your phone while your boy's sick, when he *needs* you to look after him, guess what?"

"You'll—"

"I'll report you. Good guess. Now get out."

Max's fist clenched, and Charlie thought for a moment he was going to take a swing at him.

*Do it*, he urged silently. *Then I can break your nose.*

But the fist unclenched. The other hand slid his phone back into his pocket.

The man left his office, his balding head a brilliant, fiery crimson.

Charlie collapsed into his chair, the fight rushing out of him but the anger still pulsing, still searching for somewhere to go.

Without thinking, he pulled his notebook from its hiding spot in his drawer and wrote Jamie's name. Then he added his number, that huge number that somehow—impossibly— corresponded to the precise number of days one sweet little boy had left on earth.

Simon Lopez's number was counting down.

Edna Bradley's had hit zero.

Charlie dropped the book on the desk, suddenly aware of what he was holding and not wanting to touch it a moment longer.

A little black notebook, full to the brim with death.

# 4

Charlie woke on Saturday morning with a yellowing bruise on his cheek, a hint of a hangover, and a number in his book that he couldn't quite remember writing.

The bruise just below his eye was Genevieve's mark. Despite all the blood, the cut from the glass bottle she'd hurled at his face had only been small and was almost better. But what had been a faint red patch on Friday morning was a yellowy purple by Saturday and was just getting started. Charlie estimated it would be at its most vibrant by the time Monday morning rolled around, when he'd be back with patients and joining the mourners at Edna Bradley's funeral. It probably wasn't what the notice in the *Marwick Daily* meant by "wear a touch of color," but Edna would've *loved* the story of how he'd got it. She'd always liked Gen.

So the bruise was expected. The hangover was not.

Charlie hadn't intended to go anywhere *near* the Marwick Hotel. He'd actually planned to go straight home, close the curtains, and open the notebook. He was going to read those names again and examine the numbers that had all taken on a new, troubling significance. But when he called Nick Selby to pull out of tennis, Nick had reminded him that it was their second-last match, and if they won this one they'd be playing for the title the following Friday night. And Knight/Selby had been engraved on the Marwick a-grade trophy seven years in a row, and unless Charlie was on death's door, Nick intended to make it eight. So a distracted Charlie took to the court behind the community hall as clouds of moths swarmed the old floodlights overhead.

And he had to admit—slogging a ball as hard as he could while picturing Max Clayton had actually felt kind of good. And when he won their match with an ace that would've taken Max's head off, and Nick declared dinner was on him, he didn't object, thinking it might distract him for a couple of hours.

It didn't.

Charlie had glanced at the door so many times that Nick asked him if he had somewhere else to be. Charlie couldn't confess that he was watching for Gen, half expecting her to waltz right on in. And the meal did nothing to take his mind off the numbers either, not when four separate drinkers all dropped by his table with questions about dodgy knees and sore hips. They were easy to pick: they were the ones walking his way with a large scotch whiskey that he hadn't ordered. And after he'd helped them, they'd stayed to watch him down his drink, as though the debt wasn't paid until he'd finished every drop. He wanted to tell them there was no debt. After all, he didn't even *like* whiskey, let alone drinking doubles.

He massaged his temples, feeling the aftermath of the night's work. Squinting against the bright morning light streaming through his window, he pulled out the notebook and flipped through the pages. Underneath his final patient from Friday afternoon were five more lines of text, all messier than anything else he'd written. The first four were the patients from the pub, the ones who paid for their consults with drinks, even though he would've helped them for nothing, and not just to spare himself the hangover.

But the last one... Well, that one was different.

*Don Penrose.*

Next to his name was the number 5.

Charlie screwed his face up as he tried to remember. He knew who Don was, of course, and he remembered spotting him at the hotel, along with the other members of the Marwick Woodturners. The Woodturners all had the gristly look of hard workers who'd spent most of their lives outdoors. They were eight or nine old blokes who gathered every Wednesday and Friday to make stuff from timber at the community hall and then graduated to the pub to quench their thirst. Three of them were Charlie's patients. Don wasn't; he saw MaryAnn Steiner instead, though not for much longer. Don Penrose had been in a battle against prostate cancer for years, and judging by his gaunt cheeks, it was a fight he was going to lose.

In five days, apparently.

And now Charlie remembered. Poor Don had pushed himself up from his stool, loudly denouncing prostate cancer for its effect on his bladder, and before anyone knew it—before

Don knew it, most likely—he tripped and was on the ground. The bar had gone silent, and Charlie had been the first to his side. He remembered lifting Don gently to his feet and vaguely recalled the room turning gray. Five days wouldn't have come as a surprise. It could just as easily have been three or one or none. Don Penrose, Charlie suspected, was on his farewell visit to the Marwick Hotel, having one last drink with his Woodturner pals.

So that explained the newest numbers in the notebook. He must've recorded them after he stumbled home. But it didn't help with any of the other questions buzzing about his head like those moths bothering the lights at the tennis court. So many questions, but they all relied on a gigantic leap of faith: that these numbers were truly linked to the lives of his patients. And on that front, as extraordinary as it seemed, Charlie couldn't see any other option. Not just because he'd ruled out some medical cause, but because the *evidence* supported it. He didn't like to think of Edna Bradley as *evidence*, but in a clinical way, that's exactly what she was. So if Charlie could get over the biggest hurdle—actually believing that this was happening, and it was happening to *him*, of all people—then a million other questions floated to the surface. Where were the numbers coming from? How accurate were they? What was he supposed to do with them? Should he tell anybody? Would anybody even believe him? So many questions, and a severe shortage of answers. He didn't even know where to start looking for them, and the whole thing began to feel like a horrible, confusing dream, one that came with a prickly headache and no real way out. Except, maybe, that distant speck of light that came from his departure.

So he swallowed two Advil and started packing. Because putting his life into boxes might make the move more real. Make that distant speck of light a little bit closer.

When somebody knocked on his door on Sunday afternoon, Charlie looked around his living room in a panic. Six or seven large cardboard boxes sat in various stages of completion. Two of them had already been taped up, and he'd scribbled *Living Room* across them in handwriting so bad that they may end up not just in the wrong room, but on the wrong continent altogether. Why on earth had he started in the most obvious room in the house, when his departure was a secret to everyone—especially those most likely to visit him?

It would be his dad, just swinging by for a beer, or to see whether he'd mown the lawn yet. Sundays were his day off—no house showings, no auctions. Prime visiting time. It pained him to do it, but Charlie didn't move. He'd have to give Malcolm a call that night and tell him he'd been out.

*Or I could tell him the truth.*

Another knock, louder this time, which was odd, because Malcolm Knight only ever knocked once.

Then a third; the kind of knock he'd seen on TV, just before police bashed through the door of a suspected drug den.

He relented, walked down the hall, and opened the door a crack—three inches at most, aware that it looked like he was up to something. Which he was.

"I knew you were home," Genevieve said with a grin. Her teeth were so white and her lips so full, and Charlie knew he was in trouble. But then her smile vanished. "Oh God. Your cheek."

She leaned in close, peering with dismay at her handiwork, and

Charlie saw genuine sorrow in her eyes. "I'm so sorry, Charlie. I really didn't mean to hurt you."

"It's fine," he insisted, still half hiding behind the door. "Honestly. Looks worse than it feels."

Gen raised one delicate eyebrow, and Charlie noticed she had a hand behind her back.

"Are you trying to act tough with me, Charlie Knight? Because you weren't so tough when you were under attack in my kitchen." She shook her head. "Seriously, I feel awful. I was bringing you a peace offering, but it kind of seems like it's not enough now. Even if it *was* your favorite, once upon a time."

"You're not going to throw it at me, are you?" Charlie asked, and Gen laughed. It was a beautiful sound: high and clear and full of light. No *haw-haw-haw* here.

"That depends. Are you going to invite me in?"

*The boxes.*

"I can't, I'm sorry. It's a mess in here. Spring cleaning."

"Please," Gen scoffed. "I've had seven years with a flatmate who's never even *heard* of spring cleaning. I'll give you a hand." And then she pushed the door open and strode past Charlie, and he smelled citrus and summer. It was the same aroma he'd noticed in Gen's grandmother's hallway, the one that overpowered the menthol residue of Ruth Longstaff's cigarettes.

It was, he decided, a very nice smell.

In the hand Gen had hidden behind her back he spied a foil-wrapped tray, which came with its own aroma of something fresh-baked and rich. Genevieve was heading for the kitchen, but to get there, she would pass through the living room.

He chased after her.

"Gen, really, I'm okay. I don't need help."

"It's the least I can do, Charlie, since I broke your face. And I thought...well, I thought that maybe we should talk about—"

He caught up to her, grabbed her wrist, and the same thrill shot through him. But it was too late. She was staring at the boxes, staring at the books and trinkets and all the stuff that he was packing for his new life. For his adventure.

"What's going on, Charlie? Are you moving?"

He searched his mind for an answer that didn't involve the truth and came up completely blank.

"Yeah," he admitted. "In about five weeks."

"You're not leaving Marwick though," Gen stated, as though this was a given. As though the biggest move Charlie was capable of was across town, perhaps closer to the river. Or maybe— heaven forbid—back to his parents' place.

"I am. Leaving, I mean."

Gen spun to look at him, her eyes growing wide.

"Where are you going?"

"London. Emergency medicine." He didn't need to dress it up for Genevieve. No embellishment required.

Something flickered across Gen's face. Confusion, maybe, or something else. Charlie couldn't be sure, because it was there for just a fraction of a second before it was replaced by a grin, huge and beautiful.

"Charlie! You're doing it!" And then she was hugging him, and he was enveloped in that summery smell. At last she pulled away and held up the tray. "The brownies can be a celebration then. I wish I'd brought wine too, now." She smiled mischievously at him, that eyebrow twitching up again. "I won't take it personally or anything. The moment I move in next door, you're packing up. One in, one out. Keeping the population stable."

"Move in? Aren't you just back for a visit, to see Ruth?"

She shook her head, and her hair swished across her bare shoulders. Charlie looked away.

"Nope. I'm buying it from her. The thought of someone else getting it and painting it orange or something, or worse, knocking it down." She grimaced. "I have to, Charlie. I've always loved that place. Lot of good memories, you know?"

Charlie did know. In an instant he was back there, gazing up into the stars above Marwick, and seeing all of them at once: clear and bright and *everywhere*. Sitting with Genevieve on the front steps of that house, absorbed by the twinkling and the inky blackness and the chance of spotting a shooting star. They'd seen one at last, a brief, brilliant burst of light that dazzled for a second or two, but in Charlie's memory, sitting there with Gen, that moment had lasted for hours. Days.

"Hey, I might get your dad to help with the sale. Reckon he'd do it? For me?"

"I think—"

"Wait, what did your parents say about you leaving?"

"I haven't said anything."

Gen winced. "You thought it was them at the door, didn't you? And you were just going to sit in here and pretend you weren't home. Really? That's not the Charlie that I…" She trailed off.

"Yeah?" he prompted.

"That I remember," Gen finished. Her cheeks pinked. They both knew it wasn't what she was going to say.

Charlie took the tray of brownies and uncovered them, largely for something to focus on, so that he wasn't looking at Gen. Wasn't looking at those dark eyes and her flawless skin.

Genevieve Longstaff, back in Marwick. And in his house. Again.

There was so much he wanted to ask her, and yet something was stopping him. All his questions had little red flags waving at him, like they were anchored to something unpleasant, something that made him feel uneasy, and he just couldn't quite put his finger on what it was. It was more than the fact that she was back and he was leaving, because it was something he needed to do and something she'd already done.

Something they had planned to do together.

"I'm sorry again about your cheek," Gen said as she picked up a small stone vase that Charlie had never actually used. *Why am I even taking it with me*, he wondered, as Gen deftly wrapped it in newspaper and placed it in one of the open moving boxes.

"It was just a reflex thing," she continued. "Shame it had to be patchouli. It's one of the more expensive ones."

"Expensive what?"

"Oils," Gen replied. "Get this. I'm an…" She cleared her throat. "*Oils lifestyle consultant*. Aromatherapy. I got into it about eighteen months ago. And you know what, Charlie? Don't laugh. I'm actually pretty good at it."

Charlie had no doubt that she was. Gen seemed to be good

at most things she put her mind to. Once she'd decided something, there was no stopping her. And no talking her out of it.

She picked up another trinket: an ugly ceramic cactus that
had sat on Charlie's coffee table for years.

"I gave you this," Gen exclaimed, turning it over carefully.
"Can't believe it's still in one piece. Actually, I can't believe
you've still got it."

"Course I do," Charlie murmured. He didn't need to dissect
every part of his life. Not now. "Essential oils? And you make
money from this?"

"It's just on the side for now. Nine to five, I'm still in marketing." She pulled a face, and even that was beautiful. "I start
back in Abercrombie tomorrow. But the oils… That's fun. Nice
people, they run a bunch of retreats and training sessions, and
I've built up a good network. Well, I did have a network. I guess
I'm starting again." She shrugged.

"It kind of sounds like a cult," Charlie teased. "Who gets to
be supreme leader?"

"Please. Essential oils have health benefits. I still take my
meds, obviously, but I don't think it's a coincidence that I hav-
en't had a seizure in a year. *At least* a year, actually."

And suddenly the alarms went off in Charlie's head, great
big shrieking alarms that were so loud, so completely obvious
that he wondered why he hadn't thought of it before. *That* was
the source of the red flags, the reason he couldn't pick the right
question to ask Gen. A vague sense that he needed to be careful, because he'd forgotten entirely about the numbers, and the
trigger, and his little black notebook.

But he also knew why he'd forgotten all about it: because

*Genevieve Longstaff* had been on his doorstep, in his living room, helping him pack his boxes, and preparing him to blast right back out of her orbit.

*Don't ask anything else about her epilepsy. And if she tries to say more, stop her.*

He would run out of the room if he had to, because even looking like a complete idiot would be better than the alternative. Better than finding out how many days Gen had left on earth. He couldn't bear the thought of adding that name to his notebook and then counting down the years and months and days until her end. Knowing it about the patients he'd seen was tough enough, but to know it about the people he loved? What an unbearable pressure to make each moment count. To make every day perfect.

So Charlie changed the subject, thankful that she'd mentioned it in passing and hadn't been asking his advice. There'd been no trigger for the colors, for the number, and he steered the conversation back to a trigger-free zone.

"So why'd you come back?" It sounded way too blunt, maybe even as though he didn't want her there. But if Gen noticed, she didn't say anything.

"Honestly? I think I was getting homesick. Not even homesick, really, I just kind of knew it was time to come home. I was going to do it anyway, and then an opening came up back in the office at Abercrombie, so I took it as a sign. The money's the same. And with Grandma going into care, I thought I could keep an eye on her. But still, Charlie—I wasn't expecting *you* to be leaving. I kind of had this image of knocking down the fence, making one big backyard."

"What, like a commune? You know what that sounds like, Gen."

Then she laughed, and it was that pure, happy noise again, and he told himself *five weeks.*

*You need to do this, Charlie. Five weeks.*

He'd already missed his chance once. He couldn't let it happen again.

# 5

There was a ghost standing at reception, pale and empty. Charlie spotted her as he ushered in his fourth patient, one eye firmly on the clock; four was all he could fit in if he hoped to make it to Edna's funeral on time. Edna Bradley had never tolerated tardiness, so he had reason to believe the service would start at ten sharp, and heaven help any latecomers.

So he was moving quickly, bringing patients through, treating them, seeing them out, then writing down their number. One would pass away in his sixties, the others would make it to seventy and beyond. All many years away.

His sighting of the figure at the reception desk was just a distracted glimpse: a grief-stricken, middle-aged ghost of a woman, with sunken eyes and a mouth that had forgotten how to smile. But when Charlie came back to the counter after his fourth and final patient, she was gone.

Vanished.

"Toby?" he asked, and the young receptionist looked up at

him with that doughy expression that never seemed to go away. It gave him a dazed, slightly naive air, and Charlie had a feeling that patients went out of their way to avoid him and book their appointments through Lisa instead. It made Charlie feel oddly protective of him, even though Toby was old enough to take care of himself. "Was Deb Anders here before?"

"Yep." Toby's floppy hair bounced on his forehead. "But she didn't have an appointment. It was a walk-in."

"Oh. Right. Was it urgent?"

"I don't know. She didn't go into it. It was awkward, Doc," Toby admitted, squirming a little. "I didn't know what to say to her."

"I would've tried to squeeze her in if I'd known she'd just turned up."

"Not about the appointment," Toby said. "About...you know, Hayley."

Charlie eyed Toby curiously. He was twenty-two years old, and at moments like this, could pass for sixteen.

"Just say you're sorry."

"But I didn't do anything."

Charlie sighed. Maybe fifteen.

"Not sorry like that. Sorry for her loss."

"Oh. Okay. Next time, then." Toby looked back at his computer, clearly wanting the conversation to be over.

"Hang on, Toby... What did you actually say to her?"

The young man fiddled with his keyboard. "I didn't want to say the wrong thing. So I didn't say anything."

"Toby!" Charlie exclaimed. "You can't just ignore it. Her daughter died, mate. You should say something. It's just what you do."

"All right, Doc. Next time."

Charlie thought about Deborah Anders as he drove to Abercrombie (a little too fast; he was still watching the clock), wondering what she might have wanted. A counselor, maybe, or perhaps some sleeping pills. The frail, waif-like figure in reception had looked exhausted. Broken. Three months of nonstop grief will do that.

The mourners gathering for Edna were at a different stage of the process. Grief was still a fresh wound for them; the sudden news of her lonely death at Marwick Aged Care and Hospice had sliced through half the town, and many of them had made the drive to the earth-toned chapel at Abercrombie. Charlie didn't know what Edna would've made of being farewelled in Abercrombie; she'd been Marwick born and bred. *And died*, he supposed forlornly. But the crowd wanting to see her off wouldn't have fit in any Marwick venues. The community hall topped out at fifty people. The front bar of the Marwick Hotel could squeeze in maybe a dozen more. Edna was a victim of her own popularity.

Charlie sat in the back of the room as the eulogies were delivered. Edna's son, then a distraught granddaughter, then an ancient man who—once upon a time—had been Edna's boss at Marwick Primary School. He started his speech by reciting Edna's favorite poem in a rumbling bass, the rhythm almost lyrical. Charlie closed his eyes, and the words washed over him. The poem finished, and there was silence.

"But I believe the greatest tribute to my dear friend is the number of her former students who've come to say farewell to her today. If Edna taught you at some point during her career,

I'd ask you please to stand." The man's voice still resonated with the authority of a teacher; the headmaster, used to being obeyed.

Charlie got to his feet. From his position at the back of the chapel he saw dozens more do the same.

And there, off to the left, a couple of rows from the front, he saw a seated woman, dressed in black. Lorraine Knight. His mother, sitting with her crew: the overlapping parts of the Venn diagram marked *Lorraine's golf friends*, *Lorraine's Marwick friends*, and *Lorraine's friends who knew Edna*. And even that narrow group took up two pews.

"Remarkable." The speaker clapped his hands, beaming at the crowd. "Edna would've loved to see this. Then she would've asked if any of you had ever seen a comb in your life. And she might've asked about that shiner on your face, Doc."

Charlie felt the entire congregation turn to look at him as one. Well, almost as one; the last to turn was his own mum. Suddenly the room felt too small: three hundred sets of eyes staring at him, staring at his face. He gave a little smile.

"Edna always spoke her mind," the long-retired principal of Marwick Primary continued. "And she taught generation after generation to do the same thing. I think that's a legacy to be proud of. That, and her shortbread."

The crowd laughed, and Edna Bradley's former students started to sit again, until only Charlie remained standing. He sat too, but not before he'd taken in the coffin at the altar, its polished timber covered in flowers of every imaginable color. It was beautiful and bright. It was Edna.

The speaker mentioned something about how unexpected Edna's death was, about how he'd thought she would outlive him, and probably half the room too. This brought murmurs of agreement.

"But that," he said sadly, "just wasn't to be."

And the weight of his words hit Charlie like a stone.

Of everybody in the room, of everybody who knew Edna, only one person could have known that the end was speeding up on her.

If only he'd realized earlier what that number meant.

Maybe he could've saved her.

The thought played over and over in his mind through the rest of the service, through a closing hymn and then as Edna's coffin was carried from the chapel. It continued to roll about in his head as he gave his condolences to the family. He looked for his mother and spied Lorraine with her back to him, deep in conversation with a woman he didn't recognize. So he returned to his car, still turning the thought around, examining it from all angles like a fresh-dug gem, dirty and raw, searching for the place to cut. And it was still there as he began the drive back to Marwick, back to the clinic, where he'd see more patients and have more life expectancies come tumbling down the chute from who knows where. What was he supposed to do with that information, apart from write it down? Apart from download it out of his brain, onto the paper, where it just sat, heavy with responsibility that seemed far beyond him.

He didn't want to know when Gen would die. Did he want to know it about *anybody*?

Charlie Knight was playing God, and he felt wholly underqualified for the role.

A chill shuddered through him, through the whole car, and

as Charlie reached the highway he killed the air-conditioning and opened the window instead. The wind rushed in and swept the chill right out, and he was happy to leave it behind. To leave Abercrombie behind him too. The city often seemed so *busy*, almost *angry*; the kind of place where a wonderful human like Edna Bradley could be farewelled and forgotten all in the same day. Charlie always felt somehow lighter on the homeward drive. It might have been three lanes of traffic in both directions, but there was something about the lanes moving toward Marwick that seemed smoother. Happier, if it was possible for cars and trucks and asphalt to *be* happy. He moved into the middle lane, wind still buffeting him through the open window, and he thought of Gen. He thought of her carefully wrapping the ceramic cactus in newspaper and placing it in a box marked *Living Room*—a living room that would be impossibly distant from her own.

With one hand still firmly on the steering wheel, he touched his cheek, feeling the tender spot that marked Genevieve's sudden return to his life. She'd got him a good one with that glass bottle. But what difference did one extra drop make to the ocean of pain between them?

A car passed him on the left at the same moment as another slipped by on the right, both driving fast but not *too* fast, all heading toward Marwick. At some point Charlie must have eased off the accelerator and was now sitting well below the speed limit. *The Gen effect*, he thought, not unhappily. The two cars moved ahead of him easily, one in the left lane, one in the right, and he noticed distractedly that they were both Mazdas. In fact, they were almost the same shade of iridescent blue, although one was a newish SUV and the other a hatchback with sun-faded patches. Within seconds they were three, four, five car lengths in front of him, keeping perfect pace with one another, perhaps unaware the other was even there.

What happened next seemed inevitable to Charlie: both drivers did exactly what *he* would've done had he blown past a slow-moving car. The SUV on the right indicated to move left, and the hatch on the left indicated right, each readying to move into the middle lane—Charlie's lane. He watched idly as the indicators on both cars blinked, almost in unison: *on off on off on off.* Then, as though drawn in by a central magnet, they started to merge.

Two cars. One lane.

With a flash of horror Charlie saw what was happening.

"Stop! STOP!" he yelled, knowing he couldn't be heard, his words swallowed up by the roaring of the wind through his open window. He leaned heavily on his horn; it blared long and loud but just too late.

The cars—the big blue Mazda and its smaller sibling—came together in an instant. A harsh, shocking moment of contact, then they bounced apart. The SUV swerved back into the right lane, but the hatchback overcorrected. Then it was upside down.

It rolled once, twice, three times along the highway, each barrel roll marked by the torturous scream of twisting metal and glass exploding on asphalt. Charlie's teeth clenched as he stepped on his brakes, the howling wind replaced by the deafening screech of his own tires.

He stopped. The SUV in the right lane stopped too.

Then, at last, as though not wanting to be the only one still moving, the tiny blue hatchback ran out of momentum. It ground to a halt on its roof, midway through its fifth roll, and all was still. And quiet.

Charlie pushed his door open, the only noise now the blood kerthumping in his ears, then his feet pounding on the road. And as he reached the little car he noted something funny: it had stayed neatly in its lane, even on its roof.

*One of those weird things you pay attention to when your heart's going a million beats a minute.*

Then he saw the occupants.

And the blood.

# 6

When he was fresh out of medical school and still getting used to the *Dr.* appearing in front of his name, Charlie had landed a job in the emergency room at Sacred Sisters of Unity Hospital in Abercrombie. And he'd loved it—more than he expected; more than he even thought possible—and only left the hospital because he'd been asked to do a favor. Had he known that a twelve-month favor would extend another seven years, he may have given his mum a different answer. He'd found the ER to be deeply fulfilling, well beyond a simple hit of dopamine from patching someone up and sending them on their way. He was helping people in crisis, right when they needed him the most. In a single hour he'd stitched up a child's head from a full-speed collision with a dining table, wiping away tears and somehow getting her to laugh. He'd moved to the room next door and diagnosed a heart attack in a frightened-looking man complaining of tingles in his hand, then treated a stoic older lady whose handle had come clean off her cup of tea.

He remembered cutting off her sodden pants and the skin of her upper thighs peeling away with them. He'd winced, but the woman had stared straight ahead.

He saw the complete range of trauma in the emergency room of Sacred Sisters, but the thing he found most confronting was car accidents. There was something so unpredictable about them. Something so shocking. A family could be driving along, singing or bickering or laughing and then be *completely* wiped out, T-boned at an intersection by a kid in a Subaru who'd only looked at his phone for a second. Just long enough to miss a red light or a stop sign. Just long enough to put a steering wheel column through the chest of the other driver.

And that was the other thing that troubled Charlie about car accidents. The level of injury was so extreme, and at the same time so inconsistent. He could see two people in the same accident, one with a twisted piece of metal lodged in their spine, the other with a scratch on the shin, a barely-there line of bloody dots the only evidence they'd even been in a crash. But in his experience, the former was more common than the latter. Especially at high speed, like when accidents happened on the highway. He'd seen the aftermath before. But until this instant, on the way home from Edna Bradley's funeral, he'd never witnessed the moment of impact.

It took a few seconds on the highway between Abercrombie and Marwick for Charlie to get his bearings. The tiny blue Mazda was in its lane, but on its roof, facing the wrong way, and for a moment he wasn't sure if he was looking at the driver or the passenger. Either the windows had been down or the glass had blown out, but he could see straight through into the cabin of the vehicle. Two people were strapped tight into their seats, suspended upside down like bats in a cave. Vampire bats, maybe. There certainly was a lot of blood. Charlie knelt next to the car and stared at its occupants.

The bat nearest to him let out a groan; it was the driver. The steering wheel was visible under the saggy pillow of the airbag, smeared a grisly red. The man moaned again, eyelids fluttering as he reached up with one hand, searching for something near his waist.

Footsteps crunched across broken glass.

"Jesus Christ. I'm so sorry," a man said, panting. "I didn't see them, not until we hit and...ohhhhh. Oh no. Oh no. Are they dead?"

Charlie knew that voice. He swiveled around. It was Marty Harris, the owner of the Marwick Hotel. Marty was a nice guy, a decent guy. A great trivia host. Could pull a good beer. Careful driver too. Not that it really mattered at that moment, of course. In fact, none of it would make a jot of difference to whether the upside-down man with the glassy, fluttering eyes survived.

"Marty," he said. "I'll need your help."

Marty blinked at Charlie kneeling beside the car. Recognition flashed across his pale face, then instant relief.

"Christ, it's you Doc. Ain't that lucky," he said, and Charlie suppressed the desire to shake this nice, decent man by the shoulders and yell in his face that no, nothing happening right now could be described as lucky.

"What can I do?" Marty asked. "Pen's already calling the ambulance." He gestured back to the SUV.

"Give me a moment, Marty," Charlie said. He shouldn't

move the driver; there was a significant risk that his spine had been crushed or twisted or something, and just a little tweak could be enough to land him in a wheelchair for the rest of his life. But he was also worried about the car. Steam—or was it smoke?—was wisping out from the engine bay, and the smell reminded him of the fuel pumps at the Abercrombie South Express Stop, where the gas station coffee was one buck and just strong enough to get a tired doctor home to Marwick after fourteen hours in the ER. The fuel pumps on the forecourt always stunk, and that same smell now conjured an image in Charlie's mind: a drip, drip, drip somewhere in the mangled wreck, and that wisp of steam becoming a plume of smoke.

*Better alive in a wheelchair than cremated in a car.*

He leaned in through the window and took a closer look at the driver. Charlie guessed he was maybe a few years younger than himself, perhaps early thirties. The passenger in the other seat was a woman, long blond hair hanging perfectly straight, touching the roof. She looked like a photograph snapped mid-loop on the Lightning Strike, the part of the roller coaster Charlie had always loved the best when he was ten, screaming next to his dad till his throat was sore. But there were no shrieks of delight from this girl (or of pain, or of terror). She was silent.

Still.

Dead.

Charlie turned back to the man, who was now moaning softly. Blood was coming from somewhere he couldn't see, running right up his body, across his face then dripping off his hair, pooling on the car's ceiling. *So much blood*, Charlie thought.

"Mate, what's your name?" he asked. The man just groaned,

hand still groping around weakly. Charlie realized what he was doing: he was feeling for the seatbelt clasp.

"Don't!" he urged, and the hand stopped moving. "Unclip it and you'll break your neck. We'll lift you out, but you need to tell me—where's it hurt?"

The driver opened his mouth, and Charlie stared as the deep crimson stream that coursed up the side of his face was replaced by a dull gray, as though a graphite dye had dripped into the blood flow. The airbag, once a clean puffy white with shocking red smears, faded out of focus for a moment as the contrast changed: dirty cream with slate-colored smudges that were just seconds earlier the color of fresh, warm, sticky blood. Out the corner of his eye Charlie saw the blue paintwork of the Mazda shimmer slightly like a mirage. And it stayed like that, not quite in focus, and if he hadn't known prior to the crash that it was blue—almost the same shade as the SUV it collided with—then he wouldn't have been able to identify it from the hazy, blurry, colorless scene in front of him.

Then in an instant all the color returned, and the pressure that had built behind his eyes disappeared. In its place was a number that he couldn't quite see, but felt as plainly as the sun on his back.

18963.

Charlie couldn't make his brain work fast enough to convert the number from days into weeks, into months, into years, but he didn't need to. The man hanging from his seat in the crumpled car had a long time left. He would survive this.

The driver moaned again and pointed to his waist. *Source of the pain*, Charlie thought. *The blood too.*

"All right. Mate, you're gonna be okay. We're gonna lift you out."

With some difficulty Charlie and Marty pushed him up into the seat to relieve the pressure on the seatbelt, then unclipped him. The man screamed, a hoarse, pained yell as he was lifted roughly out through the window and laid onto the roadway a safe distance from the Mazda.

More cars had pulled up behind the wreck, and people were climbing out of their vehicles, some running over to help, others walking slowly as if drawn forward by the commotion but not wanting to look *too* enthralled. One girl—Charlie thought she couldn't be much beyond her teens—wasn't even trying to hide her excitement and held her phone out in front like a camera-man in a war zone. He glared at her. She ignored him.

Quickly Charlie checked the man over, searching for the source of all that blood. He found it in his lower abdomen—an ugly gash about six inches long in his belly. It was deep. He showed Marty how to press the jagged wound.

"No, harder. Like this," he said, leaning into it with all his weight, and Marty swallowed nervously. He nodded and took over as Charlie leaped up and ran back to the smashed car. The driver would survive. Now for a miracle with the passenger.

A man and a woman were already kneeling at the window, and as Charlie approached, the ashen-faced woman stood.

"It's too late," she said.

"Are you sure?" Charlie asked, almost begging her to be wrong, but with an awful feeling she was right.

She nodded.

"I'm a nurse. There's no pulse. Not breathing either."

Charlie heard the air rush out of him, his hope for a miracle evaporating. He felt utterly useless; so much for helping people in crisis. He'd seen the entire accident unfold in front of him, the twisting and the rolling of the car and each impact as it bounced along the highway. He'd seen the young woman's life end.

"I think we should get her out," the nurse declared, stepping back from the window to make way for Charlie.

He knelt on a carpet of crumbled glass and looked through at the passenger. She was about the same age as the driver. Maybe they were married. Her lips had a moist shine to them, and he wondered if she'd been applying gloss when they rolled; such a completely ordinary thing to be doing at the end. She was beautiful. And so still.

A wave of sorrow broke over him, forcing its way down into his lungs, threatening to suffocate him. A deep, horrible feeling, like he had personally let this young woman down.

He took her hand and held it. There was no response.

Charlie trusted the nurse's judgment; he really did. But pure force of habit made him press his fingers against the girl's wrist, searching for a pulse and finding nothing. She was gone.

He took her hand again and closed his eyes, feeling the devastation build, just as a swirling, shifting pressure took up inside his head.

His eyes flicked open. The woman's blond hair had faded to a silvery sheen.

Why, when she was dead?

He felt the number as a whole before he knew each individual digit.

Five of them.

Five digits. Thousands of days.

Her life was still measured in years, not seconds.

Charlie felt his own heart skip, then it started hammering out a fierce rhythm as adrenaline took over.

*She wasn't going to die.*

"Help me lift her," he said, and the man who'd been with the nurse bent down unquestioningly. Together they wrestled the passenger free from her seat, laying her as gently as they could on the road.

Without hesitation, Charlie started compressions on her chest. Five presses in and he felt the sharp crack of a rib beneath the pressure of his hands. He ignored it and kept going.

Six, seven, eight, nine, ten.

"What are you doing?" the nurse asked.

"I don't think…" Charlie puffed, "she's gone."

The nurse didn't respond, not to Charlie, but somewhere behind him he heard her whisper to her companion: "Yes, she is. She's not coming back."

Twenty-two, twenty-three, twenty-four, twenty-five.

He kept the compressions going, pounding away at the woman's chest, and when he got to one hundred, he started counting all over again.

Sixty-six, sixty-seven, sixty-eight.

His arms ached and sweat dripped off his face as he pressed and pressed and pressed, the crowd gathered tightly around. If Charlie's life had been a hospital drama on TV—one with romance and intrigue and so many rare, improbable diseases— this moment would've had a thrilling soundtrack. But it wasn't

a TV show, and the only soundtrack was his own rapid breathing and the constant drill of the cicadas by the highway.

He kept going.

Ninety-nine, one hundred. Start again.

"Paramedics are almost here," he heard a woman say. It was
Pen, Marty's wife, who'd called the ambulance from the safety
of their SUV.

"Good," the nurse replied from the vicinity of the driver, the
one with the six-inch gash exposing his intestines. "This one's
not looking great."

Charlie didn't speak. He had no breath left for words; his
chest was burning.

*Just keep the rhythm.*

*She won't die.*

Eighteen, nineteen, twenty, twenty-one.

Thoughts flickered in and out of his head. Sometime during
his eighth set of one hundred he felt a surge of gratitude that
he'd kept up with his morning runs. That he still played tennis
as often as he did. Because his lungs were straining and his
muscles were aching and complaining, but he could do this,
because he had to do this. Because he knew she would survive.
A hundred more compressions—*just keep going. She won't die*—
and he asked himself for the thousandth time where the numbers came from. Why they were beamed into his brain. From
where. From what. From something? Then another rib cracked
under his hands and the thought slipped away. *Just keep going.*
He kept pushing.

Finally, after fifteen minutes that seemed to stretch into
hours, he heard the sirens bearing down on him. Multiple

sirens, in fact; the wailing amplified as the noise bounced off the highway and vehicles and trees and suddenly they were there. A hand was on his shoulder, pulling him backward, and a fresh set of arms took over, then another, then a defibrillator was applied. A beep and a thud.

Charlie sat by, arms wrapped around his knees, head down, breathing hard. He looked up at the sound of a stretcher being lifted, wheels rattling across the road toward an ambulance, back doors open wide like a gaping mouth. He saw the woman disappear inside, just a mess of blond hair and medical equipment, and he offered up a silent prayer that the number—the vision, or whatever it was—was right, and that she hadn't died right there in a Mazda hatchback on a three-lane highway between Abercrombie and Marwick.

The paramedic pushing the stretcher turned to close the ambulance doors and saw Charlie. Their eyes met, and there was a moment when the medic clearly realized this man sitting alone on the road had been the one performing CPR when they arrived. He slammed the door shut before raising a hand to Charlie.

Not just a hand. A thumbs up; he was an emperor, decreeing that this one shall live.

They'd got her back.

Then the vehicle was gone, racing in the direction of Abercrombie, lights strobing and siren blaring.

Charlie sat for a few more minutes, watching the commotion subside as the other ambulance carrying the driver left too. Three police cars had arrived, and a fire engine, and Charlie felt a weight of responsibility lift physically from his shoulders.

Slowly he climbed back into his own car, shut the door, and started to shake uncontrollably.

He hadn't been able to save Edna Bradley. But maybe he'd balanced the ledger.

# 7

Charlie finally fell asleep at about three o'clock in the morning. At ten past six, somebody thumped on his door.

"Dad!" He rubbed his gritty eyes. "What are you doing here?" He blinked groggily at his father, who—in the early morning light—was looking old. The lines spreading from his eyes and mouth were more defined than ever. It was some comfort to Charlie that those lines came from the smile that often creased his dad's face. Aging with humor, Malcolm described it.

Despite the early hour, Malcolm was wearing a suit, the same combination of jacket and open-necked shirt that he'd worn for as long as Charlie could remember. It was his uniform to sell houses. It worked well and had become almost synonymous with his personality: laid-back, affable, but still there to get the job done. He could talk to anybody, and they'd talk back to him, instantly at ease, and before they knew it, they were off to inspect a four-bedroom place with two bathrooms and space to park their RV in the backyard, even if they didn't *have* an RV. That's how good Malcolm Knight was.

"Morning, mate. I'm heading in to work early but wanted to stop by and say congratulations!" He clapped his son hard on the back.

"Oh." Charlie's mind went blank for a moment. "Sorry, Dad—what for?"

"*What for*," Malcolm repeated, smiling and shaking his head in wonder. "The accident. Mum showed me the video last night. I wanted to ring you then, but it was a bit late."

Charlie didn't quite understand that. It was eleven minutes past six. The sun was barely up. Marwick was silent and still and *asleep*. Not even the cicadas were awake yet. Who thought knocking on someone's door at six o'clock was a more palatable option than ringing late? He grinned. His dad did, that's who. Probably assumed Charlie would be heading out for a run.

"Thanks, Dad. But what video are you talking about?"

"The one on the internet. With the girl on the road, and you were doing CPR. You looked like a movie star, mate. Mum wasn't sure it was you at first, but I said I knew that hair anywhere. God, we're proud of you."

*There's a video online.* Was that what he was saying? On YouTube? On the news?

"Might have to make the party a joint celebration—Mum turning seventy and you saving lives, yeah?"

It still sounded like a terrible idea to Charlie.

"I don't know. Maybe let's just leave it to Mum. It's her day."

Malcolm's laugh was loud, and it echoed up the street.

"I think she'd do it, Charlie, if that's what you're worried about. She actually wanted to come and congratulate you herself, but she had an early round booked, so said she'd head straight to the course. That's if she ended up going, I guess. She hadn't left yet, I think her shoulder was a bit stiff. And she said she had a headache."

Charlie frowned. He'd examined his mother himself and couldn't find any reason for her mysterious headaches. He'd come to the conclusion that they either came on when there was an opportunity to visit her son or if her rebuilt shoulder was giving her grief. Sometimes she got lucky and it was both. A hole in one.

But if her shoulder *was* hurting… Charlie felt an old, familiar worry bob to the surface.

Malcolm must have read the expression on his face.

"I think her shoulder's fine. No pain or anything, just a bit stiff. She's okay, mate. Anyway, just wanted to shake your hand and make sure you were all right."

*Ah*, thought Charlie. *It's a welfare check too. Can't do that over the phone.*

"Hey, there's a new girl starting at the office next week. She seems nice. Pretty too. Kind of reminds me of your mum when we were dating."

"Dad. Really?"

"Yeah, I know, I know. But if you're interested, her name's Christine. She's working in leasing, but she said she wants to do sales, so who knows—might take over from me when I go. Plus she's got fifteen thousand followers on social media."

"Dad, do you even know what a follower is?"

"Not a clue," Malcolm admitted with a grin. "But she told me about it in her interview, and it sounded impressive."

They laughed the same laugh, and Charlie wondered if he was looking at himself in thirty-five years: a slightly weathered, cracked version of himself. Same nose. Same jawline. Although, in a slightly unfair twist of fate, when Charlie's hair had started turning silver, Malcolm's had remained the same rich brown, with only a slight scattering of gray above his ears. Charlie must have gotten it from his mother instead. *That'd be right.*

"Wait a minute, Dad. How old is she? Christine?"

"Um, maybe midtwenties? Twenty-six, if I had to guess."

"Dad, I'm thirty-eight!"

"Oh, I know, mate. I wasn't really suggesting it, I suppose. Guess I'm on the lookout for you. And in my defense, it's kind of hard to picture you as anything other than about fifteen, playing with your mates in the pool at home. I've cleaned it, by the way, for the party. Looks *incredible.*"

Malcolm Knight's pool always looked *incredible.* And on those rare occasions when time allowed, so did the garden, and the wide expanse of lawn surrounding the house, trimmed and green like it was ready to feature in a magazine. Charlie looked at his own patch of grass: overgrown and overrun by weeds. The green thumb must have skipped a generation. It wouldn't matter for much longer though; his new place in London, the one he'd put a deposit on, only had a balcony.

"Anyway..." Malcolm Knight said, eyeing the grass as well, absentmindedly scratching behind his ear. "I'd better be going. Half a dozen inspections—on a *Tuesday*, can you believe it?"

He paused, as though Charlie would appreciate just how unusual it was for potential buyers to look at houses on a Tuesday.

"Yeah. Wow," Charlie said, still picturing the apartment he'd inspected online. One bed, one bath, and a long way away.

*Just tell him. He'll be fine. Probably never expected me to stay this long anyway. Not once the crisis was over. Tell him, and then we can have a cup of coffee and I can show him the apartment and he can tell me if I've overpaid.*

His dad chuckled and put an arm out to hug his son.

There was blood on his hand.

Just a little smudge on two fingers, the ones that had been scratching behind his ear.

"Dad! You're bleeding."

Malcolm examined his hand. "You're right." He put his fingers back behind his ear, feeling for the source of the blood.

It was such a natural thing to do, for Charlie to take a look. Perhaps he would've been more careful if it wasn't six o'clock in the morning. If he'd had more than three hours sleep. If he'd been thinking about his dad and the black notebook and the numbers, and not about the shoebox flat he was moving into. Maybe then he might've dodged it.

But he didn't, so Charlie squinted at the spot behind his dad's ear and discovered when his father would die.

The light spilling from the hallway dimmed, its golden glow dulled, but outside the house very little changed; the yard and street were already a flat gray color, caught in the transition from night to day.

Distantly Charlie noticed Malcolm's hair now resembled his own, the color washing out of it like dye under the shower. And the sensation was there too, pushing, straining behind his eyes, trying hard to enter his field of vision, as the number crystallized. It wasn't painful, really, not anymore—just crowded. So much pressure as the feeling of a number rolled and spun and then nothing. Gone.

"How's it look?" Malcolm asked.

"Uh, yeah..." Charlie said uncertainly, blinking and peering closer. "Yeah, it's a mole. Looks like you just scratched the top off it. Probably nothing to worry about, but I'll check it again when it's healed. Just don't touch it again if you can avoid it."

"Got it, Doc," said Malcolm, smiling. "How about that, treated by the hero of the highway. You've got today's paper, haven't you?"

"Dad, it's not even six thirty—when was I going to get the newspaper?"

"It's what they're calling you. Hero of the highway. You're the full front page. I'll have to get you to sign one for me." Malcolm kept talking, but Charlie wasn't really listening.

*Four digits.*

Relief was rushing through him.

4116.

4116 days. More than a decade. What, eleven years?

His dad, Marwick's leading real estate agent, arguably the unofficial mayor of the little town, had another decade. Slightly more. He'd make his mideighties. Another decade to retire, to stop hosting six inspections on a Tuesday, to start traveling like his wife kept asking, to mow his lawn and weed his garden and clean his pool so it always looked *incredible*. To do all the little things that his long-delayed retirement would allow.

Malcolm started making his way back down the path toward his car, dodging the cracks where weeds now thrived. He walked carefully, warily, and Charlie realized why. His dad, the sure-footed agent who probably knew by heart the front path of every house in the district, was worried about tripping in the dim gray of morning. Scared of his toe catching on the uneven path and taking an inglorious spill right there in his son's overgrown front yard.

Malcolm Knight wasn't a young man anymore. Those smile lines on his face were deeper than ever, and his movements were slower, more deliberate.

He still had another eleven years left. But there was nothing in the little black book that said they'd be eleven *good* years. And what possible value did it serve having another decade if he couldn't make the most of it? Or worse: *could* make the most of it, but chose not to. Chose to keep working in a job he'd already done (and done well) for so many years. A job where he had no mountains left to climb, nothing left to prove, because he'd had *his* spectacular.

So in that split second, Charlie made a decision.

"Hey, Dad?"

Malcolm turned.

"Why didn't you retire?"

"When? Last year?" His dad waved a hand dismissively. "Time wasn't right. Soon, mate. Probably five years. The market's cyclical like that. I can't leave them in a downturn. A bit longer and I can hand it over."

Charlie shook his head and stepped toward Malcolm, the concrete path cool under his bare feet. He was dressed only in boxers and a tee, but it didn't bother him; the early morning air was fresh against his skin.

He felt invigorated. There was urgency to this.

*This is the right thing to do.*

"I don't think you should delay it again. You've planned it for so long. It's time, don't you think?"

Malcolm gazed at him curiously. "Is this about the mole, Charlie?"

*In a way, yes.*

"It's not about the mole. The mole's not a problem." *How do I make him understand?* "These six places you're showing today: What do you get out of them? Would it change anything if somebody else took them instead? Christine, with all the followers. Why couldn't she do it? Dad, I've seen you cancel holidays with Mum because of work. Maybe it's time to let the balance swing back the other way."

Malcolm looked surprised, perhaps not expecting his son to confront him like he was Marwick's answer to Tony Robbins. And for a few moments it seemed like he was considering it. But then something caught his eye.

"The cleaners left a window open."

"Sorry?" Charlie asked.

Malcolm pointed next door, to Ruth Longstaff's old house, soon to be purchased by her granddaughter.

"The window's open. The cleaner must've done it. You got your key handy?" Malcolm put his hand out. "I'll duck in and close it. Window like that's an invite to thieves."

"It's not the cleaner. Genevieve's back."

Malcolm's eyebrows shot up, and his eyes darted from Charlie to the open window, then back again.

"Oh is she?"

"Yeah."

"Since when?"

"A week or so. She's moving back, buying Ruth's house."

A cautious smile crept across Malcolm's face.

"This is good news, right? Charlie, this is *great* news."

Charlie didn't answer. He couldn't, because to do so would reveal to his dad that he wasn't sticking around to be Gen's neighbor, to knock down the fence, to pick up where they left off.

It was impossible to pick up where they'd left off, anyway.

"Does Lorraine know she's back? Your mum loved Gen. Obviously."

"Why would Mum know?" Charlie knew he was sounding defensive. "I mean, she might. She talks to everyone." *Everyone but me*, he wanted to add. "But I haven't said anything about Gen buying the place."

"All right, all right. Does she need a real estate agent to help with the transfer?"

"Former agent. You're retiring, remember?"

Malcolm laughed. "I didn't agree to that."

"Please, Dad." The passion returned to his voice, and Charlie wondered if his dad would notice. If he'd ask *why. Why the rush, Charlie?*

"I'll think about it. Honestly though, mate, kinda feels like I could keep doing this forever."

*Well, for eleven years,* Charlie thought. *And then what?* Malcolm left, and Charlie weighed up going back to bed, where he could stare at the ceiling some more. But that urgency was still there. So instead, he pulled on some clothes and laced up his sneakers. He wanted to move, he wanted to move *fast*, and he took off at a run. A left turn at the end of his street, then right, and suddenly he was on Marwick's main street, flying by a row of locked-up, fast-asleep stores. He ran past the newsstand, the only shopfront already open, and nodded at Rick behind the counter. He didn't stop for a copy of the newspaper. He had no need to see himself on the front page. There was the Marwick Hotel, run by Marty Harris, who was probably still sleeping off the trauma of the accident—likely the first time Marty had used his bare hands to stop blood oozing from a six-inch stomach wound. Maybe Marty wasn't sleeping; maybe he was doing what Charlie had done, and was staring at the ceiling above his bed, tracing the cracks in the plaster while his mind did somersaults. But Charlie's sleepless hours hadn't been spent picturing blood, or the collision, the car cartwheeling along the highway—the highlights reel for an action film.

He'd been thinking about the girl with the glossy lips and the dead-looking skin. She was alive. She was in hospital in Abercrombie, and she was alive, and getting better. If the same accident had happened a few weeks earlier, and Charlie had been in the same place, right behind those two Mazdas when they came together, then she would've been dead. Because the reason—the *only* reason—he'd thumped on her chest for so long was because he knew she was going to live, that she had decades still to go. If the crash had been two weeks prior, when the cicadas were still warming up, when Charlie had no mysterious numbers squeezing into his mind, then he would've agreed with the nurse who said she was a lost cause. And the young woman would surely have died.

Right?

*That* was why Charlie couldn't sleep. Because the girl with the glossy lips had shown him that the numbers—whatever they were, wherever they were coming from—were something he could use. When that pressure had built, and the color inside that little car had drained away to gray, Charlie had felt a number, and he'd used it.

He'd saved that girl's life.

It was what made him need to run—a strange euphoria, a bizarrely exultant energy that just had to go somewhere in the early morning. And in this case, it was into the streets. Charlie darted across the road and into the wide expanse of parkland opposite the pub, under the sign that said *John James Memorial Park* in fancy copper swirls, and pounded along one of the paths that wound their way between the trees. He had the whole place to himself. He breathed hard, sucking in the cool, clear air, barely slowing as he shot out the other side of the park. And ten minutes later he was at the river, at the old wooden bridge with the dirty white railings that he'd clung to as a kid.

Now he stopped and leaned over the railing to catch his breath. Below him, the river flowed by silently, the edges bound by thick patches of grassy reeds. A narrow track was flattened fresh through the thicket, and Charlie grinned. The bridge kids must've been out again yesterday afternoon, just like last week.

Slightly early too, like the cicadas. Two unmistakable signs of Marwick's summer.

He took his shoes off before he was even aware of what he was doing. Then he pulled off his shirt and threw one leg over the railing, and then the other. He perched for a moment on the top, sitting on the dusty wood, fourteen years old again in a heartbeat. The river caught the first rays of the sun, glistening like a long ribbon of glass as it wound its way around the edge of the town. Somewhere he heard a car start and two dogs barking madly at each other, probably as they led their owners to the park Charlie had just run through. Marwick was waking up.

*Maybe I'll miss this*, Charlie thought.

Then he jumped.

He hit the water feetfirst—Charlie at thirty-eight wasn't attempting the backflip he'd mastered at fourteen—and the cold water snatched his breath away. The force of his fall carried him deep below the surface, and he searched for the bottom of the river with his feet, just as he'd done as a kid. He kicked out and found nothing. He came back up for air and floated on his back for a minute, feeling the current gently tug at him, and the early sun warm his face.

Charlie left the water using the same track someone else had made, picking his way between the reeds, up and around and back onto the bridge to retrieve his shoes and shirt. He left a trail of wet footprints, his shorts dripping brown river water, and suddenly wondered what he was thinking. He hadn't planned to jump from the bridge, hadn't intended to go for one last dip in the river, and now he was soaking wet, and a fifteen-minute jog from home.

A car—the first he'd seen all morning—appeared at the far end of the narrow bridge, and his heart sank. He recognized the silver Audi; after all, it was parked next to his own car every day at Marwick Family Clinic. The window rolled down.

"Charlie? What are you doing?"

"Hi, MaryAnn. Just cooling off. Been for a run."

Dr. MaryAnn Steiner looked like she didn't believe him, though he wasn't sure why. The evidence was all there, dripping on the bridge.

"Right," she said. "You'll be in today?"

"Sure will."

"Because we had to push some of your list from yesterday afternoon. When you didn't make it back."

MaryAnn had a unique way of phrasing things. Charlie's absence on Monday afternoon had hardly been his fault: he'd been asked by a police officer to go back to the station, where he'd given a full statement about the accident, even drawn a diagram of how it had all unfolded. He'd described the medical help he'd provided, and in exchange, the officers gave him an update from the hospital: the young woman was going to be okay. She was going to survive. (This was information Charlie could corroborate, but obviously didn't.)

"Yeah. Sorry about that."

MaryAnn looked satisfied, as though she'd extracted the apology she'd so desperately needed, and they could all now get on with their day.

"I'd offer you a lift, but if you're halfway through your run, I better leave you to it."

Charlie eyed the immaculate leather seats of MaryAnn's car,

the real reason she wasn't inviting a soaked, shirtless, shoeless colleague to join her. Every part of her car looked as though it'd just left the dealership, even the child seat in the back, which MaryAnn used—very rarely—to ferry her granddaughter around. Charlie suspected she left it in there for the appearance. The caring grandmother, the business owner. The old-school family doctor, who turned a blind eye to some things and came down hard on others, and the deciding factor was how long she'd known you. It was a sliding scale, and Charlie had seen how far it went; fifty-odd years of friendship bought an awfully blind eye to some awfully dangerous things. Just ask Lorraine Knight.

*Maybe I won't miss this after all.*

*Four and a half weeks. Then on to the spectacular.*

Charlie pulled on his shoes, knowing his still-wet feet would probably blister, and set off again, jogging at a more sedate pace now. That odd euphoria that had fueled him before was fading, dampened first by the cold of the river and then his encounter with his boss.

As he opened his front door, he heard his phone beep. It was still upstairs by his bed, exactly where he'd left it when his dad had knocked on the door, startling him from sleep.

He had four messages from four different people, and as he unlocked his phone, wondering what on earth was going on, a fifth arrived.

His pulse increased a little. It'd been a long time since he'd seen Gen's name appear on his screen. Years, in fact. He was surprised she still had his number.

Feels like I'm living next door to a celebrity. You need an agent?

Charlie responded: What are you talking about?

Gen's text back was short, just three words.

You've gone viral.

# 8

Charlie didn't really care that he reached eight million views by the time he arrived at work, and nine million by the end of his first appointment.

And when a radio station in Abercrombie called the clinic, asking if the doctor who'd saved the woman's life on the highway would be available for an interview on what it was like to be a hero, he turned down the invitation. He had a patient to see.

"Morning, Simon."

Marwick's self-diagnosis king was in his favorite seat, deep in one-sided conversation with another waiting patient. That young man was in work boots and a municipal council reflective vest, and looked like he'd much rather be filling potholes than listening to Simon Lopez.

Simon stood up gingerly, making one last point to his captive audience.

"And I do it all through Amazon. All I do is pack them up and send them out. It's the best thing when you're sick a lot."

Charlie smiled wryly, because the truth was that Simon Lopez had hardly *ever* been sick. He'd had chicken pox when he was six, apparently, which had earned him three weeks off school. Simon had described scratching at the itchy lumps until they'd scabbed, then he'd scratched them some more. The scars were still there, tiny faded pockmarks on his arms and legs, and a handful sprinkled across his cheeks. Charlie had filled in the rest of the story on his own. He pictured little Simon's friends gathered round him on his first day back in class, poking and prodding at the raw, red marks. The attention he'd received was like a hit of pure sugar to a kid, and the only way he'd get his next dose would be to battle some other disease. He doubted if Simon had ever felt completely well again after that.

"Come on through," he said, and as they sat down in his office, Charlie clicked on the icon next to Simon's name. The screen exploded with medical records. He scrolled through without really looking; he already knew the contents. *Counseled and encouraged psych assessment* appeared at regular intervals: one, two, three, four, five times. More.

About once a year Charlie attempted to explain to Simon that he was in fact a relatively healthy man—and that he may benefit from the assistance of a therapist to find out why he felt otherwise. But Simon wasn't there for a referral to a shrink. He wanted something he could *see*, a diagnosis he could tackle with a team of doctors. Something that would land him in a hospital bed, where he'd be hooked up to a drip, and could complain about the food and rate his pain on a scale of one to ten. The whole shebang.

"All right, Simon," Charlie said. "What's the problem today?"

The color changed, the pressure built, and then it was back to normal.

"Well, you're the doctor here, Doc, but if I had to guess I reckon it could be my kidney. At least, I think that's what it is. I looked it up. Every time I move I can feel it pulling. Hurts pretty bad, actually."

He watched Simon demonstrate his pain, twisting a little to each side and grimacing as he did so, as though the expression on his face would decide whether or not he had a tumor growing on his kidney.

*I could circumvent this, you know. If I told him.*

And Charlie wondered how that would sound.

*Simon, you've got nearly forty years left. You're not going to die from a pain in your side—not today, at least. Go and live and stop looking for death. It'll come in 14,183 days. Count them down if you need to. But don't waste time waiting for it.*

"Simon," he started. "What did your dad die from?"

"Oh. Um, lung cancer. When he was fifty. Pretty young."

"Yeah, that's young," Charlie agreed. "And how many cigarettes was he smoking?"

"I dunno—probably close to two packs."

"A day?"

"Yeah, every day. When he got sick he made me go and get them for him."

"Right. And your mum?" Charlie knew exactly how healthy Mrs. Lopez was. She'd been his patient for approximately the same time as Simon, although unlike Simon, he only saw her twice a year at most.

"She's pretty good thanks. Wish I had her health."

"All right. Either your mum or your dad have a history of kidney disease? Kidney cancer? Any dialysis or anything like that?"

Simon shook his head.

"What about your grandparents?"

Same reply.

"Okay. Simon, I think it's pretty unlikely you've got a kidney problem. These things—"

"I don't know, Doc," Simon interrupted, red-faced as he realized where Charlie's questioning had been leading. "When I googled it, it said something like 80 percent of—"

"Simon, stop googling your symptoms. I think Google's got you figured out. Lie down on the bed for me, mate."

Simon took off his shoes without being asked—he'd done this before—and climbed up onto the examination bed where he lay face down. Charlie gently pressed into his back with two fingers, and Simon jerked away from the pressure. Charlie stifled a laugh. Take a normal reaction, double it, and you've got the response of Simon Lopez, determined to prove he's dying.

"All right, roll over. You've pulled a muscle. Your kidney's fine." Simon's face fell, and Charlie saw real disappointment there. Disappointment that his illness could be fixed by some Advil and a couple of days of light duty. Disappointment that this wasn't *it*—the Big One. And Charlie knew right then that Simon would just keep searching until he finally found it, until it finally happened.

Thirty-eight years from now.

And an idea came to him.

"Hey Simon, before you go—can you give me another look at your thumb?"

"My thumb?" Simon repeated, confused. Then his eyes lit up. "Oh! Yeah, of course." He sat up (with ease, Charlie noted) and thrust out his hand. The thumbnail Charlie had inspected the previous week looked a little darker than the rest of his nails, but it was a long way shy of black. It wasn't going to come off anytime soon.

But still—he could use this.

"Mmmm," he murmured, sounding very serious.

"What is it, Doc?" Simon asked, and the desperate anticipation in his eyes triggered fresh sympathy in Charlie.

"You can do something about this, you know."

"But you said it wasn't infected. Has it gotten worse? I thought it might have, Doc. It felt like something was different last night. When I press against it like this—" He squeezed his own thumb and inhaled sharply.

"Mmmm," Charlie repeated, even more gravely. "Take me through it again. How did it happen? It was the gate, wasn't it? At the park?"

Simon nodded vigorously. "Yeah, last week, after trivia at the pub. I thought I had food poisoning, so I went home early—and if I cut through the park, it's about ten minutes quicker. And yeah, the gate didn't latch like it's supposed to, and *this* is what happened instead." He held up the offending digit.

Charlie peered closely at the thumb, purely for show.

"So what's the problem, Doc? It's an infection, yeah? Staph? Has it turned septic?"

"I don't think so, Simon," Charlie replied. "But what we've

got here is a chance to treat the cause, not just the symptom. You know, this wouldn't have happened if the latch was working."

"And the lights too," Simon added. "The main light at the gate's been playing up for weeks. Can't see what you're doing."

"And the lights too," Charlie agreed. "So you might be the first, but it's probably going to happen to other people. Dangerous." He paused, trying to look nonchalant. "I wonder whether the park committee needs a bit of a shake-up. Put public health as a priority. Make that place a bit safer."

He glanced at Simon, worried that he might've overdone it, that Simon would see straight through him. The John James Memorial Park committee met weekly, and mostly consisted of Marwick elders of Edna Bradley's vintage. They drank tea, they ate cake, and they talked about everything *but* the park they were supposed to be preserving.

"Yeah. Good idea, Doc—maybe someone should join the committee. Not me though. I don't think I'm well enough to take anything else on at the moment."

"That's fair," said Charlie. "And there'd be a lot of work. I ran through the park this morning—the grass was halfway to my knee. I reckon if they don't mow it more regularly, they'll end up with snakes now it's getting hot."

"Snakes? You reckon?"

"Absolutely," Charlie replied, thinking of his own grass and his dad's warning. *Thank you, Malcolm Knight.* He wondered just how far he could push it. "How long 'til we get our first snakebite?"

Too far?

Or maybe just far enough.

"Snakebite," Simon repeated. "Did you know, Doc, that between the three hospitals in Abercrombie, they only have enough antivenom to treat four snakebites at any given time?" Charlie didn't know that. He wondered how on earth Simon had managed to uncover that fact, and also wondered just how many snakes Simon was expecting to be attacked by.

"So if five people were all bitten, they'd have to decide who gets treated," Simon continued. "What a choice, huh, Doc? Four people live, one dies. Knowing my luck, I'd be the fifth in the queue. You're absolutely right—if that grass gets any longer, the park will be overrun with snakes. And ticks too. Lyme disease." He shuddered.

*Overrun with snakes.* That wasn't quite how Charlie had put it, but he'd only planted the seed. He watched as Simon bent down and laced up his shoes without wincing.

"And you know what I saw the other day, Doc? Kids—little kids—on the swings without hats. I almost wanted to say something to their parents about skin cancer. You know that's when the damage is done, right, Doc? When the kids are still small. If the committee was thinking—*really* thinking—they'd use this year's fundraiser to put a shade up over the swings and the slide."

"Well then," Charlie said. This had gone better than he expected. The ladies of the park committee would probably relish a bit of young energy at the table. It would be someone to spoil with baked treats, plus they'd benefit from Simon's organizational skills; after all, he ran his own business, while also maintaining a detailed catalog of every known illness and the symptoms to watch for. "Something to consider, Simon."

"Yeah, Doc. It is." The look on his face suggested he'd finished considering it.

In between patients, Charlie made himself a cup of tea in the clinic's small kitchen. He was deciding on a biscuit when there was a voice behind him.

"You've dried off."

He spun round. MaryAnn was standing in the doorway, wearing the same semi-scowl that he'd seen on the bridge that morning. It was, Charlie believed, her default expression.

"Yeah. I haven't jumped off the bridge in twenty years. Probably wait another twenty before I do it again. Though I think my backflip days are behind me."

There was a tiny twitch in the corner of MaryAnn's mouth, and Charlie knew it was as close to a smile as he was going to get. MaryAnn stood next to him at the bench and put a teabag in a mug.

"I saw your video."

There was no praise accompanying the statement; it was just an observation, like acknowledging that the sun was out or the cicadas were loud. There was no admiration for his stamina, his resuscitation technique, or the simple fact that he'd brought a woman back from the dead. MaryAnn poured boiling water into the mug.

"Lorraine sent me the link. She rang just after I saw you on the bridge, actually. I was the six millionth viewer or something like that. A bit ridiculous, don't you reckon?"

"Mum called you? About me?"

"Yes, she was on her way to golf." She shook her head. "Even though she said her shoulder was stiff. I love that woman dearly.

But if I *ever* get that way about golf—actually, if it looks like I'm even *thinking* about picking up a club—you have my permission to slip a couple of hundred milligrams of oxy in my tea. Just do away with me."

The words hung in the air between them. Charlie couldn't look at her; he wanted to take his tea back to his office, close his door, and just not be in the same room as MaryAnn Steiner.

"Oh come on, Charlie. You need to lighten up. Let it go, yes?" She scooped her teabag out of the mug and squeezed it hard between her fingertips. Dirty brown liquid dribbled into the cup. It looked like river water. "It's a joke, Charlie. You understand that? You know what a joke is?" She tossed the teabag into the sink and walked out, muttering to herself.

Charlie picked up MaryAnn's used teabag and put it in the bin.

Of course he knew what a joke was. He just wasn't quite ready to laugh at that one.

Not when he could still picture MaryAnn bellowing with rage, trying to decide whether she was going to hit him or fire him.

No, Charlie doubted he'd laugh at that joke anytime soon. It had cost him too much already.

It was a long day, with extra patients squeezed in to make up for his Monday absence. And he recorded them all in his black notebook: thirty-three patients, with numbers ranging from five years to more than six decades.

Not just numbers: life spans.

The high ones were no problem at all; just keep them on track, keep them healthy. Keep them happy too, if possible. But the low numbers were a little more troubling. The patient with just five years left was in her late eighties, and Charlie suspected she might've been delighted to know she still had another half decade left in the tank. By the time the end rolled around for her, goodbyes would probably have been said, and thank-yous, and her family would be reflecting on the ups and downs of her long, long life. Because that death would be expected, like Don Penrose from the Woodturners, nearing the end of his fight with his prostate. But what if that woman's number—five years' worth of days—had belonged to someone younger? To a kid, like little Jamie Clayton with the eternal sore throat? Or to someone that he loved?

What if it belonged to Genevieve Longstaff?

What would he do then?

The lights were on in her house next door when he pulled into his own driveway, and he was tempted to knock on her door. To ask her how her first couple of days in the Abercrombie office were going and whether she'd conned any of her colleagues into a monthly delivery of essential oils. He could do all of that, surely, without triggering anything; none of it seemed to fall under the banner of medical care. But if she mentioned her epilepsy again, or complained of a post-work headache, or even suggested he rub her shoulders, sore from hunching over her computer all day, he'd have to shut it down. And then he'd have to race out of the room quickly, before it all started to change. Before the colors disappeared.

*Come on, Charlie—be honest*, he told himself. *If Gen asked you for a shoulder rub, you're not running anywhere.*

But he would have to. Because he didn't want to know.

As he unlocked his front door, he spied a note peeking out from under the doormat: a Knight Realty business card. He flipped it over to see familiar handwriting scrawled on the back.

*Charlie—*

*Dropped by for a beer to celebrate but you must be working late. Life of a hero.*

*Love Dad.*

*PS. Lawn still needed that trim.*

And now Charlie noticed the smell: the air was rich with the fresh, green scent of just-cut grass. He'd been so distracted that he'd walked straight past it in the dark. But suddenly he had an image of Malcolm Knight in his selling-houses suit, wrestling Charlie's lawn mower around the front yard in the day's dying light. He might have lingered while trimming the edges, taking longer than normal to sweep up the clippings in the hope of catching his son so they could spend a few minutes together.

"Thanks, Dad," Charlie murmured to nobody. Maybe to the quiet night sky, already crowded with stars.

"He did mine too," a sheepish voice said, and Charlie looked across. Gen was peering at him over the fence. He could only see her eyes and the hair piled up high on her head, but he could tell she was smiling.

"Did he?" Charlie replied with a chuckle. "How did that happen?"

"I got home when he was halfway through yours. And we

got chatting, and the next thing I know he was mowing my lawn."

"That sounds like Dad."

"He hasn't changed a bit, Charlie."

"I don't know. I think he's looking his age right now. You'd notice it, wouldn't you? Being away for so long."

*So long. Seven years.*

"Maybe. But he's still a sweetheart, isn't he?"

Charlie grinned.

"He's good with a lawn mower, but I don't know about a *sweetheart.*"

"Well, he always was to me." Gen disappeared for a moment, and Charlie heard rustling and a thud. Then she was back, higher now, having found something to stand on. She tilted her head slightly. "He…um…he didn't seem surprised to see me. Had you mentioned it to him, by any chance? That I was back?"

*Have you been talking about me, Charlie?*

Charlie was grateful for the darkness as his face reddened.

"Yeah. He dropped by early this morning. Really early. And he saw your window was open, and I told him why. Otherwise you were going to have a visitor letting himself in, and I couldn't risk you chucking something at him." Gen rolled her eyes, and Charlie continued. "He wondered if you needed some help transferring the house title from Ruth to yourself."

"Yeah, he offered that to me too. In exchange, your dad's getting twelve months of free oils, starting with helichrysum."

"Never heard of it."

"Neither had he. But Malcolm Knight's about to have the softest skin this side of Abercrombie."

They both laughed. Charlie knew his dad would've helped Gen for nothing, because that's just the kind of person he was. But Genevieve wasn't about to accept any favors. The dawn of a new currency, maybe: essential oils, replacing Edna Bradley's shortbread.

"I'll give it to him on Saturday," Gen said cautiously.

"Saturday?"

"At the party for your mum. He invited me." Gen studied Charlie's face, looking for a reaction. He didn't give her one. "Should I go, Charlie? It'd be nice to see Lorraine again. I haven't seen her since…" She fell silent.

"Since you left?"

"Yeah. Since then. I did tell your dad I'd have to check with you, but he insisted. Quite convincingly, actually. That man could sell anything, I reckon. He's kind of my idol now."

"So you'll go then? To the barbecue? If Dad's invited you, you might have to. He's a bit persistent." Charlie sighed. She needed to know what she was committing to. Malcolm wouldn't have told her. He may not have even considered it. "But you should probably know—things are different now, Gen. With Mum, I mean."

"Different?" Gen adjusted her grip on the fence. "How so?"

"We don't really talk. Or rather, she doesn't talk to me." It was, Charlie knew, a very one-way thing. "Honestly, I think she blames me for what happened."

"No way." Gen looked incredulous. "How was it your fault?"

Charlie shrugged. *Fault* and *blame* were two different things, as far as he was concerned. He wasn't at fault for what happened to his mum. The fault lay with Lorraine Knight herself and with MaryAnn Steiner, and maybe also with golf, of all things. But not with him. And blame without fault was meaningless. He couldn't do much about how his mum felt. But he also didn't have to stick around anymore to wear it.

He looked to the stars, more now emerging in the growing darkness. The moon was rising too, a glowing half-orb surrounded by pulsing pinpricks of light. One of the dots was moving: a satellite tracking a steady path across the sky. Gen was watching it too.

"It's beautiful, isn't it? I didn't see it like this the whole time I was away. We had a great view, this rooftop area where you could see half the city. I could actually see my office from my own building, which is kind of depressing when you think about it: just a constant reminder of where you'll be the next day. But it was an amazing view of all the buildings, the lights, the streets. It feels like I shouldn't complain, cos I know I had it pretty good—but it was almost *too* bright, you know? I could barely see the moon. And certainly nothing like this. Nothing like it at all." She sighed heavily, gazing at the display above them. The stars were so clear and bright, there was no light to drown them out, and they kept on coming, more and more and more, speckled through the Milky Way's dusty haze.

The satellite reached the horizon and it was gone.

When Gen spoke again, her voice was quiet.

"Do you still watch for shooting stars?"

Charlie felt a lump in his throat. He nodded.

"And when you see one. Does it still—"

"Remind me? Every time."

"I didn't see one the entire time I was there, Charlie. I think that made it even worse. Made the grieving even harder."

Silence.

*This* was the blame he could own. Because this *was* his fault. Neither of them spoke, and the silence stretched into minutes. Charlie kept watching, hoping to see a shooting star blaze into existence while they stood there, staring. Because the timing would have been perfect, like a movie.

But his life wasn't a movie, and as much as he wanted it, there was no movement in the night sky. Everything was still.

"So what do you think, Charlie? Am I coming to the party?" Gen asked, her voice bright once more. "If you're okay with it, I thought maybe we could go together. Just for the carpool," she added. "I can be your designated driver."

"I'm hardly getting drunk at my mum's seventieth," Charlie said, finally smiling. But there was something enticing about walking into the party with Gen by his side. More than just a carpool. More than just an icebreaker with his mum. "Be warned though—you haven't seen a frenzy until you've seen a doctor arrive at a family barbecue. Comes with the job. Every aunty and every cousin will have something they need me to check. Prepare for interruptions all night."

"I remember what it's like, Charlie."

Charlie felt his cheeks burn again and looked away from her, up toward the artwork that stretched from one side of the sky to the other.

"I've missed this," Gen murmured.

Charlie couldn't be sure, but he wasn't convinced she was only talking about the stars.

"Night, Gen," he said.

"Good night, Charlie."

And he wondered—for just one, brief second—if the deposit on his flat in London was refundable.

# 9

He blamed it on his scientific brain, but Charlie liked to divide his patients into categories. Kind of like a medical census.

There was the hypochondriac, of course: Simon Lopez, with his endless googling of symptoms and the catastrophic conclusions before he'd even made it past the waiting room.

The ambush, often a mum with a couple of kids, where one appointment suddenly covered three people, each with a different complaint. He had enormous sympathy for those mums. They always looked frazzled, and they kept their questions short. To date, he had never once enforced MaryAnn's one patient per appointment rule. He doubted he ever would.

There was the Trojan horse, where the first five minutes would be spent talking about a headache or a cough, before the real reason for the appointment was coaxed out. Charlie had developed a sense for when there was something else—often something a little embarrassing—lurking beneath the surface. He did his best to put those patients at ease. He took it quite personally if they left his office with their question still unasked.

And then there was the biennial gang: the kind of patient who would bring a shopping list of queries, run through everything in fifteen minutes flat, then drop off Charlie's radar until the next appointment rolled around in a couple of years. Those patients were good value. No-fuss patients. Salt-of-the-earth patients.

Like Glenn Forrester.

"Morning, Doc," Glenn said, pulling a crumpled piece of paper from the back pocket of his jeans as he hobbled across the office and eased himself into a chair. *Well, there you go*, Charlie marveled. *He's actually brought a list.* "Sorry it's been so long. Haven't needed to make the trip into town much, really."

"Good to hear, Glenn. Means you're keeping well," Charlie replied. Coming into town was much less of a challenge than Glenn made it sound. He had three hundred Angus cattle grazing on easy green slopes just outside Marwick, not far at all from where Charlie's parents lived. Malcolm Knight drove the ten minutes to his office near the Marwick Hotel every single day, and Malcolm was a good decade older than Glenn Forrester. If *he* managed, clearly the trip wasn't too taxing.

"Figured it was probably time. My knee's gotten pretty bad."

"What do you mean?"

If Charlie had started a stopwatch at that very instant, he could have timed how long it took for the room to switch to monochrome and back. The colors gushed out of the jelly beans and the posters and Glenn's navy checked shirt and then flooded back with barely a pause at low tide. He didn't need a watch to know it was fast—and getting faster, smoother, less of a disruption. Three or four seconds, tops. And the number emerged just as quickly.

Not bad—Glenn had another twentysomething years still to run.

"I tripped over Louie a week or so back. Went down like a sack of potatoes." Charlie assumed Louie was an animal of some sort, probably a dog. Glenn, with his grizzled gray beard and leathery, wind-whipped skin, didn't really seem like a cat person. "Twisted my knee up. I've been walking on it all right, but it's getting a bit tricky to put my jeans on, you know?"

"Right..." Charlie said warily. It took a lot for Glenn Forrester to admit defeat or even ask for help. "Well, can you get them off and hop up on the bed there for me, and we'll see what you've done."

Glenn peeled his jeans down over his knee, and Charlie couldn't stop himself from gasping. The joint was almost double its usual size and ringed with purplish-black bruises.

The farmer laughed.

"What do you reckon, Doc? Did I do a good job?"

"Glenn, how on earth have you been walking on that?" he asked. "No wonder it's painful to get dressed."

"Mmm. Yeh, it's not easy. The hardest part's actually driving the truck. Can't get the clutch in all the way. You probably heard me coming—I was stuck in third most of the way here."

Charlie examined the knee more closely, prodding gently and watching as his patient recoiled. There was no exaggeration there.

"You're going to need some scans, I'm afraid. And I don't think surgery's out of the question. If it happened a week ago—"

"More like two, I think."

"Even worse. If it happened two weeks ago, and it hasn't gotten any better, then you might have done some damage to the ligaments. It's a pretty simple procedure, but it'll have to happen in hospital."

"Yeh, I won't be having an operation. Don't have the time right now. Not while I'm on my own out there. Too much to do."

Glenn was talking as though being alone on his property was a temporary status, like his wife was away for the week visiting her sister and would be back soon and then it would be all hands on deck. Glenn's wife wasn't visiting anyone at all; Charlie knew she'd died six years ago, because he was the one who'd admitted her to hospital when her pain got too much to manage at home. Of course, he hadn't been receiving the numbers back then, but he didn't need them to see that Carol Forrester didn't have long left. He'd seen it, Glenn had seen it, and then she'd died. Right on cue. He'd attended the funeral, where Glenn had stared at the ground, looking uncomfortable in a black suit he'd probably last worn to his daughter's wedding. Charlie remembered the tears streaming down Glenn's cheeks before getting lost in the tangle of beard. No, Glenn Forrester was alone on his property and would be for some time.

Another twentysomething years, in fact.

"Glenn," Charlie said gently. "This isn't going to get better on its own. You'll need to have a scan so we get an idea of the damage. Will you do it?" Glenn said nothing. He struggled back into his jeans and limped over to the chair.

"Glenn? You'll do that?" Charlie repeated, and his patient gave a stiff nod. "Okay. Now what else did you have?" He gestured to the folded piece of paper on the desk. Glenn opened it, attempting unsuccessfully to smooth out the page. Upside down, Charlie could make out a numbered list written in blue ballpoint pen. Item one simply said *KNEE*. It had been underlined so many times the pen had scored the paper.

"Ah, I think that's it, Doc. Just the knee," replied Glenn. "Got a few other errands to run while I'm in town."

Charlie saw number two on the page. *LOUIE.*

"Okay. You sure there's nothing else I can do while you're here?" he asked.

"Not unless you're a vet too." Glenn chuckled, but it was a hollow, sad sound. "Got Louie in the truck."

"Oh. Is he all right?"

Glenn shook his head.

"Nah, mate. Cat cancer apparently." *Well, there you go,* thought Charlie. *Louie isn't a dog, and Glenn* is *a cat person after all.* "Vet didn't think he'd even make Christmas. Proved him wrong, didn't we? But he's stopped eating, so I don't think he'll be coming home with me. Still, how's this—he might be on his last legs, but he spent a few hours mousing in the shed yesterday. Same as any other day, just a bit slower. Caught a couple of them too," he added, eyes shining with paternal pride. "Anyway, we're seeing the vet at eleven thirty. You know he's twelve, yeh?"

Charlie didn't know that. Up until thirty seconds ago, he didn't even know Louie was a cat.

"Twelve. Not bad for a cat."

"Nah, not bad at all," Glenn agreed and stood up slowly.

He was almost at the door when Charlie called to him.

"Don't forget those scans."

Glenn nodded.

"And mate—good luck with Louie."

"Thanks, Doc," Glenn replied, and pulled the door closed behind him.

*Poor guy*, Charlie thought. Glenn Forrester had an appointment to see the vet at half past eleven, and he'd hobble in with Louie and hobble out without him. Then he'd drive home in an empty truck to an empty house—no wife, no cat, just a swollen knee and two adult kids who only dropped by three times a year.

Oh, and twenty-two years left on the clock.

Charlie could help fix the knee, but it was only part of the problem. The other part couldn't really be fixed with surgery.

Charlie sighed, and checked his phone. A message from Gen.

Those stars last night. Beautiful.

There was a row of emojis, a little face with starry eyes, then: You sure you're okay with me coming on Saturday?

He thought about it for a moment.

Of course. Besides, Dad's already invited you. I can't un-invite you. That'd be rude.

Then he sent a follow-up.

Shouldn't you be working?

A rapid response.

Shouldn't YOU? Supposed to be finishing a client brief but all I want is to log in and check my oils orders. Feels wrong to do that. Hey, do you still do trivia on Wednesdays?

Charlie frowned. Doctor Google had disbanded shortly after Gen left town, and he'd been back maybe once or twice since then, making cameo appearances on other teams. He had nothing against trivia at the Marwick Hotel. It was a fun night. Marty Harris was a good host. But it just hadn't been the same.

No. Why? You want to go?

He was already sifting through names, putting together a team in his head, when the response came:

Definitely. It's a date.

Was it? It was a throwaway line, just Gen being Gen. She said the same thing to colleagues and to her grandmother. He was overthinking it.

But still.

*Four and a half weeks.* Not the time to start dating. And they were kind of past the dating stage, anyway.

His tennis partner Nick was busy, so Charlie roped in Lisa from reception, and when Toby saw that Lisa was going, he put his hand up too. They were discussing team names, and Charlie was explaining the origin of Doctor Google, when MaryAnn walked in. Her eyes narrowed at the trio as though she'd caught them plotting a coup, and she now had to decide who to execute first. Out of sheer awkwardness, Charlie asked her if she'd like to join them at the Marwick Hotel.

"No. God no," she exclaimed, and Charlie thought he saw Lisa exhale in relief. "Can't think of anything worse. Not because of you three, obviously. But I'm too old to be at a pub on a Wednesday night."

"How do you know if you don't go?" Toby asked, seemingly unaware that the invite had been token, at best.

"I've been to the Marwick plenty, Toby. You know Wednesday nights used to be live music? I'm talking years and years ago, mind you. You should ask your mum, Charlie. In the eighties we'd go every week, and they'd either have a band or an open mic. There's a photo somewhere of me and Lorraine singing "Islands in the Stream." Obviously she was Dolly, I got stuck with Kenny. Don't know *where* Malcolm was. Then you came along, Charlie, and we all stopped going, and now they have trivia instead. Not saying you're to blame. But you *might* be."

MaryAnn's lip curled up, and Charlie realized she was making a joke. He smiled politely. Try as he might, he couldn't picture it: his mum and MaryAnn with big hair and microphones, belting the number out and having a grand old time.

Still, he was thankful she'd turned down the invitation, until the first trivia question that evening was about that very song. As Marty Harris read it out to the crowded front bar of the Marwick Hotel, Charlie felt a little guilty that he hadn't made MaryAnn feel more welcome. She would have enjoyed the coincidence.

The trio from the clinic sat around a small table, an answer sheet in front of them. Charlie kept one eye on the door, watching for Gen to arrive.

"You know the answer to this one, don't you?" he said to Lisa, who was tapping a pencil against her lip thoughtfully. Toby's eyes followed it like a metronome. Like he was hypnotized. "Kenny Rogers, Dolly Parton. It's what MaryAnn was talking about today."

"You forget we're a different generation." Lisa grinned as she wrote the answer.

"It's not my generation either!" insisted Charlie. "How old do you think I *am*?"

"Forty-five?" Toby guessed, dragging his gaze away from Lisa.

"Toby! I'm thirty-eight."

"Oh. Sorry, Doc. It's just…you know, the hair."

"I like the hair. A silver fox, right?" said Genevieve, running her fingers through it playfully. Charlie had missed her coming through the door, missed her picking her way through the crowd, and now the sight of her sitting down next to him just seemed slightly surreal. She was glamorous, confident, perfect—and completely at home. Because she'd already had her adventure, and now she was back, just as Charlie was ready to leave for his. "Sorry I'm late. And just so you know—Charlie's looked like this since he turned thirty."

Charlie rolled his eyes and introduced Gen to his colleagues. The trivia host flicked on the microphone again.

"The next one is for the doc," Marty declared, the loudspeaker squealing as he stepped in front of it. "Oops, sorry. Doc, how many views you up to now?"

"That better not be the question!" someone from another team yelled. Charlie recognized the heckler. In fact, he recognized every person on the team, which was entirely made up of teachers from Marwick High: lifelong students of geography and history and world leaders, the kind of things that made them unbeatable at pub trivia.

"It's not, it's not," assured Marty. "I'm just curious. Not often we have a genuine hero *and* a celebrity here. How many views, Doc?"

Charlie felt the heat creep into his face and dismissed the praise with a wave, focusing intently on the double whiskey in front of him. Payment from another trivia player, who'd hit him with a question about her vertigo before he'd even sat down.

"Sixteen million," Gen called out.

"Traitor," he hissed at her, and she grinned back.

"Sixteen million!" Marty repeated. "How 'bout a round of applause for the doc, everyone?" The bar erupted in a storm of cheers and whoops. The loudest came from a group of older men with a trivia sheet in front of them, but no answer written down. The Marwick Woodturners had an empty stool at their table, where Don Penrose normally sat. Charlie pictured Don's remaining days, written in a drunken scrawl in his notebook. He was probably in palliative care at that moment. Family only, gathered around his bed, waiting for that final breath. It may have already happened. And maybe Don had insisted the rest of the Woodturners still come to the pub. Because life goes on.

"Sorry to embarrass you," Marty continued. "But just wanted to say here, in front of everyone, thank you for what you did on Monday. On the highway. I don't think many people could've done CPR for as long as you did. Heck, I don't think many people would've even started."

*Well, I don't think many people have a direct read on when some-one's supposed to die,* Charlie thought. *Probably had an unfair advantage.*

"Anyway, a medical question—and if anyone thinks I'm being biased, take it up with the owner." A ripple of laughter around the room. Clearly they'd heard the joke before; Marty Harris *was* the owner, along with the trivia host, security guard, maintenance guy, and barman. "Where in the human body would you find the patella?"

The team of teachers was straight on it, and as the noise in the bar reduced to a murmur, Charlie whispered the answer to Lisa. Only the Woodturners kept talking at their normal volume, arguing about some issue with the state of John James Memorial Park. Grass too long, trees too big. Too much playground equipment. *Just wait 'til Simon Lopez gets his hands on it,* Charlie thought. Or hoped.

"So how do you guys know each other?" Lisa asked Gen, while their answer sheets were being marked.

Gen glanced at Charlie.

"I used to live here. I got a job after college at an advertising agency in Abercrombie, and I moved in with my grandma."

"Ah, right. So were you a patient?"

Gen burst out laughing. "No. Not a patient. We…uh…we lived next door to each other. Kind of like we are now."

*Kind of. But not quite the same, was it, Gen?*

"Did you hook up?" Toby asked, and Lisa threw the pencil at him. It bounced harmlessly off his arm, but he looked wounded.

"Toby! You can't ask that," Lisa insisted.

"Why not?"

"It's not polite."

"It's fine," Gen said. "Isn't it, Charlie? Yeah, we were together for a little while. Then I got a transfer and had to move."

Lisa turned to Charlie, enthralled. "And you stayed behind?"

Her eyes were wide, as though she was witnessing the retelling of a drama. A Shakespearean drama, with betrayal, and dishonor, and death.

She didn't know the half of it.

"Yeah," he said. "Something like that."

Marty Harris materialized at their table.

"Here you go, team. You're neck and neck with A+." *Of course the teachers would be called A+,* thought Charlie. He looked at the answer sheet, and the answer to the second question leaped out at him. The patella. The knee. Full marks.

A grossly swollen knee in a quiet, lonely house.

Marty started the next round. "What's the biggest snake in the world? And I'm talking overall size here, weight and length, all of it."

Charlie could see the high school teachers debating the response, hands waving and pointing, measuring up imaginary snakes.

"I know this one," Toby announced, sitting up straight. "Green anaconda."

"Are you sure?" Lisa asked, holding the pencil tight. She seemed reluctant to commit the answer to paper just yet. Not when it came from Toby.

"One hundred percent. I've got a whole book about them. The teachers'll say the reticulated python, *everyone* makes that mistake." He laughed, as though he couldn't believe anyone could be so ridiculous. "The python can be a bit longer sometimes, not much, but the green anaconda is twice its weight. Overall size, it's the biggest."

"Sounds good to me," Charlie said, standing up. "Nice one, Toby." The young man beamed as Lisa wrote *green anaconda* in neat letters. "Sorry everyone. Can you excuse me for a couple of minutes? I need to make a call."

Gen looked at him curiously, then Lisa continued the grilling, unpacking the untold saga of Charlie Knight and Genevieve Longstaff. Charlie left them to it. If Gen wanted to tell her everything, she was welcome to do it. It was as much her story as his. Even if it meant Lisa and Toby might look at him differently when he returned.

Out the front of the pub a couple of drinkers on the veranda nodded to Charlie, holding up their beer in a silent salute. It was cooler out here—not much, but a little. And it was quieter too. The cicadas had called it a day, handing over to the night shift of crickets and frogs in the park opposite the old hotel. They were nice sounds.

Charlie pulled out his phone, but before he could dial, a hand rested gently on his arm. He jumped, and the pale, ghostly figure by his side started too.

"Deb. I'm sorry, I didn't see you there."

"That's okay, Doctor Knight. I'm the one who crept up on you."

"Please Deb. Call me Charlie."

"All right, Charlie." Her voice was shaky, soft, and as she spoke she fiddled with her hair, winding it around her finger. The thin, shoulder-length ponytail was greasy from her touch. "I saw the video of you with the woman. The one Marty mentioned before."

Charlie nodded.

"And I just wanted to say… Well, I guess I just wanted to say well done. Or congratulations, I suppose. I don't really know *what* to say. Not in these circumstances."

"Oh. Thanks, Deb," Charlie replied. "Yeah, it's one of those things, isn't it? Not really something Hallmark makes a card for."

Deborah Anders smiled, or tried to; it was a haunting, vacant expression that stopped a long way short of her eyes. Those sad eyes, framed by lines that Charlie thought had multiplied, deepened in the last few months. "No, it's not. But I saw it and

I had to say something. Cos there's a mum somewhere who still has her daughter because of you."

*Not because of me. Because of the numbers.*

Deb's sunken eyes were glassy now, and Charlie just wanted to give her a hug, wanted to give her a squeeze, as if it would somehow help the situation. But she was already backing away.

"I'm heading off. It's all a bit loud. Don't think I'm quite ready for trivia just yet."

"Of course. Deb, can I walk you home? Just so you get there safely."

She attempted that gaunt, thin smile again.

"Thanks, Charlie. It's very kind of you. But I drove tonight. I'm going to have a glass of wine, watch *CSI*, and go to bed."

*Skip the TV show and hit the pillow,* Charlie wanted to say. *You look like you could sleep for a year.* But he didn't. He still wanted to hug her though.

"All right, Deb. Oh, by the way—Toby mentioned you dropped by the clinic the other day. Is there—" She held up a hand, waving off his concerns.

"No, no. It's fine." The crickets across the road almost drowned her out.

Charlie squinted at her in the dim light coming from the pub, and he knew she wasn't telling the truth. Of course she wasn't *fine*, but at the same time, if it was something as simple as sleeping pills or a grief counselor, then all she had to do was ask. And she knew that.

No, there was something else. Deb needed *something*.

But then she turned, shuffling away.

"Whenever you're ready, Deb—just swing by. I'll fit you in, I promise. For what it's worth, I'm still so, so sorry for your loss. I think about you a lot."

"Thanks, Doctor," she mumbled and was gone, the conversation over—brief, concise.

Just like the death notice Deborah had posted in the *Marwick Daily* for her daughter, snatched away at twenty-four. Hodgkin's lymphoma, the cancer she'd had as a teen and *beaten*, only for it to apparently sneak back and finish the job once she was all grown up. How horrifically cruel.

When Charlie had seen Hayley's name listed among the Births, Deaths & Marriages in the *Daily*, he'd felt his heart squeeze. The three or four lines of newsprint seemed a shocking mistake; that part of the column was usually reserved for the elderly. He'd never treated Hayley, she'd always gone to a doctor in Abercrombie, but he was still swept up in that tidal wave of grief radiating out from a household in the community. From Deb's household. And now Deb was going home to that house, to a detective show and what looked like another sleepless night. Those lines in the *Daily* had made Charlie's heart hurt, and now, watching a childless mother walk away so aimlessly, so lost, he felt the squeeze all over again.

She drove off, and Charlie stared after her until the car turned a corner.

Another lonely, empty house. It was what had brought him outside.

*Patella, knee, cats, Louie.*

He dialed the number.

"Hello?" The voice was gruff. A television blared in the background.

"Glenn. It's Charlie Knight, from the clinic."

"Oh. Hang on, give me a sec." The TV went silent. "There we go. What's up, Doc?" Glenn Forrester gave a slight chuckle, and Charlie smiled.

"I was just calling to let you know I booked you in for a scan on Friday. Three o'clock. Can you make it?"

Silence.

"Glenn? You there?"

"Yeh. I'm here."

"Can you do three o'clock?"

"Yeh. I can do that. You didn't have to book me in, Doc. I could do it myself."

"But were you going to, Glenn?" Charlie said with a grin.

"No," Glenn admitted. "Thanks, Doc. Three o'clock. Got it. Thanks for the call."

*Patella, knee, cats, Louie.*

"Before you go, Glenn. How'd you get on with Louie?"

"Ah. Not good, Doc."

"I'm sorry to hear that," Charlie said, and he meant it.

"Thanks mate. He had a pretty good run though. And it's not like he knew what was about to happen. Not even when I had to hold him down. Probably thought he was about to get the thermometer up his backside. Poor bugger."

"Yeah," Charlie said. "And didn't you say he spent yesterday catching mice? Like he always did."

"Caught two of them, did I tell you that? He was a terrific mouser."

An image formed in Charlie's head: Louie the cat, stalking a mouse in the shed just outside the house where Glenn now sat alone. In his mind, Louie was slow, his body old and sore, but still quiet—slinking up to the mouse on silent paws then springing. Oblivious—of course—to what was about to come for him the next day, the appointment at the vet and the end. Just doing what he always did.

But now Glenn Forrester was alone.

He was going to be alone for a long, long time.

He had twenty-three years ahead of him. But Charlie was concerned about the next month, the next week. The next few days, when the house would seem quieter than ever before.

The knee could be fixed with surgery. But maybe there *was* something Charlie could do to fix the other issue.

"Glenn, I know you probably haven't thought about it much, but you're going to have a problem soon."

"With what, Doc? My knee?"

"No mate. With the mice. Now that Louie's gone, I reckon that shed will be overrun pretty quickly."

"Mmm. Yeh, you might be right."

"You'd have stock feed and everything in there, wouldn't you?"

"'Course I do."

"The mice'll go wild for it, won't they?"

"Yeh. Always." Glenn replied.

There was silence on the other end of the phone, and Charlie let it build.

*Might not fix the problem, but it'll help.*

"Maybe I should get another cat," Glenn said at last.

Charlie murmured his agreement. "Probably makes sense."

"Probably."

"You know what, Glenn?" Charlie asked, remembering the knee scan appointment, and how Glenn needed a little extra nudge. "My old man was saying something about seeing a litter of kittens the other day. You could even get two."

"Kittens. We had Louie from a kitten. Look how he turned out. Best mouser I ever had."

"Sure was. And Dad was saying these ones need a home pretty quick. Maybe you could get them on Friday, when you head in for your scan."

"Yeh. Might do that."

"It's for the mice, Glenn."

"Yeh. All right, Doc." Silence again. "For the mice."

Charlie said goodnight to Glenn and dialed one more number.

"Hi, Dad. Sorry to call so late. Need some help and thought you might know. Any idea where I could find two kittens by Friday?"

# 10

Charlie woke feeling good, free of hangovers, and thinking of cats and mice and the black book that was rapidly filling up. They'd lost at trivia—a close second, so it was barely a loss, really—but that hardly mattered. Because he felt *good*.

He threw on some clothes and asked himself whether he would have suggested Glenn Forrester get a kitten (*two* kittens, actually) if it hadn't been for the number he'd recorded on the page. *Maybe.* Although he suspected most doctors—including himself, pre-numbers—would've just arranged for the knee scans and left it at that. But he didn't. Because he'd seen what was ahead for Glenn and decided he shouldn't do it alone.

The sun rose over Marwick, and Charlie pulled on his sneakers.

He needed to run.

Right now, while the day was still cool, and while that incredible feeling was still surging through him.

It was like somebody—maybe Somebody, with a capital S,

like the big guy God himself—was sitting upstairs with a ledger of all the souls on planet earth. And for just a split second a channel opened between whoever that was and good old Charlie Knight. And when that channel opened, when the connection was nice and solid, a number was sent tumbling down the chute, just like that. Spat out like a printout from a spreadsheet, one no mortal eyes should ever see. One that shouldn't even exist, but that Charlie was given special access to, as long as he could make sense of it. As long as he could figure out how to use it.

*The end is already set. But the days before that are still in play.*

As unscientific as it was, maybe there was something in Louie the cat's approach to life. He spent his final day chasing mice around a dusty farm shed, lurking behind tractor wheels and feed bins, then pouncing on his tiny, squeaking prey. Grim, gory, but perhaps a bit inspiring too.

Glenn couldn't change the outcome, so he left Louie chasing mice.

Living right up until the end.

And if Charlie knew when the end was coming, shouldn't he help others chase their mice too?

He ran past the empty pub, where he'd been just hours before. Gen must have given Lisa and Toby a simplified version of their story, because the only accusation when he returned to the table was that he'd abandoned the team when they needed him. And he supposed they were right; they'd missed three questions that he could've answered, if he hadn't been running an impromptu clinic on the footpath outside the Marwick Hotel. Then they'd claimed their second-place prize and vowed to come back and take down the teachers the following week.

Now, as he crossed the road and flew through the park with its dodgy latch and only slightly too-long grass (he really *had* overstated it to Simon) he realized he was on his own countdown. He had four more weeks in Marwick—four more Wednesday nights in which to demolish A+ and secure victory for Doctor Google. Four more weeks before he jetted off for St. John's Private Hospital and the job he'd won a second chance at.

Charlie increased his pace.

He was lucky to get another shot. He knew it, and he appreciated it, even though he hadn't just pulled out last time on a whim. Still, there'd been two hundred other applicants, all of them passionate about emergency medicine, all of them good at their jobs. So maybe the panel had seen something in him, something that had set him apart from the rest.

*Well now I've got something that sets me apart. Not that I can tell them about it.*

Charlie ran faster still, sprinting in the opposite direction to the bridge. He wouldn't go near the river today, just in case the urge took him again and he leaped off the railing. He'd had his last hurrah on the bridge. Now he just needed speed.

Charlie was the first to arrive at the clinic, and he checked his patient list. No Simon Lopez, but give it time. The day was new and could still bring many ailments. Snakebites, Lyme disease, sore thumbs. The world was Simon's deadly oyster. He smiled to himself, alone in his office.

The smile widened as he spied Abbie's name. One of the favorites he wasn't supposed to have. One of the ones he truly didn't want to leave behind.

Charlie had been looking after Abigail Wilson since she was

sixteen, when she first came in with her parents. She was now twenty-one, but her mum still made her appointments—not because Abbie was lazy or anything like that, but because it was one of those social skills she hadn't quite mastered.

Who needed to do that when she'd mastered so many other things?

At her first-ever visit, she'd sat opposite Charlie and read a book, sandwiched tight between her mum and her dad, a protective shield against all the harm that the world could do to a girl like Abigail. Mrs. Wilson later confessed to Charlie that she'd wanted her daughter to see MaryAnn Steiner. "A lady doctor, you know. For lady things," she'd said. But Dr. Steiner hadn't been taking on new patients at the time, so the Wilsons had wound up in Charlie's office instead.

Fate, maybe.

And Charlie had been so grateful for it. He'd never met anybody like Abigail before.

At that first visit—a double-, perhaps triple-length appointment—Charlie remembered talking and talking and talking, explaining procedures and answering questions in a curious mix of coded language laced with pop culture references so that only Abigail's parents would understand, and then blunt, honest, medical terminology for Abbie.

He'd checked her over thoroughly: looked in her eyes, listened to her breathing. Searched her skin for suspicious moles. Creating a baseline for future care. He explained everything he was doing, and Abbie nodded. Listening, learning, then back to reading.

"She hasn't had her boosters yet," Mrs. Wilson had said,

looking pointedly at Charlie while Abigail's eyes darted from the novel in her lap to the posters on the wall. She seemed to focus on the circulatory system, and he could see her mouthing the words on the chart, even from across the room. *Clearly no problems with her eyesight*, he thought.

"Got it," Charlie replied. "We can do them today if you want."

"But don't mention the method of delivery." Mrs. Wilson mouthed *needle*.

"Abigail?" said Charlie, and the girl turned toward him. "You can pull it off the wall and look at it up close if you want."

"That's okay. I can read it from here. I've got 20/20 vision in my left eye and 20/15 in my right. 20/15's even better."

"It is," Charlie agreed. "You'll have no problems reading it then. Circulation is really interesting. Did you know blood's a slightly different color depending on which way it's going? If it's heading away from the heart and lungs, it's a really bright red, full of oxygen. Coming back, it's much darker."

Abigail raised her eyebrows as she studied the fact, hanging there between them. Then she nodded approvingly and moved on to the next poster.

Later in the appointment, Mr. and Mrs. Wilson had looked at each other, and at an unspoken signal, Abigail's dad stood, patted his daughter reassuringly on the hand, and then walked to the door, pausing on the way to admire the plastic skeleton that hung behind it. It had been a graduation gift from Charlie's parents: Charlie suspected they'd googled "gifts for a new doctor."

"Hey Abbie, did you see this? Awesome."

Abigail wandered over as her father slipped out the door, closing it quietly behind him. She grabbed the skeleton's hand and started tracing the ridges of the plastic bones with her finger.

"Be careful with that, Abbie," Mrs. Wilson warned.

"It's all right," insisted Charlie. "He's pretty tough. Must drink plenty of milk."

Abbie giggled, and Mrs. Wilson frowned.

"Where do we stand on birth control? Not for now. Abbie's not interested in boys yet." Abigail screwed up her nose, her finger now tracking the bones of the skeleton's wrist. "I think she'll be ready *physically* a long time before she's ready here." Mrs. Wilson tapped the side of her forehead. "But if it does happen, we want her to be safe, you know?"

Charlie looked at the teenager peering through the gap between the skeleton's ulna and radius and wondered what constituted *ready* for a girl like Abbie. He was, he realized, in awe of her; in the time she'd sat in his office she'd already finished the novel she'd carried in with her (depleted, empty, like the darkened blood heading back to the heart), and swapped it for a new one pulled from her mother's bag (fresh and red and full of oxygen). Abbie answered every question, and she understood the words he was using, and knew about 20/15 vision and milk making bones strong, but behind it all there was a naivete to her. Her intelligence probably exceeded that of her parents, and his own too, but it was wrapped in an almost childlike demeanor. Any other teenage girl would have rolled her eyes at his milk joke, or just ignored him. Instead, Charlie could've fired off facts about the plastic skeleton she was exploring, and she would've filed those facts away, waiting for the perfect opportunity to wow the kids at school with the stunning revelation that the body's entire skeleton renews itself every ten years. But she wouldn't find the perfect opportunity—probably wouldn't even know what the *perfect opportunity* looked like—and so would use it at another time, the *wrong* time, when those other kids at school were talking about the stuff sixteen-year-olds preferred to talk about. The innocence of her struck Charlie hard and stayed with him. He knew, right from that first appointment, that she'd be the ideal training ground for bullies wanting to test out new material—an off-Broadway rehearsal before they hit the big time. No wonder her parents had spun a cocoon around her.

Mrs. Wilson accompanied her daughter on every visit to see Charlie until Abigail was about nineteen. By then she carried her own bag, a net tote that bulged with the sharp corners of one, two, maybe three books. She was chatty, she was happy, but there was still a beautiful simplicity to her.

"How's school going, Abbie?" he'd asked on her first solo visit. He knew Mrs. Wilson was waiting in the car outside, and he pictured her whiling away the time with one of Abigail's novels. He imagined her eyebrow raising at the graphic descriptions of sex and fairies and blood oaths—typical fodder for a young woman, but a young woman like *Abbie*? Better tighten that cocoon.

"Good. Nearly finished, did you know? I'm graduating this year. Hey, you should come to the graduation!"

Charlie smiled. Abigail was the oldest in her class by at least a year. Sometime, a long time ago, she'd been held back, clearly by a teacher who mistook her innocence for something else altogether.

"It's very exciting. How are the other kids? Everyone being nice?"

She pulled a face. It was identical to the one he'd seen three years earlier, when Abbie's mum had mentioned boys.

"Most of them. There's a couple of *bitches* though." It sounded almost clinical—a child repeating a swear word they'd overheard their parents using. "But I don't let them bother me. Mum says people use words to hurt because fists leave bruises."

"Your mum's a smart woman," Charlie said, and Abigail nodded, already looking around the room for material to read.

"Hey, you got a new poster!" she exclaimed, pointing to a diagram of the endocrine system on the wall. "That's for hormones, right? Bet you wish you had those," she said, turning to the skeleton, still hanging happily from his hook.

"He'd probably settle just for skin, Abbie. I don't think he's too picky." She'd laughed at that until tears streamed down her face, and by then of course, Charlie had joined in.

So on the Thursday morning after he'd told Glenn Forrester to get a pair of kittens, after he'd set a new record time for a lap of the town, he was delighted to see Abigail's name on his patient list. She was, as always, perfectly on time, as though still trying to prove to her parents that being allowed now to walk on her own around Marwick would have no effect whatsoever on her punctuality. But when he called for her in the waiting room, the Abbie Wilson who stood up was a vastly different Abbie from her previous visit six months earlier.

"Wow, Abbie. Your hair!"

She grinned at him. Gone was the straight brown hair with a fringe that looked like it'd been cut using a ruler. In its place was a ruffled nest of peroxide blond spikes so bright they were almost white.

"Mum helped me. You like it?"

"Very much. You look very…" Charlie searched for a word. The style jarred with her pale skin, but that didn't matter in the slightest. What mattered to Charlie was that Abbie loved it. "You look vivacious."

"Vivacious," Abbie repeated slowly, sounding out the letters. "Vi-vay-shuhs. Oh, I like that." Charlie had a feeling she'd be using it again soon. And often.

Abbie swung a backpack across her shoulders with a grunt.

"Books?" Charlie asked.

She clipped the two straps together across the front of her chest, set for what looked like a backpacking adventure through Europe rather than the eight steps from the waiting room to Charlie's office.

"Uh huh. I'm going to the library after this."

"Good idea. Spend the day in the AC. Come on in, and tell me what I should be reading."

He closed the door behind her and she unclipped her backpack, swinging it to the ground with a thump.

"Dad said to say hello! We had breakfast up the road this morning, I walked and met him. It was *hot*—UV of nine today, but I don't think it's there yet. Probably four or five at the moment. Still need sunscreen for anything above three." She darted between topics without taking a breath. "Dad usually has pancakes when we go out, but not today. He said he just felt like pigging out on bacon. That's what Dad said. *Pigging out*. Get it? And he showed me a video of you, by the way. Did the girl live?"

It took Charlie a few seconds to catch up. "Oh. Yes she did. It was pretty close though."

"Wow. CPR, huh. Good thing you had that," she said, pointing to the poster of the circulatory system, the same one she'd examined without leaving her seat five years earlier.

Charlie laughed.

Sweet and smart and innocent.

"Yeah. I suppose so. Now, Abbie. I'll do the normal checkup first, and then if there's anything else you want to…" He trailed off, distracted.

It wasn't the colors leaving the room that did it. There wasn't much color left in Abigail's hair anyway, and the shift to gray was just as he expected.

He was used to it.

And usually he'd push on through.

Usually his patients noticed no change in him at all.

But that was because he could normally keep talking, chatting away like nothing was happening. Keep talking as the pressure expanded in his brain. The squeezing, squirming sensation that spat out the feeling of a number: how many days until the heart stopped beating.

He couldn't hide it this time.

Abbie tilted her head slightly, waiting for him to continue, her eyes wide and curious.

But Charlie said nothing, unable to speak, unable to think, unable to move.

It wasn't the colors.

It wasn't the pressure.

Charlie stopped talking because Abbie Wilson had just one day left.

# 11

Charlie waited alone in his driveway, trying to shake off the overwhelming sadness, and a horrible, bone-deep feeling that he'd made the worst decision of his life.

The stars—which knew nothing of his anguish—grew brighter in the darkening sky, and he picked out Sirius, then Venus too, glowing near the moon. All completely indifferent to the yawning, empty sorrow that was sucking in everything around Charlie. A miniature black hole, here on earth.

He kept glancing at the fence, hoping once again to see Genevieve's face appear above it. Maybe that would help. But her house was dark, and all was quiet, and Charlie was very much alone.

And as much as he didn't want to admit it—it was probably better that way.

He'd almost called his dad as he drove home from work. And when he couldn't quite bring himself to press the "dial" button, he'd considered driving to his parents' house. Just to be near them.

He wanted to walk in unannounced, like he used to. He wanted to hug his mum and for her to hug him back. If his life had been a midday movie—like the ones they'd watched together when he was home sick from school—he could've done it. And she would've asked him what was wrong, and between them all, they would've made it better.

But his life wasn't any kind of movie, let alone a midday one. There was no crowd-pleasing ending here; quite the opposite. So he didn't ring his dad, and he didn't drive to his parents' house, and he didn't wait any longer in his driveway for Gen.

Because he was afraid that if any of them asked if he was all right—and detected any kind of a tremor in his voice, a slight waver of uncertainty—he wouldn't be able to hold anything back. And what would he say then? *I told a girl today that she's going to die tomorrow and it's unfair and it's awful and now I'm not sure if I've done the right thing?*

He hadn't been quite so direct with Abigail, and because he wasn't direct with her there was a good chance she may not have understood. May have missed the subtlety of what he was saying. Because he wanted her to live like Louie the cat—chasing her mice up 'til the very end. But it seemed completely, utterly unfair when she'd barely started chasing them at all. Hadn't even figured out what her mice were yet.

Most of the other patients in his black book could still measure their time in *years*. And they were patients who were already living lives, normal lives—working and shopping and raising families and kissing and getting drunk. Abbie was special. Abbie was different. She had a backpack full of books, a new hairdo, and a whole lot of stuff still to experience.

She hadn't even started yet.

And she had a single day.

Charlie had managed to pull himself together relatively quickly in the appointment, once the posters on the walls regained their colors and Abbie's skin had stopped looking so gray and dead. And because Abbie trusted Charlie, she certainly didn't question why he started conducting every test he could think of. He was searching for the *why*: *why* her time was about to run out. Because if he could find a simple cause, then maybe there was a simple fix. Something to help cheat the system—if the system *could* be cheated. But he also had another motive. He needed to buy some time of his own while he figured out what to say.

Blood pressure, eyesight, reflexes. He pulled an ECG monitor from the procedure room, and even got Abbie to do a spirometry test, puffing away into a tube until her face was flushed and sweaty.

Everything was normal.

And then when it was all done—after every test, every procedure—he was left alone in his office with Abbie, still clutching her backpack of books she was due to return to the Marwick Library. An innocent, sweet young woman who trusted him entirely and had barely had a chance to live yet.

So he told her.

"Abbie, can I ask you something?" She'd nodded, somehow still enthusiastic after the barrage of tests. "Is there anything you've always wanted to do?"

"Fly," she said without hesitation, and Charlie smiled sadly. "Not like that."

"Oh. But you asked if there was *anything* I wanted to do. And I've always wanted to fly. Just stand there, then jump and take off. No wings or anything, and not on a plane. I know it's not possible, obviously, cos birds have hollow bones and ours are heavy and full of marrow, but still." Abigail was on her feet, knees slightly bent, demonstrating her launch position. She looked like a ski jumper racing down a slope, about to soar off the jump and take to the sky.

"Actually Abbie, I'm with you there. Be good just to fly straight over the traffic. I reckon you could get to Abercrombie in about five minutes. And imagine the view."

"Yeah! I'd like to fly along next to a train. A steam train, like in *Harry Potter*. But that's not gonna happen."

Charlie cast around for the right thing to say. How do you shift the conversation from flying and wizards to telling some-one they're about to die?

"All right. So let's put flying at the top of the list. But is there anything else you've always wanted to do—something that doesn't need magic? I don't know, like a food you've never eaten, or...or a book you've been waiting to read?"

Abbie cocked her head again, eyes searching his face for something. Charlie guessed she was trying to figure him out, hunting perhaps for a meaning she was missing, or worse, a joke at her expense. The suspicion hurt his heart. She was looking for it, because it's what usually happened.

"I'm serious, Abbie. Everyone's got something they've been holding on to, waiting for the right moment. I just think that if you've got one of those things, do it. Do it today, if you can."

Silence.

"Can you think of something? You don't have to tell me what it is."

Abigail nodded.

"Okay. Now, are you still living with Mum and Dad?"

"Nuh uh. I'm in number seven. Mum and Dad are number 13. We're both prime numbers."

*Oh no. She's living alone.*

"They bought me a new TV for my birthday. I've got Netflix and everything now."

Charlie breathed out slowly. "Right. Abbie, it might be a good idea to stay with your mum and dad instead tonight."

"But there's new episodes of—"

"I know, I know—but trust me. Have I ever done the wrong thing by you, Abbie?" She considered it for a moment, then shook her head. "So stay with Mum and Dad tonight. Stay at number 13. Have breakfast with them in the morning. And give them a big hug and tell them you love them."

Abigail looked confused.

"I do that every day," she said simply, and Charlie thought for a second that he might cry.

"Okay. So that's what you're gonna do then. Spend tonight with your parents, and do something you've always wanted to do. Deal?"

"Deal." Abigail thrust out a hand, and Charlie shook it. His own grip was clammy. He hoped she wouldn't notice.

"Thanks, Abbie," he said. "Hey, how about I get some new posters before you're in next?" The cheeriness in his voice sounded so forced, but Abbie grinned and stood up, bag of books over one shoulder. She hadn't clipped the straps across her chest again, and Charlie sensed she was distracted.

Unknowingly planning her last day on earth.

He'd written Abigail Wilson in his notebook, and carefully recorded a *1* alongside her name, feeling like he'd done the right thing. But it seemed so absurdly unfair. Abbie trusted him so much that she hadn't even asked *why* she had to hug her parents. *Why* she should stay with them, and tell them she loved them.

If his brain was acting as a radio receiver for fate, picking up messages like Morse code tapped out in his skull, then fate really sucked.

Charlie could barely remember anything else from the rest of the day. He'd filled another page in the book, although if he'd been asked to recount any of the patients or their complaints he wouldn't be able to do it. And then he'd waited in his driveway for Gen to come home, and she hadn't, so he'd gone to bed, unable to shake the sick, sad feeling in the very pit of his stomach that kept telling him he'd done something wrong.

Charlie didn't sleep much that night. In the few short hours that he *did* sleep, he dreamed—unsurprisingly—that he was flying. He stood with his feet together, knees bent, then pushed off, soaring up, up, up, gaining more speed until at last he leveled off, cruising high above the grass. He could see far below a row of puffy white trees that seemed to be moving along with him; it was a train, smoke billowing out above and behind as it raced along the ground, not following any tracks, just charging wherever it chose.

It was a dream, of course, so then he was falling, plummeting toward the soft cushions of the smoke puffs. He had something on his back—a parachute—and he pulled the cord, only to feel a strap tighten across his chest. It was just a backpack, full of sharp edges, and as he tugged at the cord again and again the strap across his chest got tighter and tighter and tighter and he couldn't breathe.

He woke to a damp pillow.

His first thought was not of Abbie but of Genevieve Longstaff, and an almost shameful relief that she no longer shared his bed. He'd never cried in his sleep before.

How would he have explained it, without resorting to the truth?

# 12

Malcolm Knight had done a fine job with Charlie's lawn. Whenever he mowed it himself, Charlie had a habit of cutting great whorls into the grass, the blades digging in at an angle and leaving miniature crop circles dotted across the yard. He liked to blame the lawn mower, a shifty configuration of gears and cogs that meant the system was stacked against him. But Malcolm had used the same machine, and as Charlie stood on his back deck, clutching a cup of coffee, he had to admit that the lawn mower was not the problem. His lawn lay smooth and flat under a shimmering dew, not a crop circle in sight.

He inhaled deeply, feeling like he should have gone for a run. But he wasn't even sure if he had the energy to stay on his feet, let alone jog across town. It was already getting warm, and the cicadas had been at full volume for at least half an hour.

There was a puff of breeze that smelled like summer, like oranges and blossoms. Then the fence rattled, and two hands appeared, clinging to the wooden palings.

"Morning!" Gen exclaimed, peering over the top. She looked impossibly sunny; the complete opposite of how Charlie felt. "I thought I heard you out here. You ready for some news? You have to promise not to judge me for it. All right? I'm going to—oh." She stopped, and the smile—that wide, beautiful smile—disappeared. "Charlie, you don't look so good. Is everything okay?"

*No. Nothing's okay.*

"Hi, Gen," he replied. "Yeah. I'm all right."

It was a lie. Abbie Wilson was either dead or about to die and no, Charlie was not all right, not in the slightest.

"Anything you want to talk about?" She adjusted her grip on the fence. "I've got bagels. I can come over if you want?"

*Yes. Yes, more than anything. Please come over.*

He shook his head. "No. Thanks though. You have some news? Promise not to judge," he said, forcing a smile.

"Okay..." Gen's voice lacked the vigor of before. "I'm handing in my notice."

"You're quitting? But you just transferred back."

"Yep, and now I'm done. It's gotten so *boring*, Charlie. I don't know why, I think I was feeling the same way before I moved home, and maybe I thought the change would be enough. But now I'm here, I just want out, you know? So adios, nine to five. I have to give four weeks' notice, which will start in what, two hours? Then I'm counting the days 'til I'm free."

*Counting the days.*

Charlie grimaced into his coffee, and blinked back tears that were suddenly threatening to fall, right there in front of Gen.

"You sure you're okay?" she asked, and he nodded.

"Just a lot going on at work." *Say no more, Charlie. Because you won't be able to stop.*

He could see Gen didn't believe him, but after a moment she continued. "I can make enough from the oils now, I think."

"You think? You don't sound convinced."

"I don't think. I *know*. Even since I've gotten back, the orders have been really strong. Lavender oil in particular. I don't know whether it was the universe trying to tell me something, but three days ago someone posted on a Facebook group about using my lavender spray on their kids, and I've had every stressed-out mum in fifty miles DMing me. So yeah, it's enough to keep me going." She looked straight at him, eyes sparkling. "I'm so excited, Charlie. It's the right move. I know it is."

"Congratulations, Gen. That's great news." Charlie knew he sounded flat. He also knew that—even if he didn't think it *was* great news—there was no talking Genevieve out of her chosen course of action. He'd tried once before, seven years ago. But they'd both been grieving, neither thinking straight, and Gen had used those exact words: *It's the right move.* Gen needed to leave, that had been clear to Charlie. Needed to be away from him. She'd told him not to cancel his ticket—but it had seemed a little halfhearted. It was hard to argue with Charlie's claim that staying behind would actually save a life.

"Thanks, Charlie." She gave him that smile again, and he felt a flutter. "I wish you weren't leaving. Demolishing this thing would've been fun." She patted the wooden fence, then stepped down and disappeared from sight.

Her voice drifted through the palings and into his yard. "Hey, you should come over after work, and I'll give you a bottle of the lavender spray. It's good for sleep. And if I'm feeling generous, which is unlikely, you might even get 5 percent off."

Charlie laughed; he couldn't help it, and he hated himself for doing it.

It felt like a betrayal. How dare he be happy, how dare he *laugh* when Abbie was dying?

By the time he dragged himself out the door he was sure he'd be the last one to the clinic. But that wasn't the case.

"Toby's still not here," Lisa reported quietly to Charlie after the first patient had come and gone.

"Is that right?" MaryAnn Steiner asked behind them, and both Charlie and Lisa jumped. "Leave it with me."

"No, I'll call him," Charlie volunteered quickly. "There'll be a good reason, I'm sure. Maybe there was another bird."

MaryAnn scowled. Toby had once missed the first two hours of his shift because he'd run over a pigeon on his way to the clinic, and insisted on taking it to the vet even though it was already dead.

*Already dead.*

*Zero days left.*

A chill crept up his spine.

He dialed Toby from his desk. The call was answered on the first ring.

"Lis, I'm on my way. Thanks for covering." Toby sounded panicked.

"Toby, it's Charlie."

"Oh. Sorry, Doc. Been a crap morning. Couldn't get out my driveway cos all these cars parked me in. And I know I was already late, but I wanted to bring Lisa a coffee and there was

like four people in front of me at the café and I had to wait forever. Nearly there now." A noise, then he swore under his breath.

"Toby?"

"Spilled it. Looks like I've wet myself. God, what a mess."
More swearing.

"Just don't rush. Get here when you can."

He hung up and put his head on his desk. He wanted to go
to sleep. No, more than that, he wanted to call Abigail Wilson.
It was like waiting for a prisoner on death row to be injected.
He knew it was going to happen at some time today—her
counter was at zero—but there was a sick sense of anticipation
in not knowing exactly when. He just wanted to hear her voice.
He wanted to know if she'd done that thing she wanted to do,
and hugged her mum and dad, and told them that she loved
them—even if she did that every day already.

Charlie's hand hovered over the phone. If she answered, well
at least he'd know she was still alive. For now. And if she *was*
still alive, then maybe the number was wrong.

It *could* be wrong, he told himself.

*Couldn't it?*

Only one way to find out. He picked up the handset, but
before he could dial, there was a knock at his door. Lisa peered
through the crack.

"Come in, Lis. Just spoke to Toby."

"Is he all right?"

"Yeah, he's fine. But when he gets here, just ignore his pants."

"Uh…right. Will do. Can you take a walk-in? A pretty deep
cut. There's a lot of blood. I've already put him in the procedure
room."

"Could MaryAnn do it? I'm just about to make a call."

"She's with another patient. Sorry, I told them you'd be there right away. The dad got really mad last time."

He sighed. If fate was real, and was capable of sending him the exact number of days his patients had left, then maybe it was capable of standing in his way too. Of stopping him intervening. Abbie, the girl who had the least time of them all, would have to wait.

Charlie followed a line of crimson dots to the procedure room, like a gruesome trail of breadcrumbs. Lisa was right. There was a lot of blood.

"Jamie Clayton! You just can't keep away from the place, can you?"

In the bright, sterile light Charlie could plainly see where tears had tracked down the little boy's pale cheeks. His left hand was wrapped in what had once been a white cloth but was now streaked with blood: some fresh, some already dry and brown. Charlie made a show of staring straight at it.

"Let me guess. Sore throat again?" he said, sitting down next to Jamie, who—almost against his will—started to smile.

"No!" he cried. "It's my hand."

Charlie paid little attention to the fading of the room, the dulling of the color and then the sense of a number that emerged from the fog; Jamie already had his name in the notebook. The new number aligned with that entry, minus a bunch of days.

He picked up Jamie's good hand.

"Your hand? What's wrong with it? Looks okay to me. Jamie, you have to stop coming in here if there's nothing wrong. I'm very busy, you know." The boy snorted with laughter.

"No, it's this one!" He raised the blood-soaked cloth.

"Where were you hiding that? You need to see a doctor!" Charlie exclaimed. He glanced at the corner of the room, where a sullen figure sat with his arms folded. Max Clayton, Jamie's dad, looked unimpressed with Charlie's antics. But his phone was nowhere to be seen.

Jamie's tears welled up again as Charlie injected anesthetic around the wound. But the boy blinked hard and while Charlie stitched, they chatted about school and breakfast and *Rusty Rivets*. A distraction, partly, but Charlie was also fishing for information. Finally—accidentally—Jamie confessed to trying to cut his own apple, and instead of slicing into the piece of fruit, had carved neatly through his palm. End result: a perfectly grisly flap of skin hanging from his hand, and a tsunami of blood and tears.

"Done! Now don't tell anyone, but I ran out of thread so had to use some of your hair instead. Come back and see me in a few weeks and we'll give your hand a haircut, all right?"

Jamie nodded, wide-eyed, and as Charlie started to clean up the mess of bloody rags, father and son walked back to reception. Charlie saw Max rest a hand on his son's skinny shoulder. He may have just been steering him, but Jamie leaned in against his dad, almost by instinct. And Max didn't take his hand away. He didn't pull out his phone either.

The hum of noise from the waiting room told Charlie he was running *very* late, courtesy of a six-year-old's attempt to cut an apple. Charlie only needed a few minutes to call Abbie, to make sure she was alive, but it was as though time itself was conspiring against him.

There was a drop-in from a drug company sales rep, a man who pushed his psoriasis treatment with evangelical zeal. Then MaryAnn needed his opinion on a patient, an older woman who'd somehow managed to get a grass seed stuck in her eye, where—remarkably—it had germinated. MaryAnn winked at Charlie, and he realized she didn't need his input at all, she just thought he might like to see the little green shoot starting to emerge. The patient looked uncomfortable with the extra attention, and in that moment Charlie loathed MaryAnn Steiner.

Five times he went to call Abbie, and five times he was interrupted, once even when he had the phone to his ear. With each interruption the dread got a little heavier, the gloom a little deeper. Then, at the beginning of a much-delayed lunch break, he was at last able to dial her number.

It rang. And rang. And rang.

He let it ring until the phone cut out on its own. Thirty, forty rings, and no voicemail. She'd never set one up, apparently. It kind of made sense.

Charlie felt it wash over him: the horror, the sadness, his skin rippling in tiny goose bumps as he realized that somewhere in Marwick, Abigail Wilson—a girl who deserved better—may have been lying cold and still. Undiscovered. Alone.

He'd found no medical reason for her to be dying. He supposed there was always a hemorrhage, or some hidden heart condition, or something else that lay dormant beneath the surface, like a volcano, waiting for the moment to make its grand, fatal entrance.

And there was another alternative, one he'd afforded little space in his head because it was so far removed from his control, but having almost ruled out a medical episode, now seemed far more likely. Abbie was going to fall victim to an accident of some kind. She'd be bowled over while crossing the road, backpack full of books. Or she'd choke on a sandwich, or slip in the shower, or a million other senseless ways a healthy person can be snuffed out without warning. But Charlie hadn't heard any sirens, hadn't heard any panic, so maybe it hadn't happened yet. Maybe Abbie still had time. Maybe the number was wrong, and she'd live to a grand old age. Maybe fate was late, just like Toby that morning.

Just like Toby.

An alarm bell. Something dinging loudly at the thought of Toby. At hitting a bird? At the coffee stain, the spill that'd spread across his pants because he was panicking, rushing to get to work?

No. It was something Toby had *said*.

Charlie jumped up so quickly that his chair tipped backward, thudding into the wall behind him. He raced out to reception, and Toby swiveled to face him.

"Toby. This morning when I rang you—"

"Yeah, I'm sorry about that. It wasn't really my fault—"

"Doesn't matter," Charlie cut him off. "You couldn't get out of the driveway because you said there were cars parked across it?"

"Oh yeah! Five or six cop cars in my street. An ambulance too. But yeah, I thought about honking at them so they'd let me out, but it just didn't seem right you know?"

"Do you know what they were doing there?"

Toby shrugged. "Didn't ask them. Most of the cops were down next to the water."

"You're on Riverview, aren't you?" Charlie asked, already sure of the answer. It was, as the name suggested, the only street in Marwick that afforded a view of the ribbon of water that wound lazily around the edge of the town.

"Yeah. Well, my mum is. I'm not really living with her, just staying for a couple of months until..." Toby was still talking as Charlie ran out the back door of the clinic and jumped into his car.

It took just three minutes to get to Riverview Parade; Marwick was, after all, not a big town. If there had been five or six cop cars there this morning, they were long gone. Just one solitary station wagon remained, its wheels straddling the curb near where the houses ended, just before the bridge. The lights on top of the wagon were off. The emergency—whatever it was that had delayed Toby—was over. Charlie pulled up behind the vehicle and got out, fighting the bile trying to rise in his throat.

He spied an officer down by the water's edge. The river under the bridge wasn't wide, maybe three or four car lengths across, and the water looked so still that the current barely created an eddy as it crept by the solid timber pylons. Long grass ran down to the edge of the bank, merging with a thick patch of reeds to create a natural barrier to the water. Some of the reeds had been flattened, trampled down, creating a path to the river's edge. It was the trail some of the kids had made so they could get out of the water after somersaulting from the bridge above.

It was the trail Charlie had used too.

The sole officer was bending down amid the flattened reeds, collecting little yellow markers and stacking them in a pile.

Charlie hurried through the grass, and the officer turned with a start.

"Hi, Luke," Charlie said. Luke Hart was a regular patient: six-monthly checkups as required by his job. High blood pressure, a touch too much belly fat. Hadn't been in for a while, so no number yet.

"Afternoon, Doc. Sorry, you snuck up on me. You all right?"

*All right? You tell me, Luke. Is everything all right?*

"Uh, yeah… Luke, what's going on?"

The officer shook his head firmly, perhaps for the benefit of his boss, who wasn't there and couldn't see him. Up close his eyes shone with the thrill of a small-town gossip.

"Drowning," he said in a low voice. Charlie stared at the water in horror; it was so quiet and smooth, the afternoon sun bouncing off the surface at an angle that made the river look like liquid gold. "Body's long gone, if that's what you're looking for. I'm just packing these up and I'll be out of here too."

"So what happened?" Charlie croaked with a mouth that had gone dry. He knew what had happened. But he needed to hear it all. Needed to have it confirmed.

"Sorry, Doc, I can't say much. But don't worry, it wasn't *murder* or anything like that." Luke sounded almost regretful. "No big investigation. Just an accident. Early this morning."

"Do you know who it was?" Charlie tried again. A whisper this time.

"Oh yeah, of course we do. All her clothes had her name on them. And her parents were here earlier. The boss brought them down, apparently they wanted to see where she was. I dunno. If it was my kid I couldn't think of anything worse."

From a great distance Charlie heard his breath whistle out between his teeth. He tried to breathe in, to replace it, but he could only get air in short, desperate bursts; a panic attack, maybe—but he'd never heard of one feeling so *wet*. Like *he* was the one underwater.

It was her. It was definitely her. Charlie had known it was coming, but now it had happened. It had crashed through from the theoretical, hypothetical, imaginary pressure in his head—a scrawled line in a black notebook—to an actual, terrible, thing. A forever thing.

And beneath it all, a horrible gnawing feeling that he should've saved her.

"Luke," he heard himself say, again from a distance. "It was Abigail, wasn't it? It was Abbie."

Charlie wasn't expecting an answer. He hadn't really been asking a question, just stating what they both knew. But Luke winced at the name.

"Doc, you didn't hear that from me. But word'll be out soon anyway, you know how these things get around, and I'm guessing she was your patient? So…well, yeah. I think it's worth checking in on her folks if you can. They weren't in a good way when they were here."

Charlie nodded bleakly, barely registering the gross understatement by the officer. Of course Abbie's parents wouldn't be *in a good way*, whatever that was. They would be distraught. Devastated. How could they be anything else?

"I didn't actually talk to them, but we could all hear them. They just kept asking Sarge why she went in the water. God, you should've heard it when they saw her clothes up on the bridge. Never heard anything like it. They *howled*, can you imagine? Both of them. Awful. Watch your foot, Doc," he said, bending to pick up a yellow marker near Charlie's shoe. The marker had a black 9 stenciled on it. Nine pieces of evidence, Charlie supposed. *Nine little yellow gravestones for Abbie.*

"I dunno," Luke shrugged, staring up at the bridge above and the dusty white railings. "I guess we all did it when we were kids. But it's probably not something you'd do if you can't swim, you know?"

"What?"

"Yeah, she couldn't swim apparently." Luke wiped the sweat from his forehead with his sleeve as Charlie felt the ground fracture beneath him. "Not the smartest thing to do, I reckon. Not that she deserved to die for it, obviously."

*She'd jumped off the bridge.*

*Alone.*

*When she couldn't swim.*

"Hey, guess how deep it is in there. In the middle." Luke was pointing into the river.

Charlie didn't need to guess. He'd felt around with his feet when he'd jumped on Tuesday morning, and hadn't found the bottom. *Deep*, was the answer.

Deep enough.

"The divers were saying it's fourteen or fifteen foot. Makes sense, I suppose. Probably why it looks so still."

Charlie had stopped listening long before that.

*Abbie did it because I told her to.*

He nodded his thanks at Luke.

*I told her to do something she'd always wanted to do.*

He stumbled back up the grassy slope to the car.

*And now she's dead.*

His tongue was thick and heavy, and he felt the hours-old coffee churn in his stomach as he fumbled for the door handle.

*I pretty much told her she had a day left.*

He was still sitting in his car, holding down his vomit, holding himself together when Luke returned to his station wagon and drove off, giving Charlie a too-cheery wave.

Charlie was still sitting there, staring down at the river as the pieces finally settled.

It was because of *him* that Abigail Wilson had only had one day left.

And now, because of Charlie, she had none.

# 13

When Charlie was about seventeen, the *Marwick Daily* had briefly swung its weight behind a campaign on its front page. His dad had shown it to him at breakfast one morning, holding up the newspaper with a mischievous grin.

Two-thirds of page one was a picture of the bridge's narrow wooden deck, and at least a dozen kids perched on top of the splintery rails, looking for all the world like a row of starlings on a wire. But these starlings all had bathing suits, sun-streaked hair, and huge smiles that were completely at odds with the ominous headline above.

## CALLS TO BAN BRIDGE JUMP AS INJURY FEARS GROW

"Read it," Malcolm urged.

Seventeen-year-old Charlie did as he was told and finally realized why his dad's eyes were gleaming. He read aloud a quote from Dr. MaryAnn Steiner.

"*'I see them every day when I drive over the bridge, and I don't want to see them in my surgery.' Dr. Steiner warned that people jumping from the height of the bridge risked neck injuries, broken bones, and even concussion from head clashes.*" Charlie looked at his dad. "Since when did MaryAnn get so *boring*?"

"Keep going," said Malcolm. "There's more."

"Okay. *Local resident Lorraine Knight said she*—" Charlie stopped again. "Wait—did *Mum* talk to them too?"

"I think they did it together. Keep going. Out loud."

"*Local resident Lorraine Knight said she has lived in Marwick all her life and is worried that more children than ever before are risking their lives to cool down. 'Every summer there's more of them. Surely it's only a matter of time before someone breaks a leg. Or worse,' she told the* Daily."

Malcolm let out a hoot.

"I don't know where those two have cooked this one up from. I feel like slipping an anonymous tip under the *Daily*'s door. Maybe a photo of two young women who spent *weeks* every summer jumping off that bridge, then sunning themselves on the grass next to Riverview Parade. Treated it like their own private beach. Your mum got quite the tan."

"Gross, Dad."

Malcolm grinned at his son.

The *Marwick Daily*'s campaign didn't go anywhere, of course. Calls for the bridge to have higher railings were rejected, for the same reason the bridge itself had never been widened or replaced with something newer: it cost too much money. But even the suggestion of two big signs warning of injury (*or worse*, as Lorraine Knight had put it) just fizzled out. Probably because winter rolled around again, and kids stopped jumping. And besides, the *Daily* had really blown it all out of proportion, because nothing bad had actually happened.

Not yet.

Not until Abbie.

*Or worse*, Charlie's mum had told the paper. Was that what she had in mind? That someone like Abigail Wilson, who couldn't swim, would be so entranced by the sight of all these kids—the starlings—jumping, *flying* from the bridge, that she'd want to do it herself?

No. There was only one Knight who could see the future, and it wasn't Lorraine.

Charlie drove away from the river without knowing where he was driving to. He couldn't go back to work, back to where he'd made the decision to tell Abbie. Where he'd chosen to listen to the swirling mess in his brain, to see the number emerging, and to tell her to seize the day. He'd fooled himself into thinking he was Robin Williams, climbing on a desk, demanding his pupils make their lives extraordinary. As though Charlie's life was a movie.

So he didn't drive back to the clinic. He didn't even call MaryAnn Steiner to tell her he wasn't coming back. What a conversation that would've been:

"Hey, MaryAnn, remember how twenty years ago you and mum warned that someone might get hurt on the bridge, and you couldn't get anyone to listen? Well, bad news: it happened. But don't worry, it's not your fault. It's mine."

And he couldn't go home either; it was too quiet there. Already the noise of the road beneath the tires wasn't enough to keep Abbie's voice from bouncing around inside the car.

*I do that every day*, she'd said, when Charlie had told her she should give her mum and dad a big hug. That she should tell them that she loved them.

*I do that every day.*

He switched the radio on, an unfamiliar song with unfamiliar lyrics beaming in from Abercrombie, and cranked the volume up to silence the voice of the girl *he'd* killed. If her voice was this loud in the car, it would be deafening at home, where his only company was a load of half-packed boxes.

And so he drove. He didn't have a destination in mind; he just drove. And considering Marwick's size, it didn't take him long to complete two, four, six laps of the town. He was looking for something. *Somewhere* to go. Somewhere that wasn't work or home.

He spied a cluster of cars at the front of the Marwick community hall, door open wide at the top of the concrete steps. The Marwick Woodturners would be holding their Friday gathering, sharing a couple of six-packs as they carved chess pieces and fruit bowls out of redwood chunks. They'd be talking nonsense and swapping stories and the room would be full of noise. Charlie slowed and turned on his indicator.

One of the Woodturners was on the hall's porch, leaning against the well-worn balustrade. He held up a lit cigarette in a clawlike hand, and Charlie almost swerved into a parked car. Don Penrose, with his gaunt, cancer-stricken body, was waving at him. Don, who'd taken a tumble in the pub a week ago when Charlie had had too many whiskeys. Don, who was in Charlie's notebook with a messy 5 scrawled next to his name, that Charlie couldn't actually remember writing, could barely remember *receiving* in the first place. Don, who according to that number, was supposed to have died two days ago. And right then, when he should've felt relief that a drunken mistake had given this poor old man a slight stay of execution, Charlie felt only anger: anger at the patients who'd swapped scotch for advice, anger at himself for accepting the drinks, anger that he'd written the number down wrong. That he'd left off a digit before the 5. It should've been 15. Maybe 25. Anything higher seemed unlikely.

*Does it matter?*

*After Abbie—does it matter?*

If he was so desperate to correct the error in his notebook, he could just pull over. He could ask Don how he was doing and then watch as the orange glow on the cigarette's tip turned gray. Then he'd know for sure what number he'd intended to write: 15, 25, 35. Find out which digit he'd missed. But why? What would Charlie do with that information?

Maybe he'd hint to Don that he should be visiting his grandkids, seeing them one last time, for one last cuddle from Pop. And then, on the way back, on day 15, or day 25, or whenever, Don's car would be cleaned up by a semitrailer, crushed to oblivion because Charlie sent him out to say his goodbyes. Maybe take his wife out at the same time. Two more souls on Charlie's conscience.

He turned off his indicator and drove on by, giving Don a wave without looking at him.

Charlie got to the end of the street and turned left. Right would have taken him back to the bridge and the river, and he wasn't going there. Left took him toward the center of town.

Around the park, then the little strip of shops and restaurants. The newsstand, where he sometimes bought the *Marwick Daily*. And the pub.

Charlie pulled up outside the Marwick Hotel, radio still blaring away. The old two-story building seemed to bulge out over the street, held back only by the huge veranda where he'd called Glenn Forrester and been startled by Deborah Anders. The space was lined with tall tables where patrons could lean and drink beer and gaze across at John James Memorial Park. Those tables were mostly empty, waiting for the after-work rush.

*This'll do*, Charlie decided. He could hide away in the bar for an hour, have a drink, and not be bothered—safe in the workday hum of the pub. He counted three lonely men in the front bar, each sitting within sight of a small TV where greyhounds chased a blurry streak around a track. Like Charlie, they weren't looking for a chat. But it was better than being alone.

"Oh. Afternoon, Doc." Marty Harris looked up from his cleaning, surprised. Charlie could see Marty's wife, Pen, in the bistro, wiping down tables after lunch. "You all right?"

Charlie nodded but didn't ask him the same question. Marty might have a headache, or a sore back, or *something* he wanted advice on, just like he'd done after trivia two nights earlier. Charlie already knew his number—and he didn't want to see it again. Didn't want to see *anybody's* number again. He wouldn't say anything that might flick the switch and send the front bar into monochrome.

"Can I get you a drink?" Marty asked brightly. Clearly news of Abbie's death hadn't made it to the pub just yet.

*Give it time.*

"Thanks."

"Whiskey, yeah?"

Charlie shook his head.

"Beer's fine, Marty. I'm not much of a whiskey drinker."

"Oh," replied Marty. "I've been telling people to buy you a double if they're gonna ask advice." He laughed heartily at that. "Figured we both win that way." He chuckled again, but Charlie didn't join in.

He chose a table, not the same one where Doctor Google had sat for trivia—that one was too close to the door, too close to anyone who might come in. Too vulnerable. Instead, Charlie found himself a spot in the corner and stared at his glass, amber bubbles rising lazily to the hyped-up sound of greyhounds racing at Abercrombie.

Charlie felt a vibration in his pocket and pulled out his phone. *Work* flashed on the screen, and he sent the call to voice-mail. *Work* appeared again, the vibration somehow sounding just a little bit more urgent. He ignored it. The third call came not from *Work* but from MaryAnn's own number, and Charlie smiled humorlessly. She probably thought he was ignoring the calls from reception but couldn't possibly ignore the boss. He banished her to voicemail too, and switched his phone off.

He couldn't talk to MaryAnn; not yet. Because MaryAnn would tell him to take the afternoon off if he absolutely had to, to get his head together, and to come into the clinic ready to go on Monday morning. And he didn't know how to do that.

Not when that clinic held a notebook full of names. People he knew. People he cared for. And each with a number he'd been trying to use, to help his patients live better lives: happy lives, full lives, like Louie the cat, chasing his mice 'til the end.

*So much for that plan.*

It'd lasted only until Abbie came to see him, and he'd been too…too *stupid* to see what was happening. There was nothing wrong with Abbie. *He* was the cause of her death.

He couldn't make that mistake again.

He should have just left Abigail Wilson reading her library books, the grown-up ones with romance and fairies. Watching Netflix on the TV her mum and dad had given her for her birthday, safe in her own house with a prime number on the mailbox. Walking round town with her backpack. Meeting her dad for pancakes and bacon. Gaining independence by inches.

Maybe she would've survived.

The door of the pub swung open, and a small group staggered in: teachers from Marwick Primary. They waved to Charlie in the corner, before slumping at a table and sending up a delegate to order wine. They were followed by two men in fluorescent yellow shirts and big, dirty brown boots; both were his patients (of the every-two-year variety). They nodded at Charlie but left him alone.

Another beer appeared.

"Anything you want to talk about?" a voice asked. Marty Harris: barman, fix-it guy, trivia host, and therapist.

"Nah, mate," Charlie said quietly. "Thanks though. You'd better get back—looks like you're getting busy."

Marty grinned. "Friday drinks, Doc. This is where we make our dough."

Charlie nursed that beer until it was warm and the room

around him was crowded with teachers and tradies and Rick from the newsstand and the baristas from both cafés in town. Then a second wave hit: the Abercrombie commuters, returning from the office, walking into the Marwick Hotel with an almost audible sigh of relief. They ordered food and bought rounds and settled in as the sky outside darkened.

Charlie needed to leave.

The pub was noisy enough to keep Abbie's voice at bay, but it'd been a minor miracle that the only interruption to his isolation had been Marty Harris bearing another drink. Nobody had sidled up yet, double whiskey in hand, to ask about their aching back or itchy scalp—a curious class of complaints that somehow managed to be urgent enough for an on-the-spot consultation, but not so urgent that they'd make an appointment at the clinic. He frowned at his beer. Maybe it wasn't a miracle after all; maybe his body language, hunched over a glass in a dark corner of the room, was sending a very clear signal, a very un-Charlie signal: *leave me alone.*

Charlie watched as Marty poured a drink for Rick from the newsstand, only to bump the glass as he passed it across. Beer sloshed over his hand and over the bar, and Marty emptied the glass and started again.

"Don't tell the boss," he said with a wink, and Rick laughed, because of course Marty *was* the boss, so who was he going to tell? And in that instant Charlie was envious of the publican. No thoughts of life and death, no pressure. Just making the same jokes and making his dough.

Then, like a change in the wind, the mood shifted.

It was something tangible and real, as if a stranger wearing a big black cloak and carrying a scythe had just strode in, tapping people on the shoulder and whispering his news as they sipped their wine. It rippled around the room, dulling conversations, as patrons turned to each other and murmured, "Have you heard?" One woman—Mrs. Lambert, the second-grade teacher at Marwick Primary—started to cry softly, comforted by a colleague. A couple of people stood, drinks unfinished, and just walked out.

Charlie knew what'd happened.

They'd found out about Abbie.

He took a sip of his warm beer, simply because he didn't know what else to do. It was flat and awful and exactly what he deserved. He sunk down into his seat, bracing for the glares in his direction. Glares that said *you did this*. Glares that labeled him a killer.

But they didn't come. Of course they wouldn't. Nobody knew what he'd told Abigail Wilson. Nobody but him and Abbie.

The mood in the bar gradually picked up, but it was nowhere near as exuberant as before. Even the music Marty was playing through the speakers seemed a little quieter, a little more subdued. The door swung open again and again—people coming in for dinner, people going out, heading home, ready to start their weekend. Then a man shuffled in, eyes lighting up at the sight of Charlie in the corner.

Simon Lopez.

If ever there was someone oblivious to body language, it was a hypochondriac spotting a doctor alone. Unguarded.

"Hi, Doc, how's your day been?" he said, flopping uninvited into a vacant seat. He looked pale as always: the skin tone of a man who worried himself sick. But he was smiling. For Simon, this was very unusual.

"Actually, Simon," Charlie said, standing. "I was just leaving. You can have the table if you want."

"Oh. Right." Simon sounded disappointed. "Hey, just quickly, before you go—" Charlie braced for the inevitable. A twinge in his ankle, maybe, or a pain in his chest. "Look out the window."

Charlie followed where Simon pointed.

Twilight had turned the outdoors purple. A couple of cars drove slowly up the street, headlights on, and beyond them, Charlie could see the fence surrounding John James Memorial Park. The lamps were just starting to blink on in the park, tracing the paths that wound between the trees.

"What am I looking at, Simon?"

"The grass! Can't you see it?"

Charlie squinted through the darkness.

"I think I can…"

"You're talking to the newest member of the park committee, thank you very much. And first order of business was getting the grass cut. I told them what you'd said about snakes, and they were all very worried, particularly when they heard about how little antivenom they've got at Abercrombie. There's only enough for *four* people, did I tell you that, Doc? The committee was *really* worried about that. And next thing you know, we voted, and then the grass got mowed."

"Is that right, Simon? Well done, mate. You've had a win there." *Or encouraged a whole committee of old ladies to live in fear,* Charlie thought. But either way, it was a result.

"Thanks, Doc," Simon said proudly. "It's looking nice. Just thought you might like to see it."

Charlie pushed in his chair, waiting for Simon to stop him with one more quick request. Maybe a script for medication.

"Have a good night, Doc."

And that was it. With a little wave to Simon, Charlie weaved through the crowd, head down, avoiding eye contact, and then he was out on the street.

But he still wasn't ready to go home, to wallow in that quiet house where all he'd hear would be his own voice and the advice he'd given Abbie. The advice that had led her onto the bridge where they'd found her clothes, all neatly labeled with her name.

*Everyone's got something they've been holding on to, waiting for the right moment. If you've got one of those things, do it.*

He wanted—needed—to be where he could still hear and see other people.

So Charlie crossed the road and pushed open the gate to John James Memorial Park, almost jamming his finger in the dodgy latch that was surely next on Simon Lopez's hit list.

Simon had been right about the grass: it looked soft and inviting. It smelled nice too, and Charlie sat, leaning against a tree, digging his hands into the short green blades. The grass was cool to his touch, and he breathed deeply.

Then he made a decision. The only decision he *could* make, given what he'd done. Given what might happen again.

Charlie stayed there for an hour, eyes closed, anchored to the peaceful heart of the town. The empty swings creaked slightly whenever a puff of warm breeze caught them. A chorus of crickets struck up, and as one dropped away, another seemed to take its place so there was always a constant thrumming in the background. And over it all, Charlie could hear shouts and laughter coming from the Marwick Hotel. When he opened his eyes he could see people moving about on the veranda, standing at those tall tables, drinking, eating.

He was hungry.

Charlie found himself wondering what Mr. and Mrs. Wilson were eating for dinner. What do you eat on the day you lose your daughter? Anything at all? Nothing? Would grief sustain you until a neighbor or friend or relative drops by with a foil-wrapped plate and you eat it, simply because your body is now trying to keep *itself* alive? Did it really matter? A few streets away, a man and woman had just lost the very thing that had given them purpose. They'd spent more than twenty years protecting Abbie from all the dangers out there, not knowing the danger that would snatch her away was someone that she trusted. Someone trying to play God with a gift he didn't understand.

Shoes crunched on the gravel path, the crickets falling silent as the footsteps moved closer.

"If you're trying to hide from me, next time climb the tree." She was a shape, a silhouette in front of one of the lamps. It was the same outline he'd seen in the doorway of the kitchen next door, just after she'd peppered him with tiny glass bottles. A perfect silhouette. "Nobody ever looks *up* in hide and seek," Gen said. Then she sat next to him, leaning against the tree, so close that their shoulders pressed lightly together. The fresh-cut grass was starting to dew, but if she noticed the damp underneath her, she didn't mention it.

"Charlie, what's going on? Are you all right? I saw your car and thought you were in the pub," she said. "If you *are* hiding—you know they can all see you, yeah?"

Charlie didn't know that, but he didn't really care if the whole town was watching him sit under a tree in the park. Something terrible had happened, and he was to blame, and now he'd made a decision.

A big one.

"A patient died today," Charlie said. He sounded hoarse.

"They're all talking about it inside. Just awful." Gen paused. "I didn't realize she was a patient of yours. Charlie, I'm so sorry."

"Did they tell you she was only twenty-one? And, Gen, she was different, you know? Just so...so *sweet*. And clever. And funny too." He took a deep, shuddering breath, and let it out slowly. "It's my fault."

His inner thoughts had escaped on the exhale.

"Charlie. She drowned. That's not your fault," Gen murmured, and her fingers entwined with his. "You forget that I know you. And if she was *your* patient, then she was in the best possible hands."

Charlie didn't say anything else. He'd already said too much.

They sat, backs against the rough bark, listening to the crickets as they resumed their chorus. Gen rested her head gently on Charlie's shoulder, a touch that was so familiar and yet so foreign to him.

She smelled like citrus blossoms.

"I quit my job," she said in a voice barely louder than the soundtrack of the park. "Four weeks' notice. Then that's it."

*So she's done it*, Charlie thought. Took the leap. Not that he could judge, really.

"I know you laugh, but I can make a go of this, selling oils. It'll work out. I've got a feeling, you know?"

Charlie said nothing, afraid to ask her anything at all, in case he crossed a line that only he knew existed. But the silence grew heavy, even with the crickets chirping away, and Gen turned to Charlie, seemingly mistaking his lack of response for disapproval. The scowl only made her look more beautiful; her face—just inches from his—was framed by the soft glow of the lamps along the path. The dappled moonlight painted her hair in a silvery sheen, and Charlie thought how easy it would be to kiss her. To lean forward—only slightly—and fall back into something that had been so intense, and so perfect, right up until it wasn't. Because Gen was leaning in too, and maybe everything would be okay.

But what good could that possibly do, to reignite something old when he was about to leave for something new?

When he *had* to leave?

Reluctantly he pulled away.

"Gen, I need to tell you something."

He felt her body tense.

"I'm going to leave early."

"What do you mean?"

"I mean, I'm moving next week. To London."

"Why, Charlie? You don't start work for another four weeks. We have a whole month."

He climbed to his feet and put out his hand to help Gen up. She didn't take it.

"I know. But I think it's best. After today, obviously. And things have been awful with Mum. I just need to get out. I need to be somewhere else. I need to *do* something else."

*Something spectacular.* Because killing Abigail Wilson had fallen far short of spectacular.

Neither spoke as they walked slowly back to their cars. Moths bashed frantically against the lamps lining the path, just like they did at the tennis court, and Charlie realized he'd missed his Friday-night match entirely. Knight/Selby wouldn't be engraved on the Marwick doubles trophy for an eighth time after all. Nick Selby would be furious.

To Charlie, it felt like the least important thing in the world.

"It'll still be there in a month, you know," Gen said at last. Charlie held her car door open as she climbed in. "The hospital, I mean. Your job. It's not going anywhere."

"I know, Gen. But neither am I."

He drove home behind her and waved across their fence as Gen went to her door. She waved back with a sad smile and disappeared inside. Now entirely alone, Charlie threw himself headlong into packing the boxes still scattered in the living room, hoping to silence Abbie's voice in his head with a flurry of activity. He moved on to the kitchen, filling box after box with utensils he barely used and crockery that seemed excessive for a single man with no partner, no kids.

Maybe he could leave it all behind. Get out, travel light, start all over again. After all, he was leaving in a hurry.

Everything Charlie had said to Genevieve that evening was true—he really did feel like he was treading water in his career, and the situation with his mother had become unbearable—but he'd left one element out. The most important reason for his departure was the deep, horrible fear that Abbie wouldn't be the last. That he would find out how long Gen had, or his mum, or a friend, or a patient that he'd looked after for years, and despite everything that'd happened with Abbie, he'd do it again. He'd inspire them to live, and lead them into their own death.

St. John's Private Hospital came with a major advantage: there were no personal connections there. It would be like the highway crash all over again. He could use his gift—which was not a gift at all, he decided, but an ugly, murderous curse that showed no signs of abating—as a kind of psychic triage. Emergency medicine with a little extra insight. And without any connections or obligations to his patients, he could just do what he was very good at: patching them up, sending them on their way. The sooner he could start, the better.

Charlie pulled out his phone, still switched off from the pub. He turned it on, ignoring a flood of alerts: missed calls and messages from work and from Nick Selby, wondering where his doubles partner was. Instead he opened his email, typed out a few lines to his new employer, and hit *send* before he could reconsider.

But now it meant he had to tell people. Tell MaryAnn. Tell his parents, which was a conversation he wasn't looking forward to, and one he was delaying until after his mum's party.

The party.

Tomorrow night.

He groaned just as his phone pinged.

What am I supposed to wear to this thing tomorrow? How formal is it, do you reckon? I haven't seen your mum in years. Kind of want to strike the right tone.

It was as though Gen was inside his head.

He thought of her spotting him in the park, across the road

from the Marwick Hotel. He would've looked so strange, the doctor sitting alone under a tree in the dark. The same doctor who'd spent the afternoon watching a beer warm up as the bar filled with locals. Filled with friends, with people he knew, but people he couldn't even look in the eye for fear they'd trigger something. A number.

And he realized: if that's what he was like in the front bar of the hotel, then a barbecue for his mother, teeming with family, and kids, and friends who'd been in their lives *forever*, was a bad idea. A terrible one, in fact.

Sorry Gen, he texted. I think I'm coming down with something. I'm probably not going to make it tomorrow night.

But Genevieve Longstaff knew him too well.

No way Charlie. You seemed okay an hour ago. Is it cos you're leaving? Are you dodging them? If you're serious about skipping town, you need to see them.

A minute passed, then another message.

Besides—your dad invited me, so I'm going. And I'm not walking in on my own. Go to bed, and we can talk outfits tomorrow.

It finished with a smiley face, and despite himself, Charlie smiled too.

Then one more.

If it's about your mum…we can do it together. I won't leave your side. Promise.

He sighed and responded. Then he put down his phone and headed upstairs with an armful of empty boxes, ready to tackle his bedroom—the only things he really did need, if he was going to ditch and run.

He packed for hours, wishing he felt tired enough to sleep.

At two in the morning he took a sleeping pill and stared at the ceiling.

At six, as the ceiling was turning gray with the day's early light, he took another one.

Then at last he slept and dreamed of nothing.

Not even the calamity that was coming his way.

# 14

Four glossy silver balloons were tied to the mailbox. They strained against their strings, desperate to sail away, away from this place and disappear into the sky. Charlie knew how they felt.

They turned at the balloons and crept up a long driveway lined on both sides with trees.

"Wow," breathed Gen, leaning forward as she drove, and it took Charlie a moment to realize what she was staring up at. The trees soared high, branches touching overhead as the car passed beneath, a natural green tunnel that had formed over so many years that Charlie had never marveled at it. Now, for the first time, he found himself in awe of his dad's patience, planting and tending to the trees over *decades*. Malcolm Knight had been playing the long game.

"It's still amazing," Gen murmured. "Every time."

"Yeah. I guess it is." They turned a slight bend in the driveway and parked at the front of the house, wedged in amongst the cars of more punctual guests. Charlie blamed the pair of sleeping pills, combined with exhaustion, for their own tardiness; he'd woken to Gen, his designated driver, hammering on his front door at one minute past five. It was the longest he'd slept in years. He'd thrown on a shirt and pants, but hadn't had time to shower or shave.

"Don't look, but I think we're being watched," Gen whispered as she climbed out of the car. She gestured up into a huge beech tree, a subtle jerk of the chin. Charlie glanced upward, into the branches, just in time to see two small faces disappear below the window of a dilapidated tree house. He grinned.

"That would be my cousin's kids. Two of them, at least."

"The twins? How is that possible? They were only babies."

"It's been a while," he replied simply. "Hey, grab those seedpods."

Gen did as Charlie instructed, following him around the base of the trees, scooping up the little hollow pods that had fallen before winter. They were now dry and brittle. They'd do nicely.

"Did you get enough?" he asked, and Gen showed him two handfuls. He nodded, impressed, and patted his own bulging pockets. "You should be good at this. You've got an arm on you. Ready?"

"For what?" Gen asked.

"Hey, boys!" Charlie yelled.

The two faces reappeared at the tree house window, just a small square cut into the wooden wall.

"Now, Gen!" With a loud battle cry, Charlie pitched a whole handful of seedpods directly at the tree house.

"We're under attack!" the boys screeched, almost in unison, and Charlie heard them fall to the floor. He dug into his pockets and threw seedpod after seedpod at the tree house wall, most of them exploding against the old timber with a satisfying bang. The twins squealed at every impact. Then Gen joined in and lobbed three straight through the window.

The boys inside shrieked in mock terror.

They popped up at the gap, a picture of sheer joy, each of them holding one of Gen's seedpods, and flung them back at the attackers. One fell a long way short, but the other bounced off Charlie's leg.

"I'm hit!" He collapsed to the ground, clutching at his chest. "They got me. I'm gone."

The boys howled gleefully. "Attack us again!" one of them yelled.

"Later. I need to go and recover first. Nurse?" he said to Gen. "Take me to the field hospital."

She helped him to his feet, and with an arm around her shoulders, Charlie limped away from the beech tree, off toward the house. Gen was staggering under Charlie's weight. It didn't help that she was laughing almost as much as the twins.

"How do you do that?" she asked. "I think you just became their favorite person."

"Hey, you're the one who spotted them. I'm just glad the tree house is still getting some use. It's probably full of spiders."

"The boys didn't seem to care," Gen remarked. "But I half expected them to fall through the floor when they first hit the deck."

"It'll be fine, it's sturdy. I slept in there when I was a kid. It was the best."

"With your friends?"

"Actually—don't laugh. It was with Mum. I was maybe seven or eight? We were supposed to go camping but then Dad was asked to fill in at a conference or something last-minute. I don't remember exactly what it was, I just remember being devastated that he had to go—so Mum set up sleeping bags in the tree house, and we camped in there for three nights straight. She even brought all our food out and we ate there too. We read books, she taught me to play rummy and a bunch of other things. We went swimming a couple of times each day and then came back and slept in the tree. Honestly, it was the best time."

He took his arm from Gen's shoulders and led her down the side of the house, past the pool, toward a swell of music and voices coming from the backyard.

They rounded the corner and Charlie stopped dead.

He'd never seen it look so good. Somebody—his dad, he assumed—had strung festoon lights between trees in the yard, giving it a twinkling, festival atmosphere, while underfoot not a blade of grass dared to grow out of place. Two large tables covered in white cloths heaved under the weight of an assortment of mismatched plates and bowls and platters, the contributions of the forty or so people that already gathered in small groups. Some of them were just standing, admiring the view from the yard: gentle hills dotted with patches of trees, and in the distance, the shimmering roofs of Marwick.

*So many people*, Charlie thought, and felt—for a moment—the previous night's despair start to gnaw at him again. But Gen was right. He had to come, he had to do this. *Just get through it. Get through this as though nothing is wrong.*

And maybe he'd get lucky. Maybe nobody would ask his advice.

"Charlie! You're here!"

"Hi, Dad," Charlie said, and then his dad was wrapping him in a hug, and Charlie was lost in the familiar smell of his father: the light scent of his aftershave that might well have been bought in bulk thirty years ago and dabbed on every day since. The worn smell of a suit—a selling-houses suit—that had probably witnessed a hundred, two hundred sales of humble three-bedroom bungalows and countless hobby farms. Charlie felt like he was a kid again, back when he was trouble free. Long before he was a doctor, long before he had the numbers, long before he'd killed someone.

It was the first time he'd ever felt homesick.

"And Gen." Malcolm kissed her on the cheek. "You've just increased the party's glamour by about two hundred percent."

Gen's cheeks pinked a little, but she gave a slight twirl, making the skirt of her cream summer dress flare out. Charlie had to agree with his dad. Gen stood out amongst the crowd. The straps over her bare shoulders showed off her perfectly toned arms and smooth skin. Her hair cascaded down her neck, and strappy sandals twisted around her ankles and halfway up her calves. Genevieve Longstaff had always been gorgeous. But seven years apart had made Charlie forget just *how* beautiful she was.

"Thanks, Malcolm. I feel a bit overdressed—Charlie was supposed to let me know the dress code, but he slept late."

Malcolm raised an eyebrow. "Did he now? Gen, you're not overdressed. I'm just sorry your date's never heard of an iron or a razor."

"Oh no, she's not my date," Charlie blurted out. "We came together, but we're not *together*. Not like that. We just carpooled. You invited Gen separately, remember?"

"Oh, that's right." Malcolm smiled, apparently enjoying Charlie's discomfort. "I did too. Senior moment. Although speaking of age—Gen, I think you promised me something, didn't you? Guaranteed to make me look thirty again?"

"Helichrysum. Yes! Sorry, it's in the car. Give me one minute." She dashed off, and Charlie watched her go. As soon as she was out of sight, he turned back to his dad.

"Dad! What are you doing? You know we're not together!"

"I know, I know. I'm just having a bit of fun."

"Yeah, at my expense."

"What other kind of fun is there?" Malcolm asked innocently. He eyed Charlie closely, and his forehead creased with concern. "Charlie, is everything okay? You seem a bit...off."

"I'm all right, Dad. Still in shock about Abbie, I think." It was true, but it was only half the story.

"Yeah, of course. Awful news. I dropped round to see the Wilsons this morning. Took them something to eat. They're not doing too well." Charlie was reminded, once again, that his father was a fundamentally good man.

Gen reappeared, arms laden with goodies. She handed Malcolm two small glass bottles, along with a bottle of wine.

"And I made these too." She held out a tray of brownies. Malcolm closed his eyes and inhaled.

"Oh, Gen. I remember these. You didn't have to do this."

"Well, you said to bring a plate! And uh, Charlie—since we didn't, you know, come *together*, then you'll have to find your own. Imagine that, turning up to your own mum's party empty-handed." She shook her head disapprovingly, and Malcolm roared with laughter.

"Don't worry Gen, the doc here will be earning his keep. Reckon you might have a bit of work to do this evening, Charlie. Lexie's here with Finn and she's gonna come and find you. It's his ears again. Heard her tell your mum before."

Charlie frowned, haunted by his own words to Gen across their fence: *You haven't seen a frenzy until you've seen a doctor arrive at a family barbecue. Comes with the job.*

He peered behind his dad, at the crowd of relatives and friends. He couldn't see Lexie or her little boy anywhere.

*Prepare for interruptions all night,* he'd said.

The interruptions might come, he just wouldn't be able to help them. But what was he supposed to do if Lexie cornered him and just started talking? Once the color ran out, once the green grass turned gray, there was no stopping it. And if a low number burst out of the swirling fog for Finn, the poor little boy who walked around tugging his ears at every family function he'd ever been to? What would Charlie do then?

Suddenly his mind was filled with a picture, a scene he'd never witnessed but his imagination still conjured in horrifying, hypercolor detail. Through a thick tuft of river reeds he could plainly see two legs and the lower part of a torso. The top half was concealed by the reeds that held it loosely in place, loose enough that the body—the pale, very dead body of Abbie Wilson—could bob slightly as though still possessing some need, some desire to move. To fly. But she was so white, so lifeless. He blinked, and the image was gone.

"Charlie, are you all right?" Malcolm asked.

"Yeah, sorry, Dad. I'm fine," he lied. He wasn't all right, not at all.

"I'm sure she doesn't like asking. But you know, it's just good to have peace of mind. Right. I better fire up the barbecue. Hey, Charlie, if you get a chance, say hi to Cate—she had something she wanted your opinion on. Her boys are around here too somewhere," Malcolm said, eyeing the swelling crowd.

"They're in the tree house," Charlie replied.

"'Course they are. I thought I could hear them before, making a lot of noise about something. That was you, wasn't it?" Malcolm grinned and excused himself, leaving them alone.

Gen turned immediately to Charlie.

"You completely zoned out there. Are you—"

"I'm okay, Gen." He blinked again and saw the corpse of Abbie in the brief flash of black. "I just don't want to work tonight, you know? It's a party."

"Maybe it won't happen." She gazed at the crowd, and at the tables full of food, and at the decorations. "Gosh, look at those lights, all the way to the back fence. Did your dad do it all, do you reckon?"

"Probably. He does a good job."

"Amazing."

Charlie nodded. His parents' house, his childhood home, looked incredible. Inspection-ready, Malcolm called it. But there was something he'd noticed as he'd gathered seedpods under the beech tree and then again as he'd led Gen down the side of the building. And even now, standing in the manicured backyard, he could see it again, and it bothered him.

It was the stuff around the edges; the neat and careful grooming had a finite line to it. The long, straggly grass just beyond the yard. A fallen branch near the beech. A hedge untrimmed on the far side of the house, missed by most, but noticed by someone who'd used that hedge as a hiding spot when he was a kid. Charlie knew his dad, and he knew Malcolm was at his happiest when he was working in his own yard. He could only imagine how much it would irk him that these little things— the last 5 percent—were being left undone. Jettisoned because he had six inspections to run on a Tuesday. Because he kept delaying his retirement, worried about leaving his colleagues in the lurch.

"Okay. You can't put it off any longer. Time to find your mum," Gen declared. "Let's wish her a happy birthday before it gets too chaotic." Charlie followed, dread growing with every step. They circled the whole yard without any sign of Lorraine Knight, and Charlie dismissed the feeling that she was deliberately avoiding them, that the search was starting to resemble an old comedy film, and every time they turned a corner she darted around another one. If only they had a row of doors in a hallway, they could take turns running through them in different combinations. Go full slapstick.

"There she is!" Gen pointed to the deck at the back of the house. Lorraine Knight was walking down the steps toward the grass and her party. She wore a flowing blue dress and held a very full glass of champagne, every inch the guest of honor. Gen crossed the yard, Charlie still tagging along behind, and Lorraine saw her. Her eyes lit up.

"Genevieve!"

She darted across the lawn, careful not to spill her drink, and embraced Gen.

"It's been *so long*. Malcolm told me he'd bumped into you, but that was all. He didn't say what you were doing, how long you were visiting Ruth, and he *certainly* didn't tell me you were coming tonight. What a perfect surprise."

"Happy birthday, Lorraine," Gen said. "Malcolm invited me. When he mowed my lawn."

Lorraine laughed. Charlie hadn't heard that sound up close in a long time.

He missed it.

"Of course he did. Sounds like Malcolm. Gen, we have to get you a glass of champagne."

Charlie suspected his mum didn't even *mean* to do it. But for just half a second her eyes flicked down to Gen's midsection. Drawn by a memory. Because Charlie realized that the last time the pair had seen each other, Gen hadn't been able to drink at all.

"I'm not much of a drinker, but Mal bought something very expensive, and I feel like he'll be offended if we don't have it." Lorraine looked around for her husband and shrugged. "Don't know where he's gone. Tell me. How's Ruth doing?"

"Uh, not great. It's why I'm moving back, really, to try to help if I can. But Grandma's getting good care where she is."

"*Moving?* So this is permanent? Wonderful news. Ruth will love having you back. She didn't mention anything to me— but I suppose I haven't actually seen her for three weeks. Let me see. Yes, before Edna died. Maybe four weeks even—I took over a big pile of magazines. I was thinking about taking her some cake tomorrow, actually, since she can't make it tonight.

Maybe you and I should go together, wouldn't that be fun? But you're right. Good care. The staff are all so nice there. Is there anything else she needs that I can help with?"

Lorraine Knight had always been a good talker and a good listener, and whenever she spoke with somebody, they always had her full attention. But as Charlie watched his mum nodding, laughing with Gen, he got the distinct impression that she was actively avoiding looking anywhere else. Looking his way, in particular.

He sighed and took two steps forward. He stood next to Gen and waited for a pause in conversation. With Charlie there, it came quickly.

"Happy birthday, Mum."

"Thanks, Charlie," she said, presenting a cheek to him. He kissed it and gave her a quick hug. It was like embracing a scarecrow: stiff, unfeeling. Designed to repel.

"You've got a great turnout," he said.

She waved off the compliment. "Most of my friends from golf aren't here yet. There'll be more then."

"Still—nice to see so many people for your birthday. And you've got perfect weather for it."

"Can't take any credit for the weather, Charlie."

Two for two, both batted away. It might have been hurtful, and it *had* been, when it first started. But now Lorraine was just following the script for their interactions for the last seven years, a script she'd written herself. Charlie was used to it. It wasn't fair, it wasn't right, but it just *was*. And it was one of the reasons he'd set up the online job alerts, sat for three interviews, and then said yes without hesitation.

Lorraine had already turned back to Gen.

"Gen, I feel like I've been right there with you for the last—how long has it been?"

*Come on, Mum. You know this*, Charlie thought bitterly. *It's the same time you've been punishing me for your own mistake.*

"Seven years," Gen replied, glancing at Charlie.

"Seven years," Lorraine repeated, without skipping a beat. No pause, no recognition, no awkwardness. Just on with the conversation. After all, Lorraine Knight had always been a good talker. "Whenever I see Ruth, the first half hour is a full update on everything you're doing. She paints quite the picture, though if I'm honest, I'm not completely sure she understands half of it. But she gave the impression you were taking London by storm."

Gen laughed, embarrassed. "She's been known to exaggerate a little, my grandma. She fills in the gaps very well, and I reckon she's probably made my job sound a lot more exciting than it was. But I had fun. It was a cool place to live, and there are parts I'm going to miss, definitely. Did a lot of traveling. It's nice to be home though, and starting new things."

"Oh? Still in advertising?"

Charlie watched his mum take another sip of her champagne; the glass had been full when she came down the stairs. Now it was half-empty, with a cluster of pink lipstick smudges around the rim. Maybe he was making her nervous. *Sorry, Mum.*

"No, I resigned yesterday! I'm going out on my own. *Complete* change of pace—aromatherapy. Selling essential oils. I got into it last year, and I love it. And just a heads-up: I may have traded some oils with your husband. He's helping me with Grandma's house, and I'm helping him look forty years younger. Or so he reckons."

"Of course he does! He'll use it to convince himself he can just keep on working."

Charlie knew his dad had no real intention of retiring. Not unless his little pep talk after checking that mole did the trick. But he suspected his mum was right; Malcolm Knight could easily use rejuvenated skin as a reason to go for a few more years. Sell a few more houses. Help his colleagues through a rough patch. Meanwhile that grass around the edge of the yard would grow longer, and that hedge would lose its shape altogether, and Lorraine might just leave him and travel the world on her own.

"I'll bring you some samples sometime, if you like?" Gen offered, and Lorraine nodded eagerly. "The lavender spray has taken off. It's for relaxation mostly; I'm seeing a lot of parents using it on their kids. But there are so many different oils, and so many benefits. I was telling Charlie last week that since I started using them, I haven't had a proper seizure, not even the—"

Charlie didn't hear the rest of Gen's sentence, because he was gone.

He bolted from the conversation, away from the discussion of seizures and epilepsy and the inevitable question he knew would be coming from Lorraine to Gen, because she was a good talker and a good listener and a good person like her husband: "And how *is* your health?"

He would listen to the answer, and that would be the trigger. And he wouldn't—absolutely *couldn't*—find out. Not when a body bobbed in the Marwick River, caught in the reeds of his imagination every time he closed his eyes.

He found himself in the middle of the crowd of guests, all eating and laughing and having a grand old time. Some of them looked mildly surprised at Charlie's sudden appearance in their midst. His uncle gestured toward him, clutching a beer.

"Music a bit loud for you, eh, Charlie?" he asked, and Charlie realized he had his hands over his ears. Paranoid. Terrified of hearing something, of the grass going gray and the pressure building and him doing it all over again. Another Abbie.

He lowered his hands slowly and forced a laugh. "Yeah."

His uncle laughed too, then beckoned Charlie to come closer.

It was the beginning of an onslaught.

# 15

His rescuer wore a cream summer dress.

"Charlie, I'm sorry—can I snatch you away for a second? I need to show you something."

Gen took a shell-shocked Charlie by the arm, and with an apologetic smile, steered him out of the crowd. She didn't say another word until they'd reached the far corner of the yard, where the manicured lawn ended at a low hedge. Beyond was an open expanse of countless shades of green, all folding into one as the last afternoon light glinted off the distant windows of Marwick, then vanished.

"I don't really have anything to show you. But as your designated driver, I feel a sense of responsibility for your safety."

"My safety?"

"You've watched David Attenborough before, haven't you?"

"Of course."

"Well, I don't know which one it was on, *Planet Earth* or something. But it was this big, injured fish in a river. Might have had a dodgy fin, though I could be thinking of *Finding Nemo*." She shrugged. "But here was this big fish, and then these piranhas just *swarmed* all over it. I don't know if they used time lapse or anything, but a minute later, there was just a fish spine bumping along on the riverbed. And a bunch of happy piranhas." Gen grinned at him. "I just had this image of a Charlie skeleton, stripped bare. I shouldn't compare your family to piranhas. Might be a bit unkind."

But it wasn't just Charlie's family. It started that way, with his uncle asking about gout. Charlie fended him off, saying it was getting too dark for a proper examination, but that he could see him one day soon at the clinic. Uncle Ted's face lit up when Charlie assured him there'd be no charge for the consult. This, of course, wasn't true: there wouldn't be a consult at all, because he wouldn't be going back to the clinic. And even if his uncle followed him to London, he still couldn't help him.

But then another woman—a friend of his mum—had pulled out her phone, ready to show him photos of an infection lurking somewhere on her body. Then he told a colleague of his father that without seeing his medical records, he couldn't possibly advise him on whether back surgery was a good idea. Then— almost unbelievably—another one. Every time he turned, someone was hovering.

He'd been eyeing escape routes, searching for salvation, when Gen had arrived. And he'd never been more relieved in his life.

"Thanks, Gen."

He looked back across at the party: the number of revelers under the strings of lights had swollen since they arrived. Maybe these were the golf friends his mum had alluded to.

Gen's car would surely be boxed in by now, surrounded on all sides. He was trapped.

Charlie's mum was easy to pick in the throng, her bright-blue dress like a beacon. Her champagne flute had been refilled, and she was chatting animatedly to somebody Charlie couldn't see, hidden behind the uncle with suspected gout. Then the mass of people shifted slightly, and he saw it was MaryAnn.

Of course it was.

Almost as though they sensed him watching, both women glanced in his direction, then away again when their eyes met. Lorraine put her free hand over her ear, and Charlie got the distinct impression she was talking about *him*. About his rapid departure from the earlier conversation. MaryAnn was laughing.

"Why's nobody bothering *her*?" Charlie asked.

"Who?" replied Gen.

"MaryAnn. She's just standing there, surrounded by people, and nobody's asking her advice on anything."

"Charlie, these people are *your* family, not hers. And if they're not technically family, they're your mum and dad's friends—so they probably see you as family anyway. They're comfortable with you, and you've never said no before. But"— she hesitated—"it's not always this bad, is it? I remember you being asked questions; I don't remember there practically being a queue."

Charlie shook his head.

"This does seem worse than usual." Though perhaps he was just more aware of it now. He'd never been to a family barbecue that came with the risk of finding out if Uncle Ted would make it to Christmas. Or maybe—maybe—it was something else altogether, something a bit more sinister, something that made a chill scurry down his back, despite the warmth of the evening. Maybe it was fate conspiring against him, throwing everything at him to really test his mettle. Just like it did when Abbie had died, and a thousand small interruptions had stopped him from calling her. Not that a call would've made any difference. Fate had already done its thing by then, working through an agent called Charlie Knight.

"I don't blame people for coming to you instead of MaryAnn," Gen added. "She's always seemed kinda prickly. It'd be like asking a cactus for advice."

Charlie laughed, which still seemed so wrong, considering how he felt, and what he'd done. But being near Gen had always made laughing easy. Almost inevitable.

"Do you want to go back across?" she asked.

"No." Charlie was emphatic. "Absolutely not." What he really wanted to do was go home. A close second was hide in the tree house, but that space was probably still occupied by two boys who'd resisted Charlie's seedpod attack and might be plotting revenge.

And what about London? Was that option three? Get as far away as possible, as quickly as he could?

"All right. Stay here," Gen instructed. "I'm getting you a drink."

The strings of bulbs twinkled overhead, drawing attention to the huge, open sky—the darkened sky now, with its first scattering of stars—but the sight of Gen being engulfed by the crowd of partygoers made Charlie feel claustrophobic. Trapped by the very thought of those people wanting his help, standing between him and the car. He turned and looked out instead toward the distant cluster of lights; the only sign of Marwick as night fully took over. One of those lights, he thought, would be the Marwick Hotel. Another would be the flickering lamp over the front gate at the park. And one would belong to a house where a mum and dad sat in silence, not knowing what to say or do, because everything seemed a bit pointless now. Maybe one of the lights would be from Abbie's bedroom, the room that was still set up even though she'd moved to number seven. Just in case she wanted to come home.

The darkness wasn't good for Charlie's imagination. The pasty, waterlogged skin amongst the reeds. He found himself wondering if Abbie's body had really been bobbing in the reedy shallows. Maybe a driver passing over the bridge had spotted her floating face down in the deeper water. Maybe she'd sunk to the bottom. He swallowed hard. Hadn't Luke Hart said there'd been divers? It didn't matter. The only thing he knew was that he couldn't do it again.

St. John's Hospital would be safer. No connections, no obligations. No accidental deaths.

A tap on his shoulder, and he spun around, expecting to see Gen with a glass of wine, but finding someone else instead. Someone with a child in tow.

"Oh. Lexie. Hi."

"Charlie! I saw a video of you saving a woman's life. I was a very proud—um, what exactly would I be? Second cousin?"

"I think so." *Say no more, Charlie.*

"You did it for *so long*! And did you read some of the

comments on the post? Someone even called you a *heartthrob*. I didn't know people still said that. Haven't heard that one since we were kids. You and JTT, huh? A pair of heartthrobs." She cackled into the night.

Charlie wasn't listening. He was looking instead at the small, miserable child standing at his cousin's elbow, wearing a *Paw Patrol* T-shirt and a gloomy expression. This was a kid who didn't want to be at a party full of grown-ups. He wanted to be at home. *You and me both, buddy.*

"Say, Charlie, I know it's a party and everything, but his ears. Would you mind having a quick look—"

"I can't," Charlie cut her off. "I'm sorry, Lex."

"But he just keeps pulling at them. He's been so *bloody* whingey!" She mouthed the last few words, as though sharing an adult moment with Charlie would make him empathize with her and help her out. As though a lack of empathy was the problem. Charlie looked again at Finn. The kid stared back dolefully and rubbed his ear.

*The reeds.*

*The bedroom light still burning.*

*The Wilsons eating alone, asking what could possibly have made a girl who couldn't swim jump into a river.*

They were asking the wrong question: it wasn't *what* had made her do it.

It was *who*.

He shook his head, jaw set firmly.

"I'm really sorry, Lexie. I've left my bag at home. It's got my otoscope in it." She blinked at him. "It's the thing I look in ears with."

Lexie pushed Finn forward by the shoulders.

"But Lorraine said you'd—"

"Lexie! Just stop, okay?" His voice was harsh now, and Lexie fell silent, eyes wide. "I'm sorry. I just…I just can't tonight."

He spoke to the grass at their feet, so his cousin wouldn't see the shame on his face. Then he looked at the stars, at the merry festoon lights, at the shadowy trees looming over the house, at Gen walking back across the yard. He looked at anything but the little boy with the sick, sad eyes.

"Come on, Finn," Lexie said quietly. "Let's go see if there's any of those brownies left."

Lexie led poor Finn toward the tables of food. She glanced back over her shoulder and caught Charlie's eyes. Her expression was hard to read. Disgust? No, not quite. More like betrayal. He felt the guilt twist tight around his stomach.

*I should've helped him. But I can't.*

*I can't do this.*

*I need to get on the plane.*

But it was about to get worse.

"Sorry I took so long," Gen said, handing him a glass. "I ran into your mum at the drinks table. I think she might be a bit tipsy—she grabbed me to show me the cake and nearly pulled me right into it. Charlie, it is *huge*. I know she loves her golf, but, seriously." She held out her arms. "It's this big across, and twice as long—a miniature putting green. How your dad got it here from Abercrombie, I have no idea."

Charlie grimaced.

"You're not all right, are you, Charlie." It wasn't a question; at least, Charlie didn't think it was. Gen just knew him.

He stared into the blackness between the house and Marwick. Somewhere in the dark—tucked away in one of the dips—was Glenn Forrester's house, with two new kittens and a shed full of mice. And above it all, the full expanse of the night sky.

Gen put her arm around his waist, and for a moment he worried about the message it sent to the rest of the party, like a glossy magazine cover breathlessly declaring CHARLIE AND GEN ARE BACK ON. But the wine had been flowing, and the glasses were full, and Charlie doubted half the guests could even see them in the shadows at the end of the yard.

There was something about her touch that put him at ease, that made him feel lighter. They could've been anywhere at that instant: standing in their driveways, following a satellite across the sky. Sitting on the front steps of Ruth Longstaff's house, when Charlie's hair was still mostly brown, watching for shooting stars. Lying on the grass in the park, talking about London, and some unexpected news, and how even that wonderful surprise just seemed to be part of the plan, because Charlie's new hospital had a world-class maternity unit and everything would be perfect. Then that phone call outside a vacant lot in Marwick, and those shooting stars became a symbol of what they'd lost. Then there'd been Lorraine, and MaryAnn, and the ambulance, and suddenly nothing was perfect anymore.

"Let's get out of here," Gen said, and Charlie agreed.

They were picking their way through the crowd—Gen leading the way, Charlie a few feet behind, eyes down—when it happened.

"Charlie? Charlie!" His name neatly filled the break between songs, and at first Charlie thought he was hearing things.

Lorraine Knight barely spoke to him, let alone called to him across a party.

"Charlie!" the voice called again.

And there she was, the beacon of her blue dress guiding the way. She waved at him; not a friendly, good to see you kind of wave, but a wave that said "Yes, Charlie. Believe it or not, it's me." A little splash of champagne sloshed out of her glass and scored a direct bullseye on her right foot. Lorraine looked down, puzzled, then up to the lights strung above her. She shrugged.

"Charlie!" She beckoned him over.

Lorraine was flanked by a semicircle of near-identical women, whose ages seemed to vary by no more than five or six years. MaryAnn Steiner would have fit right in, but Charlie couldn't see her. Right on cue, "Islands in the Stream" started drifting out of the speakers, and he wondered if that's where MaryAnn was, gearing up for an encore performance of their pre-Charlie nights at the Marwick Hotel.

*If only.*

"What's this about?" Gen asked under her breath.

"I have no idea," Charlie replied. "But I…uh, I don't think it's going to be fun. You might want to keep your distance." He took a deep breath and approached the group of ladies.

Gen stayed by his side.

"Hi, Mum," he said. He decided it was uncharitable to observe just how much the women resembled a coven of witches.

"Charlie, do you know my friends from golf?"

*Ah*, he thought. *It's the golf crowd. MaryAnn would run a mile.*

"Of course you'd know them. This is Rosemary, Sylvia, Anne, Ann with no 'e,'" she added to the titters of some of her friends.

"Louise, Donna, and Lib." Charlie nodded at them all. Two of them were patients of his, but he didn't think he should reveal that. Some of the others he didn't know, which wasn't a surprise. His mother had a whole life built around Abercrombie Links. It was one full circle in Lorraine Knight's Venn diagram.

"I just wanted to say, Charlie, how nice it was to see Gen again. Thanks for bringing her."

"Right. Okay, Mum." Something wasn't right here. More than just his mother acknowledging his presence. "Well, Dad actually invited her."

"He did? Yes, he did. That's right. To Mal, then." Lorraine raised her glass, and Charlie watched her take a sip. He wasn't the only one who noticed how far the level dropped in the glass; one of the women, maybe Donna or Lib, was watching closely too.

But it was another one—Rosemary, a patient—who spoke next.

"I saw your video, Charlie. Lorraine sent it to us, but I've seen it on Facebook as well. You're everywhere. Made me quite proud to know you." A couple of nods.

"Thanks, Rosemary. Feels like a long time ago now. And it's all a bit embarrassing, you know? I was just doing my job." He was edging away, anxious to be out of there. "Good to see you all. We're just heading off."

"Before you go, Charlie…" Lorraine said extravagantly, and Charlie felt his guts tighten. What was going on here? "We're supposed to be playing on Monday, and Sylvia's wrist is giving her a bit of grief. Show him, Syl."

*No.*

The woman Lorraine had identified as Sylvia turned toward Charlie, arms forward, shoulders back.

"It's just when I move it like this—" She started to demonstrate the motion, holding an imaginary golf club, even adjusting her grip on the air.

*Quick. Stop her now.*

Charlie shook his head violently, freezing Sylvia midswing.

"I'm really sorry, Sylvia. I can't help tonight."

Sylvia looked at him quizzically, then started to demonstrate again, as though he hadn't even spoken. Her backswing saw her imaginary club reach halfway to the festoon lights before Charlie stopped her once more. Sylvia lowered her arms, confused, and Charlie backed away. He needed to get out. He knew what was happening.

*Run. Take Gen and go.*

Lorraine stepped forward, cheeks flushed red. Charlie wasn't sure if he'd caused that, or if they were already that color when she'd called him over.

"Why not, Charlie?" she asked innocently. "It's just her wrist."

"I...um...well it's very dark out here, and for one thing my insurance doesn't cover consults out of work," Charlie replied, searching for something that might convince the murmuring group of women. Surely they'd believe the insurance story. Everybody had heard about doctors and malpractice.

"Oh don't worry about your insurance. Sylvia's not going to sue you for improving her tee shot. Are you, Syl?" Sylvia confirmed that no, she wouldn't sue Charlie. Satisfied, Lorraine took her friend by the arm and started to lead her up the steps onto the back deck. "Come on, Charlie. We'll do it inside where the light's better."

He didn't move. "No, Mum. I really can't. I have to go."

Lorraine slowed. "Inside, Charlie. It'll only take a minute."

"No."

Now she stopped and let go of Sylvia's arm. "Is there a problem?" she asked, turning to face Charlie, still smiling, but on her thin lips it seemed distinctly dangerous. Sylvia scurried away, back to the safety of the semicircle of golfing ladies. Charlie didn't blame her.

"Mum, there's no problem. Really, I promise. But this is your birthday. Let's not spoil it with work."

"Last chance, Charlie."

"Last chance for what?" It was out of his mouth before he even realized it, and suddenly he was thirteen again, arguing with his mum about homework or going into town to swim with his friends or about watching too much TV. *Home Improvement*, maybe, with JTT, Lexie's old heartthrob. Wasn't that one filmed in front of a live studio audience? Kind of like Lorraine and Charlie had right now. He felt Gen put her hand on the small of his back. The message was clear. *Careful, now.*

Lorraine held up one long finger in front of her own face. She squinted at it for a moment, then pointed directly at Charlie.

"I think you need to apologize to Sylvia. And the rest of my friends."

"I'm not apologizing to anyone, Mum. I shouldn't have to work at a party—"

"*My* party. Not *a* party. *Mine.*"

The music was still playing, Kenny and Dolly still crooning

away, but every guest within a growing radius had stopped talking, pretending not to listen but all completely enthralled by the night's entertainment. Charlie heard someone attempt to start a conversation, only to be shushed by their companion.

"Mum, I think I should just go." He turned and a path instantly cleared, the narrow avenue between family and friends shattering any pretense that the crowd wasn't listening.

"No, Charlie. You need to say sorry. Not just to me or Sylvia. I think everyone here deserves to hear it. You turn up to my birthday—my *seventieth* birthday, did that even occur to you?—looking like you've made no effort whatsoever. Too busy to shave, or iron a shirt or, or…" Her voice trailed off. For a few brief, hopeful seconds it looked like it was all over, that Lorraine Knight had run out of steam. But Charlie knew the steam behind this engine had been building up for a long time. All it took to pull the chocks from the wheels was two-thirds of a bottle of French champagne.

"Did you know, *Charlie*, that Finn has an ear infection? Of course you did, because you could tell just by looking at him, the poor kid. But did you *care*? Not from what Lexie told me. You know Finn's *four*, right? And…and Ted?" Lorraine scanned the crowd for Charlie's uncle. "He's got *gout*, you know. Not that he was allowed to talk to you about it. His toe is so swollen and red…and…and he's *limping*, Charlie. And you barely looked at him. Oh yes. I've heard it *all* tonight."

She looked around at her guests, and Charlie thought she was realizing she was on full display, that everybody at her party was now watching the guest of honor's off-the-cuff speech. Some had their mouths agape. Others shuffled their feet uncomfortably. But no, Lorraine wasn't looking at them. She was looking *for* someone.

"You know there are other doctors here, Charlie, but you're the only one who struts around like you're God or something. Can't even have a normal conversation with people. You know what it is, Charlie? It's *selfish*."

Charlie felt a spark of anger. Like a flint, chip, chip, chipping away inside.

"Selfish?" he repeated quietly, almost hoping he'd misheard her. "Mum, did you just say I'm selfish?"

She nodded, and the flint chipped again. This time the spark caught, and the flame flickered up, twisting and curling inside him.

"Right. Okay then." He swallowed. "Mum, you can say a lot of things about me, but one thing I've never been is *selfish*."

Lorraine rolled her eyes.

"Really Charlie? What about Finn? And Ted? Charlie, selfish barely begins to cover it."

The fire surged up inside him. Charlie felt Gen's hand again, firmer now on his back. *Careful, Charlie. Careful. Don't say anything you'll regret.*

"Seven years ago, Mum. When I stayed. Was that selfish?"

Lorraine's face blanched.

She closed her eyes, just for a few moments, and when she reopened them, Charlie saw a dozen different emotions at once. They played across her face, all that champagne dulling her ability to hide them away: hurt, anger, frustration, exasperation.

And behind them?

Shame.

Humiliation.

Charlie was sure he was the only one to see those, because he was the only one watching for them. Because he'd seen them before, all those years ago, when he saved her. When she first pushed him away.

And now she waved a hand at him, doing it again.

"Just go, Charlie."

"Mum, I think I've sacrificed enough. I'm leaving. Monday, maybe Tuesday. I've got a job, and it's the job I want, and I've taken it. In London. So I guess this is it."

"Charlie," Gen whispered. "Don't. Not here."

Lorraine heard. "Why not here, Genevieve? Did you already know about this? Did you come back to get him? Should've gone with you in the first place. Staying here was an overreaction, Charlie."

She shifted slightly on the steps, as though she'd been knocked unsteady but was finding her feet. Back in control. Always in control.

"An overreaction," she repeated, reassuring herself. "You helped MaryAnn out for a year. And then you were supposed to go. But you didn't, and that was *your* call, nothing to do with me, so don't try to shift any of the blame this way. You were supposed to leave. And it's long overdue."

Her timing was magnificent. The final notes of "Islands in the Stream" died away, and the silence was complete. The entire party now watched in astonishment.

Lorraine lowered her voice, an invisible spotlight narrowing on her.

"Why wait 'til Tuesday?"

Another few seconds of silence, then the next song burst out of the speakers, as if responding to a signal from the stage. Charlie stared at his mother, who seemed to be shaking, trembling with a self-righteous anger. Behind her, Charlie's dad ran from the house, drying his hands. Malcolm had clearly caught just the final few sentences, and his horrified eyes darted between his wife and son.

Charlie looked at his mum, wanting to say something but without any idea what, and then the opportunity passed and Lorraine was back down the steps, hurrying to the safety of her golf friends. A woman—Ann, maybe, the one without an 'e'—wrapped her arms around her, and others reached out, comforting with a touch. Not all of them joined in; one of Lorraine's friends—a shorter lady with a soft-looking face—was watching Charlie with a curious, almost sympathetic expression. He spun around, and there was MaryAnn Steiner, one eyebrow raised and her mouth open, about to protest. Charlie couldn't understand why she was protesting, when she was complicit in the whole terrible thing.

Then Gen had him by the hand and was leading him around the house, back past the pool, and between the dozens of cars parked haphazardly across the grass and among the trees. The tree house was quiet and full of shadows, abandoned by the twins for the comfort of the living room. Beyond that, far above, the stars still dazzled, but Charlie didn't look up, part of him worried that if he opened his eyes too wide, the tears that were prickling at the corners of them would come out.

As Gen started the car and carefully threaded her way

between the parked vehicles, Charlie stared back over at the front of the house.

*An overreaction.*

Seven years, and he could still see the ambulance pulling up, and the stretcher, and the paramedics running.

The panic.

Seven years, and he could still feel that fear, of losing her, of not having done enough to save his own mum.

But that was a long time ago, and Charlie's focus was now firmly on what lay ahead. On London. On moving. On his black book, full of death. His little glimpse into the future.

Although if Charlie could *really* see the future—not just numbers, not just a sense of how many days, but a real, vibrant, watercolor picture of what was going to happen—he might have seen something else.

He might have seen that same ambulance, pulling up again.

# 16

Rick at the newsstand was watching Charlie run, staring at him as he pounded closer. It made sense, really. If anybody was going to have already heard about the disaster at the party, it would be the man who traded in news for a living, who sold newspapers and threw in his own opinion for free—the personal touch you couldn't get from reading the news online.

As Charlie neared the newsstand, he spotted the stack of *Marwick Dailies*, not really expecting to make the Sunday edition with a bombshell that was only hours old, but still harboring a seed of paranoia. DOCTOR LEAVES IN DISGRACE; RUINS MOTHER'S PARTY, or something like that. And maybe there'd be a picture somebody snapped on their phone: Lorraine in her blue dress, pointing one long finger straight at Charlie. Imagine that. Rick would sell a squillion. And then with the added scandal, hand-delivered at the newsstand: *I saw him running along the street the morning after. He looked like he didn't have a care in the world. Talk about callous! Heartless! Let him go, we don't need him here.*

But the front page wasn't about Charlie, or about Lorraine, but some high achiever from Marwick High, off to make the town proud at the national championships. Doing something special. Doing her *spectacular*.

Charlie nodded at Rick, Rick nodded back, and then Charlie was past the newsstand and running around the outskirts of the park. He might've imagined the front page and Rick's extra commentary, but it was—in part—correct.

Charlie did feel free. Not quite without a care in the world, but certainly lighter. His secret was out now: his parents knew he was leaving, MaryAnn knew he was leaving, and nothing would change his mind. Not this time.

Even his house was nearly ready for his departure. Gen had suggested a nightcap after the party, a chance to dissect Lorraine Knight's savage words for her son. But Charlie had turned her down, unable to analyze anything without a plausible reason for refusing to treat his family and friends. That was a secret he'd be taking with him to London, and so he'd found himself alone inside his half-packed house, wide awake after sleeping all day. Body still buzzing, wired from the party's stunning finale, he packed, and packed, and packed. Driven to get it all done, to squeeze every last morsel of his life into boxes, taped up, ready for shipping to a new city and a new life where it didn't matter if he knew when someone would die, because he didn't know them and wasn't going to tell them. He was packing with purpose. He'd slept for a few hours, and now he ran with purpose too.

He was running to the bridge.

Charlie wanted to see it one last time. Wanted to see it in the crisp morning light, so that his final memory of it wasn't of the little yellow evidence markers that had dotted the reeds by the water. He wanted to see if anyone had left flowers or a note. A pile of books, maybe; that would be a fitting tribute to Abbie.

But he didn't quite make it to the bridge.

He was running hard as he rounded the final bend, almost sprinting now that the finish line was coming into sight. He looked ahead to the old wooden deck spanning the water and stopped on the spot. The bridge was already occupied. Two people stood at the rail, shoulder to shoulder, their hands resting gently on the dirty timber beam.

Abbie's mum and dad gazed down into the water.

They were talking too, but Charlie couldn't hear what they were saying. He didn't want to, because he suspected they weren't talking to each other.

They were talking to Abbie.

He watched them chat away, as though she was right there with them. They took it in turns, laughing a little, smiling, crying. It was heartbreaking, and it was beautiful.

The morning was so still, so peaceful. The water glistened, its surface smooth and unbroken, a perfect mirror of the cloudless sky above. A lone cicada buzzed alongside a hushed chorus of morning birds, and the only other sound beyond the distant murmur of conversation on the bridge was Charlie's ragged breath. Not that Abbie's parents noticed him. As far as they were concerned, they were the only people on earth right now.

He felt like he was intruding, just by being there, by witnessing this moment. So he backed away, slowly, and when he reached the bend, he started to run back in the direction he'd come from.

Charlie bypassed the main street and the newsstand—he didn't need Rick staring at him again, judging him for what happened at a party the guy wasn't even invited to. But Charlie did cut through the park, admiring Simon Lopez's grass: still short, still snake-free and *safe*, but tinged with brown. It needed some rain. The whole town needed some rain, really. But clearly the plain blue sky had other plans.

Charlie jogged slowly toward his house and knew something was different the moment he turned onto his street. His front gate was ajar slightly. He'd closed it behind him when he'd first set out, he was sure of it.

It was open because somebody was waiting for him, sitting on his doorstep.

"Toby?"

The young man jumped up, startled. "Doc. I...um...sorry, I didn't think you were... I thought you were still asleep."

Charlie checked his watch. "Mate, it's seven o'clock on a Sunday. What are you doing?"

Toby ran his hands through his hair. It flopped straight back into place. "Sorry doc. I didn't want to bother you. I was gonna wait 'til you got up, then knock, so I've just..."

"Just been sitting there?" Charlie finished. *Careful now*, he reminded himself. *Careful what you ask him.* Toby was wearing blue jeans and a tee; he wasn't out exercising. In fact, he looked more like he'd been out for the night. All night, perhaps—his round, doughy face was gray and tired.

"Uh huh," Toby nodded.

Then he started to cry.

Charlie wanted to stand back. He wanted to stay at the gate and let Toby cry it out—whatever *it* was. He had to, otherwise that threshold, that line he couldn't cross, would be right at his toes, and he'd be tripping over it, and a number would be squeezing its way into his head for Toby Brennan.

Toby sobbed. He swiped roughly at his face and turned away, embarrassed by his tears. Now he was facing Charlie's front door, and Charlie could see his whole body shaking.

And he couldn't just watch, just wait until it was done.

He couldn't.

"Toby," he said gently, taking a few steps forward. He put an arm around Toby's shoulders. The younger man didn't pull away. "What's up, mate?"

"I've messed up, Doc. Big-time."

"Okay. Want to come inside and tell me about it?"

It was around then that the world went gray, that Toby's brown hair suddenly matched Charlie's, and then the pressure in his skull grew, fast and hard. Then it was gone, and all it left behind was the sense of a number. An absolutely huge number.

One day, Toby Brennan would grace the front page of the *Marwick Daily* as the town's newest centenarian. Assuming, of course, that he stayed in town and that the newspaper was still around and still printing stories about locals turning one hundred. Charlie knew with certainty that Toby would reach the milestone; he had no such insight into the survival of the *Daily*.

He unlocked the door. His house bore a passing resemblance to a mausoleum now: empty rooms and an echo that followed them as he showed his guest to the living room.

Toby took in the stacked boxes, the rolled-up rug, even the television, whose power plug hung lifelessly (pulled out a little prematurely during Charlie's packing rampage).

"Are you moving, Doc?" he asked, his own distress momentarily forgotten.

*Ah*, thought Charlie. Toby hadn't been at Lorraine's seventieth. This was all news to him.

"Yeah, I am. I've got a new job. I'm leaving this week."

"A new job?" Toby repeated slowly. A conversation with him was a little like shouting across a valley; Toby was taking in the sight of Charlie talking, observing his lips moving and his hands waving, but the words wouldn't arrive for another second, and the understanding of those words another moment after that. Some of the patients found it a little frustrating when they were booking new appointments. Charlie didn't; he knew it was just Toby's way. "So you're *fully* leaving."

"I am."

Charlie threw back a curtain, and light flooded in.

"You want a cup of coffee, Toby? Haven't packed that away just yet." He grinned at the young man and was relieved to see him smile back.

"Yeah, thanks Doc. I haven't been to bed."

They moved to the kitchen, and Charlie weighed up the best approach. Dive straight into the trauma or work around the edges?

*Do what I'd do with any patient. Ease into it. Build the trust.*

"How are the lizards?" Charlie asked as he started making coffee.

"Oh yeah. They're good," Toby replied, his shoulders relaxing for the first time. "Got a third one now, a green tree monitor. Some guy in Abercrombie was selling it for two hundred bucks. I got it cheap—those things usually go for a thousand. Sometimes more."

"Aren't they protected? Monitors? They've got them at the zoo in the reptile house."

"Oh. Nah, don't think so." Toby fell silent. "Crap. I hope not. Hey, don't tell anyone, yeah? Just in case."

Charlie pretended to zip his mouth shut. An image burst into his head: his dad doing the same thing when Charlie was a kid, and there was something they were keeping between them. Malcolm had always pretended to lock the zip on his mouth, then swallow the key. *How did he swallow it if his mouth was zipped?* Charlie wondered.

"Mum wasn't too happy about it," Toby confessed.

"About the new lizard?"

"Yeah. I think she wants me to move out soon. I was only staying a little while anyway, so it's probably fair enough." He blinked, a slow, heavy-lidded blink that somehow made him look even more tired.

Charlie sighed, and handed Toby a cup. "What's happened, Toby? Why haven't you been to bed yet?"

"I messed up, Doc."

"You mentioned that. What happened?"

"It's Lisa. I…uh…" He took a shuddering breath, his whole body rigid. "I like her."

Charlie hid a smile. Toby's crush on his colleague was not news. Not to Lisa, not to Charlie, not to anybody.

"Right. As in, you *like* her."

Toby nodded. "And last night we were talking, and I had a couple of beers, and I decided to ask her out."

"Ah. Okay. At the pub? Or were you texting, and—"

"Texting? You sound like my mum. No offense," he added quickly. "Nobody texts. I just DM'd her. On Instagram." He thought about it for a moment. "That's where you send a message directly to—"

"I know what a DM is." Charlie laughed. "So what did you say?"

"I asked her if she wanted to come over to my place." Which was, technically, Toby's mother's house. With Toby's mum still in it, sharing a roof with her son.

"And what did she say?" Charlie had a feeling he knew the answer.

"She said she couldn't this weekend, but maybe another time." Toby sipped his coffee and winced. Either at the heat or the memory, Charlie wasn't sure. He waited for more, but his guest had clammed up.

"I'm guessing that's not where it ended," he prompted.

Toby shook his head, and when he finally looked up at Charlie, his cheeks were burning scarlet.

"I feel like such an idiot, Doc. I mean, I think about it now, and it's pretty obvious she was blowing me off. 'Another time' means *never*, right?"

Charlie nodded. "I think so. Sorry, Toby."

The young man groaned and buried his head in his hands. "I'm such an idiot." His voice was muffled.

"I think you're being a bit hard on yourself, mate. It's really not the worst thing in the world. She's not keen, you move on. There'll be others. Yeah, it's a bit awkward, but—"

"Doc, last night…I thought it was a *yes*." A pause. Long and uncomfortable. "I sent her some pics."

"Pics? As in, photos?" The reality of what Toby was saying dawned on Charlie. This might be worse than *awkward*. A lot worse.

Toby nodded, looking up, but not able to meet Charlie's eyes.

"Not your…" Charlie nodded toward Toby's groin.

"No way!" he exclaimed. "Well, kind of. I was…I was in my boxers." His face was now an unusual shade of puce.

"So you took some photos of yourself in your boxers and sent them to her?"

Toby groaned again, louder this time. "Not exactly." He pulled his phone out of his pocket and flicked through the images stored on it. Then, without warning, he turned the screen toward Charlie. The picture was an extreme close-up of a pair of navy blue satin boxer shorts. They were pulled tight, and through them, Charlie could clearly see the outline of Toby's genitals.

*Jesus Christ.*

"I see," Charlie said, frowning. "And how many…"

"Three or four. Doc, I've messed up so bad. Lisa said she's going to quit. Said she can't work with me. She said I completely misinterpreted the nature of our relationship." Charlie had a hunch the last part was a direct quote from a message. Likely one that Toby had read and reread all night, searing it into his memory. Burnt into the part of the brain where shame lives.

"I went to her house after," Toby admitted, his voice quiet.

"You did *what*?"

"I walked to her house. I know, Doc, this was stupid, it's all completely stupid. But I went there, and I messaged her again, cos I thought that maybe I could sort things out if I could just talk to her in person. But she wouldn't come out, and then she blocked me. So I went to the park, and I've just been going over and over and over it again in my head and I'm just such an idiot. Then I came here. Cos I don't know who else to talk to. And I don't know how to make it better. I was gonna wait 'til eight or so, then knock. I didn't know you were already out running."

Charlie looked at Toby, at his blotchy cheeks and the distress in his eyes, and he wondered just how dark his thoughts had been in the park. At two, three, four o'clock in the morning, when everything was always at its most grim. A problem like this one, which looked manageable once the sun was up, took on a different shape in those early hours. And for a kid like Toby, alone in the dark, it could feel like a dead end. Terminal.

"I'm glad you came to see me, mate. We can sort this out."

His words were a trigger of their own. Toby's face slackened with relief, the tension leaving his jaw, and he slumped over the kitchen bench, motionless. Charlie waited a minute before speaking again, concerned that if he left it any longer, the young man may actually fall asleep.

"Can I ask you something, Toby? It's personal."

"I just showed you a photo of my junk. I think you can ask me pretty much anything."

"Good point." Charlie smiled gently. "Mate, have you had a girlfriend before?"

Toby sat up. "Not really," he said. "Not like that. It's embarrassing, you know? Twenty-two and still a virgin."

"So what made you do it? Even if you thought she'd said yes, that she wanted to come over sometime. Why'd you send her a picture of your…well, your boxers?"

Toby thought about it, looking for an answer in his coffee cup and not finding one.

"I dunno. My mates send them all the time. Proper ones, you know? But I…I didn't wanna take everything off, so I left the boxers on."

Charlie nodded. Somehow he'd never actually thought of Toby as having any friends, least of all young men his own age. And especially not buddies who sent pictures of their private parts to women.

"Well, the first step will be to give her some space. Especially if you went to her house overnight. You've apologized for it all, haven't you?"

"Yeah. Of course. In like, ten messages."

"Okay. You need to give her some space, and give her some time. She knows you're sorry. And then tomorrow, at work, you can see how she's feeling. You'll probably need to apologize again. And it'll mean more, not in the heat of the moment. More sincere. Lisa is a very, very decent person. Think about how she would feel in all this."

Toby considered it. "Will you help me, Doc? Tomorrow?"

Charlie wasn't expecting that. "I can't, I'm sorry. I've finished up at the clinic. I'm leaving on Tuesday."

"Okay." Toby nodded forlornly and got to his feet. "Thanks for the coffee, Doc. And for the chat. And I'm sorry for calling you old. You know, with the DMs and texting and stuff."

"I barely noticed, Toby." He showed him to the front door. "Do you want a lift home?"

Toby shook his head. "I'm gonna walk. Good luck with the rest of the packing," he said, looking down at the path. "Oh… and you won't say anything, will you? That stuff about me and girlfriends?"

Charlie zipped his lips again, and this time mimed locking them too. Toby looked relieved. Just as he'd done when Charlie had told him the situation was fixable.

*We can sort this out*, Charlie had said.

But now he was leaving Toby to sort it on his own. Even after Toby had waited on his doorstep, and asked for help. He was abandoning him.

He sighed. "Hey, Toby?"

Toby turned, seeming even more exhausted in the morning sun. Charlie felt tired just looking at him.

"I'll see you tomorrow."

It took a second, then another, but then a grin stretched across Toby's face. "Thanks Doc." His step noticeably lightened as he left.

*Just Toby*, Charlie promised himself. *No patients.*

Unless there was an extremely compelling reason to see one, of course.

And there was.

# 17

MaryAnn was livid.

"What am I supposed to do now?" she fumed. Charlie shrugged—not in a petulant way, but in a way that hopefully made it clear he wasn't going to bail her out again. Not this time. Her eyebrow was arched, and he considered the possibility it had stayed that way since Saturday night. She'd looked furious then too, when he turned around after his mother's tirade to find MaryAnn listening with her eyebrow halfway to the stars.

"Get a temp in. From Abercrombie," he replied simply, and she rolled her eyes.

"Why do you even want to leave anyway? Is it money? We can talk about salary." She stood with her arms folded: a diminutive security guard, blocking the door out of Charlie's office. Charlie hadn't even intended to set foot inside this room. He wasn't planning to go any farther than reception, but MaryAnn apparently had other ideas.

"It's not about money." *It's about doing something* spectacular, he thought. Dr. Matthew Rowan, changing lives in his serious neurologist's office. Genevieve Longstaff, immersing herself in one of the creative capitals of the world. And good old Charlie Knight, tending to coughs and colds in the same town where he'd learned to walk. "Emergency medicine. Crisis stuff. I want to do it again, MaryAnn. I'm good at it."

"You're good at *this*. Come on, Charlie. I gave you a chance."

"I did you a favor! You were in this exact position eight years ago, and Mum begged me to come work with you for a year. It was supposed to be for twelve months. I was supposed to leave seven years ago. I didn't, but now I am."

MaryAnn's face clouded over, and Charlie thought she was about to prosecute the same case that his mother had made at the party. That staying behind last time had been an overreaction, that Lorraine Knight was fine. But she didn't say it—maybe because she *had* said it at the time, back when Lorraine *hadn't* been fine. She'd bellowed it, in fact, in this very office, insisting Charlie leave. Accusing him of questioning her integrity and her character. Accusing him of being disloyal and undermining her, when all he was doing was trying to keep his mum alive.

Because keeping his mum alive had meant threatening to report Dr. MaryAnn Steiner to the medical board.

Keeping his mum alive had meant telling MaryAnn that he was staying, that he'd keep working at the clinic, to keep an eye on them both.

But after all the ugliness, after all her insults and her bluster, clearly MaryAnn had benefited from him staying so long. That's why she was so red-faced now and offering to review his salary. Maybe she'd expected him to stay for life. Maybe Matt Rowan had been right, in between all the *haw-haw-haw*s, when he said Charlie was probably MaryAnn's retirement plan.

"Fine."

"Fine?" Charlie repeated. What did that mean?

"I'll get a temp. But they won't be as good as you, and the patients aren't going to like them as much, and it's going to make everybody's life harder. Mine and Lisa's and Toby's." Charlie doubted if MaryAnn had any idea what would make Lisa's life harder or what would have any impact at all on Toby's life. To do so would require knowing something *about* their lives.

Lisa and Toby were good again; as much as they could be when one party had sent unwanted pictures of his groin to the other. Toby had been waiting for Charlie outside, not wanting to walk in alone. The air in reception had curdled like milk the moment he entered; Lisa was *not* happy to see him. But Toby had apologized, and it had been the most heartfelt, most sincere thing Charlie had ever seen. He hadn't cried, not this time, but he wasn't far off it. Lisa had accepted the apology and reassured Toby that she'd deleted the pictures. And she wasn't going to quit. Never had been, Charlie suspected. Because if it came down to that, it would've been Toby out the door, not Lisa.

But it was done now, and all resolved without MaryAnn Steiner having the faintest idea of what took place right under her nose.

"So am I getting one more day of work out of you?" she asked, still blocking the door.

Charlie shook his head.

"I'm going home. I've got more things to pack, then my flight's tomorrow night."

MaryAnn left the room without another word.

*Is that it?* thought Charlie. *An unceremonious end.* He started to follow her out, carrying only his stethoscope and a framed photo from his desk, when he remembered one more thing: something small and black in his desk drawer. Best not to leave that behind, where his replacement could discover it. Everything else, the temp was welcome to keep: the skeleton behind the door, Abbie's favorite posters. The lot.

He pulled the door closed behind him, just as a voice carried from reception. Toby's voice.

"Sorry, but he's not here anymore."

A response, too quiet to hear.

"I know, right? Friday was his last day."

Another response. A quick one. Then Toby: "And…by the way…meant to say this last time. I'm sorry for your loss."

And with that, Charlie knew who Toby was talking to. That mumbled, whispered voice belonged to the wraithlike figure of Deborah Anders.

He hadn't seen Deb since the night outside the pub, when she'd suddenly appeared out of the shadows to thank him for saving the girl in the video. And before that, when he'd glimpsed her at reception after she'd just turned up, hoping to see the doctor without an appointment. Toby had turned her away because there wasn't time, and he'd done it without acknowledging the elephant in the room: the grief she carried with her, the grief that oozed out of every pore.

Charlie stood outside his office, one hand on the door

handle. The other held his notebook, which now felt extremely heavy. Unnaturally heavy, like it was weighed down by all the days, all the years of life it contained. All the responsibility.

And maybe this was fate having one last crack at him before he left Marwick for good. *Send the grieving mother in. The one he promised to see if ever she needed him. Just swing by, he said. So swing on by and see what he says. See what he does. See if he stuffs this one up too.*

And even though it was all in his head, Charlie lifted his chin, his grip tightening on the door handle. That same flint, chipping away inside. An angry, defiant flicker of flame.

He called out to reception as he pushed his door open again. "Deb. You just caught me. Come on through."

*Cop that, fate.*

Charlie lifted his window, and the cicadas' hum filled the room. But as Deb shuffled in, he nearly closed it again; the gentle breeze that wafted through threatened to sweep her off her feet.

Deb perched almost weightlessly on the seat opposite him, his final patient in this room. She smoothed the creases out of her pants, then tucked her hands under stick-thin thighs, as though she needed something to hold them in place. Charlie recognized the sign of a compulsive fidgeter, and wondered how much it had worsened in the last few months.

Deb was fifty-three, he knew that, but her appearance was that of a much older woman. Her hair was pulled back in the same thin, oily ponytail she'd worn when he'd seen her outside the Marwick Hotel; the roots were faded, giving her hair a distinctly two-toned effect. Her bloodshot eyes had sunk deep into her skull, and her skin was drawn and gray. Translucent, almost. Like a ghost.

This was a woman who hadn't slept properly in a long time. A very long time.

He started with the only thing he could think of. "Can I just say again," he offered gently, "how sorry I am that you're going through this?"

Deb nodded; it was just another variation on "I'm sorry for your loss," which she'd probably heard so many times it was as natural a greeting as *hello*.

"Cancer is...well, cancer is cruel. I'm so sorry. And I want to help you."

Tears welled in Deb's eyes, and Charlie slid a box of tissues toward her. The colorful print on the box—interlocking circles and shapes, all bright, tropical colors—became black and white as he moved it. He ignored the change. He ignored the swell of pressure inside his skull, focusing instead on the lines on Deb's face, the deep valleys etched into her skin by sorrow. He tried so hard to ignore the sense of a number that emerged, to pay it no attention, to push it to one side unseen. But it was there, inside his own head, and even if he tried not to think about it, it was still *there*. And when at last it wormed its way into his consciousness, it left him with a new kind of sadness, different to what he'd felt for Abbie Wilson, who'd had so little time left.

*Oh, Deb. You've got years of grief ahead of you.*

"Thanks, Doctor. I mean...Charlie. It is. Cruel, I mean." Deb's voice was hoarse. Each word sounded like it took something from her.

Charlie waited. "Take your time. Grief's a tricky thing. And it has a way of coming for you when you least expect it."

Deb nodded, dabbing at her nose with the tissue, and Charlie was ashamed of the relief he felt that his words had hit their mark. One of his greatest fears as a new doctor had been speaking convincingly on death. His knowledge of grief had largely come from books, until Gen and that call outside the vacant lot about two blocks from the clinic. But even then he half expected bereaved patients to turn his words around: *What would* you *know, Doc? That's not real grief, mourning a baby that you never even held.* But it *had* been real, because it had changed their lives, and it had hurt, and only somebody who'd gone through that themselves would understand. Until that phone call, and until the awful, awful guilt had kicked in, his knowledge of grief had been theoretical. But now, he supposed, he could point as well to Edna Bradley and Abbie Wilson. The grief for them had been real too. And in Abbie's case, it had a habit of creeping up on him.

"I'm just…" Deb started, before clearing her throat. It made no change to her voice. "I'm…I'm not doing too well. I'm sorry for just dropping in like this. I was driving past, I'm supposed to be getting milk, and now I'm in here. I don't really remember the bit in between. I don't know…" She pulled another tissue from the box and started twisting it round and round and round her finger. "I think I might need something to help me get to sleep. Please."

Charlie nodded. "We can do that. How much sleep do you reckon you're getting at the moment?"

Deb gave a fragile shrug, her shoulders barely moving.

"I don't know. A couple of hours maybe? I've tried to get to sleep in my own bed but it's just...it's just not working. So I've started reading in Hayley's room, just sitting on her bed, I don't get into the sheets or anything. But I just sit there and read, and sometimes I nod off. Maybe around two o'clock. Sometimes three. And then when I wake up I can't stop thinking about her and I can't close my eyes again so I read some more." A deep, rattling breath. "And by lunchtime I'm just so tired that I'll fall asleep at the table. The other day I didn't wake up 'til it was dark, and I'd already missed watching my shows. I...I didn't sleep at all that night."

Charlie wanted to reach across the desk and take her hand. She'd been battling this on her own for too long. "Deb, I can help you. What you're describing is chronic insomnia, and the way it works is just to keep on compounding. It just gets worse, your sleep cycle gets right out of whack, and it'll make you sick. I can prescribe some pills to get you to sleep and to keep you out through the night."

"Thank you," she whispered and pulled another tissue from the box.

"But Deb," he continued softly. "If you only treat the symptom, the problem's just going to keep coming back. There's a reason you're not sleeping. I think it might be worth speaking to a grief counselor too."

Deb nodded. "I got a brochure from the...from the *funeral* home." She pronounced it like a foreign word. A word she didn't understand but knew was burdened with unbearable sadness. "They gave me some numbers to call. But I haven't done it yet."

"You should," Charlie urged gently. "When you're ready to talk about it."

Deborah started winding the new tissue around her finger. Round and round and round, like reeling in a fish. Then back the other way. Charlie was writing the script for sleeping pills, but out the corner of his eye he kept watching her. She was sitting so upright, so stiff. Like a bird, ready to fly away at the slightest rustle or scrape. He wasn't expecting her to relax, of course, but usually after the patient had said their piece there was a change, like a deflation. Problem shared, problem halved, right? But Deb was the exact opposite. She had the look of someone holding something in.

*I've seen this before*, he thought.

A Trojan horse.

One of the patient types, alongside the ambushes, and the biennials. Booking in with a headache, but really wanting to talk about something else, something personal. Often—though he doubted it was the case this time—it was something about sex, something they were embarrassed by but just couldn't put off any longer in case it ended up killing them. Sometimes it was depression or abuse. Wanting to say more but not sure how to begin.

Charlie had developed a keen eye for it, and Deborah Anders was—without question—a Trojan horse. And now he had to coax it out of her. He wasn't leaving Marwick with this unfinished.

"Deb?" Charlie prompted, his voice soft, expecting some resistance. But it was all the coaxing she needed.

Deb let out a great, racking sob and bent forward, leaning

over, her whole body shaking as the pent-up energy burst out. Charlie didn't say a word. Instead, he walked around the desk, sat next to her, and held her trembling hand.

They sat like that for five minutes, and Charlie didn't say a thing.

When Deb finally spoke, her voice was barely a croak. "She wasn't even sick anymore."

Charlie exhaled. "I know. It shouldn't be allowed to happen like that." He'd known Hayley had Hodgkin's lymphoma as a teen; Deb had talked about it at a long-ago appointment, back when her hair wasn't greasy and her arms and legs didn't look like they'd snap if she sneezed. Deb had been triumphant on that visit, glowing, because Hayley had come through the other side. But when he'd seen the death notice in the *Marwick Daily*—those three or four brutal lines in the classifieds—he knew what it meant. The cancer must have returned. It sometimes did. Like lightning, lured back for a second strike.

"No, you don't understand. She wasn't sick anymore!" Deb repeated. "The lymphoma. It was gone—fully gone. *Complete remission*, they said. How's that fair?" She blew her nose, and Charlie waited some more as she pulled yet another tissue from the box. "It might have made sense if she...if she *went* while she still had it, while she was sick. But she was better, she was working, she'd started as a nurse and everything." More tears.

Charlie sat in silence, expecting her to continue, to tell him what had claimed her daughter's life. But Deb was crying too hard to talk.

"Deb," he said, when at last she'd settled. "Can I ask—what

was it then, in the end? If she was in full remission? If she wasn't sick again?"

Another sob, then Deborah reached down to the handbag by her feet, pulling out a couple of sheets of paper, folded into four. She handed them to Charlie. It was a printed email that appeared to have been carried around for some time, with dog-eared corners from being read and reread and little wrinkled stains from where tears had dripped onto it.

He read the postmortem report, scanning for the reason Hayley died. *Cardiac arrest. Likely attribution: cardiotoxicity from historical chemotherapy.* Charlie felt his own chest squeeze.

"So the cancer treatment weakened her heart. It made her better and then she went anyway. Oh Deb, I'm so sorry. You're right. That's not fair. None of it is."

He put his arms around her and hugged her tight, feeling the sharp ridges of her shoulder blades. She was wasting away. Grief was destroying this mother.

When she said nothing else, he slowly extricated himself and sat back down on the other side of the desk. "I really do think it's worth talking to one of those counselors. You've been through trauma, one that a mum should never have to deal with. But they can give you some strategies and things to help, otherwise it won't get any easier. Not even with time."

Deb just nodded, twisting another tissue around her fingers. The same motion she'd used before to distract herself. To hold something in that she just *needed* to say.

"And I've got you a script for some sleeping pills. Don't take more than one a night, and don't take it too late either."

Deb nodded again but didn't stand. She wound the tissue one way, then back the other. Over and over. She was perching once more on the edge of the chair, even more lightly than before.

This Trojan horse was still hiding something.

"Deb?" Charlie asked, putting down his pen. "Is there…is there anything else you wanted to talk about? About Hayley or something else?"

"It's about Hayley," Deb said in a ragged whisper.

It was her tone that drew him in. Up until that point Deb's words had been hoarse and quiet. But this was different. Almost panicked. Her eyes, sunken and raw, darted from side to side as though looking for intruders, anyone who might overhear. She stared at the open window, and Charlie got up and closed it without a word.

"Please don't…you know, think I'm crazy or anything. Or that it's because of the whole sleep thing, because it's not. I've been thinking about this nonstop since it happened." She took a deep breath, and when she spoke again her voice was softer still. Charlie had to lean across the desk to hear her.

"Are there warning signs?" she whispered. "Like, specifically for what happened to Hayley?"

*Oh no. Poor Deb*, Charlie thought. *She's blaming herself for missing the symptoms.*

He shook his head. He had to reassure her. *This* was what she needed from him. "Not if they weren't picked up by her oncologist or her GP. In older or more unhealthy patients it can sometimes be a bit more obvious, but for young people—even fit young people—heart attacks like that can come right out of the blue. And when they do, sadly, they're often fatal. Tell me, was she keeping all her appointments with her GP? And the specialist?"

Deb nodded, her sunken eyes almost bouncing in her skull. "Six monthly with her GP, annually with the specialist. They're both in Abercrombie. Hayley said neither of them had any concerns. No red flags. Nothing, Charlie! The oncologist was only a few weeks before it happened too. Would they have noticed if something was wrong?" There was a dreadful desperation in her voice now.

"Yes, most likely." He searched for something else. Something to prove that this was not preventable. That Hayley had just drawn the shortest of all straws and that Deb had not failed in the one duty she regarded above all others: keeping her own daughter safe.

"She was in pretty good shape? Exercise, food?" He knew the answer to this. He'd seen Hayley jogging through the park.

"I fed her well, Charlie. I really did. She was saving for her own place, so she was staying with me. I *know* she was eating, and getting sleep, and she was at the gym most days, and she even started running. She was *better*," Deb insisted, tears threatening once again. Charlie doubted she could have many tears left.

"Yeah. By the sounds of it, she was," he agreed. "In that case, I think it's pretty unlikely there were any symptoms beforehand."

His tone softened, becoming even more gentle, reassuring. This was what she'd come for. He looked straight at Deborah. "Deb, her doctors didn't miss anything. *You* didn't miss anything."

Silence.

"You didn't," he said again. "I *promise.*"

"But that's what I don't get then," Deb replied. Her voice was barely audible now, and she squeezed her eyes shut tight. She looked like she was summoning strength, summoning courage from somewhere. Courage to say something.

Her eyes sprang open.

"How did she know she was going to die?"

# 18

Charlie packed his toaster, kettle, and half a dozen utensils from his kitchen drawers neatly into a box, taped it up, and then scribbled something that resembled *Bedroom* on the side. His mind wasn't on the job at hand.

Instead, it was fixed firmly on his *other* job, the one he was leaving behind. And one patient in particular. If Deborah Anders was the last he'd ever see at Marwick Family Clinic, then he'd picked a doozy to go out on.

Charlie had walked in his front door and dumped everything he was carrying on the kitchen bench: ground zero for the final stages of packing. Deb's words were ringing in his ears, just as they'd been when he left the clinic. Just as they'd been on his drive home.

*How did she know she was going to die?*

When Deb had first said it, Charlie had frozen, convinced that he'd misheard her. She was, after all, speaking softer than the insects that thrummed outside the closed window, softer even than the hiss of the air-conditioning vent above their heads. But she'd repeated it, a little louder this time. He hadn't misheard.

*How did she know she was going to die?*

Then, finally, after a thousand assurances that he didn't think she was just sleep deprived, Deb revealed why she'd asked. It was as though she'd decided she could trust Charlie, and nobody else, and with that decision her voice firmed up, and the bottled-up truth came pouring out of her in a rush. Deb was certain, beyond all reasonable doubt (as they liked to say in her favorite shows), that when her daughter went to bed for the last time, she'd given her a clue.

"I don't know if it was deliberate or if it just kind of slipped out, but she said it. She definitely said it. I was watching TV, and she came in, she was already in her pj's, and she put her arms around me and gave me a kiss on the cheek. She always did that, always went to bed earlier than me, because I liked to stay up watching *NCIS* or *CSI*, one of those. It was *NCIS* that night, the night when it happened, and I haven't been able to watch that once since, you know? But—and this is going to sound really stupid, but I may as well keep digging, I've dug so deep already—I keep wishing I was in the show. In *NCIS*. See? I know it sounds like I've gone a bit mad, but if I was in that show, I could get them to do that thing they always do where they enhance the image and zoom in and take out the background noise. And then I could watch it again and hear her say it. Because I know, *absolutely*, that Hayley didn't say good night to me." She stared with stricken eyes at Charlie. "She said goodbye."

Charlie had held her gaze, so many questions burning, but Deb wasn't finished. It was more than just the words, more than just a whispered farewell, half heard over the TV chatter.

"It's instinct," Deb said. "Mother's instinct, I think it's called. It's probably not a medical thing, Charlie, but it's real, I promise. When she said goodbye, I can't tell you how I know, but I just do. There was something so deliberate. So…" She fished around for the right word. "So *final* about her."

And then she'd slumped back in her seat, for the first time since she'd arrived. The Trojan horse had no more secrets.

Deb had left Charlie's office with a script for sleeping pills and three separate promises: that he believed her, that he wouldn't tell anyone what she'd said, and that he was somehow going to figure out how Hayley knew that she wouldn't wake up. What Charlie didn't tell Deborah Anders was that he wanted to know the answer to that question just as much as she did.

He lost count of how many boxes he mislabeled throughout that afternoon as he mulled it over. And he nearly missed the vibration of his phone on the bench and had to scrabble through the piles of stuff waiting to be packed. He scooped it up just in time.

"Hi, Dad."

"Charlie. How are you doing today, mate?"

"I'm all right. Thanks, Dad." *Actually, I'm distracted as heck. Any thoughts on how Hayley Anders knew she was going to die?*

"Good to hear. Better than yesterday?" Malcolm had called on Sunday too, a welfare check in the wake of the party. That call had been brief, and Charlie suspected it had ended because Lorraine had walked back into the room.

"Listen," Malcolm said when Charlie didn't answer. "I've talked to Mum about Saturday night. About what happened."

"Right."

"I know she feels bad. She doesn't normally drink, and she said some things she shouldn't have. I think she'd just had Lexie in her ear about you not looking at Finn—"

"I didn't have my otoscope."

"And Ted had a go too, about his gout, and I think it just got a bit much. She doesn't actually think you're, you know, selfish. I think that was the champagne talking. And I bought it for her, so you can blame me, really." Malcolm chuckled.

"I don't know, Dad. I think Mum forgets what it was like. How bad it was. I couldn't leave her—she almost died."

"She hasn't forgotten, mate. She's embarrassed. And I don't know why, but you remind her of it."

"Why me? Why do I get the blame for this? Why not MaryAnn? She's the one who put her on the pills in the first place."

"I don't know, Charlie."

There was silence on the other end of the phone.

"I know what you did for her, mate," Malcolm said quietly.

"Yeah?"

"Yeah."

"Thanks, Dad."

"Now—can I give you a lift to the airport tomorrow?"

Charlie grinned.

"I thought you were going to try to talk me out of it."

"I can if you want me to. But this isn't a spur-of-the-moment thing, is it, Charlie? You didn't just decide on Saturday night that you were going to up and move."

"No. I've been thinking about it for a long time."

"You should've said something. Did you overpay for your new place?"

"Probably."

Malcolm laughed. "So what time can I pick you up?"

"Thanks, Dad. But Gen's already offered."

"I know which one I'd choose. Can't convince her to get on the plane with you, Charlie?"

"Dad. There's nothing happening there."

"I know, mate. I'm just teasing. She's got her hands full with Ruth. And the new business. Speaking of which, pass on a message for me. Tell her I've tried the oil, and I'm changing my name to Benjamin."

"Benjamin?" Charlie asked.

"Button. By the time you come back to visit, I'll be in my twenties again."

They hung up, Charlie still smiling. Malcolm Knight was clearly keen to smooth things over before his son left town. Ever the salesman, ever the diplomat. But there was still the unavoidable fact that it had been his dad who called him, not his mum. She was probably still finishing a twilight game at Abercrombie Links, checking on Sylvia's wrist after each swing, because Charlie's mum was a good person like that.

There'd be no goodbye from Lorraine Knight.

And he thought of another mother, Deb Anders, and the raw grief as she sat in Charlie's office, mourning her daughter, craving some closure over her last words. His thoughts turned unexpectedly bleak: If *he* died, would Lorraine Knight cry? He didn't know the answer. He didn't have answers about anything, really.

*How did Hayley know she was going to die?*

He tipped out the contents of his cutlery drawer and turned the question over and over and over, his scientific mind looking for the logic and finding absolutely nothing. Only one tiny sliver of information that Deb had shared stuck out, a jagged edge on an otherwise smooth surface. One small similarity between Hayley Anders and Charlie Knight. Their jobs. Charlie was a doctor, Hayley had been a nurse, whose career was just sputtering to life when she died in her sleep.

And a strange possibility occurred to him.

What if Hayley had suffered from the same thing Charlie was dealing with right now? She worked in a similar field— what if she'd predicted the deaths of the people she'd looked after, just like he was doing? And then, somehow, she'd predicted *her own*, and had known it to be true, with the same certainty that Charlie had known Abbie Wilson would die? How terrifying. How completely and utterly horrible to know her time was running out, but not know how it was going to happen. And then when nothing had taken her on her final day, she'd gone to sleep, knowing the end must come during her dreams.

That was why she'd said goodbye.

Charlie needed to talk to the people who knew her, who'd worked with her, who'd cared for her and been cared for *by* her. Maybe she'd said something to one of them, some idea of where it had come from or what it was. Maybe she'd told someone else how long they had left too. Someone like Abbie.

A sharp knock echoed through the house, and for some reason Charlie pictured his mother, that long, accusing finger now curled in a fist, hammering at his door. Dropping by after golf, coming to see him off. Maybe even to say sorry.

*Well wouldn't that be something.*

But it wasn't Lorraine, and when he saw who it was instead, Charlie didn't mind at all.

Genevieve Longstaff stood on the front step, straight from work, and simply stunning. Her hair was twisted up into a knot, and huge gold earrings swooped down toward a pale green romper. In her hands she juggled a large paper bag, a bottle of wine, and a pair of wineglasses impossibly balanced between two slender fingers. She looked very glamorous for someone seeing out four weeks' notice at a job she didn't want to do anymore.

A flutter in his chest. Maybe she hadn't done it for the office. Maybe she'd done it for him.

"What's all this?" he asked.

"A farewell dinner. I thought I should bring the glasses too, because yours are probably packed away. Take them, would you, before I drop them?"

Charlie led her through the empty hall.

"I'm loving what you've done with the place. Minimalist. Though I'm *not* loving the idea of new neighbors. What if they're not keen on knocking down the back fence?"

"Why will you even need to, if I'm not here anymore?" Charlie countered slyly. "Unless it was never about me and all about the commune."

"Oh, it was always about you," Gen teased back, and Charlie felt his breath catch. There was a buzz about her, an energy that fizzed in the way she was talking, the way she was standing.

Even the way she was looking at him seemed different. "Have you still got the table and chairs out the back? Or have they been dismantled already? Let's take this out there. Better than eating surrounded by boxes."

Gen set out the food while Charlie poured the wine, and they toasted to London as the stars came out.

"I hope you're ready to not see them for a while, Charlie," Gen said. "At least not properly. Not like this. Drink it all in tonight—you're lucky the sky's so clear."

"Don't know whether it's luck," Charlie replied. "I can't actually remember the last time it was cloudy, let alone raining. You're right though. I'm going to miss it."

He glanced across at Gen, who was staring into the heavens. It wasn't the only thing he was going to miss.

Dessert was a chocolate tart, the pastry flaky and the filling rich and gooey, made by Gen herself. She poured the rest of the wine into their glasses as Charlie ran his finger around the edge of his plate, scraping up the final smear of chocolate, enjoying the moment. It was peaceful, and it was calm, and it was *easy*. Like the old days. Like it always had been with Gen, right up until the end.

And they talked, Charlie choosing his questions carefully, watching his words, dodging any possible triggers. Gen told him about the surge in orders she'd had for lavender oil, and patchouli, and mint, and how she was completely convinced now that she'd made the right choice to quit. He told her about the call he'd received from his dad. Then they talked about how neat the lawn was, and how loud the crickets were, and whether Charlie would be wearing scrubs at his new job.

Then there was quiet.

Gen swirled the last mouthful of wine around her glass, before downing it in one gulp. "I don't want you to go."

Charlie sat up straight in his chair. "What did you say?"

"I don't want you to go. I know you have to, but I don't want you to. I want you to stay here with me."

Charlie exhaled, long and slow. This was the buzz he'd felt from Gen, from the moment she'd knocked on the door.

"Gen…" he said softly, but stopped, unsure of what else to say. She was right there, so close, pupils wide in the dark. If his life was a romance—a comedy, maybe, with Drew Barrymore playing Gen, and a revolving cast playing Charlie—this was where he would kiss her. Gently, silently, under the stars, and it would be happily ever after.

But this was not a romance, and certainly not a comedy. There was far too much death in Charlie's life for it to be a comedy. And most rom-coms didn't have the leading man petrified of learning when the girl he adored was going to die.

"You don't have to say anything, Charlie. But *I* need to say something, and it's not to make you change your mind. I just… I couldn't take you to the airport tomorrow without telling you."

"Telling me what, Gen?"

"That you're the reason I came home."

Charlie felt a rush of heat, racing through his body. "But I thought…"

"Yeah, there's other reasons too. But if I had to rank them, Charlie Knight would be at number one. Then it's a long way to second."

*Gen had come back to Marwick for him.*

"You need to do this, Charlie. You keep saying it, and I agree. You need your chance to have an adventure, to have a career outside this place. But I…I don't know if I can wait. Not this time."

"What do you mean?"

"You know I waited for you, right? When we were supposed to go together, last time? I get it. I completely understand—if you hadn't stayed, your mum would be dead. It's that simple. And your dad would've been alone, and he's way too nice a guy for that. You did the right thing. And maybe if things had been different, I could've stayed too, and waited here. But I just couldn't."

Charlie knew why. He'd always known why.

"Because of me." His voice was strained.

"What?"

"Because of me," he repeated slowly. And then something he'd never admitted out loud to anybody. A weight he'd carried for the last seven years. "Because we lost the baby. And that's on me."

"On you? What are you talking about, Charlie?"

*Careful, Charlie*, he told himself. *There are triggers everywhere.* And with an enormous effort he pulled himself together, checking each sentence before he uttered it. The heat that had surged in him after Gen's revelation had cooled, and behind it was the same fear of saying the wrong thing, of asking the wrong question, of going too far. Of discovering her number. But they were talking about the past, about history, so maybe it would be okay.

*Please let it be okay.*

"Because I didn't take care of you. I didn't take care of *him*. I thought we were safe, we were well into the second trimester. And I should've known better than anyone—it's my job, and I let you down. You were at a higher risk—"

"If I had a seizure—which I didn't."

"It doesn't matter. It was my *job*, Gen. There could have been warning signs, something I missed. I should've taken better care of you."

"I didn't *need* you to take care of me, Charlie. I had it under control! Nothing you could have done, and nothing I could've done, was going to change the outcome. They told us that, remember? It just wasn't meant to be. Please don't tell me you actually thought I blamed *you* for it. Did you?"

Charlie did think that. Because he blamed himself, and had done so since the moment Gen called to say something was wrong. He still knew the exact spot on the pavement where he'd heard his phone ringing, the exact tree he'd stopped running under to answer the call, the overgrown vacant block he'd been in front of when Gen asked him how far away he was, because there was blood. And from that moment on, he'd blamed himself. Because his job was to save people, to help them, and he hadn't done it. So it had been the most natural thing in the world for Gen to blame him too, and to need some time alone.

He nodded. "You left."

"I had to! I blamed myself too! I needed to get away. *Everybody* here knew I was pregnant. And they just kept asking how the baby was doing. How I was feeling. Whether I wanted a boy or a girl. How long I was going to work for. And I couldn't keep explaining what had happened. It broke my heart every single time. But then it all happened so quickly, when your mum went into the hospital, and you were so focused on that, and I just needed to go. Just to get away from the questions and the pitying looks. I needed some space. But you also said you'd only be a few months, and then you'd come. And we spoke every day for the first few weeks. And you might not have noticed but then it went to maybe twice a week. Then a couple of times a month. Then you stopped calling, and I stopped calling, because it became very, very, *very* clear to me that you weren't coming anymore. And suddenly, what had been *our* plan to go to London so you could work at St. John's and I could do something huge in advertising, became *my* plan. On my own. So I moved on."

There was so much Charlie needed to say. So much that might help to explain *why* he hadn't followed, why he'd been glued to Marwick for so long. He wanted to tell her how he'd done it to even the score. That he'd thrown himself into saving his mum, because this was a life he *could* save, and maybe—maybe—it would make up for the one he couldn't. And that by the time he was sure his mum was okay and wasn't going to slip away again, it was too late for Gen. The weekly calls had become monthly, and then they'd stopped. Gen had moved on, so he did as well.

There was so much he wanted to say, but he was sailing so close to the trigger already. So close to the pressure building in his head, and that number squeezing its way into his mind, and once that process started he couldn't do a thing to stop it.

So much to say. But he settled for what really mattered.

"I'm sorry, Gen. For everything."

"I don't need you to be sorry. I just need you to understand.

I loved my time there. It was fun. Really fun. But I missed you every day. And the work wasn't what I thought it would be. Do you know what was the most successful campaign I worked on the entire time I was there? Actually, the most *satisfying* too, which is probably even worse?"

He shook his head.

"Convincing a hundred thousand families to join a site where you rent musical instruments for school. Seriously. It's not even to *buy* a recorder, it's just to borrow one for a year. I am single-handedly responsible for a hundred thousand kids attempting to play 'Three Blind Mice.' Half the parents in Europe probably want me arrested." She laughed: a glorious, joyful noise that seemed to hang forever in the night sky. He loved that laugh.

Actually, he just loved Gen.

"So why are you telling me this now?" he asked her, still choosing his words carefully.

"To put my cards on the table. I should've done it long ago," she said. "I should've called you up. I should've come home to visit. But there was something keeping you here, and I didn't want to be the one to pull you away from it. Just like I don't want to be the one to keep you from doing whatever it is you need to do now. But at least this time, you know where I stand. And whatever happens, happens. Leave it up to fate."

Charlie knew his life wasn't a romantic comedy. He knew it wasn't *any* kind of movie. So did it really matter if he'd missed that wide-eyed moment when he *should* have kissed her?

There *was* no script, and he had no regard for fate.

So he leaned across and kissed Genevieve Longstaff, something he hadn't done for seven years, but it was like no time had passed at all. Her lips felt exactly the same, and the smell of citrus and summer took him away.

*Spectacular.*

Then she pressed back against him, and he forgot all about packing boxes and catching flights. He forgot all about numbers and guilt and death and all of it.

Gone in an instant.

He woke first and listened to Gen breathing. The soft rhythm of it, which was still so familiar to him after all this time.

She'd come back because of him. And now he was leaving.

*It would be so easy to stay*, he thought. It would be so easy to send another email off to St. John's Private Hospital and say, *sorry—something's happened, and I can't accept the position*, and then he could just stay right there in bed next to Genevieve and never, ever leave.

Except for the numbers. The curse that had killed Abbie Wilson—or used him to do it, leaving *his* hands stained. Charlie knew, right down deep in the pit of his stomach, where all good intuition came from, that he couldn't be around the people that he cared for. The risk was just too great that he'd do it again.

Gen stirred and rolled to face him. She was even more beautiful in the morning.

"I have to go to work," she said forlornly.

"Do you have to?" Charlie asked, not wanting to say the rest: I'd like one more day with you, before I go. He didn't want to say it, because to do so would acknowledge he was still leaving, and shatter the morning's fairy tale feel.

"I do. They're wringing every last drop of value out of me, and I have calls all day. So as much as I'd like to stay right here," she said, pulling on the clothes she'd worn when she knocked on the front door, "I'm going to make us coffee."

Charlie followed her downstairs, trying to remember every single detail of how she looked at that moment. To store it all for when he was miles and miles away, and she was no longer waiting for him.

"Where are your mugs?" she asked Charlie. "This is a disaster. One, two, three…" She counted out eight boxes. "And not a single one has *kitchen* written on it." Charlie laughed and started digging in one of the cartons. Gen tackled another one, rummaging through the mess.

As he searched, Charlie tried explaining his packing system, which really wasn't a system at all, because he'd been distracted when he'd packed the boxes and had no idea where anything was. But after a minute he realized Gen wasn't listening anymore. He looked up.

She was reading something she'd found in a box. Something he'd thrown in on top of the coffee cups and forgotten all about.

"Charlie?" she asked, her voice uncertain. "What *is* this?"

Gen held it up for him to see.

It was a notebook. Small, black, and deadly.

# 19

The minutes after Gen left his house were the quietest of Charlie's life. He could almost hear the synapses firing in his brain, the little currents sparking as they carried a single question: *Did I do the right thing?*

And each one held the same conclusion: *yes.*

When Gen held up the notebook, he was sure his heart had stopped. Just for a second. Then it kicked back in, pounding at double time, because he'd forgotten all about the book, tossed carelessly into a box with the things he'd brought home from his office and his coffee mugs and coasters. And now Gen had found it.

His panicked instinct was to lie. And he'd almost done it, flipping through the possible options: it's just patient notes, it's a list of medication doses, it's a reference for a filing system.

But as he'd looked at Gen's puzzled expression, then down to the book in her hands, he'd changed his mind. Not just because she'd come back to Marwick for him. But because when she'd found him in the park after Abbie died, she'd sat on the damp grass without hesitation. And when his mum had torn strips off him for being selfish, Gen's hand had been resting on the small of his back.

So he told her.

"It's how many days they've got left."

The confusion on Gen's face deepened. "With you?"

"Not quite."

And there, surrounded by mislabeled boxes, Charlie explained everything.

She didn't believe him. And why would she? The whole idea was preposterous, that out of all the people in the world, Charlie Knight would be the one to have a direct line to God, or the guiding hand of fate, or the Grim Reaper, or whoever it was who decided that time was up.

But he told her anyway. He told her about the colors— about how they would leach out of the room, and then the pressure would build in his head. She put her own hand to her temple as he was talking, as though she was feeling that swelling sensation herself. He told her about Edna Bradley's lonely death in her shower and about Simon Lopez's number ticking down.

A shadow of skepticism still darkened her face.

And then, voice trembling slightly, he told her about Abbie.

"Oh no. Charlie." Gen opened the notebook, scanning the pages for Abigail Wilson's name and the single digit recorded alongside. She found it, and dropped the book entirely. Threw it down onto the bench like her fingers had been scorched.

*Now* she believed him.

"I thought I was doing the right thing. I just wanted her to do *something*. Make the most of it. And it killed her."

Gen put her hand on his arm. "Charlie. You didn't know she couldn't swim. And you didn't tell her to jump off the bridge."

"I might as well have."

"No." Gen shook her head firmly. "You didn't know what she was going to do. I don't think you can wear that. You just told her to do *something*. What'd you call it? Catch her mice. Only you wanted to help her catch a bigger one." Charlie smiled thinly. "I'm sure you're not the first doctor to try to help someone, only for it not to work. You did your best." Gen's eyes were deep and sincere.

Charlie didn't know what to say, but he couldn't agree with her. *His best* would have been to keep Abbie alive. And it wasn't as though she was sick, and the treatment he'd recommended just didn't work. She'd been healthy, and the treatment had killed her. Like he'd prescribed poison.

Gingerly Gen picked the notebook up again. She flicked through the pages, driven by what Charlie suspected was a morbid curiosity. She was looking for something.

"So..." Gen started, still searching. "Do you know when *I'm* going to die? Wait." She looked up. "Do I even want to know?"

"It's not in there. And if I did know, I wouldn't tell you."

"How have you avoided it?"

Charlie laughed grimly. "Remember the party?"

"When you ran away, covering your ears? Yeah, I remember. I think your mum does too."

"Well, that's how. No medical care. I just have to shut it all out. I can't ask questions, I can't help anyone, and if they ask me, I have to ignore it." He sighed. "So when that plane leaves tonight, I'll be on it. Seat 14C. Probably drinking my weight in gin."

"Even after everything I said…"

"Even after everything you said last night. I can't run the risk, Gen. Of you, of Mum, of my friends. Anyone I care about. Even anyone I *know*, really."

Gen tilted her head. "Are you *exiling* yourself, Charlie?"

"When you put it like that, I suppose I am. Makes it sound kind of grand, doesn't it."

"It does. Heroic, even." She grinned and leaned in. But there was something about her lips, something about the way she kissed him that told him just how sad she was. Charlie Knight was going into exile, and he was doing it alone.

Gen left his house at a little after seven to get ready for work, and it was *quiet*. But in those silent moments, he didn't regret telling her. Not one bit. Sure, she'd been so doubtful to begin with. That changed, once she'd heard about Abbie. And— almost unbelievably—she still loved him, despite the starring role he'd played in her death.

*And you want to leave this behind?*

He didn't. But at least Gen understood why he had to.

He looked at the time. He had about twelve hours until his flight, a dozen boxes still to pack, and a call he needed to make.

"Hello?"

For a moment he thought he'd rung the wrong number. If Deborah Anders had looked a decade older than her actual age, then the phone added another ten years on top.

"Deb?"

"Yes. Who's this?"

"It's Charlie Knight. From the clinic."

"Oh. Hi, Charlie." A shaky breath. "Did...did you find out something?"

"Not yet. But I'm going to. I need some names though. And phone numbers, if you've got them."

In a quavering voice, Deb gave him the details she knew—some high school girlfriends, the doctors who'd cared for Hayley previously, and Hayley's closest friend from the hospital where she'd worked—and said she'd find the other names and numbers he wanted: her other nursing colleagues, her roommates from college, an old boyfriend. Anyone Hayley might have spoken to in the lead-up to her death. Deb didn't ask *why* Charlie wanted those names, and he was grateful for that. Because it was a long shot, full of false hope: maybe Hayley had shared a few drinks with a friend after work, and once the wine was flowing, revealed her prediction of her own demise. Or maybe—and perhaps this was more likely—she'd just said goodbye to them too. Deb also listed a few patients, ones that Hayley had mentioned by name. No phone numbers for those people, but Charlie might be able to find them online. They were another long shot, obviously, but still worth investigating. Hayley might have said something curious to those patients, something that made them wonder if she knew a secret about them. About their lives. About how long they had left.

"Thanks, Deb," he said. "How did you go last night? Did you get any sleep?" The box in front of him turned gray, and Deb's number swam into his mind. Down by a day.

"A bit. I don't know if it was the pills or the fact that you're helping me with this, Charlie."

"Probably a bit of both. I'll let you know if I find anything out." He glanced at the clock. "And Deb—I'm sorry to call so early."

"You're talking to an insomniac, Charlie. The chances of waking me were pretty slim."

He smiled as he hung up. He wasn't entirely sure, but he thought she sounded slightly younger by the end of the call. Amazing what a little bit of hope can do.

He started with the friends. The nursing colleague's phone was off (night shift, perhaps) and the first high school friend rang out. He'd have to try them both again later, at a more civilized hour. The second school friend answered, voice blurred from sleep. She was surprised to hear from Charlie, given she hadn't seen Hayley for more than a year, but yeah, it was so super sad that she died, wasn't it.

Dead end.

Of the two doctors Deborah had mentioned, one he was familiar with and one he wasn't. The name he knew was the GP who'd looked after Hayley at a clinic in Abercrombie. Deb had explained that he used to be *her* GP as well; in fact, he'd even been the family doctor for her parents, right up until they died. Deb had stopped going to him years ago. ("He was always running late," she told Charlie, as if that was more than enough reason to sever a multigenerational connection.) But punctuality mustn't have mattered too much to Deb's daughter, because Hayley had stayed on with Dr. McKay.

Charlie dialed his number and was immediately redirected

to an after-hours service. He sighed; it was only seven thirty. He left a message asking Dr. McKay to call him, but if he was as bad with timing as Deb said, it may be a long wait.

He moved on to the other doctor. Dr. Elizabeth Frawley, the oncologist who diagnosed and treated Hayley for her cancer. Hodgkin's lymphoma. Charlie knew about the disease; when he'd first started at Marwick Family Clinic, he'd inherited a patient with it, an ultra-fit man in his late sixties. That man had made a full recovery from his cancer too, only to crash his bike while cycling in his Lycra on the outskirts of town about six months later. There was still a little cross leaning against a tree just after the bridge, and someone made sure there were fresh flowers there every year on the anniversary of his death. Charlie didn't know who was doing it; he hadn't seen a partner or kids at the funeral. But every twelve months there was a small purple posy propped up against the wooden cross. He thought they were lilacs: a cloud of delicate petals left in the night.

Charlie called the number for Dr. Elizabeth Frawley, knowing her office would be unattended. He left a message on her receptionist's voicemail.

"It's Charlie Knight here. I'm a GP in Marwick. I was hoping to speak to Dr. Frawley about one of her patients, Hayley Anders. She passed away earlier this year." He wasn't sure what else to say. *I was curious if she mentioned anything about her upcoming death? Any hunches she might've shared? Premonitions? I'll take anything.* He left his number and hung up, estimating his chances of getting a call back at about fifty-fifty. Deb Anders had described Dr. Frawley as being kind, verging on a little too cheery for the dire circumstances, so maybe she'd be willing to help. But she was also a specialist physician, and every quarter-hour in her day would be scheduled already. Family doctors asking about dead patients? They couldn't get much lower on the priority list.

Still, Charlie was on a fishing expedition here. He needed all his lines in the water, and all the optimism of a fisherman. But even he was surprised how quickly he got a bite.

He made one more call—another voicemail, this time for a patient who'd been cared for by Hayley—and then he waited. He was almost tempted to just sit by his phone, to will it to ring, but time was ticking. Charlie gave up on any semblance of order to his packing, madly throwing the last items into cartons, scribbling a list of contents on the side and sealing them up. He was moving quickly, one eye on the clock, the other on his phone. Waiting, wondering. Determined now to prove his theory correct, that Hayley had predicted her own death.

When the bite came, Charlie was outside, assessing what he could feasibly leave behind for whoever moved in after him. The outdoor furniture was staying: none of it would fit on his shoebox apartment's balcony. He found himself gazing at the fence between his house and Gen's. If he was staying, it would be an easy enough job to install a gate. Knocking down the fence for a commune like Gen had joked was probably a bit extreme. But a gate? Well, Charlie and his dad could manage that in one morning, provided Malcolm didn't have half a dozen inspections planned. If he retired. Then they could have a beer to celebrate their handiwork, sitting on the back deck, and invite Gen to be the first to walk through. Maybe they'd even tie a ribbon across the gate, and she could cut it. She'd love that. Malcolm would love it too.

Charlie leaped on his phone the moment it rang. The voice on the other end was firm and clear. No small talk, straight to business.

"Charlie, it's Lib Frawley here. You left me a message?"

A fifty-fifty bet, he'd thought. This was why he left gambling to people like little Jamie Clayton's dad.

"Thanks for calling me back. It's about a former patient of yours. Hayley Anders?"

"You mentioned that. There's not much I can tell you about Hayley, I'm afraid. You weren't her referring GP."

"I know. I'm not asking about her treatment or anything like that."

"Then what are you asking about?" Dr. Frawley was curt now. Charlie had been expecting a warmer reception; after all, Deb had said she was almost too jovial for the solemnity of her job. Perhaps that was just an act she put on for patients, something to keep their spirits up when they're in the trenches. Something to distract them when the Reaper is stalking about. To give them hope.

"Uh, it's a bit strange. But…" Charlie had been searching for a way to ask the question without breaking one of the promises he'd made to Deb. He hadn't found one. "This is going to sound odd. But did Hayley ever talk to you about dying?"

Dr. Frawley coughed, like something was stuck in her throat. It was a peculiar noise. Maybe, Charlie thought, it was supposed to be a laugh.

"Charlie, I'm an oncologist. *Every* patient talks to me about dying, about the survival rate and the odds of the treatment working. Every patient, *ever*. Hayley would have asked if she was going to survive her cancer. And I told her yes. And I was right. Her treatment was successful."

"That's not really what I meant. Did she ever say anything, or I don't know, *do* anything that made it sound like…"

"Like what?"

"Like she knew *when* she was going to die?"

Another little cough. This one was clear. She was getting impatient.

"I'm sorry Charlie, but I can't help you. What happened to Hayley was a terrible tragedy, but it's also one of the *accepted*"—she emphasized this word, like she was defending a malpractice suit—"risks of the treatment. You would've seen it before, I'm sure. It could happen at any time. There's not much more I can tell you."

"But—"

"I'm sorry," she repeated. "I've got an appointment. All the best."

Then she ended the call.

Charlie stared at the phone in his hand. He'd been prepared for her to laugh at him, to tell him he was being absurd, even to question whether he was fit to see patients. But he wasn't prepared for Dr. Elizabeth Frawley to hang up on him.

Like he'd struck a nerve.

Hayley *had* said something to her.

And now Charlie was going to find out what.

# 20

Charlie's car bounced at speed over the narrow bridge, every rivet jarring his suspension, his head bobbing about like a dashboard ornament. He was traveling too fast, but there was nobody on the deck, nobody approaching it, and he was in a hurry.

He was going to learn the truth.

And once he'd uncovered what was being hidden, then he was going to race back to Marwick, pick up his suitcase, hand over his keys, get in the car with Gen, and still make his flight. Easy.

It had taken all morning, but Charlie's house was finished. The piles of *stuff* were gone, and every room was now lined with boxes. Some of them were even labeled correctly. They'd follow soon after him, which would then be the trigger for Malcolm Knight, of Knight Realty fame, to set about finding a tenant for Charlie's half-furnished home.

Charlie had called Dr. Elizabeth Frawley four more times

during the morning, and each time he'd been stonewalled by her receptionist. On two occasions Dr. Frawley had been with a patient. Another time she'd been on a call and couldn't be disturbed. When he rang the fourth time, she'd just stepped out. And no, sorry, she wouldn't be able to return any calls.

Charlie had never gone in for conspiracies for one simple reason: it meant people were lying. If the truth about UFOs, or fluoride in the water, or chemtrails spewing out of planes was being hidden, then everyone in the government, and the air force, and the water authorities, and every dentist and every pilot was telling fibs. Coordinated lies. And that, in Charlie's opinion, was unlikely. In his opinion, people tended to default to the truth.

But on this particular occasion, after one hang-up, four failed calls, and a total refusal to engage, Charlie smelled a rat. A conspiracy.

So he did the only thing left for him to do. He jumped in his car and drove much too quickly to Abercrombie.

By two o'clock he stood outside an office building in the heart of the city, lured by the sense of a lie. The building was in a cluster of medical offices—rooms for specialists and experts in their fields who all charged a small fortune for that expertise. Charlie scanned the various towers on the block, almost hearing a distant *haw-haw-haw* as he picked out where Dr. Matt Rowan had his rooms and where he'd sent Charlie through the MRI machine to rule out a brain tumor. All of the buildings had a certain sameness to them. He wasn't a gambling man, of course, but he'd have been willing to wager that every waiting room in every building on the block would be painted in the same muted tones, with framed prints of either sailboats, country landscapes, or peaceful wildlife on the walls.

Dr. Elizabeth Frawley's office had rowboats. Close, thought Charlie, and probably near enough to collect the bet. The fresh-smelling waiting room was a pastel blue color, with half a dozen empty chairs and a receptionist whose hair was pulled back in a ponytail so tight it looked like it hurt.

"Can I help you?" the young woman asked brusquely, eyes fixed on the monitor in front of her. There was a glass bowl of wrapped mints on Charlie's side of the counter, a little treat for patients as they paid their bills. Charlie spied a small pile of empty wrappers next to the receptionist's keyboard, where her long nails tapped away without missing a beat.

"I'd like to see Dr. Frawley please. If she's around."

"Do you have an appointment?" Even at a distance, her minty breath almost made his eyes water.

"No. But I did speak with her this morning, and I've tried to call a few times since then."

"Ah, you're Charlie!" she exclaimed. Now she stopped typing and looked him up and down, not even trying to hide her smirk. "I told you when we last spoke"—she studied her watch—"*an hour* ago that she'd just stepped out. Dr. Frawley only works 'til one on Tuesdays."

If the pastel walls and rowboats were designed to keep people calm, they weren't working. Charlie drummed his fingertips on the counter, next to the bowl of mints. He'd already had enough of the smug receptionist and her too-tight ponytail. Give him Lisa or Toby any day.

"Please. Is there a reason why she's dodging my calls?"

"No reason that I'm aware of. You must understand—she's very busy." Smug *and* condescending.

"I understand that, I just need to—" An idea. Matt Rowan was always complaining about splitting his time between his own rooms and patients in hospital. He spent a good chunk of their twice-yearly dinners sermonizing about how his own staff were so much more efficient than the teams at any of the hospitals in Abercrombie. Maybe Dr. Frawley split her time too: Tuesday mornings in her office and the afternoon seeing cancer patients in their hospital beds. "Where does she go on Tuesday afternoons? Is it Sacred Sisters?"

"I'm sorry. I can't give out that information."

"Please." Charlie stared straight at the young woman. "I'm not a stranger trying to get an appointment. I'm a doctor too. I'm actually a…" He paused, trying out his new title for the first time. "Senior Emergency Physician at St. John's Private Hospital." Well, he would be. In a day or two. "And I need to see her about something. It's really quite urgent."

The receptionist returned Charlie's gaze, as if trying to assess the veracity of his claims just by whoever could hold the stare the longest.

"So is it Sacred Sisters? Or Abercrombie Base?" Charlie asked decisively.

The smirk disappeared, and she sighed. She took a mint from the bowl, unwrapped it, popped it in her mouth, and then spoke around it, as though it wasn't even there.

"Abercrombie Links."

"What? The golf course?" Charlie fought a smile. The specialist doctor taking the afternoon off for eighteen holes, midweek? Dr. Frawley was dangerously close to becoming a cliché. "Thanks," he said and meant it—partly because the receptionist looked like she was already regretting disclosing the information. As the elevator doors closed, he saw her reach for the glass bowl again.

*Golf. Of course she's playing golf.*

Charlie had never been able to get into the sport. He'd tried, when he was younger. There'd been bachelor parties where they sank a beer after every hole to toast the groom, but getting horrendously drunk on the course had done very little to change his opinion. He just didn't see the game's appeal. There was a chance his time would come; he'd seen otherwise-normal people became obsessed overnight with their handicap, like a switch had tripped in their brain. For his mum, it had been the Callaway bag and clubs she'd been given for her fiftieth birthday. Suddenly Lorraine Knight couldn't survive without playing three days a week, or four if her schedule allowed. Those four-game weeks had been what tore the rotator cuff in her shoulder.

Maybe that was when Charlie's loathing of golf had really set in, when his mum's GP recommended surgery. Or when that same GP prescribed painkillers to help after the operation. Or when she kept on prescribing them after the wound had healed. Turning a blind eye, because they'd been pals for fifty-odd years, and used to lie in the sun together next to the Marwick Bridge, and friends don't say no to friends.

Maybe that was it.

He snagged the only empty parking spot amid the SUVs at Abercrombie Links and then darted across to the clubhouse building, dodging men and women loading bags and clubs into carts. *Who* are *these people?* he thought. *It's the middle of the afternoon on a Tuesday.* The clubhouse stood on a hill, offering a remarkable view across the massive expanse of land on the edge of Abercrombie that had been claimed for the city's golfers. The bright green fairways snaked their way between lines of manicured trees, and he counted five separate ponds, three with white-painted bridges arching across them. Dotted throughout the landscape were people. So many people, all in pairs and groups of four. One of them would be Dr. Elizabeth Frawley—but he didn't know what she looked like. He didn't even know where to start looking on this great spread of terrain, pockmarked with sandy craters. With that, he realized his chances of finding her were diminishing. And it was approaching three o'clock. The hours until his flight were ticking by.

Under the clubhouse, a sign in the pro shop window promised lessons, cart hire, clubs, balls—anything a golfer needed. Charlie walked in, wondering if that extended to finding missing people on the fairway. Behind the counter a man with leathery skin—seasoned by years on the golf course—nodded politely at him.

"Afternoon, sir," the man said. "After anything in particular? If you're here for a lesson, I'll need you to sign in."

Charlie rarely introduced himself as a doctor when meeting people for the first time, or when making calls, or anywhere else, really. He'd done it a bit after university, but the novelty wore off once he realized it made him sound a little pompous. He figured "Charlie Knight from the clinic" generally told people on the other end of the phone everything they needed to know.

But sometimes, as it had with the oncologist's gatekeeper, the title could come in handy.

"Actually, I'm looking for someone. I'm Dr. Charlie Knight," he said, with a slight emphasis on the *doctor*, "and I'm looking for Dr. Frawley. She's playing this afternoon and I need to find her."

The leathery man hesitated.

"It's a medical situation," Charlie said gravely, hoping it sounded sufficiently serious, and hoping that nonmedical folk generally held a bit of respect for the mystery and urgency of a *medical situation*. For all the golf pro knew, lives were at stake. Surely that trumped the privacy policies of Abercrombie Links.

The man turned to his computer. "Uh...Dr. Frawley has a tee time booked for three."

"Right. So that means she'll be..."

"Well, it means she hasn't teed off yet. Hasn't started. She's probably on the—wait, that's her group there."

Charlie whirled around. Four women were walking past the entrance to the pro shop, their backs to the door, all of them wearing black golf pants and shirts in various shades of pink and mauve.

"Which one?" he asked.

"Second from the left. The...uh...short one," the weathered pro replied, and Charlie dashed out of the shop.

"Excuse me! Dr. Frawley?" he called to the group as they walked away from him, toward the practice putting green. All four women turned, holding putters of various lengths. Elizabeth Frawley—second from the left—seemed surprised.

But not as surprised as Charlie.

He *did* know Dr. Frawley. But when he'd been introduced to her, she'd been referred to simply as Lib—one of the coven of golf friends supporting Lorraine Knight when her horrible son ruined her party. The one who'd stood back and watched him as the others crowded around his mother.

Lib had been the shortest of the group on Saturday night, and she was the shortest of the four here too. He'd met one of the other players that night as well—Anne or Ann, he didn't know which—and, anxiously, he checked the rest of the golf-ers milling about near the clubhouse. There was no sign of Lorraine with her strapped-up shoulder.

*Thank God.*

"Dr. Frawley, I need a moment. Please."

Elizabeth Frawley—Lib—shook her head. "I'm sorry. We're about to tee off, and we'll lose our spot if we're not on time."

"I've driven from Marwick to find you. I went to your office, and they said you were here. I just need a couple of minutes," he pleaded. "That's all. Just two minutes."

Anne or Ann muttered something to Lib. The breeze car-ried a snippet to Charlie. "...Lorraine's son?"

Lib nodded. "It is. He wants me to see one of his patients."

Anne or Ann held up her hands, as if to say she wasn't get-ting involved. Doctors' business. A *medical situation.*

"Please Dr. Frawley. You don't tee off for another fifteen minutes," he said, silently thanking the pro who'd gifted him that nugget of information, "and it won't take anywhere near that long. Otherwise...otherwise I'll just wait here 'til you finish and ask you again." He didn't know how long it took four women to play eighteen holes. Two hours, four hours, six? He was calling her bluff. She didn't know he had a plane to catch.

"Oh, go on Lib," said one of the other women. "You don't need the putting practice anyway. We'll meet you at the tee." Lib breathed out, long and deep. Defeated. "Right. This way," she ordered, marching past Charlie.

He followed her around the corner of the clubhouse, with three thoughts occurring to him at the same time. The first was that she was a very fast walker for someone so short. The second was that if Lib from his mother's golf group was actually *Doctor* Elizabeth Frawley, then couldn't she have just looked at Sylvia's dodgy wrist and saved them all a lot of hassle on Saturday night? And the third thought was more of a hunch than anything else, a gut feeling that something didn't seem right. Something about their exchange at the front of the clubhouse.

Lib's destination was a small wooden gazebo a short distance away from the main building. It was ringed with bench seats, where Charlie supposed golfers could gaze out over the sand traps they'd dodged and drink to their success. From here he could also see the path leading back to the clubhouse, the practice putting green—Lib's playing partners were already hunched over, concentrating fiercely—and the driving range, punctuated by the regular distant thwack of golf balls. Dr. Frawley looked around, satisfied, and Charlie realized why she'd led him here. They were alone, there was nobody in earshot, and all approaches could be clearly seen. If not oncology, she would've made an excellent sniper.

"Right," she said, positioning herself on one of the timber

benches attached to the inside of the gazebo. She gestured for Charlie to sit. "Why have you spent all day harassing Jane? Then chasing me here?"

"It's about Hayley Anders. I just—"

"I told you everything I can this morning on the phone."

Lib's mouth was set firmly, but the scowl didn't look natural on her. The lines on her face could have come from a life of smiling and laughing; the way they radiated out from her eyes suggested a face that crinkled into a grin easily. But right now, she wasn't smiling. Right now, that seemed a long way off.

Charlie tried to gather his thoughts as the older woman watched him, waiting. There was no elegant way to say this.

"Hayley knew she was going to die, didn't she? Not from the cancer," he added quickly as Lib started to object. "But she knew that when she went to sleep, she wasn't going to wake up."

Lib scoffed. "How would she have known that? I've seen the report. It was a heart attack. As I said this morning, it's a known risk of the treatment. But there would've been no warning."

"So she didn't say anything to you?" Charlie tried again. "Nothing at all? She hadn't had a…a *feeling* or anything?"

"No."

Charlie gazed out past Lib. The midafternoon sun was still high overhead, and it bounced off the ponds of the golf course like they were golden pools. Like the river at Marwick. So enticing.

A cheer came from the practice green as Anne or Ann sunk a long putt. Charlie watched them all line up to repeat it as the conversation he'd had with the group at the front of the clubhouse replayed in his mind. Something still felt wrong about it, something that nagged at him, demanding closer attention. A word, a comment, a look.

*There.*

It had barely even registered at the time, but must have lodged sideways in his head, jagging on the edges, burrowing in like a splinter because it just didn't fit.

*A lie.*

Lib had lied to the other women about why Charlie was there.

"Why'd you tell your friends that I wanted you to see one of my patients?"

Lib was quiet.

"Why didn't you just say it was about one of *your* patients? One who passed away? There's nothing wrong with that, it's not like you're telling them something they shouldn't know, and then—" He stopped.

The pieces fell into place with a thunk, catching his breath in his throat.

*Telling them something they shouldn't know.*

Why hadn't he thought of this before?

When Charlie spoke again, his voice was lower, even though nobody was around. He needed to ensure that Lib would be the only one to hear him.

Because he'd figured it out.

"It was you, wasn't it? *You* told Hayley she was going to die."

# 21

The gazebo above Abercrombie Links was a beautiful place for a revelation.

Dr. Elizabeth Frawley's eyes widened. "What do you mean?"

"Hayley saw you for a checkup a month before she died," Charlie said, sure of himself. Beyond sure. It all made sense. "Did you tell her then?"

Lib stood and walked to the rotunda exit, looking toward her friends at the distant practice green.

"I really can't help you." She made a show of checking her watch. "We're about to tee off, so—"

"I told somebody last week," Charlie said softly.

Lib turned around slowly. "What did you say?"

"I told a patient last week that she was going to die. And then she did. Because I told her."

Lib's face went white, and for a second Charlie waited for the pressure to start building behind his eyes, and for a number to emerge. But the grass on the fairways beyond them was still green, the sky a brilliant turquoise, and Lib's shirt a dusky pink. This wasn't a premonition; the colors weren't fading. Lib had just turned pale.

Charlie was right.

"So I just want to know if we've got the same thing going on here," he said.

Lib slumped on the bench next to Charlie, her tee time seemingly forgotten. The women would have to start without her.

"You told someone? And they…" She trailed off, and Charlie could almost see her gathering her thoughts, trying to put the last few minutes into a logical order. Then when she started speaking again, the words poured out quickly, like she'd been caught misbehaving, sneaking food from the fridge before dinner and was now trying to defend herself. She wasn't looking at Charlie as she spoke. Side by side, staring straight ahead. It felt like a confessional.

No eye contact, no judgment.

"Hayley… I thought she'd use the time to go on a trip or something. Tick things off her list, because she would've already made one when she had lymphoma. Her bucket list. I *hate* that name, I don't know why. But it's what they all call it, so I go along with it. Thing is though, most of my patients know their time's running out; cancer kind of does that to you, makes you face your mortality. The sick ones know what's coming, and even if they're not really well enough to make the most of the time, to get through that list, they've at least already said their goodbyes. You understand it, right? What I'm saying?"

Her voice cracked. She needed to know that Charlie was

following. He nodded, even though Lib was still looking away, focusing on a point far below them, maybe a golf cart picking its way between the trees.

"I get it. They're prepared," Charlie said. "They've been fighting the cancer, but they're not really expecting to win. So they already know the end is probably near. They're ready for that possibility."

"Exactly. But Hayley was—Hayley was an *exception*, you see. She wasn't ready for it, not anymore, because she was *better*. She'd recovered—she thought she was in the clear. I did too; I was only seeing her once a year by then. And then on her last visit, I saw—not *saw*, but you know what I mean, better than anyone, I guess—I knew she was going to die. So I...I told her. So she'd be ready." A pause. "She didn't believe me, not straight away. Of course, I don't—didn't—blame her for that. She called me, I think, four or five times a day for a week. Even more than you did." A grim chuckle. "But she trusted me, maybe because I got her through the lymphoma. So eventually she came round. Accepted it, I suppose. And then, after all that, she didn't actually *do* anything. She just stayed with her mum and kept working. So I guess it didn't make any difference."

She fell silent. A bird chittered nearby, and down on the golf course the hum of the cicadas rose and fell with the afternoon breeze. Lib breathed heavily—in, out, in, out—like she'd completed a workout. And she had, of a sort, lifting a considerable weight off her chest. Her breath wobbled, and Charlie glanced across. Lib was crying softly, a tear making its hesitant way down her cheek. He rested a hand on her arm, just a gentle touch as she started to speak again.

"I don't know if I made a mistake in telling her. I didn't regret it at the time because I thought she was going to get out there and *do* something. Instead I probably just made her scared. Living her last few weeks at home, knowing the end was coming."

"Maybe that's just where she wanted to be. At home. With her mum," Charlie said.

"Maybe," she replied.

The pair sat, and Charlie sensed he wasn't supposed to say anything else. Lib needed a few minutes, reliving it all, accounting to herself for the decision she'd made. Just like the decision *he'd* made, except all Lib had done was possibly frighten a girl. Charlie had killed one.

"She's the only one I told," Lib said at last, shifting slightly on the hard wooden bench. "I couldn't tell anyone else now, even if I wanted to. Which I don't. All the numbers are muddled up in my head. There's just too many of them. Maybe I should've been writing them down."

Charlie thought of Gen dropping his black notebook like it had scalded her fingers.

"I did."

"Did what?"

"Write them down. I recorded them all," Charlie replied.

"What, every patient?"

He nodded.

"Name and number. Dozens of them. At least a couple of hundred over the last two or three weeks. I did it right from the start—everyone I saw at the clinic, and outside too. Even my dad, and the guy who runs the pub."

"Good grief," Lib exclaimed. "Why, Charlie?"

Charlie shrugged. "At first just to get the numbers out of my head. Download them, I guess. When I didn't know what they were. And then, once I figured it out, I was...um..." Charlie felt his cheeks go hot with shame. "I suppose I was trying to look at the bigger picture. I knew how long their lives would be, and I was trying to help them make the most of it." *Catch their mice, right up to the end.*

"Until..." Lib prompted.

"Until Abbie."

"The girl you said something to. What happened?"

And so for the second time that day, Charlie told the full story of Abigail Wilson. Slowly, painfully, he painted a picture of Abbie, of the innocence about her, this bright, sheltered young woman who trusted three people: her mum, her dad, and her doctor. He told Lib how Abbie had drowned amongst the river reeds trying to do what she'd seen other kids do, all because he'd planted that seed.

*If you've got one of those things, do it.*

He repeated those words, almost in a whisper, and at that moment hated himself more than he thought possible.

"Oh, Charlie," Lib murmured. "Is that why you're leaving?"

"Mostly. It wasn't originally. Back then it was about doing something special, something *spectacular*. Like you. Now it's about not hurting anyone else. Preserving lives." *And my conscience*, he thought. "I can't look after people I know and find out how many days they've got left. What if I say something to them—even accidentally—that sets it all in motion? I can't be the reason someone else dies. But maybe I can use it, treating strangers in emergency. Like the crash on the highway."

Lib considered that. "It's not the worst idea, Charlie. If you don't have any ties to your patients, you might find it easier. And it doesn't have to be forever. Just until it passes."

Charlie spun to face Lib, breaking whatever confessional seal had kept them both looking straight ahead. But she'd said it so quickly, almost casually, that he wasn't sure he'd heard her correctly. Lib's tears had dried now, and she was gazing at the fairways below.

"'Until it passes?'" Charlie repeated, heart racing. He could hear the desperation in his own voice. *God, I hope that's what she said. Please, please, please.* "What do you mean? It's not happening anymore? For you?"

Lib looked surprised. "No, of course not. Not for a few weeks. One day it was happening with every patient, the next day it was like I'd dreamed it all. But I hadn't. I guess Hayley Anders is proof of that."

"How...how did you stop it? What did you have to do?" Charlie's mind was already galloping, charging off in very nonscientific directions: some kind of penance, a ritual, a spell chanted under Marwick's starry skies. Whatever it takes. He'd do it.

"I didn't *do* anything. It just ended. That's what I'm saying. One day it was there, the next it wasn't. Kind of like a cold, Charlie—there's nothing you can do, really. Just push through until it runs its course."

Charlie started to respond, but Lib cut him off. "The timing of it all seems a bit curious, don't you think?" She looked at him intently, blue eyes bright with an idea. She was studying this like a puzzle. Like a rare illness, and Charlie was her patient. "It started happening for you, what, two or three weeks ago, you said? Either that's an extraordinary coincidence, Charlie, or *you're* the reason it stopped for me."

"What do you mean?"

"I mean it didn't just stop. It *left*."

Charlie considered the possibility. "How long?"

"How long what?"

"How long did you have to wait? Before it stopped. Before it came to me, if that's how it happened."

"Oh, I don't know. Five months? Six? Seven? I didn't keep a record of it, you know. Not like you have." She smiled, and Charlie beamed back, because this was something he hadn't felt in some time.

This was *hope*.

Hope that the numbers might pass.

Hope that things would go back to normal.

And Gen.

He could be with Gen. Here, or in London, or anywhere on earth, and they could talk without fear of straying too far, and they could spend every night together, watching for shooting stars, knowing that if they didn't see one, they'd always have the next night. And the one after that. And after that.

Would that be spectacular enough?

"It has its own end date," he said softly. "Its own life span, then it moves on. Lib, I'm terrified of it, you know? Now that I've seen what it can do. I'm afraid of saying the wrong thing, of asking the wrong question, then the room changing and the color and all that. And the pressure too, how it squeezes into your head, and there's nothing you can do to stop it. Once it starts, it's going all the way."

"What do you mean the *pressure*? And the room *changing*?" Lib asked. "What does it change into?"

Charlie peered at her. "You know, when the numbers come through, and everything goes black and white."

Lib shook her head, eyes gleaming. "That's not what happened for me. This is fascinating, Charlie," she said, still sounding as though she was poring over the results of a medical trial. Applying a scientific lens to something decidedly *un*scientific; a phenomenon that existed well outside the laws of what was possible.

"You saw something different?"

She nodded.

"Look down there," Lib said, pointing at the largest of the lakes on the golf course. The sun was reflecting off the surface, glittering and golden. "Stare at the water for a moment."

Charlie did what he was told.

"Now close your eyes. What do you see?"

Charlie shut his eyes, but it was like they were still open—all he could see behind his eyelids was the yellow brilliance of the sun as it bounced off the lake.

"That's what I saw when I got the numbers," Lib said. "Each time I was with a patient I'd blink, and it was like I'd been staring straight at the sun. A white flash and the number was almost burnt in its place. Scared the life out of me the first few times. Thought I was having a stroke."

"Yeah, I thought I had a brain tumor."

They both laughed gently.

"So what is it, then, Lib?" Charlie asked at last. "Have you got a theory?"

"Charlie, your guess is as good as mine. It's different now, knowing you've got it. A lot more data to work with. And the *timing* too, how it ended for me and then started for you. I'm not big on coincidences, they don't fit with my line of work—if I've got a patient with a spot on their lungs and another on the liver, I'd have to be mad to suggest they're not connected. So I suppose I'm leaning toward some sort of virus or something. Don't you think it's got that living feel to it? Especially if it changed when it moved from me to you. Adapted. Though that makes it sound like it's dangerous. I kind of took it as a nice affirmation of my work, proof that I'd given people more time. A bit like God saying you're doing the right thing."

"Yeah, I'm not so sure." Charlie grimaced. *Not after Abbie.*

"Maybe not in every case. But our bodies can only go for so long, Charlie, and to me the numbers said I was helping my patients get every last day they could out of theirs. But I also like to think it was God's way of telling *me* to slow down too. There's only so much time and I should take a bit more of it for myself. All that kind of thing. Now I play golf every Tuesday and Thursday afternoon. Well, I try to. When my game's not being hijacked." She grinned at Charlie. He was right; the creases next to her eyes did come from her smile. "This is why you were acting so strange at the party, isn't it? You were trying to avoid finding out how long Sylvia's got left."

Charlie nodded.

"Twenty years," Lib said flatly. "I looked at the same wrist two months ago."

They laughed again.

"I think your mum was just testing you to see if you'd help. That was a different side to Lorraine. I haven't seen that before. To be fair, I've never actually seen her have a drink before either, let alone half a dozen. I don't know all the details of what's happened between the two of you, but I thought it was a bit rough, putting you on the spot like that."

"Lib, it wasn't just Sylvia, it was half my family. You say this thing feels alive? That night, I'd believe you. It was like it was throwing everything at me. And I was awful, I know I was. Rude, obnoxious, and to people who didn't deserve it. But I couldn't let it happen again. I just kept seeing Abbie, you know? In the water, whenever I blinked."

Lib put an arm around him and squeezed, but didn't say anything. Charlie followed her gaze down onto the course; a cart was weaving around trees on the edge of a fairway. From this height it resembled a mouse, darting between cover.

They sat like that for a while, just watching the sun play off the water and the trees sway in the gentle southerly breeze, blowing in from Marwick.

"I'd like to get the numbers out of my head," Lib said at last, her voice quiet. "They're with me, all the time. I thought they'd fade, now that it's gone—but they just hang around, bumping into each other, and I don't know whose is whose anymore. Maybe you won't have the same problem, since you wrote them down. That was smart, Charlie. Do you think it's too late for me to do that?" She didn't give him a chance to respond. "It is, isn't it? Because they're all confused for me now—there's so many of them, and I'm getting them mixed up, passing people on the street that I thought were supposed to have gone. Pray that never happens to you, Charlie, because it'll scare the life out of you—the closest thing you'll ever come to seeing a ghost." She chuckled, and Charlie thought of Don Penrose, waving his lit cigarette from the front porch of the Marwick community hall. Charlie had nearly crashed his car.

"But maybe I'll try it anyway," Lib said. "Putting them on paper. I don't like the thought of them staying up here for-ever." She tapped her head. "If you do keep writing them down though, Charlie, just don't let anybody see it. The questions would be unbearable, don't you think? I reckon everyone would want to know their number, until they find out it's less than they'd like. Better to keep it all hidden."

*Too late for that.*

"Gen found my notebook this morning."

"Oh no." Lib's hand flew to her mouth. "This was the girl you were with at the party? The pretty one, with the nice laugh?"

Charlie nodded. Gen did have a wonderful laugh.

"And? What did she say when she found it?" Lib asked.

"A lot of things. She was very good about it, all things con-sidered. She didn't run away, so that's something. She's even still taking me to the airport."

Lib eyed Charlie closely, as though weighing up her next words. She leaned back against the edge of the gazebo.

"Can I give you a little bit of advice? From someone a bit older? When I was twenty-eight I missed my chance to settle down. Well, not settle down exactly—I don't think that was ever the plan. But my attention was on other things. I was the only woman in my entire class at med school selected to specialize. I wanted it so badly, and I got it. And look at me now. I've had a great career. But I've had to do it alone."

"Why didn't he wait for you?" Charlie asked.

"She," Lib corrected, and Charlie flushed with embarrassment. "People have their own timelines and not everyone's willing to wait around for everything to line up perfectly. And I don't blame her for that. But I thought I had more time before she moved on. I didn't. So I get it, Charlie—you need to leave. But don't stay away too long."

Charlie leaned back beside her, hard up against the wooden lip of the gazebo, and considered Lib's advice. The older woman's eyes had misted a little—not crying, more an involuntary reaction as she looked back on what might have been. Her wistful sorrow reminded him of someone.

"What do I do about Deborah Anders? Hayley's mum. She came to see me. She suspects something."

"Oh. Right." Lib paused. "I'll call her."

Charlie thought about it for a moment.

"No, let me do it."

"What will you say?"

"I don't know yet. She just wants closure, I suppose. I think I can give her that."

He shifted on the bench and snuck a look at his watch. He needed to get back to Marwick.

"One more question, Charlie," Lib said, as though sensing their time together was almost up. Her tone changed, and Charlie knew immediately what was coming. "I wasn't expecting this today, but I'm glad it happened. It's like our own support group." Her eyes met his, and he was struck by just how blue they were, like two pools of perfect summer sky. "The numbers. If yours are the same as mine, they come through when you start to look after someone. To provide care."

Charlie sat silently as Lib searched for the right words, or—if she had them already—found the nerve to say them out loud.

"Did you see *my* number? While we've been talking?"

He thought about lying. He considered telling her he'd seen nothing, that there'd been nothing to trigger it, that her life span was still a mystery, like that of the anonymous golfers scurrying about on the fairways below them. But there *had* been a moment, possibly when a lonely tear had trickled down Lib's cheek, or when she'd asked his opinion about the chaos in her head, that the green of the grass had faded away, and the golden ponds had become a bright white light.

He thought about lying. But didn't.

"Yes. I saw it."

Lib closed her eyes for a long time. The warm afternoon sun fell gently on her face, and Charlie waited. Somewhere far away someone was whooping and hollering and others were clapping—a hole in one, perhaps, but it might as well have been happening on another planet altogether. The birds, the cicadas, the whickering of the trees in the breeze—it was all so peaceful and quiet and far, far away. Lib stayed still, eyes closed, a half-smile on her lips.

At last she turned to him and seemed almost grateful to see he was still there.

"Keep it to yourself, will you, Charlie? I'm sorry to ask that of you, but I'd—"

"Rather not know? Lib, even if you begged me, I wouldn't tell you."

"Good."

Charlie glanced across at the practice putting green. Lib's companions were long gone, replaced by a group of young men. They were all wearing gloves on one hand; they looked the part, but even Charlie could see from a distance that they missed more putts than they sunk.

"Think you've well and truly missed your tee time," he said to Lib.

"Ah, that's all right. I'll meet them at the nineteenth," she replied with a smile.

Charlie frowned.

"It's the clubhouse, Charlie. You really don't know golf, do you?"

"No," he admitted. "Hey, don't mention that to Mum, okay?"

"Charlie, I can promise you one thing—I'll take this whole conversation to the grave."

# 22

Gen's car was already running when Charlie pulled up outside his house. She spotted him, sprang out of the driver's seat, and pulled Charlie's door open before he'd even turned off his car.

"We need to go! You're going to miss your flight."

He had to get his bag from the house. But first he grabbed Gen around the waist and pulled her to him.

"The numbers are going to pass," he said.

Her brow crinkled in confusion.

"What do you mean?"

"They won't last forever. I'm not stuck with this."

Gen's eyes widened as it sunk in.

"It's not a permanent exile?"

"No. Not a permanent exile."

Her smile lit up the late afternoon. It was dazzling but brief, the shooting star of smiles.

"How long?"

"I don't know. A few months? A year? Maybe a lot less. But it does end. Well, it did for Lib."

"Who? Actually—tell me on the way. Charlie, we *really* need to go, otherwise you're going to miss this plane."

Suitcase in hand, Charlie closed his front door for the last time and hid his key for his dad to find. Gen was waiting by her car, bouncing on her heels.

"Come on, Charlie! We're going to be *late*."

She opened the back door of the car.

"Am I supposed to sit in the back?" he asked with a grin.

"It's for your bag. The trunk's full."

Gen almost spun the tires as she pulled out of their street. They flew past John James Memorial Park, the newsstand, and the Marwick Hotel—the fastest farewell tour in history. Then they were at the river, and something in the rear of the car clinked merrily as they jolted and bounced over the bridge.

"New stock," Gen explained. Her face seemed pinched. "Five boxes of it. I haven't unloaded it yet because I didn't think I had time."

"Sorry. I didn't realize how late it was. We...we had a lot to talk about."

"It's fine, Charlie. Really. Now tell me everything."

He told her about his search for Dr. Elizabeth Frawley—from his run-in with the mint-chewing receptionist, right through to the gazebo with views for days over fairways and ponds.

"Lib. Was she the short one at the party?"

"Yes. She stood back a little from the rest."

"Ah. I liked the look of her. Kind eyes."

Charlie recounted the conversation at the golf course as Gen passed car after car, racing along the highway. He got to the part where the numbers left Lib and came to him, and glanced at Gen, expecting to see her eyes light up, because that part of the story was what gave them *hope*. But she stared straight ahead, focused intently on the road.

Dark trees flicked by outside, just blurry smudges in the early evening.

They were moving *really* quickly.

Charlie looked at the clock on the dashboard, the orange numbers glowing bright.

"Hey, Gen? I think we're gonna be fine for time."

"What? Oh. Yeah, you're right." The speed eased slightly, but not much. Charlie checked the rearview mirror, half expecting to see flashing lights at any moment. If that happened, then he really *would* miss his flight. But there was nothing behind them except the headlights of the cars they'd passed, growing smaller in the distance.

Something was wrong. Gen was jumpy.

He'd missed it when he'd arrived home, too wrapped up in the euphoria of his conversation with Lib and the idea that everything might just have a happy ending.

And he hadn't noticed it when he'd settled into the passenger seat either. But now—almost too late—it was obvious: the air in the car was tense, Gen was somewhere else altogether, and they were just going so fast.

And Charlie couldn't ask her what was wrong. Not without triggering the numbers, and he couldn't do that now, not when he was so close to being out of there, a safe distance from Gen, a safe distance from everybody.

But maybe he could play around the edges.

"How was work?" This was safe terrain, he was sure. But Gen didn't answer that question. She answered the question she wanted to be asked instead.

"I had a call today, about Grandma. She's okay, kind of. And Charlie, I can't say anything about it to you, because you *can't know*." She sighed with frustration. "But it's just something I have to deal with, and I wasn't expecting it. Not today. Not when you're leaving, and it's just a lot."

All Charlie wanted to do was comfort her. Find out what had happened to Ruth, and do everything he could to help. He wanted to fix whatever was causing Gen's angst. But any of that would cross the line. He knew that, and Gen knew it too.

"Distract me, Charlie. Distract us both. Tell me more about Lib. What else did she say?"

But before he could even respond, Gen screwed up her nose. "Can you smell that?"

Charlie sniffed. All he could smell was citrus: lemon and orange blossom, that fresh scent that was unmistakably Genevieve Longstaff.

"No. Just your perfume. Or is that an oil blend? Your signature mix?" he teased, trying to lighten the mood.

"You can't smell that? It's like something burning." She sniffed again. "You really can't smell it?"

"Nope. Nothing."

"Well, I... Oh God. Oh no." Gen pulled hard to the side of the road, slamming on the brakes at the same time. "Charlie, you need to get out of the car, quick."

"What? Why, Gen?"

"Just do it. Quick. You can't see this."

"See what? Gen, we're on the highway. We can't stop here."

"Get out, Charlie. Now. Quick. Please."

She sounded so desperate, so panicked, that he did exactly as he was told.

He closed the door behind him and took a few steps up the gravel slope that bounded the edge of the highway. Gen had pulled onto the shoulder, but barely a few inches separated her car from the closest lane. As if to prove the point, another vehicle flew past, and Gen's car rocked, buffeted by the wind.

*This is not safe*, Charlie thought, and looked about, trying to get a fix on their location. It was familiar, of course; he knew the road between Marwick and Abercrombie almost better than anyone. But he knew *this* spot particularly well. By sheer coincidence, Gen had stopped on the opposite side of the highway to where he'd done CPR on a girl who looked like she was dead. The place where he'd become an online celebrity and been fooled into thinking the numbers were in fact a gift. A blessing.

And he thought of Lib, and her refusal to believe in coincidence, and wondered if this—stopping right here—might be fate's hand too.

He peered back through the car window. Gen wasn't looking at him; she was facing forward, hands gripping the steering wheel.

*What is going on?*

He tapped on the window, but she didn't react.

She couldn't.

Charlie froze, watching Gen's eyes flicker from side to side, little flashes of white darting about in the dark, then, without warning, they rolled right back into her head and for a second the white took over completely.

And her knee.

Her knee was twitching. Jerking up and down, and if he listened—over the sound of other cars tearing past—he could hear Gen's car rev slightly, in perfect time with those little jerks of her knee. Each one making her foot press gently on the accelerator, causing the engine to purr like an oversized cat.

*Purr*

*Purr*

*Purrrrr*

Charlie's heart leaped into his throat.

*Jesus Christ.*

The last time he'd seen a seizure had been on the floor of the emergency room at Sacred Sisters—a teenage boy shaking and shaking and shaking for minutes that felt like hours to Charlie. There was nothing he could do to help the kid: just stand by, and make sure he didn't hurt himself. No sharp edges, no sharp corners, nothing that would cut and bruise.

Gen's eyes flickered and the engine purred.

And Charlie did nothing, realizing why Gen had kicked him out of the car. She'd felt it coming on, and she'd booted him out so he wouldn't see. Wouldn't intervene, wouldn't get her number.

A car blasted its horn, the driver leaning on it the whole way past, a sharp wail continuing for a hundred yards down the highway, before finally fading away into the night. It almost deafened Charlie. Gen paid no attention.

Charlie's breath shortened. She was so close to the road. To the cars.

And the jerks of her knee. They were getting bigger. Were they getting bigger?

*Purrrrr*

*Purrrrrr*

Gen's knuckles tensed on the steering wheel, squeezing, releasing, squeezing, as her eyes rolled about, a ghoulish white in the evening gloom.

A truck—a big one—roared past, giving one short blast on its air horn before the entire car rocked and swayed in its wake. Gen didn't move, didn't react, just kept squeezing the steering wheel, eyes rolling, knee pumping. The engine revved, still keeping time with that tap tap tap of her leg.

*Purr*

*Purr*

*Purrrrrrr*

Another horn. Angry, loud, and just so close.

"Please, Gen. That's enough. Please." Charlie was begging her now, out loud, pleading with her through the shut-tight window to stop, as if she had any control at all.

Because he knew what he needed to do.

Another horn. The engine kept purring, purring, purring. Another horn.

Gen had kicked him out. But he couldn't stand by and watch. Because any moment now, Gen's car was going to be clipped by something—another car, a truck, just an inch or two too close, and then it would be all over. Gone.

"Please, Gen," he begged one more time, but of course there was no response, and then there was a break in the traffic, and with it came his chance.

He ran to her door and flung it open. Unclipping her from her seatbelt, he put one arm around her middle, another under her knees, and pulled her clear of the car. Adrenaline coursed through him, and he carried Gen as though she weighed nothing. He put her in the passenger seat, still twitching, eyes still rolling, and raced back around to the driver's side, climbing in, pulling the door shut.

Another horn. The car wobbled and shook.

Charlie threw it into gear, hit the accelerator and they leaped forward, back onto the road, and he squinted into the darkness, searching for somewhere safe, somewhere he could pull over and make sure Gen was okay. And maybe, maybe, he could somehow avoid *it* happening.

The orange numbers on the dashboard clock turned gray.

"No. No, please no. No," Charlie pleaded with someone, anyone. He looked across at Gen, at her ashen skin and the charcoal lips that had been red when he'd kissed her hello.

"No, please! Please don't!" He squeezed one fist against his temple, trying to stop the pressure building inside it.

"No!" he cried one more time, and in desperation tried something else, thinking of people, places, things—anything at all—to distract him, pull his attention away from the number starting to swirl and push insistently within his brain. He pictured his mum, and the ambulance, and the paramedics helping her to breathe. His dad, pushing a lawn mower in his selling-houses suit. Simon Lopez with his committee. Toby's blue satin boxers. Glenn Forrester. A swollen knee. Louie pouncing on mice. The day Gen left. His team playing trivia. The sun on the ponds at the golf course. The bridge. The river. The stars.

It didn't work.

Hot, angry tears ran down Charlie's face, and Gen's eyes opened again, just in time to see one splash onto the leather seat.

He'd lost.

And now he knew when her time would be up.

———————

Charlie parked across the middle of the gas station forecourt and sprang out of the car, ignoring the strange looks from other drivers filling their tanks.

"Charlie. Stop," Gen insisted again. "I'm fine."

But Charlie surrendered to his training, picturing himself in the emergency room at Sacred Sisters or at St. John's. Because that was the only thing he could think of to keep himself there, to keep his feet anchored to the ground and stop his head spinning off his shoulders and up into the night sky. He opened his suitcase, flinging clothes about until he found his medical bag. He then performed an examination right there at the Abercrombie South Express Stop, shining a light into Gen's eyes, checking her reflexes and her coherence after the seizure.

"I'm *fine,*" she repeated, pushing him away. "Charlie, that's enough. I'm okay."

And at last he gave up and slumped back into the driver's seat. The car was silent, the purring engine sleeping. He felt Gen watching him, waiting for him to say something. Instead he twisted the key and turned back onto the road.

"Wrong direction, Charlie. You can still make your flight."

"I'm not going. There's no point anymore."

"Don't be ridiculous. You know mine, but what about everyone else?"

He kept driving, now back on the open highway, heading toward Marwick. Heading home.

*I know her number*, he thought, and felt it bounce around inside his head, just like Lib Frawley had described. But there were no other numbers for it to bump into, because he'd written all of those down, and besides, as far as Charlie was concerned, only one number mattered. The one he'd learned in the final moments of Gen's seizure.

"How did you know it was coming, Gen?" The silence was too much for him. "Before it happened. What did you feel?"

"I haven't felt like that in ages. It's strange, really strange—just this vague, out-of-it feeling. Doesn't always happen, not everyone gets an aura, so I guess you could say I'm lucky, right?" She laughed. Charlie didn't. "It was handy at school, cos it gave me a bit of notice to get out of the classroom. And there's a smell too, an awful *burning* smell, and nobody else notices it, because obviously it's in my head. That was the real giveaway. When you couldn't smell it, I figured it was pretty close. God, Charlie, can you imagine if I hadn't pulled over? I could've killed us both." She groaned. "And now I can't drive for a while either."

"But why? Why today?" Charlie checked his speed. He was traveling at five under the limit. It felt positively sluggish compared to the previous journey.

"Stress, I guess." She shrugged. "I've been taking my meds. And the oils too. But there's a lot going on right now. And I know saying that to *you* feels a bit rich. But to each her own, right? Moving back here, starting in the office, quitting that job, getting the business up and running, and then everything with you. I'm not blaming you, by the way, just to be *very* clear. But it's still a lot."

"You can blame me," Charlie replied quietly. "I shouldn't have said anything, when you found the book. I could've made up a story and kept it all to myself."

Gen scoffed.

"Charlie, it's not what you said! That's not what I mean. It's not the notebook, or the numbers, or any of that stuff. It's the fact that you're leaving! Or *were* leaving. Which one is it?"

Charlie didn't answer. He wasn't leaving tonight, that much was clear. He was heading the wrong way for that.

"And Ruth?" he asked, changing the subject. "Something happened with her today. You were distracted."

"Yeah, I suppose I can tell you now, can't I? The home called me. They think she might have dementia. Showing all the signs, apparently. Add that to the emphysema, and…well, I'm worried, Charlie." Gen closed her eyes, and Charlie reached for her hand. It felt good to comfort her at last.

They were passing over the bridge, almost home, when Gen finally brought it up.

"Charlie, are we going to talk about what you saw? The number?"

"No, we're not."

She ignored him.

"I don't even know if I *want* to find out, Charlie. But I don't know how I feel about *you* knowing and keeping it a secret. If that makes any sense."

"It does—but I still won't say anything."

"Why not, Charlie? Because it kind of feels like it's not *your* information to withhold." She clenched her fists tight. "Ooh, the last twenty-four hours with you is giving me whiplash. Last night, I told you I came back for you—and maybe we were going to have a future together. This morning, you told me you could *see* the future, so you had to leave. This afternoon, it turns out you won't see it forever, so you won't be gone for long. And now you've seen *my* future, but won't tell me what it is. And now you're still here. You get why this is making me dizzy, right, Charlie?"

He pulled up outside their houses. Both were dark, but his felt abandoned. Empty.

"I don't know," Gen continued, unbuckling her seatbelt. "I can't imagine what it would be like, us planning our years together, but you knowing exactly how many I've got. Like you'd be watching the calendar every birthday, every Christmas, and I'd be wondering—is this it? Is it my last one, and you're making it extra special? Charlie, I have to be honest here. I love the thought of years and years with you. It's what I came back for. But I don't think I can do it with a massive secret between us."

Her eyes glistened, pleading with him to say something.

But Charlie's head didn't hold any words. Just that number.

"You're not going to tell me, are you?"

"I can't."

"Okay." Gen opened her door, and Charlie ran around to help her out of the car. She shook him off. "I told you—I'm fine." He watched her walk away, and it hurt him—an aching, wrenching pain, deep in his chest—to not go after her. When at last she turned around, she was lit entirely by the glow from the moon and stars above.

"Charlie? Thank you. I know what it cost you to help me tonight. But it feels like it cost us both, you know?"

He nodded. He knew.

He also knew it would be the last time he'd ever see Genevieve Longstaff, because to keep her safe, to keep her alive, he'd need to stay away from her.

She'd mentioned the cost to them both—and now he was going to pay a very high price indeed.

But he'd do anything to give Gen more than eighteen days.

# 23

The noise was coming from his front door. It wasn't a knock; more of a scratching, rustling sound. The noise an animal might make, scouting for food in suburbia. But then there was a grunt—a very human grunt—and Charlie knew for sure there was a person out there. Somebody who didn't realize the house was still occupied.

He flung the door open, and Malcolm Knight jerked upright, holding the doormat in his hands.

"Dad?"

"Charlie! Good Lord, you nearly gave me a heart attack." Malcolm repositioned the mat. "What are you still doing here? I thought you left last night."

"I did," replied Charlie. "Then I came back."

Malcolm looked closely at his son, then at his watch, and Charlie knew he'd be searching for the box with the coffee cups again.

"I was just looking for the key, thought I might check out

the place before the movers come through this afternoon. Start getting the rental ad ready."

"The movers aren't coming today, Dad. I've had to push them back a couple of days."

"Oh well, I'm here now." Malcolm shrugged. "Don't need to be back at the office for a bit. Why don't I come on through, and we can have a cup of coffee?"

Charlie smiled. He knew his dad remarkably well.

He found the right box on just the second attempt, and Malcolm leaned back in a chair as the coffee brewed.

"I scoped out your new place online, by the way. You didn't overpay. Well, maybe a little." He winked. "I thought you'd be there right now, settling in. What brought you back?"

"I…uh…something happened on the way to the airport last night."

"What, with Gen?" Malcolm asked, all humor gone.

Charlie nodded.

"She had a seizure while we were driving."

"Oh mate. Is she all right?"

"She said she's fine. But it was a bit scary, obviously. She pulled over just in time."

Malcolm winced, and Charlie guessed he was picturing an alternate scenario in his head. It was the same scenario Charlie had played out dozens of times overnight, before he moved on to a bunch of horrific hypotheticals about what might happen to her in eighteen—now seventeen—days. Each one was awful, because each one ended the same way, and Charlie didn't know how he could live with that.

"I'm glad she's okay. Is it something to be worried about?"

"It's her epilepsy. Her medication usually keeps it under control. Last night was a bit of an exception."

"Must've been terrifying, Charlie. For both of you."

Charlie nodded. *The worst part had come after, Dad.*

"If there's anything I can do to help, all you have to do is ask."

"Actually…" Charlie said, a thought occurring to him. "There is. I'm booked on a new flight tomorrow." Malcolm started to say something. "No, no, don't worry about a lift to the airport. I'm getting a cab. But I was wondering—could you keep an eye on Gen's grandma?"

"On Ruth? Sure. Why?"

"She's not doing too well right now. And Gen's feeling the pressure. The seizure means she has to catch the bus to and from work, so I don't think she'll be able to visit her as easily."

"No worries, mate. Leave it with me."

"Thanks, Dad."

Charlie handed his dad a mug. Malcolm took it, but instead of sipping the coffee, he swirled it about distractedly like it was a fine red wine. Charlie couldn't be sure, but his dad was showing all the hallmarks of a Trojan horse.

"You know, Charlie, I'm actually glad you're still here. I was going to ring you today after I'd had a quick look through… I wanted to see if you'd be comfortable with me *not* handling this place myself. Thinking of passing it over to Christine instead."

"Christine?" Charlie tried to recall the name. So much had happened.

"Yeah. She'll find you a tenant quick-smart. Probably get more for it too," he added. "She's the one with all those…people on the internet." Malcolm chuckled. "Help me out, mate—I've forgotten what you call them."

"Followers. Yeah, that's fine by me, Dad. Trying to give her a bit more experience?"

"Something like that. I've decided I've had enough."

Charlie almost spat out his coffee. All things considered, this was unexpected.

"Really, Dad? You're *actually* retiring?"

"I'm *actually* retiring." And he grinned; it was a smile that had sold a thousand houses, but this one was supercharged by something else altogether. Anticipation, maybe. Malcolm looked truly happy, and that made Charlie happy too—the first bit of joy he'd had that day. Probably the last he'd have for a while too.

"I thought about what you said the other week, and you're right," Malcolm continued. "I've got things I want to do—you probably didn't notice, but the hedge on the other side of our place is about to walk away on its own, it's gotten so wild. But really, it's your mum."

"Putting the heat on?"

"Not really. Not at all, actually. But she's been waiting a long time for this. And you got me thinking, Charlie. When we talked the other day about what it was like after mum's shoulder op and when she needed the painkillers."

*She didn't* need *the painkillers*, Charlie thought. Not for that long. She'd been *addicted* to the painkillers. There was a difference there, but it wasn't one he needed to point out. Not to his dad, who'd suffered through it just as much as he had.

"I really did think I was going to lose her there, mate. If you hadn't been there that day, I certainly would have. And afterward too, when you stepped in with MaryAnn. That was the hard part. That took guts."

"Dad, I threatened to report her if she kept prescribing them. I don't think it took guts." The contempt in MaryAnn's eyes had been soul-deep. He could still see it. Could still feel her rage.

"You stood up to your boss, Charlie. And then you stuck around to make sure. Sounds like guts to me."

That hadn't been the hardest part. Not really, though he was perfectly fine if Malcolm didn't want to talk about the *real* hardest part. They'd always let it slide between them as something unspoken, a family secret that would die with them both. Because it was Charlie's mum, and Malcolm's wife, and they both loved her.

But for two weeks after the paramedics left, Charlie had stayed at his parents' house, a thirtysomething doctor, full of his own fresh grief, sleeping on the floor outside the bedroom allocated to Lorraine Knight. At home, because she said rehab facilities weren't for people like her. Hers was a *medical* issue, she said. And what if someone found out?

So they'd filled that room instead with books and magazines and all the things she loved. A TV, to pass the time, as Charlie reduced her doses day by day. Photos and music, to take the edge off the symptoms that he knew were going to hurt. But even *he* hadn't expected it to hurt as much as it did.

The door to that room wasn't particularly thick and did little to stop the wails and the howls from coming through. Lorraine had sounded like a wounded animal, except wounded animals didn't wish they were dead. Charlie's mum repeatedly begged to die, because the pain was just too much and it just hurt *soooo bad*, and the word *bad* would rise to a scream. And then there'd be silence for a few hours, and a couple of times Charlie had tiptoed into the room then to make sure that his mother *wasn't*, in fact, dead. She wasn't, of course, but her sleeping face would be flushed and her forehead wet with sweat.

And then when the sun came up, Malcolm would relieve Charlie at the bedroom door, and the daytime would consist of a walk outside under the trees, and more bellowing and shrieking and a bit of retching into a bucket in her dry-out room.

*That* had been the hardest part, not standing up to MaryAnn Steiner.

And after all of that, once the color had returned to Lorraine's cheeks, and she could sleep through the night without screaming, and she'd started to eat again, she stopped talking to her son.

"I could've lost her," Malcolm repeated, and Charlie jumped forward seven years in an instant, back to his kitchen where his dad was drinking coffee and talking about plans to retire at long last. Because of Lorraine. "If she'd…you know, *died*, we would've left so many things unticked on the list."

*The bucket list*, Charlie thought. Lib Frawley would be shuddering.

"So how about this one, Charlie." He beckoned his son closer and proceeded to detail an itinerary that would take Malcolm and Lorraine from Greece to Italy and Spain, then on a train ride they'd been talking about for longer than Charlie had been on earth. "What do you reckon? And if she asks why we're doing it, I'm going to tell her the truth. It's to remind her that she made it through, and she's still alive."

Charlie had never heard something more perfect. And he said so.

"Thanks, mate." Malcolm smiled. The salesman, the diplomat, the poet, the romantic. And just for a moment, Charlie wondered if his dad sensed something was coming, something that made him remember the ambulance and those awful, awful weeks. Not the way Charlie could sense the future, but just a vibe, like Gen and the aura before her eyes started rolling and the car started purring there beside the highway. Charlie shooed the memory away.

"I'd better get back to work." Malcolm stood. "Have a good flight tomorrow. And if you change your mind about needing a lift, you know where to find me."

He gave Charlie a hug.

"Don't stay away too long, mate." Then he was off, the smell of his aftershave lingering in the kitchen and making Charlie question once again whether he even wanted to leave anymore.

*I have to*, he reminded himself. *For Gen. In case I'm the reason she's got seventeen days.*

But God, he wanted to see her one more time. And he did, the following morning. His last in Marwick.

Charlie was up with the sun, pulling on his sneakers, because if he couldn't sleep, he may as well run. And he ran hard and long, and was coming back through the park for the second time when he looked across and *there she was*.

Gen was waiting next to the newsstand, and at first he thought she might have been waiting for *him*. Maybe she'd seen him pounding along the paths and had deliberately positioned herself right where he'd run past. But she wasn't looking at him. She was looking down at her phone and probably didn't even know he was there.

She stood in a patch of early sun that in a couple of hours would be unbearably hot. But now, while the cicadas were still waking up, it was the perfect spot to bask, and it made her *glow*. Charlie skidded to a stop, catching his breath under a tree. The desire was so strong it was almost alive: the need to go up to her, to be next to her, to talk to her, to share that little patch of sun in the early morning. He watched her scroll on her phone, and he almost—*almost*—gave in to that urge to cross the road. Then a bus pulled to the curb and blocked his view, and when it roared away again Gen was gone. As it turned the corner, headed for the bridge and Abercrombie, Charlie couldn't help but think: what a sad way to spend her sixteenth-last day on earth. Sitting on a bus, taking her to a job that she'd already quit.

But he couldn't say anything. The urge to cross the road, to talk to her, was dangerous. Because if he did, and he put something in motion like he did with Abbie, then that would be the end of *him* too.

No. The safest thing right now was distance.

Charlie had an earlier flight this time, and by midmorning the boxes he'd opened were resealed, and his suitcase was repacked and sitting by the door. The cab pulled up outside, and Charlie patted his pockets—one last check before his final departure, because this time there was no coming back. His phone was missing. He waved to the driver, mouthed *one minute* to him, and darted back through the house.

He found it wedged between couch cushions, with two missed calls on the screen: Dad.

Charlie grinned. He knew why his dad had called. There was a special persistence about Malcolm Knight, still offering to take him to the airport, even as the cab idled outside. He punched the return call button to let Malcolm know that he really was okay for a lift, that he was just leaving now, and that he'd text him once the plane landed. He'd call later too with a full report on his new apartment, even if it meant admitting he'd paid too much and should've haggled. Should've asked for help, should've come clean about the move earlier. All of it.

It rang five, six times, and Charlie was about to hang up when finally a voice answered.

"Charlie."

"Oh. Hi, Mum." He paused, caught entirely off-guard. "Um, I think Dad called me earlier but I missed it."

"It was me, Charlie. I called you."

"Oh," he said again. "On Dad's phone?"

Then came a noise he would never forget.

Lorraine Knight started to cry.

"Mum? Is Dad okay?"

"Charlie…" she said in a hollow tone he didn't recognize. "He's dead."

---

The first sign that Malcolm Knight was unwell had come as he spooned raspberry yogurt onto his muesli that morning. Lorraine told Charlie how he'd looked a little gray.

"Are you all right?" she'd asked him, and he'd waved her

concerns away. But he'd tried to stand, only to collapse back into his chair, sweaty and panting. That, the doctors explained to her, had likely been the first of two heart attacks, a small one to get the ball rolling. The second occurred in the back of the ambulance, almost exactly halfway between Marwick and Abercrombie.

*Of course it would happen there*, Charlie thought numbly.

That one had been a beastie, the doctor had said, and Malcolm Knight—salesman, diplomat, mower of neighbors' lawns, and all-round nice guy—was gone by the time the ambulance pulled up outside Sacred Sisters of Unity. Lorraine had been in the passenger seat of the vehicle—near, but not close enough to hold her husband's hand as he died.

Charlie put his arm around his mother as she dissolved into another bout of sobs that shook her entire body. He was entirely lost for words.

They were sitting in the kitchen of the home Charlie had grown up in; a home that now seemed too quiet, too empty. The first thing he'd done after picking his mum up from Sacred Sisters was clear the breakfast table. The sight of his dad's bowl of muesli, a splat of pinkish yogurt sprayed across the table from where he'd dropped his spoon, was too much. Too visceral. Just a few hours earlier, Malcolm Knight had been holding that spoon, planning his day—who he was going to call, which listings needed an update. Deciding how much he'd trust his colleagues with today, because soon they'd be running the whole show. Maybe he'd been thinking about calling his son to offer him a ride, even though Charlie had already said no. Maybe he'd just turn up outside his door anyway.

Charlie gave his mum a little squeeze as her tears eased. A squeeze was the best he could do. He had no advice, no wisdom, no words at all. He felt like his brain—his whole body—was stuck at a point two hours earlier and couldn't process what was happening. Couldn't quite catch up, still living in a time when his suitcase was packed by the door and the cab was pulling up outside, before he knew his dad was dead. Another squeeze, and Lorraine grabbed his hand and held it in a vise grip as though Charlie would disappear too if she let go. Charlie blinked back tears of his own and remembered what he'd said to Deborah Anders when she sat in his office, dabbing at her eyes with a tissue. Something about grief coming for you when you least expect it. Grief was not just coming; it had arrived, and it was crashing over him in waves.

They sat together, not speaking, for an hour or more. Just the two of them in the kitchen, sometimes crying softly, sometimes just staring at the wall, the floor, the table where it had happened. Then, suddenly, the deathly silence of the house was broken by the crunch of car tires on the gravel driveway outside. The news had spread. The visitors were arriving.

Lorraine Knight dropped her son's hand and sprang to her feet.

---

Word leaped around Marwick about the death of Malcolm Knight, and in the following hours Charlie fielded a flurry of calls. His second cousin Lexie rang to see how he was doing; Charlie didn't know what to tell her. He'd never lost a parent before. Now it felt like things were just happening around him, happening to him, and he couldn't keep pace. Couldn't even think. Marty Harris from the Marwick Hotel rang, and afterward Charlie couldn't remember a word Marty said. MaryAnn Steiner walked through the door of Charlie's family home, not needing to knock. She wrapped Lorraine in a monstrous hug, and they stayed like that for minutes. When the pair separated, MaryAnn hugged Charlie too. But it was different for him. It was shorter, and a few degrees colder.

Charlie watched as his mum alternated between the comfort of her best friend and the protective fold of some of her buddies from golf. Two circles of Lorraine's Venn diagram in a silent tug-of-war, and he realized he didn't need to be there anymore. Didn't *want* to be there. So he left, driving under that avenue of trees his father had planted decades ago. Leaving the house that had belonged to his parents, and now just belonged to his mum.

When the knock came on his door that evening, he knew who it would be. And he thought about not opening it at all, leaving it closed and pretending he wasn't home. He'd done that once before, and Gen had almost bashed his door down. He knew he shouldn't answer it, he knew he shouldn't speak to her, but the thought of Gen standing at his door and him leaving it locked was just too much.

He pushed everything else to one side.

He needed her.

"Oh, Charlie. I'm so sorry."

A bag of food sat at her feet, but it was the only similarity with the last time Gen had arrived on his doorstep bearing gifts. Gone was the pale green romper and golden hoops and the nervous energy she'd brought with her. Now she wore jeans and a plain black tee. Her hair hung loose and her eyes were red. She put her arms out for him, and Charlie had never loved her more than he did right then.

"Are you…are you okay?" Gen asked as she unloaded the food in the kitchen.

He shrugged, a gesture that seemed completely inadequate. "Kind of numb. Shock, I guess. Mum isn't doing well."

"Oh." Gen stopped for a moment, an odd expression on her face. Then she kept unpacking, pulling containers out and handing them to Charlie. "I can't even imagine how Lorraine would be right now. She'd be taking it so hard."

"Dad came here yesterday. He was standing right *there*." Charlie pointed to a spot next to Gen. "And he was talking about retiring, and this trip they were going on, and even with all that, he still wanted to take me to the airport today."

"Of course he wanted to take you," Gen said with a sad smile. "He was a good man." She hunted amongst the boxes, searching for one marked *plates*, and gave up.

Instead they ate straight from the containers, seated together on the couch without talking. Even in silence, Gen's presence soothed Charlie, but he had a vague, grief-numbed sense of the enormous distance between them: two cushions and about a hundred light years. The weight of the unspoken conversation—of everything he'd swept aside when he'd opened the door, of everything she wanted to know, and everything he couldn't tell her—grew heavier, and he thumbed the TV remote.

He found a movie on Netflix, something light and fun and old—a romantic comedy, with Meg Ryan and somebody else— and stared at the screen, trying not to think about life without

Gen, or about his dad, or food, or planning a funeral, or his mum, or about anything really. But behind it all, something nagged at him. Something that required him to just *think* about it; to stop ignoring what was happening and just *think*. Charlie refused to give it space. The shock that had anesthetized his mind was starting to wear off, and it was taking more and more effort to keep his thoughts in a place where he could control them. He didn't want to *think*, he just wanted to close his eyes.

Grief, he realized, was exhausting.

Charlie was asleep long before the credits rolled on the film.

# 24

The next day was Friday. And it was an extraordinary day.

It began with a phone call from Glenn Forrester, of all people. The farmer with the busted knee and two new kittens woke him up.

"Hello?" Charlie's neck ached and his eyes were gritty and sore. There was a cushion under his head, and a blanket covered his legs, but he was alone. Gen must have slipped out once the movie had finished.

"Doc? It's Glenn."

"Glenn…" Charlie had been having a dream, something vivid, and maybe he was still having one. Why else would Glenn Forrester be calling him?

"They told me to call you." Glenn's voice sounded more gravelly than normal. Like he was talking through gritted teeth. "The young bloke who answers the phone—he gave me your number."

*Young bloke who answers the phone.*

"*Toby* did? At the clinic?" Charlie sat up on his couch, rubbing his neck. This didn't make any sense. Outside he could hear the cicadas in full swing, and the living room was bright with midmorning sun. He checked the time. It was just past ten o'clock.

"Yeh." A sharp intake of breath. "Thanks, Doc. When you get here, one of the cats is out. Just keep an eye out so you don't run over her. Don't leave it too long though, yeh?"

"All right, Glenn," promised Charlie, without any idea what he was promising.

Glenn ended the call, and Charlie stared at his phone. The whole conversation felt like he'd joined in the final moments of a joke, having missed the setup entirely. He was there for the punchline, but he didn't get it.

He swallowed some Advil for his aching neck and splashed cold water on his face. The fog cleared, and reality smashed into him. Malcolm Knight was dead. His dad was dead. And now he had to plan a funeral.

His phone rang again.

"Doc, it's Toby. Has Glenn Forrester called you?"

"He has. Toby, what's going on?"

"It's chaos, Doc. I said you'd swing by his place. I'm sorry, I know I should've checked with you first, but it's *chaos*."

"Toby—what's happening?" Charlie could hear noise in the background. People. It sounded like a *lot* of people.

"Lisa's printed his scans if you want to take them with you. Doc, I've got to go, someone else is calling. It's chaos." And he was gone.

Toby had volunteered him to go to Glenn Forrester's house.

And more than that: to swing by the clinic first to pick up his scans. His knee scans?

Charlie tried to call the clinic back, but the lines were engaged. *Of course they were.*

So he got dressed. He searched in his suitcase for his medical kit, and then he climbed into his car. He was supposed to be going to his mum's house. They had a funeral to plan; there were people to call, flowers to arrange, catering, songs. Christ, he had to choose a coffin. But instead of doing any of those things he drove—almost on autopilot, and certainly still in a daze—to Marwick Family Clinic, where Toby had sounded so panicked and where the scans for Glenn Forrester were waiting to be collected.

It felt like half of Marwick was in the waiting room.

"Toby! What's going on here?" Charlie asked over the commotion. Every seat was occupied, and the volume—normally a hushed, respectful whisper—was dialed right up. Patients glanced in his direction, some hopeful, others with sympathetic eyes.

"Chaos," Toby said for the fourth time, somewhat unhelpfully.

"No temp today," Lisa said, hanging up the phone. "He's got something going on at his son's school. Dr. Steiner said yesterday not to worry about getting someone else in, she could get by on her own."

Charlie looked around. The evidence would suggest otherwise.

"But now *she's* not here either," Toby said. "She saw one patient this morning, then went home sick."

"Not sick," corrected Lisa. "She just left. You *assumed* she was sick."

"I thought she looked green," Toby said with a shrug. "But she left in a hurry."

"So there's nobody else here?" Charlie asked. "No temp, and MaryAnn's disappeared. It's just you two?"

"Just us, Doc," Toby confirmed. "Not for long though. Lisa rang the agency, and there's another temp coming. They should be here soon." He eyed the waiting room. "Hopefully."

"Right. And what about Glenn? Why did he ring me this morning?"

"Sorry, Doc." Toby looked sheepish. "I was in a panic. I did tell him to call an ambulance, though, and he said he changed his mind, that he'd be okay. Dr. Steiner was running out when he called—she was literally *running*, can you believe that? I told her about Glenn and you know what she said?"

Charlie could guess.

"She said to call me."

"Yep! She said 'call Charlie.' That's all, and then she was gone. Seriously, she looked *green*."

"So you gave Glenn my number."

"Yeah. I panicked. It sounded bad. Sorry."

"It's fine, Toby." And it was. Toby was doing his best in a stressful situation. "So where are his scans?"

Lisa handed them to him.

"MaryAnn told us about your dad, Charlie." A sledgehammer, right to the guts. "We're so sorry. That's awful."

Charlie nodded.

"Thanks guys. Appreciate it. I better get going to Glenn's place." He glanced back at the waiting room. "Hope the temp turns up soon."

Glenn's farm was on the road to Charlie's parents' house, a road he'd driven so many times with one destination in mind that he almost sailed past the letterbox marked FORRESTER. He hit the brakes and swung in fast, tires spinning on the gravel. At the end of a long driveway sat three buildings: a squat brick bungalow and two large sheds, one new, one old. Drums marked "diesel fuel" were stacked neatly about, and a dull red tractor sat waiting, its nose sticking out of one of the sheds, a bale of stock feed wedged on its front tines. Just in time Charlie remembered Glenn's warning and slowed down as he approached the house. And right on cue, a ginger kitten darted from behind one of the drums, charging at something only it could see: a grasshopper, maybe, or just a speck of dust. It pounced, then looked up at Charlie's car and bolted in the opposite direction, racing back to the shelter of the house.

Charlie got out and followed it, knocking loudly on the front door. There was no answer.

"Glenn?" he called. "Where are you, mate?"

He walked to the first shed—the old one—and called again, peering into the shadows beyond the tractor.

"In here, Doc." Charlie followed the voice.

He found Glenn Forrester on the ground.

"Sorry, Doc. I shouldn't have rung you, I'm fine." He was sitting up, his back against the wall of the shed. The concrete floor was colored by a thick layer of reddish-brown dust, dirt that had blown in from outside over years and years. It was everywhere, except for a two-meter-long stripe that looked like it'd been swept clean. The stripe revealed just how far Glenn had been able to drag himself before Charlie arrived.

"What've you done, Glenn?"

"I figured if I could just get to the wall, I could pull myself up." And he grabbed hold of a shelf above him and heaved himself upright, putting all his weight onto his good leg. He wobbled, and started to tilt. Charlie lunged forward and threw an arm under his shoulder.

"See? Easy peasy." Glenn had a pained smile on his face. "Thanks, Doc."

Charlie half carried Glenn to a wooden crate nearby and gently lowered him into a sitting position. Sweat beaded on the farmer's forehead; the shed was hot, but that wasn't it. Charlie could tell he was hurting. Badly.

"It's the knee again. I got off the tractor, and I don't know what happened, honestly. I just hit the deck, and it's like someone's cracked me across the leg with a bat or something. Hurts like hell."

"Okay. I'll be back. Stay here for a second."

"Doc, did you see how far I got without you?" He pointed to the track through the dust. "I'm not going anywhere in a hurry."

Charlie raced back to his car and grabbed his medical bag. He then let himself into Glenn's house and searched through the kitchen drawers. At last he raided the freezer and returned to his patient.

"How's the pain?"

"Like a hot iron, Doc."

"All right. Take this." He gave Glenn some painkillers, then started cutting up the leg of Glenn's jeans with a pair of blunt scissors from the kitchen. "Hope these weren't your favorites."

Glenn winced as Charlie got closer to the knee, hacking through the material. Then he was past the joint, and Charlie grimaced at the ballooning flesh. He wrapped the knee in two bags of frozen peas he'd found in Glenn's freezer.

"I looked at your scans in the car, Glenn. You did tear the ligaments last time, like we thought—and I'll bet anything that you've done more damage, before it's even had a chance to heal."

Glenn grunted.

"I don't think you'll be avoiding the surgery this time round." Charlie stood and stretched his back. "Mate, you're here on your own. Why didn't you call an ambulance?"

"Not on my own, Doc. I've got the cats." He pointed behind Charlie; the ginger kitten had returned at some point, curious at the commotion.

"You know what I mean, Glenn."

"I know, Doc. I'm pulling your leg. But I didn't need an ambulance; save that for emergencies. Figured I could get myself to the truck and drive into town. It's why I called the clinic to make an appointment. But that young bloke just gave me your number instead, said you'd swing by."

*Some of Toby's best work*, Charlie thought with a smile.

Once the painkillers had kicked in, Charlie acted as a crutch for Glenn to get him out of the hot shed and into his house. He talked him through the immediate treatment and then broke the news to him.

"You need to call your daughter."

"I can't bother Ash with this," Glenn said. "She's busy."

"You *can*, Glenn. And if you don't, I will. Do either of your kids even know you busted your knee the first time?"

Glenn said nothing, and Charlie took a deep breath. This stubborn independence had led to a very lonely existence.

"Call Ash. Right now. Because you're going to need help running this place for the next little while. Are you going to do it?"

Glenn nodded.

"Really?" Charlie asked.

"Yes, Doc." Glenn rolled his eyes. "God, you're as bad as Carol was."

"Glenn, that's the best compliment you could pay me," said Charlie, quietly delighted. Glenn's wife had been a kind, wonderful person. "Now that's settled, I'm going to head off. But only once I see you dial the number."

"Seriously, Doc?"

"Yep."

"I was wrong. You're *worse* than Carol. Fine, I'll do it." Charlie watched Glenn scroll through his phone for his daughter's number. Finally, with an indignant glare at Charlie, he pressed the call button and put the phone to his ear.

"Ashie. How are you doing, sweetheart?"

Charlie left the room.

He drove away, taking it nice and steady past the sheds, watching closely for the kittens that Malcolm Knight had wrangled from somewhere with just a couple of days' notice. And he realized Glenn Forrester hadn't mentioned Malcolm's death. He hadn't offered his sympathies, hadn't said a word, because he didn't know. Charlie was probably the first person he'd seen in days.

Glenn had some lonely years ahead of him. Charlie

remembered thinking the same thing on the day Glenn had come to see *him*, the day Louie had gone to the vet for the last time. The day Charlie had written Glenn's number in his book, then vowed to help his patients catch their mice, just like Louie. That all seemed so long ago. At least now Glenn had those kittens, and if his daughter came to stay, maybe she'd—

*Glenn's lonely years. How many, exactly?*

Charlie slammed on the brakes, and the car skidded to a stop, gravel flying.

When he'd first found Glenn, legs splayed out on the shed's dusty concrete floor, he'd asked him what he'd done. Glenn had pulled himself to his feet, and Charlie had helped him. Stopped him from falling. And then Glenn had talked about the pain, that hot iron pain that felt like someone had cracked him across the knee with a bat.

*Trigger after trigger after trigger.*

And his blue jeans had stayed blue.

The dust on the ground had stayed a reddish brown.

And the cat, poking its nose into the shed, never even looked like changing to gray or black or white. It stayed the same dappled ginger it was when Charlie saw it pouncing on thin air outside.

The color hadn't faded. It hadn't run out like a plug had been pulled. It hadn't changed at all.

And Charlie had talked to Glenn without the bulging pressure behind his eyes, without the spinning and swirling mass that spat out the feeling of a number.

Because there was no number.

A minute passed, then another, and then finally he started

to drive again, and when he reached the main road, he paused. He was supposed to be turning right, to his mum's house. And he would go there, in an hour or two. But first he went left, because Toby had been in a panic, and even Lisa had looked overwhelmed. That waiting room had been *chaos*.

And he could help.

Just like Lib Frawley had said to him in the gazebo, as they stared out over golfers scurrying about the course: it came suddenly, and left just as quickly.

Whatever *it* was, it had left Charlie Knight.

Moved on.

# 25

Malcolm Knight had made just one request for his funeral. Lorraine found it in an envelope in the drawer of his desk, upstairs in the house where Charlie had grown up. Just one instruction, but it was a big one. And she told Charlie she intended to fulfill it.

Malcolm wanted to be buried on a Sunday. And not just any Sunday: the Sunday immediately after his death. Malcolm had added an explanatory note to this, scribbled in the same handwriting Charlie had sometimes found on the back of a business card, slipped under his door. Because Sunday was an agent's day off. No showings, no auctions, no sales. It had to be Sunday, which gave Charlie and his grieving mum just a couple of days to pull together a farewell. Charlie wondered if his dad would've been okay with a midweek service if he'd known what the deadline was doing to his wife. He could almost hear his response.

"God, yes. Just change it, mate. I'm hardly going to notice."

And then he would have laughed that hearty chuckle, and everything would've been okay.

But Lorraine was determined.

"No, Charlie. He said Sunday. So we'll do Sunday."

And they did. By Saturday afternoon, Charlie and his mum sat alone in the kitchen at Lorraine's house, finalizing the plans for the wake. Charlie had been listening to his mother talk about the music, and the wine, and where everybody would park, but his mind kept wandering, and his gaze kept finding its way back to the vacant seat opposite him. He knew it was where his dad had suffered the first attack, that first almighty squeeze around his worn-out heart, but it didn't feel ghoulish to be there now. Instead, it almost felt the opposite; as though by being together in the last place where he was alive and vital and *there*, there was some connection to him.

He could almost smell his aftershave, and feel his selling-houses suit.

"What do we do if it rains?" Lorraine asked.

"Mum, it's not going to rain. It's been dry for a month, and there's nothing forecast for another week. It'll be fine."

"If it rains tomorrow we'll have to move it inside."

"It's not going to rain tomorrow."

"What about the lawn? Your dad wouldn't be happy with it. He would have mowed it by now. Especially if people were coming over."

"The lawn looks fine, Mum. But I'll give it a mow, if you like."

Then she was crying again, and he put his hand on hers. Her fingers felt so frail, like the bones could crack with the slightest pressure. It was a seismic shift in just a couple of days, and worlds away from the blue-dress woman who'd pointed one of those same fingers at him in anger on the back deck.

"It's not fair, Charlie. We had so many things we wanted to do. We used to talk about them all the time, and then after…my shoulder…he'd forgotten all about them."

Charlie looked closely at his mum. Lorraine's face had aged, the lines on her forehead so deep they seemed almost bottomless. Her bloodshot eyes met his and stayed there. And he realized she didn't know any of Malcolm's plans. Perhaps she didn't even know he'd been going to retire.

So he told her.

"He was planning a trip, you know, Mum."

"A what?"

"A holiday. A big one, for the two of you."

And he recounted the conversation he'd had with his dad in his own kitchen, about the places Malcolm was going to take Lorraine. When he got to the train trip—the one they'd been dreaming of for decades—her eyes welled up again.

"Dad didn't tell you any of this, did he."

She shook her head.

"Why, Charlie? Why was he doing it? He'd already given me my birthday present." She touched her neck, where a delicate gold necklace hung.

Charlie thought about it. He knew exactly why Malcolm was taking her on the trip.

And he thought about that day seven years ago when he'd dropped by the house and found his mum unconscious in bed. She might've been asleep, except it was midday, and her eyes were partly open, and her breathing had been so shallow. Any one of those breaths might have been her last, her body finally overwhelmed by the pills taken day and night and day and night because she *needed* them. And the paramedics had come and parked at the front door, and then they'd *run*. Run, carrying all of their gear, because the only thing standing between Lorraine Knight and death had been her son, keeping her alive. All because he'd dropped by to say hello, and to tell her something. To tell her news that broke his heart: that he wasn't going to be a dad, and Lorraine wasn't going to be a grandma, and that he didn't know what it meant for him and Gen. And even though he'd done his year at the clinic, and they were supposed to do something *big*, something *spectacular*, he just didn't know what to do anymore, because it was his fault, and Gen needed to get away.

Then Charlie had found Lorraine, barely clinging to life. And he'd found a purpose.

And now he weighed up whether to tell her why Malcolm was planning the trip to Italy and Greece and Spain, and the train ride of their dreams. Whether to risk bringing it all back up again. But in the end, the decision wasn't his to make. It was his dad's, and he'd already made it. *If she asks why we're doing it, I'm going to tell her the truth.*

"No, Mum. It wasn't for your birthday. He was doing it to remind you that you made it through. And that you're still alive."

———

Charlie wasn't a meteorologist, but he was right about the weather on Sunday. It was warm and dry with a milky blue sky. *Perfect for a send-off,* he thought.

He watched as guests arrived by the dozen for the wake, parking at the front of the house before trudging around the back, solemnly clad in black suits and polished shoes and dark dresses. The twins were in the tree house, but this time Charlie didn't long to hide with them. He wanted to be amongst people. People who knew his dad and who felt the same sense of injustice that he was gone. Who felt it was rude of the grass to grow and the birds to chirp and for things to just keep happening, because Malcolm Knight wasn't with them anymore, and that deserved more of a pause.

Gen found him on the deck and gave him a hug; his cousin Lexie did the same. Then the family and friends and colleagues gathered in small clusters on the lawn, eating sandwiches laid out on tables under the festoon lighting that Malcolm had hung for a much merrier occasion. As Charlie stood alone and watched them chat, some crying, some laughing, his first thought was that his mother had been right: the lawn *had* needed that trim. He hoped he could be forgiven for the somewhat uneven job he'd done with the mower. He'd positioned one of the food tables over the worst part, where he'd accidentally scored the grass with a trio of his signature crop circles. On the whole, it looked presentable—but he was no Malcolm.

"Charlie. I'm so sorry," came a voice from behind him.

It was Lib. He'd missed her at the service, but of course she'd be here—part of the guard around Lorraine Knight, helping her to stay on her feet until the very last guest had gone and the house was silent.

"Thanks, Lib," Charlie said. He looked out over the crowd. "Good turnout."

"It is," she agreed. "Your dad was a very popular man. A very decent one too."

"So I keep hearing. It's nice to know everyone else saw him the way I did. Sometimes you wonder, you know? Whether you've just idolized someone. I guess you find out at something like this." He sighed. "I'm glad you're here for Mum. I don't know how she's going to get through this. It's just... I think it was the shock, mostly. It happened so quickly, and she saw it all. She's not ready to be a widow." He didn't like that word, *widow*. His mother's title had changed in an instant, and she had no say over it.

Lib opened her mouth to respond, then appeared to think better of it. She put an arm around Charlie, her head barely reaching his shoulder.

"We'll keep her going," she promised. "And how are *you*?"

Charlie knew she wasn't talking about his dad.

"It's gone," he said. He didn't need to say what *it* was.

"Good," she replied. "I suppose it's somebody else's turn now—but I'm glad it was faster for you."

"Did plenty of damage though," Charlie said, eyes landing on Gen, who was holding a glass of wine in one hand and selecting a sandwich from a tray with the other.

Two women passed close by, wandering into the house behind them. Charlie gave them directions to the bathroom. As soon as they were out of earshot, Lib handed something to Charlie.

"I realized the other day I didn't give you my cell phone number. If you ever need to talk about it, call me. Anytime. Don't bother going through Jane. She's everything you could want in a receptionist—your call won't get anywhere near me." She smiled, hugged him again, and went in search of Lorraine.

Charlie felt a surge of gratitude—to know that his mum was being looked after, and that he'd stumbled across someone who knew *exactly* what he'd been through, because she'd been through it too.

What would Jamie Clayton's dad make of those odds?

The adrenaline of the day—of the funeral, the wake, the raw emotion of it all, even dodging Gen when all he wanted was to hold her hand—ran out at exactly five minutes past nine that evening. Charlie was drinking a beer alone on his couch when he felt himself sinking. But despite the waves of fatigue that came again and again, something kept nudging him to the surface, a life vest that refused to let him go down. Something he'd forgotten, something he hadn't quite processed. Something he'd filed away under *Things That Need More Attention Later*, maybe when everything had slowed down. Kind of like now.

But what was it? He and his mum had put it all together so quickly, making decision after decision at lightning speed. And Charlie had talked to so many people, in so many places. Gen. MaryAnn. Lib. Lexie. Toby. Lisa. Probably all of Marwick, really. Hundreds of conversations. Thousands of kind words.

Maybe that was it.

*Maybe it was something someone had said.*

He thought about it more in the shower, hoping the running water and steam would help him as he unpicked all those conversations, looking for whatever was making him uneasy. A grain of sand that had slipped into the oyster shell.

He lay in bed, still thinking. Poring over the last few days, remembering words said to him, looks exchanged, gestures almost missed.

*What was it?*

Whatever it was, it was important and wouldn't leave him alone.

But at least—at last—it let him sleep.

———

Maybe it was the absence of conscious effort that helped; once he stopped *trying* to remember, it came to him. Charlie didn't know if it arrived like the numbers did, borne of a pressing headache at the front of his brain, because he was asleep at the time.

All he knew for sure was that he woke up with a start, heart pounding fast and loud. How had he missed it? An almost identical reaction by two people, on different days, in different locations. The only two people who knew his secret: Gen Longstaff and Dr. Elizabeth Frawley. Both times there'd been a slight furrowing of the brow, a tilt of the head, a question thought but not asked.

*Why was it a shock?*

He'd told Lib how his mother was unprepared to be a widow; how the heart attack had been so sudden. And he'd told Gen about the shock of it all, that Malcolm had been talking about retiring, and had even offered to take Charlie to the airport.

Gen had seemed confused, and now he realized why: she thought he knew Malcolm's number. The same with Lib. Neither of them could quite understand how Charlie—with all his secret knowledge of what was to come—could be caught off guard by the death of his father.

Unless it *was* unexpected.

Charlie sat bolt upright in bed. He had to check his notebook. He threw back his covers and ran for the stairs, not wasting time groping for the light switch, and he stumbled down the last three steps as his penance. The fall barely slowed his pace. He was in the kitchen, and now he turned on the lights and started tearing boxes open, searching, digging, wishing he'd been more careful in his haphazard labeling of cartons.

Then he found it.

The little black book.

Charlie's hands shook as he lifted it out and opened the cover. There was Edna Bradley, with her four days. Simon Lopez's multiple entries. The girl from the crashed car, the one who looked dead but wasn't.

And Malcolm Knight.

*4116.*

4116 days to live, from the moment Charlie checked that spot behind his ear. Less than two weeks had passed since that early morning visit, when his dad was so proud, so happy, so alive.

Malcolm Knight should have had another eleven years, and a few months' spare change.

*Eleven years.*

Instead, he was dead.

The numbers were wrong.

## 26

Charlie knew firsthand what a phone call in the depths of night meant for a doctor. It meant an emergency: a patient is dying, a baby is coming. He knew how it felt to get those calls. But with every ounce of him buzzing, he didn't check the time before he dialed her number.

"Hello?" a sleepy voice answered after just two rings. The phone was clearly close. For emergencies.

"Lib! Is that you?" Charlie was almost shouting. He was wide awake, and in a frantic, irrational part of his mind, couldn't understand why Lib Frawley wasn't either.

"Yes. Who's this?"

"It's me. Charlie. Charlie Knight." Slowly that irrational part of his brain—the part that had given him the all-clear to call Lib at two in the morning—surrendered control to logic. "Did I… Of course, I woke you up. Sorry."

"It's fine," Lib replied groggily. "I'm awake now. What's happened, Charlie? Are you okay?"

"I got the numbers wrong."

"Which numbers?"

"About Dad. I saw him a couple of weeks ago, and he got me to check a mole on his neck. It was nothing, he just kept scratching it. But I saw his number. He's supposed to be alive for another eleven years. He shouldn't…he shouldn't be dead."

There was an instant change in Lib's voice. She'd had a shot of adrenaline, delivered by phone.

"Are you sure you it was his? *His* number?"

"One hundred percent," Charlie said. He jabbed at the notebook on the kitchen bench. "It's in my book. I'd bet my life on it—the number I wrote down was *exactly* what I felt when I checked him. I even suggested he should retire, so he could make the most of the time he had left. Lib, it was *wrong*."

"I don't know what to say, Charlie. I'd call it an inexact science, but labeling it *any* kind of science might be a bit of a stretch. Though I think we can safely say…" She trailed off. "Oh my goodness. Charlie."

Something in Lib's tone thrilled him. "What is it?"

"I thought I was getting the numbers confused. Remember how I said they were bumping into each other, and I couldn't remember whose was whose? Do you remember that?"

"I do."

"I told you I saw someone who was supposed to have died. Because of their number, I mean. The closest thing to seeing a ghost, I said. And I thought that was me—that I'd got it muddled. I thought it was *my* mistake."

Charlie's arms were covered in goose bumps.

"But…but Charlie, maybe it *wasn't* my mistake. What if I

*didn't* mix up the numbers? Maybe that one was wrong too. Just like your dad's." Her voice became firmer, louder as she turned the pieces around, fitting them together. "Yes! Charlie! Think about it. Most of the patients you saw would have had somewhere between say, ten and fifty years left, right? Depending on their age."

Charlie nodded, even though she couldn't see him.

"Because that's the average life expectancy. Most people will make it to seventy or eighty. Some into their nineties. We're talking about dates that are a long way off, even decades into the future—do you think you'll be around to check if the number was right? Still holding on to your notebook so you can compare? It could be out by weeks or months, or in your dad's case, years. Maybe it's wrong *a lot*. But we just don't see the end result. We're not there to tick them off the list."

Charlie leaned against his kitchen bench, phone pressed hard to his ear, barely breathing.

"How many patients have passed away on the day you expected?" Lib asked.

"Two. Edna Bradley and Abbie," Charlie said. He didn't need to consult the pages for that.

"And then one unexpected. Your dad. That's one in three, Charlie. A 33 percent failure rate."

"No," Charlie blurted out. "That's not right."

"Sorry?"

"There was another one. Lib, I had one who was supposed to die, but didn't. And he's still alive now, as far as I know." He exhaled. "I never even considered it was the *number* that was wrong. I thought it was me. I blamed the whiskey."

Charlie flipped the pages in his book, searching for the entries he'd added after an evening at the Marwick Hotel.

"There he is," he said. "Don Penrose."

"Prostate cancer," Lib said immediately.

"You know him?"

"Charlie, I've been treating him for the last six years. Wouldn't have the foggiest what his number was supposed to be. I'd just be guessing now."

"I can tell you, because he was at the pub a couple of weeks ago and I helped him up when he tripped. When I got home I put the number in my book—it's right here. It was 5. But Don...well, he definitely didn't die five days later. He...uh...he *waved* at me, a couple of days after that. Very much alive. And I just assumed I'd left a number off, because patients kept buying me doubles."

"Don's still going," Lib reported. "Not exactly strong, but upright. He's a tough old bugger, probably looking at another two or three months—though I wouldn't bet against him lasting another six. That's an old-fashioned medical assessment, mind you. *Without* help."

Charlie smiled, and Lib continued.

"So that's one more. You know what that means, right? Don Penrose makes it 50 percent. Charlie, half your numbers have been wrong."

Lib's words sunk in slowly.

*Half of them have been wrong.*

"But why?" he asked.

She laughed gently.

"Charlie, I don't even understand why it happened to us in the first place, let alone why it's not always right. Maybe circumstances change. Maybe it *is* like a virus, a living thing—remember, you saw something completely different to me when you got the numbers. So it changes, adapts. Maybe it makes mistakes. Like all of us."

They sat in silence for some time; the soft, constant breaths coming through the phone the only reminder that somebody else was awake at this ungodly hour.

At last Lib spoke.

"I'm sorry you didn't get to say goodbye to your dad, Charlie."

"Thanks, Lib," he murmured, but he didn't think he deserved to feel cheated. After all, being misled by his special insight meant he'd just experienced death the same way as so many others: sudden and unexpected. "Sorry for calling so late."

"No apology needed," Lib insisted. "I did say call me anytime. Though I might be having a cup of tea before I go back to sleep. You've given me plenty to think about."

Charlie didn't have a cup of tea, although maybe he should have; chamomile could have silenced the mind that was racing, dissecting the idea that the numbers could be wrong. Instead he lay wide-eyed in his bed, tracking the path of a hairline crack in his ceiling as he replayed his conversation with Lib—what it actually meant for Edna Bradley, who'd died when she was supposed to. What it meant for Abbie Wilson, who maybe wasn't supposed to die at all, but did because of *his* intervention. What it meant for Malcolm Knight, who passed more than four thousand days *before* his time was up.

And, perhaps most importantly, what it meant for those who were supposed to die soon.

One in particular.

Charlie finally nodded off just as the sky outside his window lightened. He dozed for an hour or two, and when he woke again, a bright shaft of morning sun was bursting through the gap in his curtain. And in that first minute, when everything seemed crisp and clear and *simple*, Charlie made a decision.

He raced outside still wearing his pajamas. There was no need to get dressed. After all, Genevieve Longstaff had seen him in less than a tattered old T-shirt and shorts. He banged on her door, the thuds echoing up and down the street.

"Gen?" he called, not caring who heard him, not caring who he woke. This was urgent. This was a *medical situation*.

He pressed his ear against the door, listening for any response, listening for a coffee cup being placed on the kitchen bench or heels clacking on the floorboards.

Nothing. Gen's house was quiet.

Her car was parked out the front, so he figured she must still be inside. Still getting ready for work, for the drive to Abercrombie.

*No. That's not right. Gen can't drive right now.*

And he took off at a sprint, faster than he'd ever run before, bare feet stinging on the road. Still wearing his old shirt and shorts. He made it to the main street in record time, chest heaving and heart thumping. A woman walking her dog past the Marwick Hotel stepped aside to let him through; this was a man on a mission, if ever there was one. He couldn't quite see the bus stop, it was hidden by the newsstand, but he knew Gen would be there. He slowed now, trying to compose himself, to steady his breathing. To prepare his words.

He rounded the stand, and his shoulders slumped.

Gen was gone.

The bus had already left.

"Just missed it, Charlie," said Rick, sorting a stack of newspapers. "Next one's in an hour. Fifty-five minutes, to be exact. Probably enough time to put on some clothes, eh?"

Charlie had to smile, because he knew he looked ridiculous, standing barefoot on the street, sweat staining his old pajamas, breath coming in short bursts.

He turned for home and thought about calling or texting. But how would that look? What would Gen do, reading that message while sitting on a bus?

*Gen. You might have 12 days left. Or you might not. There's a 50% chance I'm wrong. It was 18 days but you lost 6 because I didn't tell you straight away. Sorry.*

There weren't enough emojis in the world to take the sting out of a message like that.

No, Charlie was going to Abercrombie to see her.

If he was going to do this, he was going to do it right.

---

Charlie held his breath as he passed a certain point on the road between Marwick and Abercrombie. That spot, he suspected, had it in for him.

But he sailed past it without incident, and the traffic swept him along, almost as though it too knew he had a purpose. He was going to see Gen.

Her office was on the fourteenth floor, and as soon as he stepped out of the elevator he was confronted by a monstrous black wall, with paint so dark it seemed to steal the light from around it. The name of the advertising company stretched across the wall in shambolic silver lettering, a display that hollered: *Creativity lives here.*

The first impression didn't last. Beyond the wall was a large open area lined with cubicles, a handful of ferns the only nod to anything organic or creative. It all seemed very serious to Charlie, a notion supported by the fact it wasn't even nine o'clock yet, and every workspace was already occupied. *And doesn't everyone look thrilled about it*, he thought.

He asked a sour-mouthed woman to point him in the direction of Gen Longstaff's desk. She gestured across the room, and Charlie weaved through the crowded floor toward a row of glass offices lining the far edge of the building. As he walked he scanned them, searching for Gen.

His nerves tightened.

*There.*

Her desk faced the thicket of cubicles, while behind her back a massive window showcasing the cityscape beyond was going to waste. Not that Gen was looking in either direction. She was concentrating hard on her laptop screen, pen in hand, scribbling notes. Charlie kept waiting for her to glance up as he crossed the office floor, for her to spy him among her colleagues and maybe to leap to her feet, the way they did in the rom-coms. But she didn't. In fact, she didn't even see him at her door, and suddenly he was in her office, standing three feet away, with just a desk between them. The door clicked closed behind him, and they were alone.

"Hi," he said, and finally Gen looked up.

Her brow creased in surprise, and she shook her head slightly, pointing to the computer screen.

"Gen, are you still with us?" a tinny voice asked.

Gen looked searchingly at Charlie, trying to figure out why he'd interrupted her meeting. He didn't speak. He didn't have to. She must have seen something in his eyes, because her own widened slightly.

"I'm sorry," she said to the laptop. "Something's come up." And she closed the computer.

"God, that was dull," she said. "Charlie, what are you doing here? Are you… Is everything okay?"

"Gen, we need to talk." Charlie watched a faint wisp of steam drift up from a gadget on the desk. It had an earthy scent.

"Patchouli," Gen said. "Good for focus and efficiency. Doesn't stop interruptions though," she added with a smile. "And yes, we do need to talk. But it's Monday morning and it feels like they're trying to load me up with every project they can think of. Punishment for quitting, maybe. How about tonight? Let's do this properly. Come to mine."

*She doesn't know the urgency*, Charlie remembered. Because it *was* urgent: he'd already robbed her of six days. He wasn't going to take any more time from her.

"No, now. It has to be now."

"You've changed your mind," Gen said, her tone serious. "About telling me. Haven't you?"

He nodded.

"Why the change of heart? And why the rush?" Charlie didn't answer straight away, and then it was too late. Too late to stop the horrible understanding that crept across Gen's face.

"Not here," she said quickly. "If it's bad news, not where everyone can see." She nodded toward the glass wall of her office and the cubicles out on the main floor. There were people everywhere: standing to take calls, typing at computers. Talking about the stranger who'd just barged into Genevieve Longstaff's office. Watching. "It's like working in a fishbowl."

She led him back through the cubicles to an internal stairwell, then up two flights of stairs to a door. It opened onto a small terrace, just a balcony with a railing then a sixteen-story drop to the city streets below. The view was impressive, but clearly that wasn't why people came here—the ground was littered with cigarette butts, spread in a wide radius around an old instant coffee can.

"Look at this. Got the place to ourselves," she said. "So. Out with it. How long?"

"There's something else you should know first," Charlie replied. He had to do this in a certain order. *He had to do it right.* "My dad—the number was wrong." He told her about his realization and the middle-of-the-night phone call to Lib. He explained it over and over again, coming back to three points: it was alive, it had left him, and it made mistakes.

"Right," Gen said slowly. "That's why you seemed so shocked about Malcolm. You really *weren't* expecting it. Oh, Charlie, I'm so sorry." She squeezed his hand. "That almost makes it worse."

"No, it doesn't. It makes it better. Don't you understand?" He wasn't even trying to hide the desperation in his voice. "The numbers aren't always right. It was wrong for Dad, and wrong for Don at the pub. Lib has had it as well. It *matters*, Gen. Tell me you get that. They can be wrong."

"Okay. Charlie, enough!" She pulled away. "I get it."

A gust of wind sent cigarette butts skittering across the terrace, and Charlie felt his stomach twist into a knot, tight and awful. He'd delivered bad news plenty of times, but never to the woman he loved.

"How long then? How long have I got?" There was a terrible curiosity to her words.

Charlie swallowed loudly. His throat was dry, and his voice came out hoarse.

"Twelve days."

One second, two seconds, three, four. They ticked by in slow motion, each seeming a little longer than the one before.

*Good. We need more time.*

"Twelve *days*?" Gen repeated softly. Charlie could hardly hear her over the traffic on the streets far below.

"But remember what happened to Dad. Fifty percent. It could be wrong."

"Twelve days," Gen said again, before her legs buckled. Charlie caught her, and lowered her to sit against the wall. He sat too, ignoring the rubbish and the grime under him. Just as she'd done for him on the wet grass in the park.

"How?" she asked.

"How what?"

"How does it happen? In twelve days?"

"I don't know. It doesn't work like that," Charlie replied gently. Gen knew that too, but he recognized all the signs of shock. Her skin had turned pallid. Her pupils were big and black.

"Why'd you change your mind? What about…what about Abbie? Is that going to happen to me?"

Charlie had been expecting this.

"I don't know. I just don't. The truth is, I really don't know if the number's right. And if it's wrong, like it was for Dad, like it was for Don and some of Lib's patients, then it should just pass you by. Day twelve will be nothing out of the ordinary, and there'll be a day thirteen, and fourteen, and the rest." He paused. "But if it's right, then you can't spend the next twelve days catching a bus to work here. Counting down your days in a job you've already quit. That's not how I'd want to do it."

Gen didn't respond. She sat there, stunned, and Charlie sat next to her, saying nothing, just breathing quietly. Deeply. Here on the terrace there was no woody patchouli oil to cloud the air. Instead it was the soft, summery scent of Gen. Of orange blossom and lemons, a smell he'd be quite happy to float in for the rest of his days.

Eventually, he took her hand.

They stayed that way for half an hour, surrounded by discarded cigarettes and baked-on pieces of gum, discolored by shoes and dirt and years of smoggy rain. Gen didn't talk or cry. She just sat there, and Charlie sat too, holding her hand.

Waiting for her.

At last, she tilted her head slightly toward him.

"Do you think it's fate, Charlie? I suppose that's the wrong question. Do you *believe* in fate?"

Charlie shrugged. He'd been a skeptic—*a man of science* was what they usually said, and it came with the job—until he'd started receiving the numbers. Then he'd been converted. It was hard not to be, when the evidence of some kind of predetermination was right there, written in his little black notebook. But now, he was back on board with the skeptics. Clinging to that 50 percent failure rate for all he was worth.

"Well, this is kind of the ultimate test, isn't it," Gen said. "If in twelve days I...well, *it* happens, then you can say—yep, these things are decided for us. But if I'm still standing on day thirteen, well then, all bets are off. And we're on our own. Uncharted waters."

Charlie laughed softly.

"One thing's for certain though," she said. "I'm not going back on that video call. I've already given my notice. Think I might finish up a little early, given the circumstances."

"Yeah, I thought you might."

"But what then?" Gen was quiet for a moment, eyes distant. "I don't know if I can handle twelve days of sitting around, waiting to find out if your visions are right."

Charlie was ready for this one too.

He told her his idea, and Gen beamed.

It was the most beautiful smile he'd ever seen.

# 27

"She's telling all her patients it was planned long in advance. She hasn't set foot in the clinic for two weeks now."

"Had MaryAnn even *mentioned* retirement?" Gen asked. "Had she said anything to you?"

"Nope. Not a word. And for something that was apparently in the cards for so long, it seemed to happen pretty suddenly." Charlie stretched out on the picnic blanket. "She saw *one* patient that morning, then bolted out the door and hasn't been back since. What does that sound like to you?"

"Sounds like a coincidence, Charlie," Gen said innocently, then poked him in the ribs. "I know how you and Lib feel about those."

"Yeah, all right," he replied, swatting at her hand. "But something happened with that patient, I reckon. The same thing that *stopped* happening to me at the same time."

Gen took a sip of her wine.

"So she got it from you?"

"I suppose so—though I didn't have any say over it. And part of me thinks I should talk to her, tell her it'll pass at some point, and her life can go back to normal. But I don't know. Maybe it happens for a reason. She actually seems really happy, planning this trip with Mum."

"What about her husband?" asked Gen.

He laughed. "MaryAnn's husband hates trains. Apparently he's more than fine for it to be a girls' trip."

Charlie closed his eyes, basking in the late afternoon warmth. They had John James Memorial Park to themselves. A magpie called softly from a branch far overhead, and somewhere nearby a lone cricket was chirping. But that was it. The cicadas had finished up for the day, and the rest of the park was still and quiet.

"Are you going to buy it?"

"Possibly. She's not asking much, considering the business she's built. But I haven't decided yet. Bigger things on my mind right now, you know?"

Charlie raised himself up on one elbow to look at Gen. The last of the sun was catching her jet-black hair, her silhouette glowing with the dying light. She gazed back at him, her face completely serene. She was a work of art, someone dreamed up by a master of paint and light and color.

Maybe that was it: Genevieve Longstaff belonged in a gallery. Where nothing could hurt her.

"How are you so perfect?" he asked softly, not intending for her to hear.

But she did, and shrugged off the praise.

"For someone on death's door?"

"Maybe not," he replied. "Hopefully not."

She lay down next to him, resting her head on his shoulder. He held her tight and they gazed up at the clouds as they changed from white to pink to the most vibrant orange the closer the sun got to the horizon. Gen turned her head, pressing her face into his neck. He felt her sigh.

Twelve days gone. None left.

Twelve days. They hadn't even gone back to Gen's office after leaving the terrace; instead, they ran down all sixteen flights of stairs directly to the ground floor, to Charlie's car, and to freedom. On the way back to Marwick, Gen had left a message for her boss, telling him she was bringing forward her exit from the company on the advice of her doctor. Then she'd switched off her phone. And once they returned home, Charlie sent another email to the HR department at St. John's Private Hospital. He explained that he wouldn't be able to start early anymore because of unexpected family trauma. The email left a lot unsaid, including whether he intended to take up the role at all. That was a decision for another day. Then Charlie switched off his phone too.

And so started Gen Longstaff's just-in-case bucket list; the kind of bucket list you have when you don't actually know if the end is coming.

Charlie wasn't sure about their first stop. Part of him worried that Gen might have been expecting something more exciting or exotic. Skydiving, fine dining, a hot air balloon high over the river at sunrise. But when he pulled up outside Marwick Aged Care and Hospice, her eyes welled. He'd made the right choice.

"Hi, Grandma," she said. "Look who I've brought. Your old neighbor!"

Charlie, Gen, and Ruth Longstaff sat at a table in the dining room, near the piano, with cups of tea and a cake Charlie had bought. Ruth occasionally drifted off, staring somewhere only she could see, and then she'd be back with them, taking a short, hungry breath from the oxygen cylinder by her side. In those lucid minutes, she asked Gen questions, and Gen told her all about the oils, about the boom in lavender demand, and Charlie just sat listening and smiling. When at last it came time to leave, he gave Ruth Longstaff a hug and felt her frail arms wrap around him.

"I told her you were still single," Ruth whispered in his ear. "I thought it might bring her home."

The next morning Charlie and Gen rose with the sun. They laced up their shoes and ran through the park, which had been mowed for the second time in just a couple of weeks. As they turned back onto their street, Charlie sensed Gen was picking up pace. He sped up too, and then it became an all-out sprint, a race back home, which ended in a dead heat. They collapsed together on Charlie's front lawn, laughing. Charlie mowed that grass later that day, and he mowed Gen's too, and Gen took a photo of him. From a distance, she said, it was Malcolm Knight. The only difference was the selling-houses suit. And Charlie's mowing wasn't as neat.

Gen unlocked the shed at the bottom of her yard, and introduced Charlie to her other love. She opened boxes and held little vials to his nose and watched his face wrinkle up as he sniffed them: ginger, thyme, yarrow, cardamom. Then slowly, carefully, she showed him how to mix the oils, describing their properties as they went, the true believer and the cynic. He kept poking fun at her, until eventually she threatened to use them as projectiles again. He rubbed his cheek, felt the tiny scar, and promised to behave.

The orders kept rolling in for lavender oil, and Charlie helped Gen package up bottle after bottle. With it came requests for her Oil of the Month, so they packed that up too, stuffing the boxes into his car until every spare inch of space was filled. Then they set out on a delivery run together, taking the scenic route between houses in Marwick and the outer suburbs of Abercrombie. They could've used the postal service, but that was for people who didn't have any time. Charlie and Gen *had* time. Not much, maybe, but they intended to spend it together.

They went to trivia at the Marwick Hotel, determined to take down A+. The team of teachers heckled Doctor Google, but nobody minded. And during a break between rounds, Mrs. Henderson—who taught history and had been ribbing Charlie after every question all night—sidled up with a question of her own about stiffness in her knee. Gen eyed Charlie warily, but he was already kneeling down, asking her to bend her leg and show him where the problem was. No whiskey required. It bought them no favors; the teachers demolished Doctor Google. But the night didn't end there.

"Ladies and gentlemen," Marty Harris announced. "I've had a special request. It's one night only, so don't get too attached to it—but who's up for a bit of karaoke? Doc, the mic's yours."

And Charlie leaped up, dragging Gen with him as the opening bars of "Islands in the Stream" kicked in. Charlie delivered a passable Kenny, and Gen a sublime Dolly. It didn't surprise him to discover Gen could sing—after all, Genevieve

Longstaff constantly amazed him. But he *was* astonished when young Toby Brennan stepped up to the microphone and performed "The Gambler" in a rich, smoky baritone. The entire bar erupted, and Charlie suspected it wouldn't be a one-night event after all.

Not one to be outdone, Gen had a surprise of her own for Charlie. As they ate breakfast one morning she tossed something on the table, right in front of him. A single black glove.

"Nope," Charlie said, throwing the golf glove back at her. "No way. Not happening."

But it did happen, and Charlie loved it: eighteen holes of golf with Gen, Lib Frawley and Lorraine Knight. He came dead last, as he knew he would, and had to buy a round of drinks for the group.

"To the nineteenth," he declared, and Lib gave him a knowing smile.

And scattered throughout their days were seven years of missed celebrations: birthdays, Christmases, Valentine's Day. They drank wine, they ate cake, and toasted each other. They planned a future, not knowing if they would have it. They talked about family, and pets, and renovations, starting—of course— with the back fence.

They went together to a house a few streets away, and Gen waited outside as Charlie went in to sit with Deborah Anders, a grieving mother who looked like she was finally getting some sleep. He told her he believed her daughter *had* known she was going to die, that she must have had a feeling, just a hunch, and sometimes—even in medicine—there were mysteries that may never be solved. A white lie, but then the truth: the fact that she chose to spend her last days there, at that house, with her mum, said something extraordinary. Deb cried, and Charlie held her. Then when he joined Gen on the street, he cried too, and Gen held him.

One warm, still evening they lit a small fire in a corner of Charlie's backyard. The flames licked and curled, feeding off the pile of dry sticks. Then, when the coals were glowing a brilliant orange, Charlie tore pages from a little black book and gently tossed them in. They watched together as the center of a page turned brown, then black, then burst alight, the flame burning out toward the edge until there was nothing left of the paper and its messy scrawl of names and numbers but a pile of hot ash.

That night, Charlie and Gen slept in the backyard, with a thin blanket the only thing between them and the stars. They lay there, murmuring to each other softly until the early hours of the morning. How could they sleep when the lights above them were so bright? They watched, waiting, and then two shooting stars arced across the sky, just minutes apart. One for the past, one for the future.

When the first raindrops finally fell, Charlie and Gen set off on a walk. No umbrellas, no raincoats. They strolled to the bridge and watched as the big, fat drops fell on the dusty wooden rails. The red dust turned to muddy streaks, dripping down onto the deck, then to the river below.

Gen squeezed his hand. Thick droplets were hanging off her long eyelashes, and Charlie thought they looked like tears. The rain came down harder, drenching them to the bone, and the river rose quickly. They watched the water now coursing under the bridge. Rushing through the reeds. Cleansing them of an image Charlie had only ever seen in his mind.

He knew he wouldn't see it again.

They went to bed early and they slept in late. They danced in Charlie's kitchen, surrounded by half-unpacked boxes, and they read together on the couch, wineglasses in their hands.

Then after what seemed like seconds, the days had rolled away. The countdown in Charlie's head—the big red number he saw every time he closed his eyes—stood at zero.

The park changed as the moon replaced the sun. The silvery light made the trees look bigger and the gate farther away. They were alone. The magpie that had been calling had long since flown off, leaving only the cricket still chirping happily.

The wine was empty, the cheese was gone, and it was time to go home. But still they lay for a few minutes more, watching the stars emerge.

"Thank you, Charlie," Gen said softly. He looked at her and found himself longing for more time. Not more minutes in the park, but more hours. More days. More years. He wanted the rest of his life with Gen Longstaff.

For the thousandth time, he issued a silent demand to wherever the numbers had come from.

*This one had better be wrong.*

*Please let it be wrong.*

"Are you hungry?" he asked. "I can cook you something."

Gen laughed. The soft, sweet noise seemed to hang in the air.

"How much do we want to tempt fate here, Charlie? You could set the house on fire. Maybe give me food poisoning.

What a way to go." She squeezed his arm. "I don't need to eat again. This was perfect. Let's just go to bed."

And so they did.

Gen fell asleep in Charlie's arms, and he followed a few minutes later. *We're almost there*, he thought as he drifted off. *Please. Please be wrong.*

———

For a few blissful seconds when he woke, Charlie lay still, his mind completely blank under the fog of sleep. Then the fog lifted, and thoughts rushed in to fill the space. The last twelve days. The park. Wine. Walking in the rain. The stars.

*Oh, God.*

*Gen.*

He didn't want to roll over, completely and honestly terrified at what he might see. But he had to.

Gen wasn't there. Her pillow was cold. Her whole side of the bed was cold.

"Gen?" he called hoarsely, praying she'd respond, that she'd just ducked into the bathroom and that nothing awful—truly awful—had happened during the night while he slept. That she'd wandered downstairs for a drink of water and fallen, slipped in the lonely dark of the house.

He called again. There was no answer.

Charlie flung back the covers and listened hard. The house was quiet. Completely, deathly silent.

He tiptoed down the stairs, unsure why he was even tiptoeing. With every step he felt his heart sink a little lower, horribly convinced that if she wasn't lifeless at the base of the stairs, then Gen would be on the couch, cool and still in front of a flickering TV.

But she wasn't in the living room; the television was dark, offering nothing. No help, no answers.

The kitchen was empty too, and as the panic rose in him, he slid the back door open and stepped onto the deck, into the backyard where they'd slept under the stars.

It was still early, and Charlie could hear a cricket somewhere in the grass along the fence. For a brief, nonsensical moment he wondered if it was the same one from the park, the one that had kept on chirping as night set in. Just hours ago, when he still held Gen in his arms, when she was warm and soft and next to him. He shook the thought free, and it drifted away with the morning breeze.

The breeze.

Charlie sniffed.

It carried something with it: something familiar.

Something summery, like orange blossoms and lemons and drinking cocktails in the sun.

A scent, coming from next door.

A scent he loved.

He tried to look through the tiny gaps between the fence palings, searching for something—someone—in the backyard on the other side. But the spaces were too narrow, the wood nailed together too tightly to afford a proper view.

*Wait.*

There: just a flash of color through those tiny paling gaps, moving quickly down the yard. He followed it. It stopped.

A moment of nothing, then two palings of the fence exploded

outward in a spray of wooden shards. Charlie shielded his face, splinters peppering his bare arms harmlessly.

"Well that was more dramatic than I expected," said a voice, and Charlie opened his eyes. Gen grinned through the hole where the palings used to be, leaning on what appeared to be a sledgehammer. "I didn't know you were there. Are you all right?"

*She survived.*

*The numbers were wrong.*

And there she was, completely alive and vital and smiling her wonderful, beautiful smile. He had so much he wanted to say. So many questions to ask. But only one came out.

"Where did you get a sledgehammer?"

She nodded toward the side of her house.

"Up there. Must've been Grandma's. But I thought the fence would give a bit more resistance. Can you imagine that: *I* make it through the night, then *you* get speared by a fence paling." Her laugh came so easily, and Charlie laughed too. "Figured I may as well make a start. What do you reckon?"

He looked at Gen, leaning on her sledgehammer, wood chips in her hair, and a single word came to mind.

*Spectacular.*

# ACKNOWLEDGMENTS

I've loved writing this book. It's taken shape over three long years, helped at every step by a very supportive group of people. Perhaps the defining quality of this group is their patience—patience as they read and reread drafts, answered a million questions, and kept pointing me in the right direction.

To my agent, Catherine Drayton, and the team at InkWell Management—thank you for championing this book and my career. I continue to be in excellent hands. And also to Orly Greenberg at UTA, who does a fantastic job representing my work for film/TV.

To my first readers—my mum, Sue, and my wife, Sian. I have no idea how many times you read drafts of this novel, but thank you a thousand times for doing it. The thing I value most—even more than the notes and the ideas—is the way you talk about the characters as though they're real people. It makes it infinitely easier to keep writing about them knowing that you're invested in them too.

I am enormously grateful to Deb Werksman at Sourcebooks. Thank you, Deb, for taking such extraordinary care of this book. Your faith in the story, your editorial feedback, your ongoing guidance, and—yes—your patience as I kept working through it has been invaluable.

The broader Sourcebooks team makes the whole publishing process look so smooth, because they do it so well. This includes the editorial team of Jocelyn Travis, Susie Benton, and Jessica Thelander; Cristina Arreola and Anna Venckus in marketing and publicity; and copy editor Lynne Hartzer, who took my extreme fondness for commas in her stride.

To my father-in-law, Dr. Tim Hamilton—thank you for reviewing the manuscript for its medical accuracy. As a GP, your advice has helped to make Charlie's work far more realistic. Any errors of a medical nature are certainly not yours. I'd like to say they're not mine either, but I've got nobody else to blame.

To my incredible family cheer squad: Mum and Dad, Sarah, Pat, Andy, Bel, Tim, and Maj; and to the friends cheer squad, represented here by: Nick, Ricardo, Tina, Adam, Bravo, Christine, Canna, Sean, and Adam. Some of you read versions of this book as it made its way through the process, sometimes many, many months after I said I'd send it to you. But every single one of you has been a wonderful support just by being excited and asking how it's going. "Slowly" has often been the answer. But we got there. Thank you so much.

And finally, to Sian: thank you for everything. For putting up with me having too-long showers while I think about the plot. For being a sounding board for my many questions and theories and complaints. And for picking up far more slack than you should have to, particularly with the kids. And while on the topic of the kids… I dedicated the book to Henry and Maeve because it was their turn—but really, because it's a novel about appreciating what you have, while you have it. And with the three of you, I'm constantly aware that I am the luckiest person in the world.

# ABOUT THE AUTHOR

Michael Thompson spent fifteen years working in the Australian media, where he won multiple awards for radio and journalism. His time is now divided between writing books and podcasting from his home in Sydney, where he lives with his wife and two children. *All the Perfect Days* is his second novel. Michael's first book, *How to Be Remembered*, was published internationally in 2023, translated into seven languages, and optioned for film.